WAKING DESIRE

"Forgive me," Reed said before Fleur could form a rebuke. "I do not know what came over me. It's been a long time since I've had any interest in a woman. And you—" he shook his head "—are a woman only a dead man could resist."

Fleur wagged her finger at him. "You are in no condition to be thinking such thoughts."

That irresistible dimple appeared in Reed's cheek. "I'm not dead yet, Fleur."

Fleur studied his gaunt features, trying to visualize what he had looked like before he had been starved and beaten. She expected he was a bit of a rogue despite his dangerous work. She couldn't help admiring his daring, fully aware that he was in no condition to follow through with his amorous intentions.

Fleur returned his grin. "There is plenty of time for that once you are back in England."

Other books by Connie Mason:

A LEISURE BOOK ®

December 2007

Published by

Dorchester Publishing Co., Inc.
200 Madison Avenue
New York, NY 10016

ISBN 10: 0-8439-5745-X
ISBN 13: 978-0-8439-5745-7

The name "Leisure Books" and the stylized "L" with design are trademarks of Dorchester Publishing Co., Inc.

Printed in the United States of America.

10 9 8 7 6 5 4 3 2 1

Visit us on the web at www.dorchesterpub.com.

CONNIE MASON

The Price of Pleasure

LEISURE BOOKS   NEW YORK CITY

The Price of Pleasure

❖ Chapter One ❖

France, 1798

Never had Reed Harwood wished so fervently for death. But then, Reed had never before wallowed in his own filth and the filth of others, in the worst hellhole imaginable. Bruised, battered and broken, he had suffered days, weeks of total darkness in a black, suffocating pit.

Reed had lost all track of time. He couldn't even recall how long it had been since Napoleon's agents had seized him, charged him with spying for England and taken him without benefit of trial to Devil's Chateau, the unofficial name of the prison perched on a windswept cliff on the coast of France. Six months? Nine months? It was impossible to judge the passage of time when one day was much the same as the next.

Though the beatings had stopped a week ago—at least Reed thought it had been a week since his arm had been broken—his body was still a mass of throbbing pain. His brutal jailors cared nothing for a man's dignity or suffering as they wielded their weapons of torture. As he had been told repeatedly by sadistic guards, he and his fellow inmates would die in this prison. What did it matter if it was sooner rather than later?

There was no reprieve. Reed had been caught, charged with spying for England and buried alive in the hellhole where he now resided. He couldn't even plead his innocence, for he had indeed been working as a British operative, assigned by a secret division of the Foreign Office to ferret out Napoleon's secrets. He had been chosen for the assignment because his French grandmother had taught him to speak flawless French. For nearly a year he had successfully posed as a Frenchman in Paris and spied for the Crown.

Then someone had betrayed him.

Reed let out a groan. It rose up and joined the agonizing sounds of misery emanating from his fellow prisoners. There were six of them locked in a dank cell strewn with filthy straw. Three buckets for human waste sat in one corner, befouling the air they breathed. Reed didn't know how many prisoners occupied Devil's Chateau, but he suspected there were many cells just like the one he now called home.

Reed raised his gaze to the single window high in the cell and breathed deeply of the meager supply of fresh, salt-tinged air. The scent of the sea air was the only thing that had sustained Reed and kept him sane. He tried not to dream of home, for he knew his destiny was to die in Devil's Chateau.

Reed welcomed death, sought it even. Why was he still alive? He tried to laugh, but it hurt too much. For some reason the life force within him refused give up. He raised his good arm, not recognizing the appendage that once was thick with muscles. His flesh had melted, revealing the bony structure of his six-foot-two frame.

He had been betrayed.

Perhaps the reason he clung so tenaciously to life was to hunt down and destroy his betrayer.

Reed heard a shuffling sound and glanced at the emaciated figure beside him. "Are you all right, Leclair?" he heard himself ask in an unfamiliar voice very different from his usual deep tone.

"As well as any man can be in this hellhole," Doctor Leclair croaked. "How is your arm? I set it the best I could with what little I had at hand."

"You did well, *mon ami*, thank you. Lucky for us Lucien was on duty when you asked for pieces of wood to use as splints. The others would have laughed at you and watched me die of infection."

The doctor sighed.

"I know what you're thinking," Reed rasped. "We're going to die anyway."

"It is true, *mon ami*. I am to meet my maker simply because I treated aristocratic patients who had escape Madame Guillotine, and you will die for spying for England. God willing, one day Napoleon will be defeated. No matter the outcome, France will never be the same after the Reign of Terror that tore our country apart."

Reed closed his eyes, wishing he could bid his brother goodbye before he breathed his last. Reed loved his brother, Jason Harwood, Earl of Hunthurst. Jason had tried to talk Reed out of taking on such a dangerous assignment, but Reed, reckless as always, had refused to listen. Napoleon was heading for war with England and Reed wanted to help defeat the self-proclaimed dictator in any way he could. Reed's proficiency in French gave him an edge over other British agents.

Reed wondered if Jason had produced an heir yet. His brother had been sickly all his life, but had seemed to rally when he had wed Lady Helen Dewbury. Perhaps taking a wife had been the turning point in his health. Reed's thoughts slammed to a halt. It didn't matter. Nothing mattered to a man hovering on the brink of death.

The door rattled. A flickering light flared near the entrance. Reed blinked, then blinked again. He must be hallucinating. He could swear he saw a female being ushered into the cell by the guard Lucien. A woman dressed from head to toe in unrelieved black, her face hidden by a heavy veil, stepped hesitantly into the circle of light.

Reed heard the doctor suck in a breath, then exhale sharply. "Do you see what I see?" Reed asked.

"*Oui*, I was wondering when she would return. It's been several months since her last visit."

"The Black Widow," Reed breathed. He had heard prisoners speak in hushed voices about the woman, but had never seen her.

The doctor's voice trembled. "*Oui*. She is the woman known as the Black Widow. I have been here a year, more or less, and have seen her but twice in all that time. I wonder who she's come for this time."

Reed watched the Black Widow through shuttered eyes as she spoke in low tones to the guard. His brow puckered in concentration. "I heard rumors about her. I understand she selects a man from among the prisoners, makes him her love slave and kills him when she tires of him."

"Hence the name Black Widow," the doctor said wryly. "I cannot vouch for that part of the story, however. What I do know is that money changes hands and her retainers carry the man of her choice away. To my knowledge, the poor hapless devil is never heard from again."

Reed glanced at his cellmates. Like him, they were pitiful specimens of manhood. Most were half-starved and near death. He couldn't imagine a woman gaining pleasure from any of these men, most of whom could barely raise their heads let alone their cocks. Did no one except he think that strange?

"Our cellmates seem to fear her; they're cringing from her."

"Can you blame them? Fear of the unknown."

The hum of voices ceased. Lucien and the woman were no longer conversing. The Black Widow took the lantern from Lucien and walked slowly into the cell. Reed tensed as she approached one of the prisoners, peered into his face, then moved on to the next poor soul.

Reed studied the pert tilt of her bottom as she bent to her task. The woman was small and shapely; not even her widow's weeds could disguise her womanly curves. Had Reed been half the man, no, a quarter of the man he once was, she would have piqued his interest. Though he couldn't recall the last time he'd had a woman, the Black Widow stirred nothing even remotely akin to desire. But he was curious. Not even the specter of death hovering over him could dim his interest in this unseemly female.

"She's coming this way," Leclair hissed. "I wonder if anyone has struck her fancy."

Reed found the energy to chuckle, though it hurt his broken ribs to do so. "Only a woman with a twisted mind would want one of us. We're filthy, broken men with one foot in the grave. In my case, one foot's in the grave and the other is ready to join it."

Reed fell silent. Talking had exhausted him. He closed his eyes, balancing on the edge of unconsciousness. A gentle hand on his shoulder drew him from the brink. Slowly he opened his eyes, blinking in the bright light of the lantern. At first all he could see was black, from the top of her head to black boots and hands encased in black gloves.

She looked into his face. Though the veil hid her features, it could not disguise the youthful outlines beneath. What would a young woman want with broken men? He could almost feel her eyes piercing into him. He breathed a sigh of relief when she moved on. But to Reed's consternation, after she looked over the last of the six men, she returned to him.

Lucien, who waited impatiently near the door, cleared his throat. "Have you made your choice, *madame*? You've rejected men in all but this cell block. 'Tis unwise to linger too long. The warden could return at any time."

The Black Widow placed the lantern on the floor near Reed's face and bent to peer into his eyes. "Are you Reed Harwood?" Her English was flawless, without a trace of an accent.

Startled, Reed rasped, "Who wants to know?"

"Answer my question," she ordered.

Reed saw no reason to lie; he was already a dead man. What more could anyone possibly do to him? "Aye, I am Reed Harwood. What is it to you?"

"It matters very much to me, my lord."

The woman rose and picked up the lantern. "This one will do, Monsieur Lucien."

Her French was also perfect, Reed noted.

"You're making a mistake," Reed said. "I am as close to death as a man can get. You will gain no pleasure from me."

"Let me be the judge of that."

Reed gave a hoarse cackle. "I am incapable of giving you the pleasure you will surely demand of me."

The woman hissed in a breath and shook her head as the prison guard joined her.

Lucien gave an incredulous snort. "You want *that* one? I beg you, choose another, *madame*. As you can see, this one is not long for this world."

"Is that your only objection?" the Black Widow asked sharply.

Lucien gave a Gallic shrug. "It matters not to me. These men—" his gesture took in all six prisoners—"are meant to die in Devil's Chateau."

The Black Widow withdrew a fat purse from her pocket and jiggled it before Lucien's greedy eyes. "I've added a bit more this time. Will you turn it down?"

Lucien plucked the purse from her fingers, hefting it in his palm. "I will take it and gladly. A humble jailor cannot afford to turn down bribes. Take the man and do as you please." He shuddered. "I cannot imagine what pleasure you will gain from him. In any case, he will soon die. You will save me the trouble of digging a grave."

Reed listened carefully to the exchange. Was he missing something? He could think of no reason the widow would choose him, or any of these men, for that matter.

"Summon my servants," the woman ordered.

As if accustomed to her demands, Lucien walked to the cell door and beckoned. Two men entered. They appeared to be ordinary French peasants, wearing rough clothing and wooden clogs on their feet.

"This one," the Black Widow said, pointing to Reed. "Be careful; he appears to be badly injured."

The two men bent toward Reed. Reed stiffened. "Do I have a choice?"

"None whatsoever," she whispered in English. "You are the one I have come for. If you wish to live, do not struggle."

Reed couldn't have struggled had he wanted to. He did, however, gasp in pain when the widow's servants gently lifted him to his feet.

"Be careful of his arm," Doctor Leclair admonished. "It's broken."

The widow stared at the doctor a moment, then nodded.

"Good luck, *mon ami*," Leclair called to Reed as the woman's servants half carried, half dragged Reed from the cell.

Reed must have lost consciousness, for when he awakened he found himself lying in a swaying cart on a thick pallet of straw, covered by a warm blanket. Daylight had fled; Reed gazed up at the star-studded sky and wondered what in God's name he had gotten himself into.

Fleur Fontaine removed her hat and veil and shook out her tangle of lustrous ebony curls. Each time she walked into that maelstrom of human suffering, she died a little inside. She thanked God her husband's death had come quickly. No man deserved to be treated like an animal, or beaten simply because he was an aristocrat. More importantly, no man deserved to die in Devil's Chateau. Unfortunately, she couldn't rescue everyone.

Fleur lived in constant fear that one day her identity and work for England would be discovered. For the past year, she had lived the life of an anonymous widow, residing in a small cottage with her servants on a sparsely populated spit of land hugging the French coast. The bribe money that facilitated the release of prisoners came from Lord Porter's agency, as did the names of the men she was to rescue from Devil's Chateau.

Lord Reed Harwood was the third man she had spirited out of the jail for political prisoners, and in the worst condition. She prayed Doctor Defoe would be able to save him, for according to the last communication she'd received, Harwood was a man of some importance.

"How is he tolerating the ride, Antoine?" Fleur asked the man riding in the back of the cart with Reed. The other man drove the wagon along a road that followed the cliff.

"He's still alive, countess," Antoine said. "More than that, I cannot say."

"We'll be home soon. Doctor Defoe should be waiting for us. I summoned him from the village before we left."

Fleur sighed and fell silent, overwhelmed by pity. Reed Harwood had suffered more than any man should have to bear. At one time he must have been a handsome man, one much sought after by women. Now he was a shell of that man, filthy, painfully thin and sick. His flesh sagged on his long frame, his gray eyes were dull and his black hair matted and lusterless.

The driver veered off onto a dirt lane. The night was so dark, Fleur could barely see the small stone-and-wood cottage until it rose up before them.

"The doctor is here," Antoine said, pointing to a horse tethered to a tree near the front door.

The door opened; a weak light leaked through. Fleur hopped down from the cart without help. A short, thin man stepped into the night and approached them.

"Did all go well? Did you find the one you were looking for?"

Though Fleur trusted Doctor Defoe, she had been instructed not to reveal the identity of the men he treated. She paid him well for his discretion, and he appreciated the extra coin.

"I found the man, but I'm not sure he will live."

"Everything is prepared. Have your servants carry him inside. I won't know what I'm up against until I examine him."

Fleur watched as her two servants lifted Reed from the cart and took him to the cottage. A plump older woman met them at the door, an expression of immense relief on her face.

"I have returned safely, Lisette. You can cease fretting now," Fleur said.

"Why must you do this, *ma petite?*" Lisette chided. "I live in fear of the day you will not return."

"You know I do this to avenge my husband's death. We will speak more later. I must attend the doctor."

Fleur hurried after Doctor Defoe and his patient, arriving in the bedchamber just as Harwood was eased onto the bed. Lisette followed close on her heels.

"Hot water, plenty of it, and clean cloths," Defoe barked. "The man reeks; his flesh is covered in filth."

Lisette hurried off to do his bidding.

"Antoine, fetch two splints for my patient's arm. You know what I require," Defoe said.

"What can I do?" Fleur asked.

"Right now, nothing." Defoe shook his head. "Look at him. The poor man's been starved and beaten. What a terrible waste."

"Can you save him? He will need nourishing food and rest while his bones mend."

Defoe said nothing as he continued his examination. "Two broken ribs," he enumerated. His probing elicited a moan from Reed. "They will have to be bound. The bruises will heal, but it may still be too late to save him. Youth is on his side; the will to live beats strong within him."

Lisette returned with hot water and cloths. She pushed

Fleur aside and began stripping off Reed's ragged clothing. "Go change, *ma chère*. I will help the good doctor while you rid yourself of the prison stench."

Lisette was right, Fleur thought. She had brought the stench of death and offal with her. "I won't be long," Fleur said as she hurried off.

Fleur took the time for a thorough wash and change of clothing. Staying in character, she donned a plain black gown with no embellishment. She would continue to wear black until her job here was finished.

Fleur's thoughts returned to Reed Harwood. He had been harshly treated since his arrival at Devil's Chateau, though he hadn't been at the prison during her last visit, about eight months ago, when she had bought another Englishman's freedom.

Did Lord Harwood know what had happened in England to make his rescue imperative? She doubted it. The communication she'd received said that he had been working as an agent in Paris and had disappeared from the face of the earth. Fleur had been informed that Devil's Chateau was one of the last places left to look for him, and it was there she had found him.

Before Fleur returned to the sickroom, she wrote a hasty note to her contact and sent Antoine to deliver it. The note reported Harwood's rescue as well as his serious condition. She also explained that if Harwood lived, it would be several weeks before he could travel.

When Fleur returned to the sickroom, Lisette had washed the patient and thrown a blanket over his nude form. With the dirt removed, it was easy to see that Harwood had once been a handsome man possessed of an admirable physique. If he recovered and regained his lost flesh, he would be an extraordinary specimen of male virility. But that was beside the point.

"How is he?" Fleur asked.

"Weak," Doctor Defoe said. "He couldn't have lasted

much longer. Whoever set his broken arm did a remarkable job, considering what he had to work with."

"As for his broken ribs and various external injuries, they will heal. I'm more concerned about losing him to severe malnutrition." Defoe shook his head. "He must be an extremely stubborn man to hold on as long as he has."

"Treat his injuries, Doctor, that's all I ask. I will nurse him back to health, and Lisette's cooking will fatten him up."

"Don't feed him anything heavy or rich at first, mind you. Broth and gruel and plenty of liquids. I'm sure he'll let you know when he's ready for solid food."

"Thank you, Doctor." She handed him a heavy purse. "I appreciate your coming out this time of night and maintaining secrecy."

"I'm no more a fan of the current government than you are." Defoe snorted. "I'll leave a salve for his bruises and laudanum. Sleep is essential to his healing; give him laudanum as necessary, but use it sparingly. It is highly addictive. I'll be back in two days to see how he is progressing."

The doctor left. Fleur looked on as Lisette fussed with the patient.

"We've done all we can for now," Lisette said, moving away from the bed.

"I'll sit with him while you prepare a nourishing beef broth. I expect he'll want some questions answered when he wakes."

Fleur pulled a chair up to the bed and sat down. She didn't know much about Reed Harwood except what she'd learned from secret communications. Harwood, working as an operative for England, spoke flawless French and had gathered valuable information for the Crown. His father had been an earl and the title had passed to his brother. No one seemed to know what had gone wrong or how Harwood had ended up in Devil's Chateau.

Fleur studied Reed's features; the dark slash of his eyebrows, the thick black hair, the full lips and sunken cheeks, trying to imagine what he had looked like before Devil's Chateau. Did he have a wife? she wondered. Was he betrothed? He appeared to be somewhere between twenty-five and thirty, give or take a year or two. Most men his age were wed or betrothed.

Fleur half rose from her chair and leaned close when Reed opened his eyes. They shone like pure silver in the candlelight.

Full consciousness returned slowly to Reed. With great effort, he opened his eyes a crack and feared he was dreaming. Gone were the rough stone walls, the foul straw upon which he had lain more days than he cared to count. It was too quiet. There was no moaning, no sobbing, no pleading. All Reed heard was blessed silence.

The overwhelming stench of death and decay was gone. He had lived with the smell for weeks, months. He sniffed the air, recognizing the scent of flowers, sweet clean linen and . . . *he was lying naked on clean sheets!*

Reed tried to speak, but no sound came forth. His throat was raw and his mouth filled with cotton.

"Would you like some water?"

Ross turned his head toward the dulcet female voice and wondered if he had died and gone to heaven. Nothing this side of paradise could sound so sweet. Reed nodded, praying his dream would go on forever.

He watched the woman tip up the pitcher on the bedside table and pour water into a glass. Then she slipped an arm under his shoulders to lift his head while she held the glass to his lips. Reed realized this was no dream when he felt her soft breasts pressing against his cheek. The water tasted sweet and pure, unlike the dark, murky liquid that passed for water in prison. And the woman smelled of . . . flowers.

"More?" the woman asked when Reed drained the glass.

Reed shook his head. "You . . . speak . . . English."

"I was born in England. How do you feel?"

"I . . . hurt, but I can't recall when I *didn't* hurt. Am I dreaming?"

"No, this is real. The doctor has already seen you and left you in my hands. If you're in pain, I can give you some laudanum."

"Later. Who are you? Where am I?"

"What do you remember?"

"Being in a dark pit and wishing for death."

"Is that all?"

Reed frowned, searching his memory. Suddenly it came to him. *The Black Widow*. He searched her face. She wasn't wearing a veil now, and what he saw stunned him. Flickering candlelight revealed the Black Widow to be young and lovely. Pale skin, ebony hair falling in curls around her face, long sooty eyelashes and full lips. She was a raving beauty.

"Are you the Black Widow?" She nodded. "I don't understand. Why would you want a dying man? What good am I to you? If pleasure is the price you demand for my freedom, I fear the price is too high. I'm in no condition to please either of us."

"It's good to know the persona I fabricated is working. My name is Fleur Fontaine. I am English by birth. My late husband was a French count; he went to the guillotine during the Reign of Terror. He arranged for my escape but was unable to save himself."

"I'm sorry," Reed said softly. "Why are you doing this? Why me? I understand none of this."

"I don't expect you to, not yet. Enough questions for now. You're in pain. Let me give you some laudanum. When you awaken, I will feed you some broth that Lisette is preparing as we speak. You are dangerously malnourished. And if you are to return to England, your broken bones must heal properly."

Reed watched as she mixed laudanum with water in a

glass and held it to his lips. He drank, grimaced and at her urging drank some more. After a few minutes, Reed's eyes grew heavy. "Fleur," he murmured. "Flower. It fits. You smell like flowers."

Fleur's smile bathed him in sunshine despite the darkness closing in on him. "And you, my lord earl, need to rest."

Hovering on the edge of consciousness, Reed wanted to tell her he wasn't an earl and that the title belonged to his brother, but his mind had shut down.

Fleur bent to brush a lock of hair away from Reed's forehead, then quietly tiptoed from the chamber. He had spoken, which was a good sign. He'd also expressed curiosity, another good sign.

Fleur made her way to the kitchen. The rich beef broth simmering in a kettle over the hearth smelled delicious. Fleur hoped that nourishing food and good care would snatch Reed Harwood from the brink of death so he could return to England in full health.

The last man Fleur had rescued hadn't been in prison long and was able to return to England within a fortnight. Fleur feared Harwood wasn't going to be as lucky. Her main worry was discovery. How many times could she bribe Lucien before the authorities caught up with her? How long before she was imprisoned as a spy herself? Fleur sighed. She couldn't think of that now. Not when she had someone more important than herself to protect.

Lisette turned from the pot she was stirring when she saw Fleur. "How is the patient?"

"He's sleeping. I gave him laudanum; he should be out until morning."

"Morning isn't very far off, *ma petite*. Go to bed. There is nothing more you can do. The broth simmers nicely and will be ready when he awakens."

Fleur yawned. "I should sit with him in case he takes a turn for the worse."

"Let Gaston sit with him tonight. He can see to his needs better than you. You need your rest. Going into that prison again must have been difficult." She gave Fleur a little push. "Go, I will fetch Gaston."

Fleur gave in; there was no arguing with Lisette where Fleur's health was concerned. "Very well. Tell Gaston to call me should he need me."

Fleur made a detour to the sickroom before retiring to her own chamber. Though his lordship was sleeping, he moved restlessly in the bed, moaning softly. She heard him mutter something and leaned close to listen. Shock rolled through her when she heard his words.

"Betrayed. Got to tell Porter. Dying . . . dying . . ."

Fleur's hand went immediately to his brow, expecting to feel the heat of fever, but his skin was cool to her touch. She could only imagine what he'd been through. Something about this man struck a chord in her that went beyond pity. Something about the new Earl of Hunthurst was different from the other men she had plucked from prison and sent on their way to England.

Just then Gaston arrived in the sickroom and urged Fleur to seek her own bed. Fleur didn't know what she would do or how she would proceed without her faithful Lisette, Antoine and Gaston. They had fled with her after her husband had been taken away and remained after she began her undercover work for Lord Porter.

"Call me if there is a change in his condition," Fleur told Gaston.

"Of course, Countess."

Fleur considered correcting him about addressing her as a countess, the Reign of Terror had stripped the title from her, but she decided her words would do little good. To her faithful servants, she would always be Countess Fleur Fontaine.

❧ Chapter Two ❧

Reed was aware of little that went on around him during the following days. He knew by Fleur's scent when she appeared at his bedside. But when he tried to bestir himself, his eyes refused to open. Somewhere in his befuddled brain he knew he was being fed laudanum. Sometimes he roused enough to swallow broth, gruel and rich puddings.

Reed always knew when the doctor paid a call, for pain occurred with each visit. But as the days passed, his broken bones began to mend, his mind cleared, and broth and gruel no longer satisfied him. During his lucid moments, he decided to forgo the laudanum the next time it was offered to him. He needed more answers than Fleur had given him, and he wouldn't get them as long as his mind remained in a fog.

The servant was sitting with him one morning when Reed awakened. After Gaston helped him wash and clean his teeth, Reed asked for something more substantial to eat than his usual fare. He spoke in French, for he'd discovered that Gaston spoke no English.

"I will fetch the countess for you," Gaston said as he hurried from the chamber.

Once he was alone, Reed levered himself into a sitting position with his uninjured arm and sat at the edge of the bed. When Fleur bustled into the chamber, he hastily covered his loins with the sheet.

Fleur spoke to him in English. "What are you doing? Are you in pain? Do you want more laudanum?"

"No more laudanum," Reed rasped. "I'm hungry. Now that I know I'm going to live, I need something more substantial than the pap you've been feeding me."

"It was touch and go for a while," Fleur admitted. "Doctor Defoe said you would know when it's time for solid food. I've been waiting for you to ask. But we can't overload your stomach with heavy fare for a while yet. Lisette will know what is best for you right now."

"Lisette," Reed repeated. "Your cook?"

"My cook, my companion, she is everything to me. She will probably suggest eggs and toasted bread to start. If that stays down, we'll proceed from there."

"I need to move around a bit," Reed said. "If I lie abed much longer, my muscles will atrophy, or what's left of them," he added wryly. He held out his good arm and shook his head. "I look like a skeleton. My brother won't recognize me when I return home."

He sent her a piercing look. "I *am* returning to England, aren't I?"

"You are indeed, my lord, but not until you are ready. Your departure will require a great deal of preparation. Lord Porter already knows you're alive and will inform me when to expect a ship to take you back to England. I've made him aware that you'll need a lengthy recovery period before you can depart."

"You work for Porter? You're an English operative?" He tried to smile, revealing a dimple in his right cheek. "So you don't take men from prison and force them to pleasure you."

Fleur laughed. "I hardly think you or any of the men I rescue are in any condition to give pleasure."

"How do you get in touch with Porter?"

"Through my contact here in France. I receive my orders from him. As you have guessed, I am an English operative."

"Who is your contact?"

"He is known as Andre. I've met him only once. It was dark, and I didn't seem him clearly. My servant Antoine carries messages between us. They meet at a tavern in the village. Andre is the one who recruited me for this mission and provided the bribe money."

Reed stared at her, able to fully appreciate her beauty for the first time since his rescue. Hints of red in her ebony hair seemed to glow in the sunlight streaming through the window. The slender wings of her eyebrows rose elegantly above a heavy fringe of eyelashes, so thick and luxurious they nearly obscured the golden flecks in her soft brown eyes. Her fair skin was as smooth and delicate as the finest porcelain. By the time his gaze arrived at her full, rose-colored lips, he realized she was staring at him with the same intensity.

Reed cleared his throat. "I need to speak with Andre as soon as possible."

"He probably can't tell you much more than I have. The rescue operation in which I am involved demands extreme secrecy. Last names are not used. I don't even know if Andre is my contact's real name. It's what we were told to call him."

"I know all about secrecy." Reed snorted. "I was an operative myself, until I was . . . exposed." Reed thought it best not to mention his betrayal until he knew more about this mission. First and foremost, he needed to regain his strength.

"I'll go fetch your breakfast," Fleur said. "As for getting out of bed, we'll see what Doctor Defoe has to say. He's coming today to check your arm. He says the bones are knitting nicely."

"What about clothing? I can't very well run around in a sheet."

"You'll have what you need once you're well enough to run around," Fleur said as she sailed out of the room.

Reed watched her trim figure disappear through the door. Though he hadn't been aware of much these past few days, he always recognized Fleur by her soft touch and her scent. Now that his mind wasn't clouded by laudanum, he realized she was a rare beauty.

If Fleur was English, what was she doing in France working for Lord Porter and the Foreign Office? Reed frowned. He vaguely recalled Fleur saying her husband had been French. *Her dead husband.* That much he remembered, but there was still a great deal he didn't know.

Suddenly Reed became aware that he needed to relieve himself. Since neither Antoine nor Gaston was with him, he decided to test his legs. He remembered that the chamber pot sat behind a screen in the corner of the room and rose shakily to his feet. Surprisingly, he was able to stand despite his wobbly knees. He took an experimental step, then another and another, until he was breathing hard from the effort. But he had reached the screen, and that was a triumph in itself.

Reed managed to accomplish his business without help, but when he emerged from behind the screen, he saw Fleur enter the chamber, a tray held gingerly in her hands. It was at that moment he realized he was naked.

They stared at each other, as if frozen in time. Reed knew that physically he was in the worst shape of his life; he didn't want anyone, particularly an attractive female, looking at him. He made a dash for the bed and its concealing sheet. Unfortunately he didn't make it. His knees buckled, and he hit the floor.

Fleur set the tray on the bedside table and wagged her head, as if he were a child and not a grown man. "Foolish man. Why didn't you wait for someone to help you?"

She grasped his good arm and helped him to rise.

"If I let myself be waited on, I'll never regain my strength."

Embarrassment raised flags of color on his cheeks. Reed had always been proud of his body. He kept himself in tip-top shape, exercising his muscles and toning his body by fencing, boxing and other outdoor activities. In England he had been known as something of a rogue and ladies' man. But now he wondered if he would ever be able to bare his body to a woman again.

Fortunately Fleur seemed not to notice his embarrassment, for her expression remained concerned but dispassionate as she helped him sit on the edge of the bed and cover himself with the sheet.

"Are you ready to eat?" she asked brightly.

"More than ready; I'm starving," Reed admitted.

Fleur pulled the napkin off the tray, revealing a fluffy omelet, thick slices of fresh bread and butter, and a pot of tea. "If you're still hungry after this, Lisette will make you another omelet."

Reed's mouth began to water, and he forgot all about his embarrassment. "This is a veritable feast, Countess."

Fleur looked furtively behind her, even though she knew no one was listening. "Royalty does not exist in France today. I'm merely a citizen, my lord. Please call me Fleur. Anything else is too dangerous."

"Forgive me, Fleur. Though I've been out of contact with the world these past few months, I should have known better. Can you trust your servants and the good doctor?"

"They are the only ones I *can* trust. Your presence cannot be known outside this cottage."

"What about Lucien, the guard at Devil's Chateau? He knows."

"If it became known that Lucien accepted a bribe to release you to my care, he would be a dead man. Lucien will say nothing, though there will be a new grave in the cemetery outside the gates. Lucien's superiors will be told it's your final resting place. I'm sure no questions will be asked."

Reed picked up the fork and dug into his omelet. The delicate herbs tempted his taste buds, awakening the appetite that had been sadly deprived in Devil's Chateau. He closed his eyes and swallowed, savoring every bite. The bread was light and fluffy; the freshly churned butter tasted like heaven. In minutes his plate was clean and he was licking butter from his fingers.

"That tasted like manna from heaven," Reed sighed. "I can hardly wait to sample more of Lisette's cooking."

"Would you like more?"

Reed hesitated. He could probably eat three times the amount he had just consumed but didn't know if his stomach could handle it. "Perhaps I should wait for lunch. Overloading my stomach might not be a good idea."

Fleur nodded. "Rest now, I'll bring the doctor up as soon as he arrives." Reed lay back against the pillows. When Fleur started to withdraw, he reached out and grabbed her arm, surprised that he still had sufficient strength to restrain her.

"Wait! There's something you're not telling me, isn't there? Why was I chosen from amongst dozens of deserving men in Devil's Chateau? Why was I singled out and taken from the prison while others were left behind?"

"You've had enough excitement for now. I'll explain after the doctor has come. Meanwhile, I'll find some clothing for you."

Reed released her arm, loath to lose contact with his lovely savior. Moments later, his eyes fluttered shut and he slept.

Fleur didn't leave immediately. She lingered awhile to watch Reed sleep. She thought he looked better, that his face had a bit more color. His incredible silver eyes had lost the hollow, half-starved look, though his face was still gaunt and his skin pulled taut across his cheekbones. Since the omelet seemed to have agreed with him, she would make sure he was fed more hearty food at lunch. He definitely needed more meat on his lanky frame.

For some reason, Fleur couldn't make herself leave Reed's bedside. He fascinated her. His face hinted at something dark and dangerous. She knew intuitively that he could be ruthless when the situation warranted and she pitied his enemies. But when he flashed that dimple, she could well imagine his appeal to women.

Fleur hadn't found another man so interesting since her husband's death, and she wondered what attracted her to Reed Harwood. She knew he was the kind of man who attracted women. Before his imprisonment they had probably fallen all over him. She'd seen his kind, had been pursued by them before marrying Pierre.

Sighing, Fleur picked up the tray and left Reed's bedchamber. When she reached the kitchen, Lisette eyed the empty dishes and smiled.

"How did his lordship like the omelet?" she asked.

Fleur set the tray on the table. "He enjoyed it very much. I think he's ready for something more substantial. He's eager to regain his strength. He tried to use the chamber pot by himself, but didn't quite make it back to bed. I don't think I've ever seen a man blush like he did when I saw him lying naked on the floor. I believe the pitiful state of his body embarrassed him."

"I wouldn't doubt it," Lisette replied. "Our guest seems like a proud man. He wouldn't want you or any woman seeing him the way he is now."

"He asked for clothing. I'm going to find Antoine and see what's available."

By the time Fleur found Antoine and explained her needs, Doctor Defoe had arrived. Fleur followed him to the sickroom, where Reed appeared to be sleeping soundly.

"Shall I wake him, *madame?*" Defoe asked.

Reed opened his eyes. "I'm awake, Doctor."

The doctor nodded. "Let's have a look at that arm. Does it pain you?"

"Not as much as it did."

"It is healing well," Defoe declared with a great deal of satisfaction. "The splints can come off next week, if you promise to keep the arm immobilized in a sling while it finishes healing. Fortunately the break was a simple one."

"Thank you, Doctor. When can I leave the bed and move around?"

"Whenever you feel strong enough," Defoe replied.

Reed smiled, his skin stretching tight over his cheekbones. "I am ready."

Defoe tapped his chin, then addressed Fleur. "I believe solid food is in order for our patient, *madame*. He needs to regain some of the weight he's lost."

"My thoughts exactly, Doctor," Fleur said. "Lisette prepared him an omelet this morning, and it seems to have agreed with him. His appetite is returning, which is always a favorable sign."

"Indeed it is. There is little more for me to do here, unless there is a sudden change in his condition." He examined Reed's bound ribs. "His ribs are knitting nicely, and the bruises are fading. The bandages can be removed when he feels comfortable without them."

Reed heaved a sigh of relief. "The sooner I can move about freely, the sooner I can regain my strength."

"Shall I return in a few days and remove the arm splints?" Defoe asked Fleur.

"I can manage, Doctor. Thank you for everything you've done. As before, this must be kept in the strictest confidence."

"I understand, Madame. And you are right about my not returning. There are too many inquisitive people in the village willing to betray their neighbors for a few paltry coins." He shook his head. "I do not know what our great country has come to."

Fleur ushered the doctor out of the chamber. After Defoe left, she returned to the sickroom. She needed to tell Reed what she had been putting off. But first she went to the kitchen to fetch thick slices of bread and butter and a mug of milk for her patient. Eating often was the only way he was going to regain his strength.

Reed's stomach was beginning to growl again when Fleur entered the chamber with a mug of milk and two thick slices of bread slathered with butter.

"How did you know?" Reed asked as he grabbed a slice of bread and took a huge bite.

"You should eat small amounts often," Fleur advised. "With Lisette's help, we'll have you fattened up in no time." She pulled a chair over to the bed. "Antoine is securing clothes for you. They won't fit properly, but they will be better than nothing."

Nodding, Reed continued eating.

"My lord, I have some bad news to impart," Fleur began.

Reed didn't like the sound of that. He swallowed hastily, giving Fleur his full attention. The black gown she wore hugged her curves and did nothing to detract from her beauty. The unrelieved darkness of mourning was supposed to make a woman look somber and drab. Instead, the black made her creamy skin glow and enhanced the reddish tint in her dark hair. For the first time in months, he felt a familiar tug in his loins.

With a concentrated effort, Reed raised his gaze from the subtle rise and fall of Fleur's breasts to her face. "Bad news, you say? I knew there was something you were keeping from me."

"I felt I should wait until you were ready to hear it. You have no idea how close to death you were when you arrived here."

Reed nodded solemnly. "I do know; I even wished for death. But as you can see, I am now fully capable of handling whatever news, good or bad, you're about to relate. Please continue. I hope you're going to tell me why you singled me out for rescue."

"Yes, and I regret I'm the one to inform you instead of a member of your family."

"Except for my brother and grandmother, I have little family left. Not close family, anyway. Go ahead, Fleur. I can take it."

Fleur hesitated, then said, "Your brother is dead, my lord. You are now the sixth Earl of Hunthurst. Lord Porter's communiqué said you are desperately needed at home to take up the reins of the earldom."

A crushing weight pressed down on Reed's chest. Jason was only a year older than he. "Jason is dead?" he asked dully. "You must be mistaken. I . . . he was well when last I saw him."

"It seems his illness was swift and deadly."

"Jason's health was never robust, but after he wed he seemed to perk up. We all hoped he would sire an heir. Grandmamma must be devastated."

"Your grandmother was the one who instigated the investigation into your disappearance. I understand she hounded Lord Porter to find you, threatening dire consequences if he did not."

A smile curved Reed's lips. "That sounds like something Grandmamma would do."

Reed couldn't believe his brother was gone. He didn't want the earldom, had never aspired to a higher station in life than the one he occupied. He had been happy to let Jason take up the reins after their father's death so Reed could continue his carousing.

"How long has Jason been dead?" Reed choked out.

"I'm not sure. I wasn't privy to that information. But it must have happened after you were captured. British agents have been investigating your disappearance for several months, although I was just recently recruited to find you. I'd already removed two men from the prison, and Lord Porter thought you might be there when you couldn't be located elsewhere. They had begun to fear you were dead."

Reed was still reeling from the news that Jason had died without siring an heir.

While Helen, Jason's wife, had never impressed Reed, Jason had seemed happy enough with her. It was Helen's sister Violet whom Reed had tried to steer clear of. Violet had openly pursued him; that was one of the reasons he had welcomed the invitation to join Lord Porter's group of spies and accepted the assignment in France.

"Are you all right, my lord?" Fleur asked. "I truly hate to be the bearer of such bad news."

"The death of a loved one is never easy to accept," Reed said. "I'm sure you felt the same about your husband."

Fleur gazed down at her clenched hands. When she looked up, there were tears in her eyes. "Pierre was too young to die such a violent death. His execution is the reason I am working for Lord Porter, though I have never met him personally."

"Will you ever return to England?"

Fleur shrugged. "Perhaps one day, when my work here is done. My family is mostly gone. There is no one left but an aunt with whom I lived before marrying Pierre and settling in France."

"So your marriage was a love match," Reed dared.

Fleur looked away, her lips clamped tight.

"I'm sorry; I have no right to ask personal questions."

"It's painful for me to talk about Pierre. He was a sweet man who didn't deserve to die."

"Do you have children?"

Fleur shook her head and rose, effectively ending the conversation. "I'll leave you alone with your grief."

Reed nodded. He did need to be alone. His brother had been a good man. Though health problems had plagued Jason all his life, he shouldn't have died so young. Poor Grandmamma, Reed lamented. She had so wanted to live to see the future heir of Hunthurst come into the world. If setting up a nursery now was dependent on him, Grandmamma was going to be disappointed. Reed had no intention of looking for a wife when he returned to England.

Being in prison had shown him just how precious life was, and he intended to make up for lost time. Settling down now was the last thing he wanted. There were too many willing women out there to be shackled to one. The Marriage Mart wasn't for him. Jason had toed the line when it came to matrimony, but Reed wasn't going to be caught in the parson's mousetrap any time soon.

Reed spent the next hours grieving Jason and recalling their times together. Theirs had been a happy childhood despite Jason's frequent illnesses. If Fleur hadn't shown up when she did, Reed would have joined his brother in perpetual sleep, leaving the earldom without an heir, except for a distant cousin from the French side of the family. In fact, he didn't know if his cousin was still alive. To his knowledge, Gallard Duvall had never visited England. If Grandmamma kept in touch with the Duvall family, Reed had no knowledge of it.

Feeling bereft and alone, Reed fell asleep, his dreams troubled. When he awakened, the sun was sinking below the horizon. He heard the click of the door latch and glanced up as Antoine entered on tiptoe.

"It's all right, Antoine, I'm awake."

"I found some clothes for you, *monsieur*," Antoine said. "I can help you dress, if you'd like. The countess said you can join us in the dining room for dinner, if you're feeling well enough."

"I'd like that very much," Reed said. "And I would appreciate your help. My arm isn't much good yet, and I am still a bit weak. But first, I'd like to ask you some questions about Andre, your contact."

Antoine gave Reed a wary look. "The countess said you would ask about Andre. Unfortunately, I know very little about the man. I meet him at the local tavern and carry messages between him and the countess. We rarely speak."

"What does he look like?"

He shrugged. "Like anyone else. He tries to blend in."

Reed frowned. "Is that all you can tell me about him?"

"I'm sorry. Our exchanges are usually fast and furtive."

Reed sighed. He would have liked to know the identity of the operative working on his behalf. "Very well, you may help me dress."

Antoine helped Reed into a pair of homespun breeches. Then Reed slid his arm through a brown shirt that Antoine buttoned over his splinted arm. After, Antoine placed a jacket of the same rough material as the breeches over Reed's shoulders and stood back to inspect him.

"You will do, *monsieur.* The clothing will fit better once you gain some flesh."

Reed leaned heavily on Antoine as they negotiated the narrow hallway that led to the rooms beyond the bedchambers. In England the cottage would be called rustic. Though undeniably comfortable, it was neither large nor pretentious, nothing to draw undue attention to its occupants.

Reed breathed a sigh of relief when they reached the large, country-style kitchen. He affected an awkward bow in Fleur's direction and sank into the chair Antoine indicated.

"Are you all right?" Fleur asked. "Perhaps you should have remained in bed a bit longer."

"I have been better," Reed said, "but at least I'm alive. Not too many days ago I prayed for death."

Fleur's smile lit up her face. "Thank God your prayers went unanswered, my lord."

"Thanks to you, Fleur. Please, call me Reed."

Conversation waned as Lisette and Gaston carried in the food and placed it family style in the center of the table. Then they all sat down together.

Speaking in French, Fleur said, "We don't stand on formality here, as you can see. We take our meals together as friends."

Reed glanced around at Fleur's friends, grateful to be

alive and sharing a meal with them. "I wouldn't have it any other way," he replied in flawless French.

"Let me help you," Fleur said as she reached for a tureen of something that smelled delicious. She ladled a generous portion into Reed's bowl. "I hope you like bouillabaisse. Fish is cheap and easy to obtain in these parts. It may be a bit spicy for your taste."

Plying his spoon with his uninjured arm and hand, Reed sipped the soup and rolled his eyes. "Delicious. I've never tasted better," he said as he dipped a piece of crusty bread into the broth. "My compliments, Lisette."

Lisette nodded, a pleased smile curving the corners of her mouth.

"You've just made Lisette's day," Fleur said. "She's determined to fatten you up."

"I promise to eat everything Lisette sees fit to serve me."

Dessert proved just as delicious as the main course. Reed devoured every bite of the flaky pastry filled with fruit. After the meal, he was more than ready to return to bed. The act of eating had exhausted him, even though he had thoroughly enjoyed every morsel, as well as the convivial company. But he could feel weakness creeping up on him.

"Antoine will help you to bed," Fleur said after glancing at Reed's sagging body.

Reed nodded, even though he wasn't yet ready to part with Fleur. The woman intrigued him. Despite the danger to herself and her friends, she stalwartly forged ahead, helping England to the best of her ability. But he was worried about her. When he returned to London, he intended to speak to Porter about the dangerous assignment Fleur had been given. The thought of her ending up in Devil's Chateau was untenable.

"Will you come to my room later?" Reed asked in English, so only Fleur would understand. "Perhaps we can talk. I get lonely."

"Of course I'll come, if you aren't too tired."

"I won't be too tired for you. Please come."

Reed managed the hallway with Antoine's help. "What the countess does is dangerous," Reed said. "She should return to England."

Antoine gave a Gallic shrug. "We all know that, *monsieur*, but she will not listen to reason. We can do nothing but look after her as best we can."

They had reached Reed's room. Antoine helped him out of his clothing and eased him into bed. "I intend to speak to her superior when I return to England," Reed said. "Fleur cannot continue to put her life in danger. If I can arrange for her removal to England, will you, Gaston and Lisette accompany her?"

"I cannot speak for Lisette, but Gaston and I would probably return to our village. Though we owe our loyalty to the countess as long as she remains in France, we are Frenchmen. If the countess leaves, we will return to our families."

"Thank you, Antoine. Without your and Gaston's help, I wouldn't be alive today."

Antoine took himself off, leaving Reed alone with his thoughts. He didn't look forward to taking up the reins of the earldom after an exciting life as a government operative. Lord Porter believed that Napoleon was on the verge of invading England, and Reed's assignment had been either to prove or disprove that theory.

But once he returned home, he would probably be expected to choose a wife from the current crop of debutantes and set up a nursery. He shuddered at the thought.

Reed enjoyed his freedom, and liked to bed whomever he wished whenever he pleased without gossips watching his every move. How could he live his life in the public eye?

A rustling noise brought Reed's attention to the other side of the room, where Fleur stood poised in the doorway.

"I thought you might be sleeping," Fleur said.

"No, I'm waiting for you. Come in and sit beside me. There's something I'd like to discuss with you."

Fleur moved into the room and pulled a chair up to the bed. "What is it?"

"Doctor Leclair. He was in prison with me. He set my arm and did what he could for me. His only crime is that he treated aristocrats and tried to hide their identities. Can you get him out of Devil's Chateau without endangering your life?"

Fleur remained silent a long time. "The guard will become suspicious if I return too soon to the prison. I have to maintain the mystique of the Black Widow in order to continue my work. But this I will promise: Once you are on your way to England, I will see what I can do for him."

"I cannot ask more of you than that. Thank you."

"It's time I left. You need your rest."

As Fleur rose and bent over Reed to adjust the blanket, something Reed hadn't thought possible happened. Her subtle scent of flowers aroused the first stirrings of desire he had felt in longer than he cared to remember. The urge to kiss Fleur, to taste her lips, overwhelmed him. Impulsively, his hand clutched the back of her head and brought her lips to his.

For the first time in months, he felt alive.

❧ Chapter Three ❧

The unexpectedness of Reed's kiss stunned Fleur. She stiffened, poised on the brink of pushing herself away. But something inside her wanted this kiss. She had missed the closeness, the intimacy of marriage, but hadn't allowed herself to be distracted by a man since Pierre's death. But this kiss, the wonderfully satisfying magic of Reed's lips, brought back all the yearnings she had buried with Pierre.

Without volition, her body softened as she gave herself up to pleasure. She knew allowing this to happen was wrong, but she couldn't seem to help herself. Why Reed? Fleur wondered distractedly. None of the other men who'd flowed through her cottage on their way to England had attracted her in the same way Reed did. They were simply hapless men who had been placed in her care before leaving French shores, never to be seen again. And so it would be with Reed.

That thought gave Fleur the impetus to do as she should have done in the beginning: end the kiss. She tried to pull away, suddenly aware that Reed's uninjured arm had found its way around her waist. No, this wouldn't do at all. Struggling against her own desire to enjoy Reed's kisses, she broke away and gently removed his arm from her waist.

"Forgive me," Reed said before Fleur could form a rebuke. "I do not know what came over me. It's been a long time since I've had any interest in a woman. And you—" he shook his head—"are a woman only a dead man could resist."

Fleur wagged her finger at him. "You are in no condition to be thinking such thoughts."

That irresistible dimple appeared in Reed's cheek. "I'm not dead yet, Fleur."

Fleur studied his gaunt features, trying to visualize what he had looked like before he had been starved and beaten. She suspected he was a bit of a rogue despite his dangerous work. She couldn't help admiring his daring, fully aware that he was in no condition to follow through with his amorous intentions.

Fleur returned his grin. "There is plenty of time for that once you are back in England. I suspect there are any number of young women whose eager mamas will actively seek your attendance upon their daughters."

Reed grimaced. "That's what I'm afraid of."

She tucked the blanket beneath his chin. "Good night, Reed. I'll send Gaston up to see to your needs before you settle down to sleep."

Fleur picked up the candlestick she had brought with her and left, closing the door softly behind her. She leaned against the door for a moment and placed her fingertips over her mouth. The warmth of Reed's lips still lingered, creating a long-forgotten tingling throughout her body. She shook her head and moved on to her own bedchamber. She was a fool to let herself be distracted by a man's lips. Especially a man she would never see after he left France.

Reed's thoughts matched Fleur's. Whatever had possessed him to kiss Fleur? There was something about her luscious plump lips he couldn't resist, and kissing her had made him feel more alive than he had in weeks, no, months. He grinned. If the opportunity presented itself, he wouldn't hesitate to kiss her again.

*   *   *

Reed continued rapidly on the road to recovery. According to Doctor Defoe's instructions, the bandages were removed from his patient's midsection. A few deep breaths proved to Reed that his ribs had indeed mended. And a few days after that, Fleur carefully removed the splints from Reed's arm and fashioned a sling to hold it in place while it finished healing.

The amount of food Reed consumed during the following days surprised even him. Within a month after leaving Devil's Chateau, he had regained much of his former weight. His hollow cheeks had filled out and his silver eyes had lost their hollow look. Though full recovery was still weeks away, he began to feel like his old self again.

One of the first signs of recovery was Reed's continued fascination with Fleur. The woman was truly amazing. Brave beyond words, Fleur put her life on the line each time she visited Devil's Chateau under the guise of the Black Widow.

Reed knew Fleur's vow to avenge her husband's death drove her, and he admired her for not wavering from her course despite the risk to herself. Every moment he spent at the cottage increased her danger. Therefore, he vowed to hasten his recovery and return to England as soon as his weak body would allow.

One pleasant evening after dinner, Fleur asked Reed if he felt like going for a walk. Reed agreed with alacrity.

"I'd like that; I could use the exercise. Will you walk with me?"

"If you wish."

"I wish. Are you sure it's safe?"

"No one will be about this time of night. We are rather isolated here. Gaston found a cane for you. It should help you keep your balance."

Reed rose from his chair slowly. Fleur departed to fetch her wrap. Gaston left the dining room and returned moments later with the cane and Reed's jacket. When Fleur arrived, she took his arm.

"Are you ready?"

"Whenever you are."

Gaston opened the door and together they walked into the night. "Where shall we go?" Reed asked.

"Down the lane a bit. The grassy area will be too uneven for you to traverse, but you should be able to manage the dirt lane without difficulty."

They strolled, arm in arm, beneath a heaven bright with moonlight and twinkling stars. Reed breathed deeply of the fragrant night air, grateful that his maker had not granted his wish to die. It seemed as if he had waited a lifetime to walk beside Fleur on a soft summer night such as this.

Despite his pleasure at being outside, Reed soon felt himself begin to tire. Fleur must have noticed his flagging steps for she said, "There's a fallen log beside the lane. Would you like to stop and rest before we start back?"

"I don't like to think I am such a weakling, but yes, I'd better stop and rest. Besides, there's something I'd like to discuss with you, and I rarely see you alone anymore."

They ambled over to the fallen log. Reed eased himself down gingerly; Fleur sat beside him. "What did you wish to talk about?" She asked once they were settled.

"You. I've had a lot of time to think. I want you to leave France when I do. It isn't safe here for you. I can't believe Porter hasn't insisted that you return to England."

Fleur glanced at him, then looked away. "Lord Porter did suggest that I return, but my work here isn't done. This cottage belongs to Lisette, a mere citizen, and I am but a simple widow. No one here is curious about me. As long my country needs me, I will remain."

"You are but one woman, Fleur."

Fleur shrugged. "I do what I can."

"How much longer can the Black Widow remain anonymous? I don't like it, Fleur. The least I can do to repay you for saving my life is to see you safely settled in England."

Fleur shook her head. "You owe me nothing, Reed. I don't do this for personal gain. Saving lives is my way of making sure Pierre did not die in vain. Go home when the time comes and forget about me. I will be fine."

Reed searched her face. If only someone loved him as much as Fleur had loved her husband. "You must have loved your Pierre very much."

She flushed and looked away. "Pierre did not deserve to die. He was a good man."

She looked so sad, so utterly alone, that Reed couldn't help himself. Reaching out with his uninjured arm, he caressed her face, tracing her lips with the pad of his thumb.

"You are flirting with danger as long as you remain in France."

She turned her cheek into his palm. "It's been a long time since a man touched me with affection." Her whispered words held a poignant note.

"Return with me to England and I'll make sure you find a man who will appreciate you. You deserve someone to love you."

"I had someone who loved me."

He brought his hand to the back of her neck, urging her closer, until he could feel the sweet touch of her breath. "You will find another."

Resisting Fleur was impossible, even for a man still too weak to do what he truly wanted to do with Fleur. She needed a virile man, but he wasn't that man yet. Had she taken any of the other men she had rescued to her bed?

Fleur held her breath. The look in Reed's eyes captivated her. She couldn't have moved if she'd wanted to. She knew he was going to kiss her, and she wanted it. Yearned for it. She'd been so lonely since Pierre's death. She hadn't realized just how lonely until Reed came along. Their eyes met and clung.

None of the other men she had rescued affected her as Reed did. What was there about him that made her desire more than the lonely life she had embraced after her husband's death?

That was her last thought before Reed lowered his lips to hers and kissed her. His kiss created arousing memories of giving and receiving pleasure, of lying in a man's arms, of being cherished.

His ravishing mouth left hers, sought her ear, then her neck. His kisses produced delicious tremors of excitement she hadn't experienced for longer than she cared to remember. With a small moan of surrender, she circled his neck with her arms so she could hold him closer, returning his kiss even though she knew she was swimming in dangerous waters.

Abruptly her senses returned and she drew away. "Are you ready to go back to the house?"

"I'd rather stay here and kiss you."

"We can't do this, Reed. One, you're not well enough to engage in this kind of activity."

"We were only kissing."

"Two," she continued, "this shouldn't be happening. Once you leave, I'll never see you again. We both need to remember that."

She rose and helped Reed to his feet. They walked in silence back to the house, where Fleur bid Reed good night and continued on to her bedchamber. Once inside, she sat on the bed and hugged herself. Reed's kisses had tempted her to act injudiciously. She didn't know what had gotten into her. She wasn't the kind of woman whose head was easily turned by someone she scarcely knew.

Besides, she had told Reed the truth. He was too weak to engage in activity of the sort he was contemplating. But what would happen when he was well enough? It wasn't difficult to tell that Reed was a man who enjoyed women. Fleur didn't dare succumb, however, for her work here was too important. Letting herself become infatuated with Reed would lead to heartache. Besides, no man could take Pierre's place.

Reed lay in bed, unable to sleep, cursing his weak body. Though his strength was slowly returning and he had put on weight since he'd arrived at the cottage, his stamina was not what it once was. Being around Fleur had awakened his libido, however. He could actually feel desire again. He'd felt a tugging in his loins despite his inability to sustain a full erection.

Reed pounded his pillow, angry with himself and with his weakness. Would he ever be able to perform as a man again, with a man's ability to do both himself and the woman of his choice justice? Kissing Fleur had proven that he could still desire a woman, and that was encouraging.

Reed finally found sleep, but not an easy one. Sexual stirrings he hadn't experienced in months plagued him. He dreamed of holding Fleur in his arms, slowly undressing her, making love to her, running his hands over her smooth skin, learning every nuance of her sweet flesh.

In the middle of the night, Reed awoke with a start and realized he was suffering discomfort. He nearly laughed aloud when he discovered the reason for his distress. He had a full-blown erection. Even though he could do nothing about it, he turned over on his stomach and embraced sleep with a smile on his face.

He was indeed alive!

The next morning, still in good humor, Reed devoured his breakfast of eggs, ham, and fresh bread and butter. The entire household ate together, engaging in pleasant conversation.

"I know I've been eating like a horse, Fleur, and I'm concerned about depleting your funds," Reed said. "Where do you get the money to put food on the table?"

Fleur placed her fork on her plate as she mulled over her answer. "Pierre knew bad times were coming. He gathered all the gold coin and family jewels he could get his hands on and insisted I sew them in the hem of one of my gowns and in the lining of my cloak, in case I had to flee Paris."

She swallowed, as if it was painful to go on. "That day arrived far too soon. Pierre insisted I leave without him. For a while, Lisette, Gaston and I stayed with Antoine's parents in a small village outside Paris, waiting for Pierre to join us. Not long afterward, I learned that Pierre had been seized with other noblemen and sent to the guillotine."

"I'm sorry," Reed murmured.

Fleur seemed not to hear. "I remained with Antoine's parents but planned to leave before my presence put them in danger. We lived on the coins Pierre had provided for me without having to sell my jewels. Soon after, we moved to this cottage. It belongs to Lisette. It had stood unoccupied after her parents' deaths. Andre contacted me shortly thereafter."

"How did he find you?" Reed asked.

"I don't know. But one evening I had gone alone to the village church to pray. Andre knelt in the pew behind me and began speaking in a low voice. No one else was in the church. He told me he knew who I was and asked if I'd be willing to help my homeland.

"At first I feared he had been sent by someone to trap me, but the longer he talked, the more I began to believe he actually was an English operative. He seemed to know everything, even the fact that Lisette owned the cottage. I didn't even know about Devil's Chateau until he told me.

"He laid his plan before me in that holy place," Fleur continued. "Together we invented the Black Widow. Andre provides the coin we use to bribe the guards and support ourselves. You are the third Englishman I've taken from Devil's Chateau."

"Each time you enter the prison, it becomes more dangerous," Reed warned. "It won't be long before the warden learns about you and puts a stop to your activities. You could die, Fleur."

"I appreciate your concern, Reed, but that day is far off. My work here is not done."

Reed did not argue. He still had time to convince Fleur to return to England. "Do you have relatives in England?" he asked.

"I haven't heard from her in some time, but as far as I know, the aunt I lived with before I married Pierre is still living in the country. When the time comes for me to leave, I will have somewhere to go. She has no other relatives, so I will inherit her home, but not for a good long time, I hope. She is a dear woman."

Reed's relief was heartfelt. At least Fleur had a place to live once she returned to England. She was also a countess, which increased her chances of finding a worthy husband.

But did Fleur want another husband? Or had she loved Pierre so deeply that she refused to consider another marriage? "You are too young to be alone, Fleur. You need someone to take care of you."

Fleur bristled. "I do very well on my own, thank you. You needn't worry about me, Reed. I do what I do for my own peace of mind. What is happening to France is horrific. Executing innocent people just because they were born with a title is unconscionable. In my small way, I am doing my part to combat this Reign of Terror."

Reed knew that arguing with Fleur was getting him nowhere. The woman had a mind of her own; no one was going to convince her to leave France until she was ready. And then it might be too late. One thing was damn sure: When Reed returned to England, he intended to chastise Lord Porter for placing Fleur in the path of danger and keeping her there.

*   *   *

Reed continued to recover at an amazing pace. He had discarded the sling and found that his bones had healed perfectly. His arm was as good as new. He was putting on weight, too. No more hollows in his cheeks, and his muscle tone was improving.

He had begun a program of exercises to strengthen his body. He ran, hefted increasingly larger rocks over his head, and performed sequences of lifting and squatting. Were he at home, he would practice swordplay and boxing, but here he had to improvise. And it seemed to be working.

Fleur knew it was time to contact Andre about Reed's return to England. Her patient's health had improved dramatically during the weeks since he'd left Devil's Chateau. With each passing day, Fleur became increasingly aware of Reed's masculine allure. He was no longer the desperately ill man she had snatched from the jaws of death. Beneath his prison pallor was a ruggedly handsome face, perfect in its imperfections.

Reed's silver eyes had regained their luster, and his laughter came easily. Fleur could tell he was growing bored with inactivity, that he thought he wasn't healing fast enough, but the difference between the man he was now and the prisoner he had been was astounding.

Reed spoke often of Doctor Leclair, the man whom he had befriended in prison, and for Reed's sake, Fleur wanted to help the doctor before it was too late. Accordingly, she summoned Antoine and Gaston, and together they planned the doctor's rescue, even though instinct told her it was too soon to return to Devil's Chateau.

Fleur said nothing to Reed about her plans and waited until he'd retired for the night before leaving in the cart with her two servants. Antoine had learned beforehand that Lucien would be on duty tonight, and she had enough money on hand to bribe him.

When Fleur reached the prison, it was not Lucien but a guard she did not know who confronted her.

"Who are you and what do you want?" the guard challenged.

"Names are not important," Fleur murmured, aware that she had blundered badly. "I wish to visit Doctor Leclair."

"Now?" He tried to peer through her veil. "It's the middle of the night. Besides, no one in Devil's Chateau has visiting rights."

Fleur shook her purse of coins before the guard's eyes. "Where is Lucien? He knows me. I pay him well to let me inside to . . . visit."

Fleur feared she had raised the guard's suspicion and found out she was right when the guard said, "Stay here while I summon the warden." Apparently, this guard was above taking bribes.

The moment the guard's back was turned, Fleur fled. "Go!" she hissed as she climbed into the cart.

"What happened?" Gaston asked.

"Something went wrong. Lucien wasn't on duty. There was a different guard, and he grew suspicious. He has gone to fetch the warden. It was a mistake to come. I should have known it, but I wanted to surprise Reed."

As they sped home, Fleur kept looking behind her to see if they were being followed. They weren't. But when she walked into the cottage, she found both Reed and Lisette pacing the hall.

"Are you crazy?" Reed berated. "I heard wheels crunching on gravel and looked out the window in time to see you leaving in the cart. I couldn't believe you would attempt another rescue so soon after my own. I sought out Lisette, and she admitted you were off to Devil's Chateau. What were you thinking?"

Fleur pulled off her gloves and veil and handed them to Lisette. "Obviously, I wasn't," Fleur admitted. "Why aren't you asleep?"

"I was, but I'm a light sleeper." He glared at her. "Did Andre send you to Devil's Chateau again? I intend to have words with Porter next time I see him." He must have caught something in her face, for he said, "Something happened, didn't it?"

"Go back to bed. I'll tell you tomorrow."

"You'll tell me now," Reed said, grabbing her arm and pulling her into the parlor, where a lamp had been left burning. "What happened?"

Fleur sighed and sank into a chair. "Lucien was supposed to be on duty, but he wasn't. A different guard answered my summons. I fled when he went to fetch the warden."

Reed cursed. "I'm going to wring Andre's neck. Who did he send you after this time?"

Fleur stared down at her hands. She knew Reed was going to be angry when he learned whom she had gone for.

"Who, Fleur?"

"Doctor Leclair, but it wasn't Andre's idea. I wanted to rescue Leclair for you. I know you are worried about him."

Reed thrust his fingers through his dark hair, mussing it beyond redemption. "I'm sorry I asked you to help him. Clearly I wasn't thinking. I didn't mean for you to put your life on the line again. What do you think will happen now?"

Fleur didn't know. "Antoine has already contacted Andre to arrange for a ship to take you to England."

"What about you?"

"Nothing will happen to me. No one in the village besides Doctor Defoe knows I exist."

Reed shook his head. "That's not true. Lucien and every prisoner at Devil's Chateau know you exist. You are the subject of much speculation. Your life is in danger."

Fleur stood. "I'm tired, Reed. We'll discuss this tomorrow."

When she strode past him, Reed reached out, snagging her around the waist and bringing her into the circle of his arms. "I worry about you, Fleur. How can I turn my back on you when I leave?"

"You won't be turning your back on me. You'll be taking your rightful place among the *ton*. We should be hearing from Andre concerning travel arrangements within a fortnight."

As much as Reed wanted to return home, he didn't want to leave Fleur. He had grown closer to her in the past few weeks than to any other woman. "I care about you, Fleur."

"Don't say anything you don't mean, Reed. I suspect that you are grateful and that you probably confuse gratitude with caring."

His arms tightened around her. He stroked her hair, her cheek, reveling in the way she made him feel. He felt himself harden and knew it was due to this special woman in his arms. The depth of his desire surprised him. An inexplicable need to have her in his bed assailed him. He'd had dozens of women, but none made him feel as Fleur did.

Was it gratitude that made him want Fleur so much? He thought not, although he was indeed grateful. No, his need for Fleur possessed every sense, every emotion. Eager to taste her again, he lowered his head and kissed her. Sliding a hand down her bodice, he deftly undid several buttons, until his fingertips encountered her warm skin.

Reed heard the sudden intake of her breath as he searched beneath her corset and curled his fingers around her breast. Right now Fleur was the only real thing in his life. He had clung to her while he was as weak as a mewling babe, but now that he was well and strong, he wanted Fleur in ways that had nothing to do with his healing.

Fleur broke off the kiss and stared up at Reed. "You're making this difficult for me, Reed."

"Come to my bed, Fleur. I need you."

He took her mouth again before she could deny him, deepening the kiss, tasting her with his tongue, savoring her with slow relish. A rustling noise followed by a gasp alerted them that they were no longer alone in the parlor.

Fleur pulled away from him, quickly fastening her buttons before turning around to face Lisette.

Lisette cleared her throat. "Forgive me, Fleur. You weren't in your chamber when I went in to help you prepare for bed, and I grew worried."

"You weren't intruding, Lisette. I was just having a word with Reed before retiring. Come, you can help me undress."

Reed watched helplessly as Fleur made a hasty exit, dragging Lisette with her. Frustrated, Reed had no choice but to seek his own bed.

Fleur managed to evade Reed during the next two days, making sure she was never alone with him. Reed thought he understood why. She was as attracted to him as he was to her and was fighting against involvement.

Reed had just finished lunch in the cozy kitchen, making idle conversation with Fleur and Lisette, when Antoine raced into the house.

"Countess," Antoine cried, skidding to a halt in the doorway. "You and *monsieur* must hide. Quickly! Soldiers, they come."

Reed leapt from his chair. "They're coming here? How do you know?"

"I went to the village this morning to purchase meat from the butcher when half a dozen soldiers entered the village. They were asking questions of everyone. They wanted to know about inhabitants of the village and outlying cottages. I lingered nearby while the villagers gave directions to several cottages in the vicinity. This cottage was one of them."

Gaston had arrived in time to hear Antoine's warning. "How soon will the soldiers arrive, Antoine?"

"Soon. There aren't many homes in this area, for the countryside is not conducive to farming or raising livestock. You and *monsieur* must hide immediately, Countess," Antoine urged.

Reed had many questions but decided to save them for later. He recognized panic when he saw it. "Shall we hide in the woods?" he asked.

"No," Fleur said. "We've prepared a better place. Follow me."

"We will hide all evidence that you and *monsieur* ever existed," Lisette said, running from the room.

"This way," Fleur said, leading the way down the hall. "We've planned well for this day, even though we hoped it would never arrive."

"Your decision to go to Devil's Chateau so soon after my rescue was ill-advised," Reed chided.

At the end of the hallway they came to a nondescript wardrobe that Reed had paid scant heed to. When Fleur opened the door to the wardrobe, Reed balked.

"This is ridiculous. We can't hide in there. The search will be a thorough one; we are certain to be found. Hiding in the woods would be better."

"As I told you before, we are well prepared for this day."

To Reed's astonishment, Fleur pushed aside a few garments hanging inside and lifted a trapdoor in the floor of the wardrobe, revealing a gaping, dark hole.

"Come on," Fleur urged as she stepped down into the dark void. "Be careful, there are four steps leading down to a small enclosure beneath the house where we can hide. Hunch over—you're too tall to stand erect—and be sure to close the wardrobe door and pull the trapdoor down behind you."

Reed had no choice but to obey. He shut the wardrobe door and groped his way down the steps. He reached up and pulled the trapdoor into place, enclosing them in total darkness.

"There is space for two to sit comfortably down here," Fleur said.

Reed felt her hands on his arm, guiding him down. His breath seized, and he began to tremble. This small, damp enclosure reminded him too much of the unending days spent in solitary confinement at Devil's Chateau, in a black hole just like this. It had been his punishment for failing to divulge the names of his fellow operatives in France.

"What's wrong?" Fleur asked.

Reed could scarcely catch his breath. He felt as if a heavy weight were pressing down on his chest. Panic stuck its talons into him and refused to let go. He began sweating profusely.

"Reed, what is it? Are you ill?"

"I . . . don't do well in tight, closed places. The memories . . . I'm sorry, I can't stay here." He started to rise.

Fleur caught his arm. Her hands followed his arm up to his shoulder, grazing his neck, until she found his cheek. Her other hand joined the first, cupping his face. Mesmerized, Reed felt his fears ease when she brought her mouth to his and kissed him.

❧ Chapter Four ❧

For a few wild moments of pure joy, Reed forgot where he was. Darkness receded; he was no longer in a black pit associated with pain and suffering. Fleur's kiss became a lifeline to reality, pulling him toward the light, where his own instincts took over.

Tugging her against him, he deepened the kiss, exploring the sweetness of her mouth as if it were his only link to sanity. He cupped her breasts in his hands, dimly aware that today she wore no corset to hinder his exploration. She caught his groan in her mouth, squeezing his arm as if to warn him that even the tiniest noise could bring disaster down upon them.

Reed heeded her implied warning, though it was difficult. He wanted to do things with Fleur that were impossible in the limited space of the cramped hole. But that didn't stop him from kissing her, touching her, caressing her sweet womanly curves. As long as he kept the darkness at bay, he could survive the terrifying memories.

And one day soon, Reed vowed, he would have Fleur naked beneath him, bringing them the pleasure they had both denied themselves. His once-dormant cock jerked and stiffened. Reed rejoiced at the knowledge that he was still capable of making love to a woman.

Suddenly Fleur went rigid against him. "Listen," she whispered against his lips.

Reed went still, listening as Fleur directed. Muted voices, accompanied by the stomp of boots and the soft shuffle of leather slippers alerted him to imminent danger.

The boots stopped before the wardrobe. Reed could hear the voices clearly now.

"What is this?" a man asked in a commanding voice.

"A wardrobe, *monsieur*," he heard Lisette answer.

"What is it doing out here?"

"My brothers moved it here. There was no room for it in the bedchamber."

Reed clutched Fleur tightly when he heard the wardrobe door open and someone rummaging about directly above them. He scarcely dared to breathe; each tiny breath he took sounded like thunder in his ears. Their combined heartbeats pounded so loudly, he feared the sound would give them away.

With Fleur's kisses no longer distracting him, reality intruded, making him aware once more of where they were. The dirt walls of the black pit in which they were hiding began to close in on him. His heartbeat accelerated; sweat drenched him. If he didn't get out of here soon, he feared he would go mad. He should have taken his chances in the woods. Now Fleur would know what a coward he was, how being entombed in dark places roused him to panic.

"Does this cottage have a cellar?" Reed heard the soldier ask.

"*Non, monsieur*," Lisette answered. "My parents built this house with their own two hands. My father did not dig a cellar."

The soldier merely grunted.

The sound of receding footsteps did little to calm Reed's ragged nerves. He needed to get out . . . now.

"I can't do this, Fleur," he whispered into her ear. "The soldiers are gone. I have to get out of here."

Grasping his arm, Fleur prevented him from raising the trap door. "Not yet. Someone will come for us when it's safe to leave. Please, Reed, you need to stay here with me."

Reed began to shiver. "You don't know. You can't even imagine what it's like for me. I spent days, weeks, in a pit barely large enough to turn around in, fighting off rats, deprived of light and companionship."

"But you're not alone this time," Fleur soothed. "Kiss me, Reed."

Reed barely heard her words. Panic sent his pulse soaring. Vividly he recalled being pulled from the pit, beaten, then returned to his private hell, broken and bruised, alone and forgotten. Though he couldn't recall how long he had remained in the pit, he did remember praying for death. After what seemed like eons they had come for him, beaten him again and then placed him in a different kind of hell with other prisoners.

Fleur knew she wasn't getting through to Reed. She could practically smell his fear. He was panting, and she could feel perspiration seeping through his clothing. If she couldn't save him from his demons, there was no telling what he might do. She could still hear soldiers in the cottage and feared discovery. Fumbling for his hand, she grasped it and placed it on her breast.

"Reed, come back to me. Kiss me."

Relief shuddered through her when she felt Reed's hand tighten on her breast. His breathing, though still frantic, slowed. She smiled when his fingers searched for her nipple, rolling the sensitive bud between his thumb and forefinger. When he found her cheek with his other hand and turned her face into his kiss, she knew she had reached him in that dark place and that his demons were retreating.

Reed relaxed into the kiss like a drowning man seeking air. She melted against him, drawing him deeper into the kiss. She opened her mouth to his tongue, surprised by her own state of arousal. She was so lost in passion, she nearly failed to hear footsteps returning to the wardrobe.

Her lips moved against his. "Reed, stop! They're coming back."

Reed went still. Fleur strained to hear the murmur of voices.

"Are you satisfied, *monsieur?*" she heard Lisette ask. "If you tell me who or what you're looking for, I might be of more help."

A male voice rumbled in reply. "Since we didn't find what we were looking for, there is no need for you to know." A moment of silence and then he asked, "How long will your brothers be staying with you?"

Fleur realized he was asking about Antoine and Gaston. The plan was to introduce them as Lisette's brothers should anyone ask.

"We will return to our wives and families soon," Gaston answered. "We came to make sure our sister is well. She has recently been widowed and moved into our parents' cottage."

The soldier muttered something Fleur didn't understand, followed by the sound of retreating footsteps.

"Are they gone?" Reed whispered.

"We can only hope."

A few minutes later the trapdoor was raised. Fleur blinked in the sudden light as Gaston's face came into view.

"Are you two all right, Countess?"

"We're fine," Fleur answered. "Is it safe to come out?"

"They're gone. I don't think they'll return any time soon."

"Thank God," Fleur said, nearly collapsing in relief. She didn't know if Reed could have held up much longer. She hadn't been aware of the darkness inside him. Or that he was fighting demons from his time at Devil's Chateau.

Gaston reached down. She grasped his hand and climbed out of the hole, ducking out of the wardrobe as the servant offered Reed his hand.

Until now, Fleur hadn't been aware of Reed's fear of closed-in places. She knew he'd been beaten and starved, but this was the first time she'd heard him mention a pit. None of the others had spoken of the kind of torture Reed had suffered. Perhaps it was something they wanted to forget. If she and Reed hadn't been forced to hide, Fleur would have never known about the inhumane method of torture the prison guards used to extract information.

"Are you all right, Reed?" Fleur asked when Reed emerged from the darkness.

"I've been better," he said from between clenched teeth. "You and your friends are very clever. That was an excellent hiding place. If it's safe, I think I'll go bask in the sunshine awhile."

Gaston sent him a curious look. "The danger is over for now, *monsieur*."

Reed nodded and headed toward the front door. Fleur hurried after him. He didn't go far. He sank down on the ground beneath a tree and lifted his face to the sun. Fleur settled beside him.

"Thank you for saving my sanity," Reed said without looking at her. "I never thought I'd react so strongly to being confined in a dark place. I feel wrung out, emotionally drained. I hope the soldiers never come back, because I don't think I could face that confinement again."

"I'm sorry; I didn't know. It must have been terrifying for you."

"I don't want to talk about it." He gave a sheepish grin. "I liked the way you tried to distract me. You're an astute woman, Fleur. I nearly lost my soul in that dark, frightening place I visit far too often in my dreams."

They sat together in companionable silence. At length Reed said, "The arrival of those soldiers should be a warning. It's time you left France, Fleur. You cannot continue like this—it's too dangerous. I can't bear to think of you locked up in Devil's Chateau, or another prison equally offensive. I shall go to the village to meet with Andre myself. He needs to know what's going on here."

"No," Fleur stubbornly objected. "I'll know when it's time to leave, and that day hasn't arrived. Don't worry, Reed. I can take care of myself."

Gaston called them in to lunch. Reed rose, helped Fleur to her feet, and they returned to the cottage together.

"By the way," Reed whispered to Fleur, "I enjoyed the kisses we shared. I want you, Fleur; that's never been in doubt. Come to me tonight."

Fleur was tempted. More than tempted. Kissing Reed had made her feel as giddy as a girl. Her body still thrummed. She wanted more, much more than kisses. But did she dare? She feared if she let Reed make love to her, she would never be the same; yearning for a man out of her reach would endanger lives and distract her. And Reed would most definitely be out of her reach, for she wasn't ready to leave France yet.

She opened her mouth to deny Reed's request but shut it when Lisette greeted them at the door. "There you are," Lisette said. "Lunch is ready and I know *monsieur* must be hungry."

Fleur gave Reed an apologetic look and followed Lisette into the kitchen.

As Reed prepared for bed that night, he thought about the pit and how Fleur had distracted him. If not for Fleur, he would have fallen apart and betrayed their hiding place. He'd had no idea he would react like that, not until he found himself enclosed in darkness so complete it had threatened his sanity.

Restlessly Reed prowled the bedchamber. His body was unsettled, his emotions ragged. Why wouldn't Fleur listen to him? Why wouldn't she take his advice? He'd been an undercover operative a long time, collecting battle plans, arsenal locations, troop assignments; experience told him it was time for Fleur to leave.

Reed couldn't sleep. He stared at the door a long time, waiting for Fleur to come to him. When she failed to arrive, he became restless and edgy. He knew he would be leaving soon and couldn't imagine leaving Fleur behind. He had no idea precisely what he intended until he found himself leaving his bedchamber and standing before Fleur's. He didn't knock. The knob turned beneath his hand, and he let himself inside. The chamber was dark but for moonlight streaming through the single window, which had been left open to the cool night air.

Reed moved noiselessly to the bed. Fleur was sleeping on her side, her black hair stark against the white pillow, her hands folded beneath her cheek. She looked young, far too young to be involved in such dangerous work. As desperately as he wanted to, he decided not to awaken her. He turned to leave.

"Reed?"

He whipped around; her eyes were open, staring at him.

"What are you doing here?" she asked sleepily.

Reed shrugged. "Honestly, I don't know. I waited for you to come to me and when you didn't, I found myself at your door."

Fleur sat up, reaching for him. "Are you ill? Were you thinking about Devil's Chateau again?"

Reed stared at her hand upon his arm and eased down on the side of the bed. "It wasn't the pit I was thinking about; I was waiting for you. I can't stop worrying about you. Today was a warning you should heed. Tell me how to contact Andre. If I can't convince you to leave, maybe he can."

"Andre is gone. He won't be back until he brings word that the ship has arrived for you."

Reed spit out a curse. "Maybe I won't leave."

Fleur sat up straighter, letting the sheet slip down to her hips. "You have to go. Your grandmother needs you. You have a duty to the earldom."

"I have a duty to my country. I was an operative before I was an earl. I can stay and help you."

Even as he said it, Reed knew Fleur was right. He had another obligation now, to his family and his tenants. An earldom was a huge responsibility. He had never wanted it, yet it had come to him and he couldn't let his grandmother down by ignoring his duty.

"Fleur," he said thickly.

Fleur lifted a finger to his lips. "The subject is moot, Reed. Do you need laudanum to help you sleep?"

"No, I need . . . you. Only you, Fleur." He reached for her. "Enduring the darkness beneath the ground today was pure hell, but you pulled me through. I want to make love to you more than I have wanted anything in my life. If I must leave without you, let me have this memory of you to take with me."

Fleur opened her mouth to deny Reed, then thought better of it. What would it hurt to make love with Reed? They were both adults, and Reed was the first man to attract her both physically and emotionally since Pierre's death. In Fleur's mind there was only one reply to Reed's need, and she could give it without speaking a word.

Circling his neck with her arms, she brought his head down to hers, the invitation implicit in her actions. Groaning, Reed joined their mouths, slowly lowering her against the mattress and covering her with his body. He kissed her until she was trembling with excitement. Knowledge of what would happen next shook Fleur to her very toes. It seemed like forever since she had felt the pressure of a man's body against hers, inside hers.

"It's been a long time for me," Reed whispered against her lips, echoing Fleur's thoughts.

"For me, too."

She saw passion tightening his face, saw his silver eyes darken. She felt her breasts flush with heat. With a rough sound of need, he took her mouth again, bringing her hips against him with one hand and with the other stroking the curves of her trembling body.

Reed rose up on his elbows and looked down at her, his face dark and intense. "You want me as badly as I want you."

"Oh, yes," Fleur replied, helpless to do anything except follow the dictates of her body.

With a strangled sound of triumph deep in his throat, Reed tightened his hold, surrounding her in the heat and scent of his aroused body while his mouth returned to hers, kissing her nearly senseless.

Although Fleur had enjoyed making love with Pierre, it was different with Reed, more intense, more powerfully arousing. Pierre had been like a calm sea in a storm, while Reed was the storm itself, seething beneath churning waves of desire. With a cry of surrender, she fell headlong into the turbulence. Only to have it withdrawn when Reed broke off the kiss and rose up on his knees. A cry of protest escaped her lips.

"Raise your arms, sweetheart. I want you naked."

Dutifully Fleur lifted her arms while Reed pulled the offending article of clothing up and away. It floated gracefully to the floor beside the bed. Seconds later, Reed's clothing joined it.

Fleur stared at his body, clearly visible in the moonlight that fell across the bed. She found it difficult to believe that this was the same bruised and emaciated man she had taken from Devil's Chateau. Though he was still on the thin side, he had slowly added muscle through exercise and a steady diet of nourishing food. Though nothing could be done about the scars, they wouldn't interfere with his life or activities.

"What are you looking at?" Reed asked.

Fleur's gaze lifted to his face. "You've made a great deal of progress in the past few weeks. You're not the same man who arrived at the cottage."

"It's all due to you and your friends, Fleur. I owe you more than I can ever repay. Now shut up and let me love you. I've been waiting for this day since I first saw you."

He lowered himself on top of her, melding their bodies together, hot skin against hot skin. She sighed as his mouth skimmed over her lips, her cheeks, down the slender column of her throat. His tongue flicked out to test the pulse at the base of her neck before moving down, licking a path between her breasts, leaving a trail of liquid fire.

Fleur moaned and clutched his head, holding him against her as his hot mouth found a nipple and sucked gently. She reveled in the naked heat and strength of him. She felt her nipple tighten, and she shivered in delight. When he moved his hand along her hip and thigh, she felt her body quicken and her blood thicken. When his hand moved between her thighs, she wanted to scream in joy. She was ready . . . more than ready; she opened her legs and stirred restlessly beneath him. Her body craved what she had denied herself since Pierre's death. And she wanted it from this man. No other would do.

His fingers splayed to clasp her woman's mound, delving into the dewy cleft of her sex. Fleur drew a sharp breath, her body stiffening.

"Relax, sweetheart," he murmured.

His husky whisper soothed her, coaxing her restless, needy body to soften even though the clamoring in her blood didn't want to wait. She burned beneath his touch, her nipples aching points of flame. She lifted her hips in silent supplication as he parted the quivering silky folds of her flesh with his fingers.

Fleur mewed softly as his fingers grew bolder, exploring her slick flesh with tender strokes, sliding inside her, probing. His fingers came away wet with her dew; he held them up for her inspection.

Her lips quivered with embarrassment. This was different from anything she'd experienced with Pierre. This was titillating, naughty, wicked. "Reed, please hurry."

Reed merely looked at her and flashed his dimple. His grin was a heady elixir. It flowed through her blood like molten honey. Instinctively she knew that Reed was an experienced lover, a rogue who lived to love and please women.

"We're not even half done yet, Fleur. It's been a long time since I've had a woman, and I want to savor the experience. For a time I feared I had lost desire forever, but then you proved me wrong."

The words had scarcely left his mouth when he scooted down her body, pressing kisses against her navel. His tongue parted the thatch of hair between her thighs, searching for the tiny hooded bud nestled there. She felt the rough pad of his tongue flick out, stroking the dewy cleft between her thighs. He licked the hidden bud. She arched up into his mouth, crying out his name.

"Reed, stop! This is far too intimate. I cannot bear it."

Reed lifted his head. "Did Pierre not love you in this way?"

She shook her head. "I would not allow it."

Reed blinked. "Why not?"

"The intimacy of it . . . was . . . too much."

"Not if you loved him."

Reed's words hung in the air as he returned his attention to the sensitive flesh between Fleur's thighs. Fleur's moans grew progressively louder as Reed used his mouth and tongue to arouse her to heights never before reached. She felt her tender flesh swell, then burn beneath the relentless lapping of his tongue.

Suddenly she was writhing with frantic need, straining toward a frenzied explosion. She sobbed, clutching mindlessly at him, the world around her shattering. With an abandoned cry, she surged against his mouth.

Stretching up, Reed's arms came around her to hold her trembling body as rapture claimed her.

Throbbing with the urgent need to possess the hot,

aroused woman in his arms, Reed wanted very much to plunge into her softness, claiming her in the most primitive way. He watched her face as she climbed down from the heights of pleasure. He wanted desperately to feel her hands upon his body.

"Touch me, Fleur. Feel how hard I am for you."

Deliberately he drew her palm over his flat belly, pressing her fingers against his throbbing sex. Her fingers curled around him. He jerked violently, pushing himself into her palm. The pleasure was almost more than he could bear. He needed to be inside her.

Now!

He spread her thighs, settled into the cradle of her hips and thrust forward. He entered her smoothly, seating his staff fully. He felt her muscles squeeze him and found heaven. He withdrew almost completely, intending to drive forward again, but Fleur must have mistaken his intention.

She grasped his hips and cried, "No, don't leave me!"

"I won't," he vowed hoarsely.

Even as he spoke, her hips tilted up, giving him better access. Groaning, he moved forward and inward, going deeper, driving harder, faster.

Fleur tensed, holding her breath. Then Reed settled his lips over hers; she tasted her scent on his mouth, a taste both shocking and arousing. Her hands clutched the broad shoulders of the man straining above her, her loins rising to meet his. She felt his body tense moments before she burst into flame. The world spun away, and she rose up to meet it.

She was only dimly aware of his husky voice urging her on, barely cognizant of the ridges of scarred flesh beneath her fingertips. Reduced to a bundle of quivering nerve endings, she clung to him, rocking her hips as her cries of pleasure filled the space around them.

Moments later she convulsed, soaring higher than she'd ever soared before, visited places she had never seen. The view from the top shook her to the very core. When she felt Reed stiffen and go still, heard his hoarse cry, she grasped his hand to welcome him to paradise.

Reed's eyes closed in sensual pleasure that bordered on pain as Fleur trembled and quaked beneath him. When she grasped his hand and clutched it tightly, he could no longer help himself. Thrusting in a raw, urgent rhythm, he felt the explosion rip through him. He cried out his own savage release, his body clenching and shuddering with pent-up wildness, finally ending his enforced celibacy.

Fleur had never experienced anything quite like what had just happened between her and Reed. She closed her eyes to better enjoy the aftermath, relishing the weight of Reed's body atop hers.

It was a memory to savor, to store and retrieve at will after Reed left. Emotionally drained, overwhelmed, Fleur felt Reed soften inside her and his weight lift away from her. He sagged to his side on the mattress, still breathing hard. During the lull, Fleur recalled the purpose of Reed's nocturnal visit.

"It won't work, you know," Fleur said.

He rolled on his side to face her. "What won't work?"

"Using sex to convince me to leave."

"You misjudge me. Making love to you wasn't my intention when I came to your chamber."

"You don't need to explain, Reed. You haven't had a woman in a long time, and I was handy. I don't blame you for what happened between us. I understand your need, although I don't understand mine."

"Didn't you enjoy sex with your husband?"

"Yes, I enjoyed that aspect of marriage." She looked at him, then glanced away. "Though I have to admit what you and I did in no way compares to what I experienced during my marriage."

"Should I be insulted?"

A long pause. "No, Reed, you have nothing to be

ashamed of. I never knew I was capable of responding as I did to you. It was . . . intense."

"You were magnificent. When we return to England, we can see each other as often as we like. We're both adults; we need answer to no one about our actions. Do you see now why I can't leave you behind, Fleur?"

Fleur saw a great deal. "I'm not looking for a casual affair, Reed. I'm not looking for a man at all. And as I told you before, I'm not leaving France until I absolutely have to."

"Fleur . . ."

"Say no more, Reed. Your grandmother moved heaven and earth to get you back home. The earldom needs an heir and you have a duty to marry well and provide one. Even if I returned with you to England, our lives would take different paths. And I absolutely refuse to become your mistress."

"I didn't ask that of you and never will."

"Are you saying you want to marry me?"

Fleur smiled when Reed appeared stunned by her question.

"I wouldn't rule that out," Reed said after a long, telling silence. "You are as well-born as I am and certainly appropriate."

"No, I'm not," Fleur confessed. "We don't really know each other, and I can't have children."

"What? You don't know that."

"I didn't conceive during my marriage to Pierre."

Another long silence ensued before Reed said with a hint of resignation, "Is there nothing I can say to make you understand the danger you would be in should you remain in France?"

"I *know* the work I do is dangerous. I'm not stupid. But it's what I want to do, what I need to do. Go home and forget me, Reed. Perhaps one day, when my work here is done, we will meet again and laugh over this little . . . episode in our lives."

"Laugh? I hardly think so."

It was true that Reed was in no hurry to wed. Spending months in prison and weeks before that working undercover had left him eager to indulge the passionate side of his nature. Before leaving England, he had gained a reputation as a talented lover. But there had been no urgency to settle down then. He wasn't the heir and had expected his brother to produce children. So Reed had abandoned himself to wicked pursuits, enjoying every one of them.

His reckless quest for adventure was what had attracted him to his current position: that of a British agent in revolutionary France. Though Reed knew Grandmamma would insist that he wed soon and set up his nursery, he had earned a bit of carousing before settling down to wedded bliss.

"You should leave," Fleur said, interrupting Reed's introspection. "Thank you for making me feel alive again. I needed this night as much as you did."

"We're not done yet, sweetheart. The night is still young; we have hours left to make up for months of deprivation."

Before Fleur knew what he intended, he dragged her on top of him and pulled her head down for his kiss.

The hours passed too swiftly as Fleur and Reed explored each other's bodies, both aware that their time together was drawing to an end. They made love slowly, with Fleur on top, controlling the movement until the very end. Then Reed took over, his wildness driving them both over the edge. Nothing was sacrosanct, nothing off limits. After, they fell asleep in each other's arms, only to awaken again before dawn and make love again.

✦ Chapter Five ✦

Fleur became Reed's lover during the time left to him on French shores. They both knew it was only a matter of days before Reed left France and Fleur continued her dangerous game.

Sensing Fleur's withdrawal whenever Reed urged her to leave France, he stopped mentioning it. Instead, he began considering the possibility of remaining in France and continuing his undercover work for the Crown. The earldom could wait for him until Napoleon's march to conquer the world was halted.

Reed's only hesitation came when he thought of his grandmother, who anxiously awaited his return. To Grandmamma, nothing was more important than preserving the earldom for future generations, and that meant he must wed. But taking a wife was the last thing on Reed's list of priorities. There was still a great deal he could do to help his country.

A fortnight after Fleur sent word to Andre that Reed was well enough to travel, a message arrived via Antoine. Reed and Fleur were seated in the parlor when Antoine relayed Andre's response. An English sloop would arrive to pick Reed up two nights hence. Andre would be waiting at the rendezvous on the beach to see Reed off. Reed received the message with ill humor.

"Why are you scowling, Reed?" Fleur asked after Antoine had delivered the message and departed. "You'll be home soon, taking your rightful place in Society."

"I never cared a fig about Society. Jason was the heir; it was his duty to maintain the Hunthurst dignity, marry and produce heirs. I never wanted the title. I was perfectly happy indulging myself shamelessly and pursuing danger and adventure. Becoming a secret operative suited me just fine." His voice broke. "I'll never forgive Jason for dying."

Fleur knew Reed was speaking from grief. He might not verbally admit it, but he loved his brother and mourned his death. Reed needed to return home and take over as head of the family. And she needed to remain in France, where rescuing men like Reed was essential to her country.

"I want to talk to Andre," Reed said. "Now. Can Antoine arrange it?"

"I doubt it," Fleur replied. "Andre appears only at a pre-arranged time and day. He won't show himself again until the night of your departure."

"Where, pray tell, is that?"

"There's a small cove about two miles up the coast. The ship will anchor in the bay and send a small boat ashore for you. There's an alternative route farther up the coast in case the first becomes unavailable to us. If the night is stormy, the ship will wait beyond the cove until the weather clears before sending out a boat. We've done this before and know how it works."

Before Reed could answer, Lisette walked into the small parlor. "Antoine tells me we'll be losing our guest soon."

"It's true, Lisette," Fleur replied. "Once our guest returns to England, his family doctor can take over his care."

"I doubt I will receive better care anywhere than I did from you and your mistress, Lisette," Reed said. "Had I remained in Devil's Chateau, I would have been dead long before now. Your simple but delicious meals were instrumental in returning me to health."

Lisette blushed at the compliment. "You give me too much credit, *monsieur*. Have you seen Gaston, Fleur? I thought he might pick some vegetables from the garden for our dinner tonight."

"Perhaps I can help," Reed offered.

"We have plans to go over, Reed," Fleur said. "Gaston can do Lisette's bidding. I believe you'll find him stacking wood behind the house, Lisette."

Lisette took her leave.

"Will you come to meet the ship with me?" Reed asked.

Fleur glanced at him and looked away. "I think not. Usually Antoine drives the cart and Gaston goes along in case of trouble. That's how it's done."

Reed nodded. "I suppose it's for the best. Keeping you safe is my main concern. Can I come to you tonight? It might be the last time for us to be together."

She lifted her eyes to him. "Come to me after the household settles down for the night."

They parted then. Fleur stopped into the kitchen to visit with Lisette while Reed went outside to help Gaston in the garden. Lisette greeted Fleur with a scowl.

"Do you think it wise to become involved with our guest, *chèrie*? The heart is a fragile thing, easily broken. I do not wish to see you pining for a man so far out of your reach. It could affect your work and *bon Dieu* knows you need your wits about you."

"I will be fine, Lisette, truly," Fleur assured her. "My heart is not involved."

Fleur nearly bit her tongue at that untruth. Though she couldn't exactly say she loved Reed, she cared about him in a way that surprised her. Fleur had cared deeply about her husband, but it hadn't been a passionate, tempestuous love. With Reed the passion was all-consuming, but Fleur knew that kind of wild passion could not last. Pierre had given her peace of mind, comfort and a warm regard that would have lasted a lifetime had he lived. What she experienced with Reed was too searing to bring peace into her life. And once her work in France ended, Fleur wanted peace and quiet.

Besides, Reed needed an heir, and she couldn't give him one. Even if he was still interested in her once she returned to England, which was doubtful, nothing would come of their relationship. London was filled with eligible debs looking for a titled husband. How long could Reed hold out against them? Not long if his grandmother had anything to say about it.

"You're not fooling me, *ma petite*," Lisette said as she poured two cups of tea and handed one to Fleur. "I know you have taken our guest as a lover. He is the first since your husband."

Fleur sipped her tea slowly. "I was lonely. Do not scold me, Lisette, for I know what I am about. Reed leaves tomorrow night—I thought you might prepare something special for supper tomorrow. His appetite is insatiable of late."

"*Monsieur* seems to have an insatiable appetite for many things," Lisette grumbled beneath her breath.

"What did you say, Lisette?"

"Pay me no heed. I just pray you know what you are doing."

Reed found Gaston in the garden, gathering vegetables. He stood and watched awhile, then offered to help. Gaston declined his offer, saying he had already picked what was needed for tonight's meal. Reed wandered off down the lane. He had a great deal to think about.

Foremost in his thoughts were the responsibilities he must shoulder as the Earl of Hunthurst. Was he up to them? Was he prepared to settle down and take a wife? That question was easily answered. No, he was not. How could a man accustomed to facing dangerous situations and living precariously be satisfied with a mild-mannered Society miss whose most daring adventure was a walk in the park with a gentleman, accompanied by her mama or a maid?

Grandmamma was going to be disappointed if she expected him to settle down and set up a nursery any time soon. None of the society debs was Fleur. Reed caught his breath. Where had that thought come from? Except as a temporary fling, Fleur wasn't for him. Despite their mutual commitment to the Crown, their lives followed diverse paths.

After a long walk, Reed returned to his bedchamber for a nap. If he was to spend his last night in Fleur's bed, he wanted to be well rested.

Reed awakened refreshed and went to the kitchen to partake of another of Lisette's excellent meals. There was even a fine Bordeaux wine to accompany the ragout, and fresh bread and a dessert to die for. Reed cleaned his plate and asked for seconds of the dessert.

Conversation centered on plans for Reed's departure. Reed listened carefully, then asked a few questions of his own.

"Will I finally meet Andre?" he asked.

Antoine supplied the answer. "*Oui*, he will be waiting for you on the beach."

Reed excused himself after the meal and went directly to his bedchamber, where he counted the minutes until the house quieted and he was free to go to Fleur. He left his chamber and walked the short distance to Fleur's. He opened the door without knocking and stepped inside, closing the door softly behind him. Fleur was waiting; she turned from the window at the sound of his entry, her luminous eyes as dark as melted chocolate in the golden glow of a single candle.

She had stripped down to her shift, a white, diaphanous garment that revealed more than it concealed. Reed stopped in midstep, his silver eyes darkening as he admired her haunting beauty. Then she opened her arms to him, and Reed walked into them.

"Fleur, I . . ."

"No, don't say anything, Reed. What is there to say that hasn't already been said? Let us enjoy the moment. They don't come very often for people like us."

"All you have to do is step aboard that ship with me for our liaison to continue," Reed reminded her.

"You don't mean that, Reed. Think about it. You and I are but a moment in time."

Though Reed knew Fleur was right, he wasn't ready for their relationship to end. "Did anyone ever tell you that you talk too much? If we have only this moment, let us enjoy it."

She gazed at him, her brown eyes soft with desire and alight with eagerness. He was charmed that she could feel and show more than one emotion at once. But that wasn't the only thing he admired about Fleur. He had never met a woman like her.

"Kiss me, Reed. I didn't realize how lonely I was until you came to us, and when you leave I shall be lonely again."

Reed didn't hesitate. He wanted to kiss Fleur as badly as she wanted to kiss him. He had thought of nothing else all day. That and how many times he could make love to her before dawn.

"You're so beautiful," he murmured, setting his lips to the fragrant turn of her neck, then to her shoulder and finally over her mouth. He thrust his tongue past her open lips and stroked inside, offering a promise of pleasure to come. Her arms circled his neck as she melted into him, returning his kiss passionately.

A deep groan escaped his lips as he ended the kiss and broke contact with her body. His gaze never left hers as he slipped one finger beneath the strap of her shift and pushed it off her shoulder. Then he released the other strap; the garment drifted down her body to the floor.

Fleur smiled into his eyes as she grasped the lapels of his

jacket and pushed it down his shoulders. He shrugged it off
as she worked on the buttons of his shirt. After the shirt
came off, he tugged his breeches down his hips and stepped
out of them. His shoes and stockings were the last to go.

"Seeing you as you are now," Fleur said, "one would
never believe you were the same man I carried away from
Devil's Chateau."

Reed sent her a wry smile. "Unfortunately, the scars on
my body tell their own story. And in case you haven't noticed, there are demons inside me that threaten my sanity
at inconvenient times.

"But this isn't one of those times," he said, sweeping her
into his arms and carrying her to the bed. He followed her
down, propping himself on his elbows so he could stare
into her eyes.

She touched his face. "I firmly believe you will defeat
those demons, Reed. Time has a way of healing all wounds.
Let me give you a happy memory to take back to England
with you."

She rose to her knees and pushed him down. She straddled him, dropping tiny kisses over his chest and shoulders.
Her mouth found his nipples, and she nibbled gently. He
arched and tried to unseat her, but she refused to budge.

"No, let me love you," she whispered. "I want to do this."

His erection strained against her bottom as she kissed a
path down his torso, teasing him with nipping little kisses
up and down his body.

A growl rumbled from his throat as Fleur's lips moved
lower, dangerously lower. She hesitated and looked up at
him, her eyes kindling with heat as she scooted back and
stroked the rigid length of his cock.

"You don't have to . . ."

But she did. His whole body trembled with delight as she
bent her head and licked the head of his cock. Then she
took him in her mouth, tasting, sucking, driving him to the
edge of madness.

When she ran her tongue the length of his cock and over the tip, he shuddered violently. And when her hand slipped between his legs to cup his bollocks, Reed tipped his head back and gasped her name through clenched teeth. Raw, primitive lust surged through his veins. He was close, so very close, but he wanted to be inside her when he came.

Fleur grew bolder, licking down and over his wet slickness again and again. Reed stiffened. She had to stop before he . . .

"No more, love. I cannot bear it."

Grasping her slender waist, he lifted her up and away, depositing her beside him on the bed. Panting harshly, he reared up and mounted her, his face stark, his silver eyes glittering hungrily. "Now it's my turn to love you."

Moonlight washed over her, burnishing her skin with gold. She was perfection, this woman who had saved his life. He covered her mouth with his, thrusting his tongue languidly inside, tasting himself on her lips. After kissing her breathless, he left her mouth in favor of her nipples, suckling just hard enough to make her arch and cry out. Her fingers clamped on to his buttocks, digging into the muscle as her breathing grew labored.

Reed slid from her grasp, working his way lower, feasting on sweetly scented flesh along the way. Parting the soft thatch of curls, he probed hungrily with his tongue, seeking the erect little nub of flesh hidden there. She made a soft gurgle of pleasure as he stroked over her clitoris again and again.

"You're as perfect there as you are everywhere else," he rasped moments before he covered her with his mouth. He worked her slowly with his tongue, flicking inside, then withdrawing as he continued to fondle the swelling nub of her femininity with the pad of his thumb.

"Reed! I'm . . . I cannot . . ."

Trembling violently, Fleur cried out and rocked beneath

him for what seemed an eternity. She was still lost in the throes of ecstasy when Reed moved up her body and thrust his cock inside her tight sheath. She arched upward, her body coming up to meet his. His body taut, teeth clenched, he rode her furiously to his own thundering climax, aware of nothing save his own pleasure.

Moments later they lay side by side, wrapped in each other's arms, sated and weary.

"I will never forget this moment," Reed promised. "Not ever, no matter what life brings. Even if we never cross paths again, I will remember this night."

Before the fingers of a misty gray dawn pushed away the night, Reed had two more precious memories to store up and savor at his leisure. He left Fleur's bed before the household began to stir and slept until noon.

Fleur was awakened hours earlier by Lisette, who swished into the chamber, sniffed delicately and opened the window.

"The room reeks of sex, *ma petite*. I trust you enjoyed yourself."

Fleur opened her eyes, blinked blearily, sat up and gave a satisfied purr. "I enjoyed myself very much, Lisette. Do not begrudge me a few moments of happiness. Chances are Reed and I will never meet again."

Lisette's expression softened. "I begrudge you nothing, *chérie*, but I fear your heart will be broken."

"My heart is well guarded, Lisette," Fleur replied, desperately wanting to believe her own words.

Fleur had always enjoyed the marital bed with Pierre, but what they'd done and how he made her feel was a far cry from what she experienced with Reed. After Reed was gone, she would have plenty of time to ponder the state of her emotions. But regardless of whatever conclusion she came to, she and Reed could be nothing more than brief lovers, like ships passing in the night.

Fleur kept busy the rest of the day, though her mind

was as dismal as the weather. A light rain had fallen all day, and fog rolling in from the sea had lowered visibility to a few feet. Today was Reed's last day at the cottage, and the weather was cooperating perfectly for his clandestine departure.

Tonight Reed would board a ship for England, and Fleur would continue on in France as if she hadn't taken him as her lover. There were so many details involved with Reed's leaving that Fleur found no opportunity to speak privately with him. They all met in the dining room for dinner that night to partake of roast beef and other dishes Lisette had prepared.

"Everything is in place for tonight," Fleur said to Reed. "Rendezvous time is midnight. Antoine will bring the cart around at precisely eleven. We couldn't ask for better weather. The fog will provide a perfect cover for the boat."

"What if the ship fails to arrive?" Reed asked hopefully.

"Then we will return home and hope for a rendezvous tomorrow night. But that has never happened. The ship has always been there waiting. Nor have we been forced to use the alternate rendezvous."

The plans set and the meal finished, Antoine and Gaston left to prepare the cart, while Lisette busied herself elsewhere. Reed and Fleur were alone at last, each dreading this final goodbye. Reed drew Fleur to her feet and led her into the parlor.

"This isn't goodbye, Fleur. We'll meet again one day."

Fleur held scant hope of meeting Reed again in this life. And she was smart enough to realize that being besotted with a man she would never see again was futile, so she forced her thoughts away from Reed to the reason she was remaining in France.

Though she would admit it to no one, intuition told her that the authorities were closing in on her. If her time was limited, she wanted to save as many Englishmen as she could. But for Reed's sake, she put on a brave face.

"One day I will return to England, and when I do, we may meet, but more than likely we will not. Perhaps you'll be wed by then, with your heir on the way. All I ask is that you remember me fondly."

"Fondly? You saved my life, Fleur. But for you I would be dead. What I will remember about you is your courage, your kindness and most of all your passion. You returned my faith in my manhood. Thank you for that, for everything."

Reed pulled her into his arms, wishing he could say something, anything, to convince her to leave with him. But he knew he would be wasting his breath. Fleur felt the same about serving her country as he. So he did what his heart and body directed. He tightened his arms around her and kissed her one last time, drinking in her taste and essence so as to remember her forever.

When the kiss ended, Fleur gave him a wave and a wobbly smile and fled. He didn't follow her. Nor did he see her again before he climbed onto the cart and left the cottage forever.

The ride to the rendezvous was damp and uncomfortable. The night was so foggy, Reed feared the cart would miss a turn and plunge off the cliff. But Antoine knew the way and kept the horse on the narrow trail. They proceeded without incident, arriving at the rendezvous at the appointed time.

Reed climbed out of the cart. "I can't see anything. If there's a ship out there, it's hidden by the fog." He walked to the edge of a steep incline and stared into the misty darkness, wondering where Andre was and if he should proceed down the slope to the narrow strip of beach.

"Welcome back from the dead, Hunthurst."

Reed whirled at the sound of a familiar voice. "Who's there?"

"Your friends know me as Andre, but you know me by another name."

A lantern flared. Andre's face came into view, and Reed recognized him as an operative he had met several times before. He was dressed in the same rough clothing as Reed, able to pass as a French peasant without difficulty. "Peter Weldon. You were in Paris the last time I saw you. What are you still doing in France?"

"I've spent the last few months searching for you," Weldon said. "I was beginning to fear you were dead when I stumbled upon Devil's Chateau. Then it took awhile to discover if you were one of the prisoners inside. It was Porter who told me about Fleur Fontaine. He knows her aunt. From her he learned that the countess was supposedly living in a cottage near Devil's Chateau. I contacted her and together we hatched a plan to get her inside the prison.

"Before she found you, she was able to rescue Grimes and Leasenby. They hadn't been there long and weren't in as bad shape as you were. Fleur and her little group have worked wonders with you, though you are still a bit thin and pale. Now it's time you returned to England and took your rightful place in Society."

"To hell with Society!" Reed blasted. "How could you place Fleur in such a dangerous situation? You sent her into Devil's Chateau without a thought for her safety."

"It was her decision, Hunthurst. She felt a need to serve her country and to avenge her husband's murder. I merely supplied the means."

"I tried to convince her to accompany me to England, but she refused."

"Fleur Fontaine is a courageous woman. Lord Porter is grateful for her dedication to the Crown. She can leave France at any time. All she has to do is contact me and a ship will come for her."

"Does that mean you're remaining in France?"

"I will remain here for as long as I am needed. Someone

has to look out for Fleur. Don't worry, Hunthurst, I won't let anything happen to her. Porter has charged me with her safety."

Reed glanced out past the breakers, where a faint light was visible. "Perhaps I should remain here, too. Porter needs all the operatives he can get."

Weldon must have seen the light, too, for he raised the lantern aloft and waved it back and forth.

"You're leaving," he said. "Your grandmother and the earldom need you." He clasped Reed's shoulder. "My condolences; I know how fond you were of your brother."

"Thank you. I never wanted the title, you know."

"I know, but often fate is heedless of our wants and desires. Shall we make our way to the beach? The rowboat should arrive soon."

Seeing no way to refuse, Reed expressed his gratitude to Antoine and Gaston and waved them off. He heard the sound of the cart's wheels as he started down the slippery incline. Weldon led the way with the lantern. The rowboat hadn't arrived yet when they reached the slim crescent of beach.

"How will they find us in this fog?" Reed asked.

"Look," Weldon said, pointing toward the water.

Reed saw a flickering light moving through the mist. Weldon held his lantern aloft, guiding the rowboat to their position.

"Actually, the fog is a godsend," Weldon said. "French ships patrol the coast quite rigorously. Slipping past their guard will be easier on a night such as this."

Reed watched the rowboat approach with growing dread. Leaving Fleur behind didn't sit well with him. A gut feeling warned him that trouble loomed for the Black Widow. Despite the fact that Fleur had chosen her own path, Reed wanted to return to the cottage and take her away, even if he had to drag her out kicking and screaming.

A rasping sound brought Reed's attention back to the present. The rowboat had reached the beach, its bottom scraping against sand in the shallow water.

"Get in," Weldon said.

"Wait," Reed said, "there is something you should know. I was betrayed. My gut is telling me someone in the organization is a traitor. I will make sure Porter knows so he can take action."

He reached out to shake Weldon's hand. "Watch your back, Weldon. At this point, we don't know who is a friend and who is an enemy."

Weldon clasped Reed's hand. "I'm surprised but not shocked. Thanks for the warning. Give Porter my regards and tell him I'll be in touch through the regular channels as soon as I have anything of importance to report."

Reed released Weldon's hand and waded to the boat. Someone reached out to grasp his arm, and he climbed inside and took a seat. He barely had time to wave goodbye to Weldon before the two sailors in the boat shoved off.

"Don't worry about Lady Fontaine," Weldon called through the misty darkness. "No harm . . ."

That was all Reed could hear over the sound of oars pushing through choppy water. Thick fingers of dense fog closed in on them. Reed saw no ship, nothing but grayness surrounding them. He was beginning to wonder how they would find the ship when one of the sailors stood and waved a lantern back and forth.

Reed held his breath as he waited for the ship to respond. Sure enough, a dim light appeared in the distance, flashing a reply. The rowboat adjusted its course slightly and continued toward the flashing light. A short time later, the outline of a sleek sloop appeared dead ahead. When they reached the ship, a rope ladder was let down and Reed scrambled up. A hand reached out and helped him over the railing. Minutes later the rowboat was winched aboard.

"Good to see you again, Harwood. Forgive me, I should say Lord Hunthurst. Welcome aboard the *Mary Ann*."

"Captain Skilling, we meet again," Reed replied. "I should have known you would be here to carry me back to England. After all, you were the one who brought me here."

"I understand you are still recuperating. The fog is turning into rain. Perhaps you should go below and rest while we maneuver past French gunships patrolling the coast."

Still pale after months in prison, Reed turned even paler, if that was possible. He couldn't bear the thought of being enclosed in the small, airless space below that served as a cabin. Just thinking about it made him shudder.

"I'll remain topside if you don't mind, Skilling," Reed said. "Prison changed me in many ways, some of which I don't understand myself. I seem to have developed an aversion for closed-in places."

"Suit yourself, Hunthurst," Skilling replied. "A few weeks in the country and I'm sure you will be your old self again."

Reed wondered if he'd ever be his old self again. His greatest fear was that he would turn into a blithering idiot if he allowed his demons to take control.

"We won't be going all the way to London this time. We're putting you ashore at Portsmouth and then we're off on another mission," Skilling said.

Reed found a seat on a coil of ropes and watched the water rush by as the sails were unfurled and caught the wind. He was going home. It was difficult to believe that not too long ago he had wished for death, had been as close to death as a man could get without being in the grave.

And then Fleur had arrived, whisking him away and nursing him back to health. But despite Fleur's best efforts, she couldn't cure the darkness that dwelt deep within him.

Night turned into dawn. With the light of day, it became evident that the *Mary Ann* had successfully evaded the French ships guarding the coast and was well on her way to Portsmouth. Reed leaned against the mast, turned his face up to the rising sun and promptly fell asleep.

Two days later, they reached Portsmouth. Captain Skilling placed a purse filled with gold coins, compliments of Lord Porter, in Reed's hands, wished him a safe journey and sent him ashore in the rowboat.

Reed Harwood, the new Earl of Hunthurst, was home.

❖ Chapter Six ❖

Reed approached the town aware of his lack of proper attire. The rough clothing he wore was better suited for a peasant than an earl. Since Portsmouth was a good-sized city and he knew the town well, he headed for the shop of a tailor he had done business with before. He didn't want to show up at Hunthurst Park looking like a poor relation.

"Lord Harwood, welcome," Mr. Sidley the tailor greeted him. "It's been a while since you stopped into my shop to make a purchase. What can I do for you, sir?"

Reed held out his arms and made a slow turn. "Take a good look at me, Sidley. Don't I look like I need a new set of clothing?"

Sidley adjusted his spectacles. "You look . . . my word, what happened to you? You're thinner than I remember, and paler. And you're wearing peasants' garb. Have you been ill?"

"You might say that," Reed said, declining to elaborate. "How soon can you make up something for me? I can't stay in town long. My brother has passed to his reward, and I am the new Earl of Hunthurst. I wish to return home looking halfway decent."

Sidley stared at Reed and obviously came to his own conclusion about Reed's disreputable appearance, pale face and weight loss. Combined with his sudden appearance in a port town, it didn't take a genius to put two and two together and figure out where Reed had been and why.

"My lord, forgive me for being unaware of your new station. Please accept my condolences on the loss of your brother. I can have a suit of clothing ready for you the day after tomorrow. I shall take your measurements now and set my employees to work immediately. Do you have any preferences?"

"A proper riding costume, I think. I intend to buy a horse and ride to my estate in Kent. I should like a blue jacket, a white shirt and buckskin riding breeches. I'll need riding gloves and boots, of course, but I'm hoping they can be purchased easily in a town this size."

Sidley nodded. "I have sufficient material on hand for you to choose from. Shall we get on with the measuring?"

Reed spent a few minutes picking out material, then stood impatiently while Sidley measured him. He would order an entire new wardrobe once he returned to London. He had clothing at Hunthurst Park that would suffice until new garments could be custom-made. Reed told the tailor to put the bill on his account, instructed him to deliver the clothing to the Red Fox Inn and left.

Reed next visited a men's emporium where he purchased gloves, a scarf and underclothing. He didn't bother with a hat, for he didn't like wearing one. He found boots that fit reasonably well at the shoemaker's. They had been made for a customer who couldn't pay, and the shoemaker was eager to find a buyer. Reed paid the man and wore them out of the shop.

A meal and a room for the night was Reed's next order of business. He walked to the Red Fox Inn, where he had stayed before, and paid for a room, meal and bath. He ate an excellent meal consisting of good English beef, roasted potatoes and apple cobbler smothered in fresh cream while his room was being prepared.

Reed was delighted to find a bath waiting in his room, along with the items he had purchased at the men's emporium, which had been delivered to his room while he ate. Reed undressed quickly and climbed into the tub, reaching for the soap sitting on a nearby bench with a towel.

Reed lingered in the bath until the water cooled, then rubbed his body dry with the towel and stretched out naked on the bed.

A pained expression crossed his face when he thought of Fleur. He intended to speak to Porter about her dangerous mission as soon as he returned to London. Porter was the only one who could order her return to England, and Reed intended to encourage him to do so.

His stomach comfortably full, his body clean, Reed promptly fell asleep. He didn't awaken until late the following morning. After a substantial breakfast, he left the inn to purchase a horse. He had good luck there, too. He found a feisty black gelding with good lines and strong teeth at the livery. The price was fair so Reed closed the deal immediately. The owner was so pleased he threw in a perfectly acceptable saddle and tack. Reed named the gelding Ebony and rode him back to the inn.

Reed spent the rest of the day in idleness, much of it contemplating Fleur and wondering if they would ever meet again. An hour did not go by without his thinking about her.

Reed's new clothes arrived early the following morning, just as promised. He donned them, pleased with the fit, and left the inn on Ebony's back after a satisfying breakfast. Reed smiled to himself. If he kept on eating like this, his new riding costume wouldn't fit much longer.

Three days later, Reed reached Hunthurst Park in Kent. He rode around to the stables at the rear of the house and turned Ebony over to a stableman he didn't recognize.

"What happened to Dobson?" Reed asked.

"He was let go after the earl's death, sir," the man an-

swered. "For some reason Lady Helen and the new earl
didn't like him."

Lady Helen, Jason's wife. Who in bloody hell was calling
himself the new earl? Something strange was going on here,
but Reed kept his questions to himself. "Who are you?"

"Potter, sir," the man said, touching his forelock. "Are
you visiting the Park?"

"I am Reed Harwood, the new Earl of Hunthurst, the
deceased earl's brother."

Potter turned white. "Lud, you're dead!"

"As you can see, I'm very much alive, Potter. Is Lady Helen in residence?"

"Aye, my lord. My lady and her sister, Lady Dewbury,
live here when they're not in London. The new earl is also
in residence."

"I am the new earl," Reed said between clenched teeth.

"But . . . but they told us you were dead."

"I beg to differ, Potter. I am not a ghost."

Reed turned abruptly and strode off. Who was this im-
poster posing as the new earl? The only male relative who
could claim the earldom if he, himself, were dead was his
distant French cousin, and as far as Reed knew, Gallard
Duvall was in France.

Reed walked around to the front entrance and used the
brass knocker to announce his arrival. Though the house
was now his, he felt uncomfortable barging in. A butler
Reed didn't recognize answered the door. Reed stepped
past him into the elegant entry hall.

"How many I help you, sir?" the butler asked.

"Who are you?"

Apparently taken aback by Reed's rude question, he
stiffened and said, "Lawson, sir. May I ask who is calling?"

Footsteps sounded on the marble staircase. Reed looked
up and saw Helen descending. She reached the bottom
landing and strode toward the door.

"Do we have visitors, Lawson?"

"Yes, my lady, but he has yet to give his name."

"Kindly tell Lawson who I am, Helen."

Helen's hand went to her throat the moment she recognized Reed. She turned white and promptly swooned. Reed caught her before she hit the marble floor; then he carried her into the drawing room. Carefully he placed her on a sofa and ordered a stunned Lawson to send for her maid. He scurried from the room as if the devil were at his heels.

Moments later a maid bustled into the parlor with a bottle of smelling salts. Reed grabbed it and waved it before Helen's nose. Helen gasped and nearly swooned again when she saw Reed standing before her. He thrust the bottle under her nose once more. Helen choked and waved it away.

"You *are* alive," she said, struggling to sit up. Her wide-eyed gaze slid over him. "You're pale and far too thin. What has happened to you?"

"Let's say I was unavoidably detained in a place where the food was abominable and the sun nonexistent. Tell me, who in blazes is posing as the Earl of Hunthurst?"

"Your cousin, Gallard Duvall. He arrived in England shortly after you were reported missing. Jason was still alive then. Jason, Grandmamma and I all knew you were involved in some kind of secret government work and when you disappeared we feared the worst. It was about then that dear Gallard arrived at Hunthurst Park seeking refuge from the turmoil in France."

"Duvall is a distant cousin," Reed ground out. "How did Jason die? I knew his health wasn't the best—he had never been strong—but wasn't his death rather sudden?"

Helen sighed. "The doctor said his heart gave out. He just seemed to grow weaker and weaker and then one day he awoke practically at death's door. He tried to tell me something before he drew his last breath, but it didn't make sense."

Reed grew still. "What did he say?"

"He gasped out but a few disjointed words before he . . . he died. He said, 'Tell Reed to look for . . .'" her words faltered, "'the truth.' And then he said—" she wiped away a tear—"'Nothing is as it seems.'"

"Is that all?"

Helen nodded. "What do you think it means?"

"I wish I knew. But if there is a truth to be found, you can be sure I'll find it. What did Grandmamma think of Duvall's showing up when he did?"

"She thought it a fortunate coincidence. How could he have known Jason was dying or that you would be reported missing? As it turned out, he's been a big help. You were gone so long, we all assumed you were never coming back. Gallard took over the reins of the earldom even though he hadn't been declared the rightful heir. The Crown is still investigating your disappearance. . . ." She let the sentence dangle. "Nevertheless, Gallard saw that the staff was lax and sacked most of them. I could not have done it myself."

"So you all gave up on me."

"What were we to think? It had been a year. Jason was gone, and Gallard was here to step in when I needed him. We all assumed he would be named heir to Jason's title."

"Even Grandmamma?"

"Well, no, not Grandmamma. She never lost faith that you would return. She sought every channel available to her to learn what had happened to you. I fear she was quite relentless in her pursuit of the truth."

"Thank God for Grandmamma. Her persistence is the reason I am here today."

"We are all grateful," Helen murmured.

Reed's words held a hint of mockery. "So where can I find this paragon who stepped in as earl when he was needed?"

"He's out riding the estate with Violet. She's been living here with me since Jason passed. They should return soon."

"I'm going up to my bedchamber. Have one of the footmen inform me when Duvall returns, and ask Duvall to await me in the study."

A pained expression crossed Helen's face. "Well . . . um . . . your chamber . . ."

Reed held up his hand. "No, don't tell me. Duvall has taken over my bedchamber."

"Well, he couldn't very well use the master suite with the connecting door. And your chamber was the second best."

"Have his things moved into another chamber," Reed ordered. "You may keep the master suite; I am quite satisfied with my former bedchamber. Besides, I'll be leaving for London very soon. The details of succession will have to be finalized and visits made to Jason's solicitor and bankers."

Reed took his leave. He had much to think about before he left for London: Jason's death and final words, the abrupt arrival of a distant cousin who had claimed the title, and the traitor who'd betrayed him. Somehow he had to fit the pieces together and solve the puzzle.

Reed walked through the hallway to the kitchen, expecting to find Mrs. Walters, the kindly rotund woman he remembered from his youth. Instead he found a thin, stern-faced man waving a wooden spoon and shouting commands at a trio of terrified young kitchen maids.

"Who are you, and what are you doing in my kitchen?" the man inquired in a French accent.

"More to the point, who are *you*?" Reed replied, refusing to be intimidated. He was beginning to see a pattern here. Duvall had sacked all his loyal retainers.

Giving Reed an indignant glare, the cook said, "I am Jules, not that it is any of your concern."

"It is very much my concern. I am the Earl of Hunthurst. The manor and everything in it is within my jurisdiction."

Jules nearly spat the words. "You are *not* the earl, *monsieur*. The Earl of Hunthurst is a Frenchman."

"Is he now?" Reed said laconically. "What happened to Mrs. Walters?"

Jules shrugged. "I do not know."

Reed turned to the cowering kitchen maids. "Do any of you know what has happened to Mrs. Walters?"

Silence.

"Do not be afraid to speak. Jules no longer has any authority in the kitchen. I'm sacking him as of today."

"You cannot do that!" Jules sputtered. "No one but the earl can sack me."

"I am Reed Harwood, the new earl; I can do whatever I please in my own home. Gather your things and get out of here."

"But . . . but . . . you are dead. Lord Hunthurst . . ."

"Mr. Duvall."

"Mr. D-D-Duvall," Jules repeated, stumbling over the name, "assured me you were dead."

"As you can see, I am very much alive."

Jules backed away and fled out the door. Reed turned back to the kitchen maids. "Now, who can tell me where I can find Mrs. Walters?"

"Mrs. Walters lives with her daughter in the village," offered one of the maids, who looked no older than fourteen or fifteen.

"What is your name?"

"Polly, my lord. Are you really the earl?"

"Indeed I am."

Polly smiled. "I'm ever so glad."

Reed smiled back. "Can you go fetch Mrs. Walters for me, Polly? Tell her Lord Reed wishes her to resume her position at the manor."

The girl scurried out the back door. Reed turned to the remaining two girls. "You two can continue what you were doing until Mrs. Walters arrives."

Reed was so confident that Mrs. Walters would return that he left the kitchen and made his way to the study. As he neared the front hall, he heard voices and headed in that direction. Three people, two men and a woman, were standing in the hall. He recognized Violet, Helen's sister, and Jules, and assumed the third person was Gallard Duvall, the upstart who had stepped into the role of earl.

Reed stopped in the doorway to listen to the conversation, which was held entirely in French.

"Who was that man who came to my kitchen and sacked me?" Jules loudly complained. "You are the earl, are you not?"

"The earldom is mine, I assure you," Duvall said, trying to calm the agitated cook. "Who told you otherwise? Who sacked you without my permission?"

Reed studied Duvall, noting the stylish cut of his clothing, his dapper mustache and unremarkable physique. Tall and thin, the man did not resemble the Hunthurst males, although they were distantly related.

Reed walked into the hall. "I sacked Jules. The man offends me. I'm reinstating Mrs. Walters as cook."

Violet recognized Reed immediately. Unlike Helen, who'd fainted dead away, Violet squealed and threw herself at Reed.

"Reed, you're alive! Thank God! Your grandmother will be so pleased."

Duvall's mouth fell open, his face turned pale and he staggered backward. He repeatedly cleared his throat, as if something nasty had stuck in it. Reed turned his glittering silver gaze on the self-proclaimed earl.

"You must be Gallard Duvall."

Duvall hemmed and hawed before saying, "I thought . . . that is, I assumed . . . I mean . . . you are an exceedingly lucky man." He stuck out his hand. "Welcome home, my lord. I only did what I thought necessary to keep the estate running smoothly in your absence."

Reed looked at Duvall's extended hand for three long heartbeats before accepting it. Why did Duvall think him a lucky man?

"I will move my things out of your chamber immediately."

"Don't bother. It's being done as we speak."

"Will you tell us what happened to you?" Violet asked, batting her blue eyes at him.

"Most definitely not, Lady Violet. My adventures are not for tender ears. Now if you'll excuse me, I'm going to my study to sample some of my brother's excellent brandy while I await Mrs. Walters."

Jules began babbling in rapid French. Duvall shushed him and pulled him into the back hall.

"We're finally alone," Violet purred, clinging tenaciously to Reed's arm. "I think I can use a brandy, too, after such a shock. Do you mind if I join you?"

Violet Dewbury was what Reed would call a man-eater, and he would definitely prefer to drink his brandy alone, so he could contemplate the curious turn of events. "I've just returned, Violet, and need some time alone. I will see you at dinner tonight—if Mrs. Walters accepts the position of cook, that is."

"Very well," Violet said, pouting. "But you do know I am thrilled to see you alive and well, do you not?" She rose onto her tiptoes and kissed his cheek. "Welcome home, my lord. I, for one, am happy to see you, even if Gallard is not."

The way Violet pushed her breasts against him was most annoying. Reed wasn't interested in Violet and never would be. She definitely was not his type. She was nothing like Fleur.

"You think Duvall wasn't happy to see me?"

Violet's long eyelashes fluttered charmingly. "Even a fool could see he wasn't expecting you to turn up." She squeezed his arm. "But here you are, in the flesh, thinner and paler than I remember but still handsome."

Reed shrugged away. "I really want to be alone, Violet. Do you mind?"

"A little," Violet objected, "but I understand. I'll see you at dinner."

After Violet pranced off, Reed found his way to the desk and took a seat behind it. He recalled his father sitting here and later Jason. And now it was his. Somehow that didn't seem right. But better he than Duvall.

Where did Duvall fit into all this? It was a puzzle he intended to solve. He was still contemplating the mysteries of his life and Fleur's appearance in it when Mrs. Walters arrived. Reed invited her inside.

"Lord Reed!" exclaimed the plump cook with chubby cheeks and graying hair. She had worked at Hunthurst since she was a young woman, and her mother before her. "Welcome home. We all feared the worst when you disappeared. Then Lord Jason died, and it didn't seem right for that Frenchman to claim the title." She threw her apron over her head. "We were all sacked and replaced with new people."

"That's what I wish to discuss with you, Mrs. Walters. I let the French cook go and would like you to return to your old position. Are you available?"

"Available? Oh, aye, my lord. My daughter has five little ones and barely enough room to house them much less me. I'd be delighted to return to Hunthurst. It's the only home I've ever known."

"What about Rogers? Do you know where our butler can be located?"

"He went to London to accept other employment."

"Ah. Well, at least you are here and willing to return. Can you start immediately? The kitchen maids need direction. They are working on dinner as we speak."

Mrs. Walters rose, apparently eager to resume her position. "I don't know what the Frenchman planned for dinner, but we'll make do for tonight."

Mrs. Walters departed. Reed walked to the sideboard, poured himself a measure of brandy and let the smooth liquid roll down his throat. Tomorrow he intended to go over the books with his estate manager, spend a few days visiting the tenants, and then head to London.

Reed was eager to speak to Lord Porter about the traitor, and to finalize the details of his succession. His
thoughts still disordered, he climbed the stairs to his bedchamber to check his wardrobe for something suitable to
wear to dinner.

The upstairs maid had her arms full of dirty bed linen
when Reed entered the chamber. She curtsied and scurried
off. Reed opened the wardrobe, pleased to find the clothing he had left there intact. Most of the things had been
hanging since he had left university and would not have fit
his more mature physique before he went to France. Now
they would suit him well enough. He wondered why Jason
had kept them.

Though Reed hoped his butler/valet was waiting for him
at his London bachelor quarters, he feared he was expecting too much of the man. He had been gone so long, he
wouldn't blame Updike if he had found a new employer.

Reed thought he looked reasonably well in his out-of-
date clothing as he headed down to dinner that night. He
had chosen a black coat and buff breeches, normal wear for
a country dinner. In the back of his wardrobe he had found
a pair of his favorite boots and wore them tonight. They
felt like old friends.

Everyone was already seated when he arrived. Despite
the excellent meal Mrs. Walters had put together for them,
Reed thought Duvall looked uncomfortable. His nostrils
were pinched, and his mouth turned down at the corners.
Conversation was sporadic, and when the dessert was
served, Duvall cleared his throat and said, "I intend to take
my leave in the morning."

"You're leaving?" Helen cried. "Wherever will you go?"

He gave a Gallic shrug. "To London, I suppose. It's time
I met some of my compatriots. I understand there is quite a
community of émigrés in London."

"I'll probably follow you to London in a few days, as soon
as I make sure things are running smoothly at Hunthurst.

Is Mr. Dunbar still the estate manager?" he asked Duvall. "Or is he another of the faithful employees you have sacked?"

Duvall shifted nervously in his seat. "I saw no reason to sack Dunbar. He's doing an excellent job."

"It's nice to know there is someone on the estate you valued," Reed drawled.

Suddenly Helen brightened. "Why don't we all go to London? Lord knows I could use a change, and I'm sure Violet will agree. The London mansion has plenty of room for all of us."

Reed stifled a groan. It was true the mansion could house a dozen people, but the idea of sharing it with Helen and Violet was unpalatable to him.

"I know I'm officially in mourning, but I can still make calls and have a social life of sorts. And you can squire me and Violet to all the evening functions."

"Oh, yes," Violet exclaimed, clapping her hands. "London is just the thing! It will take no time at all to pack, and the Little Season is about to begin. There is no one I would rather have escort me than Reed."

Reed didn't have the heart to deny them the use of the mansion since he didn't intend to stay there himself. He much preferred his bachelor quarters, where he could keep his private life private. He had purchased the townhouse when Jason announced his intention to wed Helen. The money had come from his mother's estate and had been willed specifically to him.

"You may use the London mansion whenever you wish and for however long you please," Reed said. "I will be staying at my townhouse. As for escorting you and Violet about, I may be available upon occasion but not as often as you might wish. Begin your preparations for the move immediately, for I intend to leave as soon I'm sure things are running smoothly here."

Reed excused himself and sought the privacy of his

study. He had no stomach for Violet's fawning, Helen's foolishness or Duvall's scowls. Reed sat at the desk and penned a note to Mr. Dunbar, requesting his presence at the estate office at nine o'clock the next morning, then sent a footman to deliver the message.

That done, Reed leaned back in his chair and thought of Fleur. Was she well? Was she staying away from Devil's Chateau after the last fiasco? A knock on the door dragged him from his thoughts.

"Come."

Helen entered. "May I have a word with you, Reed?"

"Of course. Please sit down and tell me how I can help you."

"It's about Violet."

Reed frowned. "What about Violet?"

"Staying with me in the country has put her social life on hold. She's an attractive woman, in case you haven't noticed. She also has a sizeable dowry. You could do worse."

Reed's eyebrows shot up. "I'm not looking for a wife, Helen."

"Your grandmother will have something to say about that. Jason and I weren't fortunate enough to produce an heir, so now it's up to you."

"I just returned home; don't push me. I imagine I will wed one day, but not for a long time. I'm not in my dotage yet. As for Violet, if she's as good a catch as you say, she will find a husband before the Season ends. Is there anything else?" he asked dismissively.

Helen rose and took her leave, her face flushed with displeasure. Alone again, Reed penned a note to his grandmother, intending to send it off in the morning. The old lady was probably chomping at the bit to see him. Porter would have already told her that her grandson was alive. Reed could well imagine Grandmamma lining up this Season's debs and heiresses for him to look over.

* * *

The following morning, Reed was informed that Gallard Duvall had left shortly after dawn. That suited Reed just fine. He ate breakfast and arrived at the estate office for his meeting with Mr. Dunbar at precisely nine o'clock. They spent that entire day and the next going over the books, which Reed found in excellent order. The day after that they rode the width and breadth of the property, stopping to talk to the tenants along the way.

The neat little cottages appeared in good repair, and the gardens and orchards were ripe with the fruit of the workers' labor. Reed was pleased. Jason had been a good landlord; he hoped he could live up to his brother's standards.

It took two more days to settle everything at Hunthurst and the outlying farms to his satisfaction. When Reed announced his intention to leave for London the following day, the women proclaimed themselves ready to accompany him. Reed packed only a few items of clothing to take with him. Everything else he intended to order new from London tailors.

The morning of their departure, the Hunthurst coach had been brought around and the boot and top loaded with the ladies' hatboxes and trunks. The ladies themselves came out of the house wearing their best black traveling costumes and feathered hats and climbed into the coach. When Reed brought his horse around, Violet asked, "Aren't you going to ride inside with us?"

God forbid. "I intend to ride Ebony to town. The distance isn't great. I will ride ahead and make sure everything at the town mansion is in order when you arrive." He saluted them with his riding crop. "Have a good journey, ladies."

Before the ladies reached the Hunthurst mansion in London, Reed had assured himself that everything was as it should be. All the old servants still held the same positions, which pleased him enormously. Apparently Gallard Duvall hadn't attempted to exert his authority in London.

Reed didn't wait around for the ladies to arrive but left for his townhouse immediately after he'd greeted the servants. Since his townhouse was just around the corner from the family mansion, Reed didn't have far to travel. He tied his horse to a hitching post, walked up to the front door and stopped. He had no key. All his personal belongings had been confiscated when he was apprehended. Though Reed knew that the townhouse was probably empty and it wouldn't do any good to knock, he did so anyway.

The summons was answered by a tall man with long white sideburns and a sparse patch of hair on top of his head. He beamed from ear to ear when he saw Reed standing before him.

"Welcome home, my lord."

❦ Chapter Seven ❦

Stunned to see his employee and friend, Reed pumped his hand and clapped him on the back. "Updike, good God, man, you're still here!"

Updike gave an affronted snort. "Where else would I be, my lord?"

Updike threw open the door, and Reed stepped inside. Everything was just as he had left it. Dear Lord, it was good to be home.

"Truth to tell, Updike, I didn't expect you to be here. It's been over a year. Everyone seems to be of the opinion that I am dead."

"Not I, my lord. I have great faith in your ability to survive even the worst of circumstances."

"What about the staff? Have they found employment elsewhere?"

"Mrs. Peabody remains, and I've managed to keep one maid to help her."

"However did you continue to pay them and yourself?"

"You left money in your cashbox, if you recall. We've managed well enough."

"So I did," Reed remembered, "but a year is a long time."

"You've paid me well over the years. I supplemented the

cash you left with my savings to keep the townhouse running properly in your absence."

Reed shook his head. How could he reward such loyalty? "I'll make it up to you, Updike."

"Your chamber is in readiness for you. Lord Porter sent word several days ago that you had reached England and would be returning to London soon. Mrs. Peabody and I didn't know whether you would be staying here or at the Hunthurst mansion, but we went ahead and prepared the townhouse for your homecoming anyway."

"Come to my study, Updike. I'd like you to join me in a celebratory drink. You don't know how close I came to turning up my toes."

Reed led the way to the study, stopping a moment in the open doorway to inhale the odor of leather, tobacco and furniture polish. The room was the most comfortable in the townhouse, complete with leather chairs, mahogany desk, fireplace, and walls lined with books.

"I'll get the brandy straightaway," Updike said, moving off to the sideboard.

Reed walked to the window and stared out at the fog rolling in from the Thames; the fire blazing in the hearth was most welcome. "How did you know to build a fire?" Reed asked. "Even I didn't know when I would arrive in London."

"I've built a fire in here every day since Lord Porter informed me of your return."

He handed Reed a snifter of brandy and lifted his own in a toast. "To your safe return and continued good health, my lord. Long live the new Earl of Hunthurst."

Reed sank into a chair, lifted his snifter and sipped appreciatively of the amber liquid. "Sit down, Updike."

"You're an earl now, my lord. It wouldn't be proper."

"It's proper if I say it is."

Updike perched on the edge of a chair. "May I ask what happened to you during your long absence?"

Reed contemplated the remaining liquid in his snifter. "I will speak of it just this once, Updike, but never again. The reason I am telling you is because there may be times when I do not seem myself and cannot be reached. Would you believe that not too many weeks ago I prayed for death?"

"You, my lord? Never!"

"It's true, Updike. The only thing that kept me alive was pain. Since you are my valet, you will see me unclothed and realize I have suffered indignities no man should have to suffer. There were days when I would have welcomed death."

Updike went white. "My lord, how ghastly for you. Were you in some kind of prison? How did you escape?"

"It was called Devil's Chateau. That I left there alive was a miracle. I cannot tell you the specifics, even though I trust you implicitly."

Reed pictured the first time he had seen Fleur in the guise of the Black Widow. Even then he knew she was someone special. How special he did not know until she whisked him away from Devil's Chateau and nursed him back to health.

"Think no more of that terrible time, my lord," Updike said, rising. "Please accept my condolences on your brother's death. And might I add that you will make an admirable earl. I shall inform Mrs. Peabody that you have arrived. I'm sure she will be thrilled. If you're hungry, she can put together a cold collation for you in no time."

Reed grinned, happy to drop the subject of his incarceration. His spirits were on an even keel right now, and he wanted to keep them that way. "A light meal would be welcome. I'll eat in my bedchamber. Since there are no other servants available, I will make do with a jug of hot water instead of a full bath. Tomorrow you can visit the employment agency and hire a full complement of help."

Reed left his study moments after Updike and climbed the stairs to his chamber. Nothing had changed, he thought as his gaze roved over the hunter green drapery and bed hangings. The dark, masculine furniture had been polished to a high luster and a fire danced merrily in the hearth. Home had never felt so good.

There came a knock on the door. "Come in," Reed called. Mrs. Peabody entered the chamber, followed by a maid carrying a tray.

"Welcome home, my lord," Mrs. Peabody said, beaming and executing a clumsy curtsey. Reed caught her and steadied her. "We never gave up on you, Lord Reed," the woman declared. "Updike, Mary—" she indicated the blushing maid—"and I never lost hope. Will you remain home now?"

"My duties as earl will keep me in England, so I doubt I will be leaving again, though I will miss the excitement of my former work."

" 'Tis grateful I am to have you home safe." Her concerned gaze swept over him. "Enjoy your food, my lord; you look like you could use a few good meals. You're far too thin and pale. The offering tonight isn't grand, but I promise you'll have better tomorrow." She beckoned to the maid. "Come along, Mary, we've a great deal to do to prepare for the arrival of new servants."

Reed ate the excellent cold collation, consisting of slices of ham, roast beef and cheese, accompanied by crusty bread and crisp apples. Reed ate his fill and had just dropped the apple core on his plate when Updike arrived with the hot water.

The valet cast a jaundiced eye on Reed's apparel. "Shall I help you undress, my lord?"

"I can manage on my own tonight, Updike. Are the clothes I left behind still in my wardrobe?"

"Indeed, my lord, and might I say they are finer than what you are wearing."

"I didn't have much choice, Updike. You wouldn't have let me in the front door had I been wearing the clothing I was given for my return to England. I've decided a new wardrobe is in order to accommodate my thinner physique."

"Very wise of you, my lord. Good night, then."

Reed washed and prepared for bed, exhausted from his long ride to London and the excitement of being home again. He knew he would have to move into the London mansion one day, but he wasn't ready yet. He fell asleep immediately, aware that he had much to accomplish on the morrow. Visits to his grandmother and Lord Porter would be his first order of business.

Across the channel in France, Fleur stared into the dark night from the front window of the cottage. She missed Reed, as much if not more than she missed Pierre. In the short time she had known Reed, he had become important to her. So important that she had let him make love to her. When she had first begun working for Lord Porter as the Black Widow, she had vowed to keep her life free of romantic entanglements. And that meant remaining aloof from the men she rescued.

But Reed had been different. Something compelling about him had attracted her from the moment of their first meeting. She admired his determination to recover despite his damaged soul, physical injuries and emaciated body. He'd inspired her, made her care for him deeply, so deeply that she forgot her pledge to keep her emotions in check.

Would she ever see Reed again? she wondered. She seriously doubted it. Since the day the cottage had been searched, she had felt the hammer of doom hanging over her. Fleur seriously doubted she could continue as the Black Widow much longer, and she intended to relay that message to Andre soon. Perhaps she could move to another location near a different prison and continue her work.

"What are you thinking, *ma petite?*" Lisette asked as she joined Fleur.

"I am thinking of many things, Lisette."

"Ah, let me guess. Is Monsieur Reed one of them?"

"Perhaps. He asked me to go to England with him."

"Why did you refuse? Did he mention marriage?"

"We both know I cannot marry him. He needs an heir, and I cannot give him one. I can better serve England here."

"It's time to leave France, Fleur, and we both know it. You feel it here—" she touched her heart—"just as I do. You risk much by remaining."

Fleur turned away from the window. "Come sit with me, Lisette." Both women sat facing each other before the hearth. "There is something I must do before I leave."

"What is that, *ma petite?*"

"I must rescue Doctor Leclair from Devil's Chateau. The man means a lot to Reed, and I want to do this for him. After that, I will consider leaving."

"'Tis too soon!" Lisette cried, clearly upset. "The authorities are suspicious. Taking one more man from Devil's Chateau might mean the end of you."

"I have to attempt it, Lisette. You have my permission to leave, if you wish. I don't want to place you in danger. I'll need Antoine and Gaston for the rescue, but they, too, will be free to leave once Leclair is out of prison."

"Leave you?" Lisette said, aghast. "Never!"

"Very well, then. I shall prepare to make another visit to Devil's Chateau. And I promise you this, Lisette, it will be the last time anyone at Devil's Chateau sees the Black Widow."

Reed awakened early and rang for Updike. The faithful valet helped him dress. Though the clothing hung on his slim frame, at least it was in step with the current styles. Mrs. Peabody served him a hearty breakfast of eggs, ham, kidneys, tomatoes, toasted bread, jam and strong tea, just the way he liked it. Reed worked in his study until ten. Updike had already departed to visit the employment agency when Reed left to call on his grandmother.

Lady Martine's dignified butler let him into the house. Reed handed him his hat, an item necessary in town though Reed disliked wearing one. Reed cooled his heels in the drawing room while the butler went to inform his mistress of Reed's arrival.

"My lady will see you in her sitting room," the butler announced when he returned. "Please follow me."

The dowager countess of Hunthurst was reclining on her chaise longue when Reed entered. Aside from having acquired a few more wrinkles, she hadn't changed much in a year. He strode to her side, bent and kissed her wrinkled cheek.

"Dear boy," she said, dashing a tear from her eyes. "I feared I would never see you again. Our family was in such disarray after Jason's death. I did everything I could to bring you back to me."

"You saved my life, Grandmamma," Reed said. "If not for you, I would have died in a place so dark and evil I do not wish to think about it, much less discuss it. I can tell you, however, that I was betrayed."

"Betrayed!" The dowager searched his face. "I can see the suffering you endured reflected in your eyes. No need to tell me about it, dear boy." She made a place for him on the chaise. "Come sit by me. Tell me how you escaped from the hellish place you described."

Reed looked away. Silence stretched between them. Then he said, "An angel came for me. She took me away even as I wished for death."

The dowager's delicate white brows shot up. "Does this angel have a name? I would like to reward her or at least thank her."

"Thank Lord Porter instead. His operatives found me."

"I can tell that talking about this is painful, dear boy. I'm just thrilled to have you home. Jason's sudden death was such a shock, coming so soon after your disappearance. I didn't know how the family was to go on. You are our last hope for an heir." She gave him a stern look. "Mind you, there will be no more traipsing about the world on dangerous missions. If you hadn't told me about Lord Porter and your work for the government before you left, I wouldn't have known whom to contact concerning your safe return. I threatened to cut off Lord Porter's private parts and feed them to the hounds if he failed to find you. I was ready to go to the king himself, if need be."

"You certainly ruffled some feathers." Reed chuckled. "And thank you for not mentioning my weight loss and paleness. I'm quite aware of how I look."

"It's nothing a few weeks of good English fare can't cure. What are your plans?"

"I must report to Lord Porter as soon as I leave here. He should know that someone within the organization is a traitor. If time permits, I intend to visit my tailor."

"I was about to suggest that very thing. Now that you are home, you need to concentrate on finding a wife and setting up your nursery. There's a commendable crop of debs this year. You could have your pick of them."

Reed rose. "Time enough to discuss that later, Grandmamma. I need to recover fully first, have a chance to look up old friends and sample some of the pleasures London has to offer before I think about marrying. I'm off now to speak to Porter. By the way, Helen and her sister Violet are staying at the London mansion. If you need me, I can be reached at my townhouse."

"You're not staying at the mansion? It's yours now, you know."

"I know, but I thought it best to keep my own bachelor quarters as long as the ladies are residing at the mansion."

"Hmmm. As I recall, Violet Dewbury is an attractive woman. Her dowry is respectable, and she is eminently suitable. You could do worse, Reed."

"Please, Grandmamma, do not push Violet at me. I'll choose my own bride when the time comes, and it won't be

Violet." He paused. "I want to discuss Gallard Duvall with you at a later date."

Reed kissed her cheek again and took his leave. White-hall was the next stop on his itinerary. He found Lord Porter's office and was greeted by Mr. Wainwright, Porter's secretary. Porter was in charge of a group of secret agents working within the Foreign Office.

"Lord Porter has been expecting you," Wainwright said. "Henry Dempsey is with him now, but I expect he'll see you at the same time since you are both agents employed by the Crown."

Wainwright poked his head in Porter's office and announced Reed. "Come in, Hunthurst," Porter said. Wainwright held the door open for Reed to enter.

Reed strode into the office, nodding to Dempsey as he shook Porter's proffered hand. He was aware that Dempsey was part of the organization but didn't know him well. Porter had told him once that Dempsey spoke flawless French, just as Reed did, and was operating in France. Apparently their paths had not crossed, for Reed had not seen him during his months on the Continent.

"Are you newly returned from France?" Reed asked Dempsey.

Dempsey appeared shaken and somewhat confused. Reed couldn't imagine what was bothering the man. "I have been in England less than a fortnight."

Dempsey stuttered as he asked, "H-h-have you been ill? I remember you as being more robust."

"It's a long story," Reed said, unwilling to reveal more in front of Dempsey. Until he learned who had betrayed him, everyone was suspect.

Porter must have sensed Reed's reluctance to speak, for he said, "I believe you and I are finished here, Dempsey. I'll contact you soon concerning your next assignment. I haven't decided yet where your services are most needed."

Summarily dismissed, Dempsey bid the men good day

and took his leave. Before he reached the door, he threw one last look back, as if something about Reed puzzled him.

"I sensed you wished to speak privately to me," Porter said, once the door closed behind Dempsey. "Have a seat. This promises to be a long and interesting conversation. Why don't you begin with your apprehension and imprisonment?"

"First, I want to thank you for leaving no stone unturned in finding me. Few people know about Devil's Chateau. I truly thought I would perish in that hellhole."

"We looked everywhere for you and feared you were dead. If not for your grandmother, we might have given up." He chuckled. "She threatened me, you know."

"I know, she told me."

Porter turned serious. "Explain how you were apprehended. You are too smart to make dangerous mistakes."

Reed's hands clenched into fists at his sides. "I was betrayed, by someone within the organization. I've gone over this again and again in my head and it's the only explanation. If Peter Weldon hadn't been so thorough in his search, I would not be alive today."

"Betrayed? Are you certain of this? Very certain?"

"There is no other explanation. I was living in a small flat in Paris, mixing with the local citizens and gathering information about troop movements and such. No one suspected a thing. When I was arrested, the soldiers addressed me by my real name during interrogation. How would they have known my name if an informer hadn't supplied it? It's obvious that a double spy is working within our organization."

"A double spy, you say? I cannot imagine it, but rest assured that your claim will be thoroughly investigated."

"How did you come to recruit Lady Fontaine?"

"I knew her aunt and recalled she had a niece who had married a Frenchman. When I learned Lady Fontaine had lost her husband and was still in France, I asked Weldon to find her and recruit her to our cause. We owe that courageous lady our thanks for bringing you and two other operatives out of Devil's Chateau."

"We owe her more than we can ever repay," Reed replied. "She is the reason I am standing here today. I was more dead than alive when she located me."

"Weldon's communication told me you were in a bad way, but I didn't realize how greatly you had suffered. Did you learn anything helpful to our cause after you were incarcerated?"

"No, there's scant information available in Devil's Chateau. It's considered a place of no return. If not for a greedy guard and Fleur Fontaine, escape would have been impossible. There are now three anonymous graves outside the prison that supposedly bear our operatives' bodies."

Porter's gaze bored into Reed. "Were you forced to divulge any classified information under torture?"

"You insult me, Porter," Reed retorted. "I gave up nothing, not even my name, though they already had it." He fell silent, fighting the demons conjured up by talk of his ordeal. "Shall we change the subject? Thinking about Devil's Chateau is something I would rather avoid. I am home—that's all that matters—and ready for a new assignment."

Porter searched his face before letting his gaze slide over Reed's thin form. "You have outlived your usefulness to the organization, Hunthurst. I wish it were otherwise, for you are a good man and have served us with honor and courage. Nevertheless, your cover has been destroyed. I suggest you devote yourself to the earldom. Rest assured, however, that I won't hesitate to call on you should your services be useful to us in the future."

"So it's over for me," Reed said with a hint of sadness.

"I fear so."

"What about the traitor? He needs to be caught before another good man is forced to go through what I did."

"Agreed. Every resource at my disposal will be used to smoke out the traitor."

"There's one more thing I wish to discuss," Reed said. "I am concerned about Fleur Fontaine's safety. Each day she remains in France increases the danger of her being caught. She's appeared at Devil's Chateau three times under the persona of the Black Widow. It cannot go on. You must bring her home immediately."

"You understand, of course, that it was Lady Fontaine's decision to undertake this assignment."

"I understand her reason for agreeing to work with Weldon, but that still doesn't excuse you for keeping her in a dangerous situation. The occupants of the cottage are already under suspicion. Fleur and I had to hide while French soldiers searched the area. You should have insisted that she leave France."

"Actually, I did. After I was informed that you had reached England safely, I sent word to Weldon about her removal to England. The last communiqué I received from him said that Lady Fontaine had one more mission to complete before leaving France."

"And you allowed it? You condoned her recklessness?" Reed exploded, leaping to his feet. "Who is the man she is to rescue? I thought all the operatives in France were now accounted for."

"Indeed they are. From the scant information Weldon relayed to me, this rescue is personal."

"That's it!" Reed exclaimed. "I'm returning to France."

"You will not! And that's an order. I don't want your grandmother on my back again. She's a veritable tigress. Besides, Weldon is there to look after the countess. If anything goes awry, he will protect her."

"Porter, I . . ."

Porter raised his hand. "Say no more. Look at you. You've scarcely recovered from your incarceration. Go home and see to your health, Hunthurst."

Reed left Porter's office in a rage. One more rescue could

prove fatal for Fleur. What was she trying to do, commit suicide?

Still fuming, Reed made his last visit of the day to his tailor on Bond Street. The tailor welcomed him warmly, and together they chose material for his new wardrobe. By the time he had been measured for clothing to fit his thinner figure, it was tea time, and he hadn't eaten since breakfast. He thought about going home but decided to have tea at White's first. He needed the company of old friends to take his mind off his frantic worry about Fleur. If there were some way he could protect her, he would move heaven and earth, but he couldn't think of a damn thing to do.

"Reed Harwood, where have you been keeping yourself?" a man greeted him shortly after he entered the staid establishment. "Forgive me, old man, I should have said Hunthurst. Your brother's death came as a shock to all who knew him."

Reed didn't want to talk about Jason. His death was still a raw wound. "I've spent the last year rusticating in the country," Reed lied. "What have you been up to, Tolland?"

"Mostly I've been trying to keep one step ahead of matchmaking mamas casting their lures out for me." Viscount George Tolland chuckled. "Your title and single status will put you in the same league as the rest of us trying to escape the parson's mousetrap. Are you in town looking for a potential bride?"

"I'm not ready for marriage," Reed acknowledged, "even though Grandmamma has a bevy of debs lined up for my inspection. I'm off to the dining room, Tolland. Will you join me?"

Tolland stroked his smooth chin. "Actually, you look like you've been starving yourself, old man. You haven't been ill, have you?"

"I've been perfectly well, thank you. Will you join me or not?" Reed asked, hoping for company to distract him.

"Another day. I have to call on my mother. She wants to lecture me on my duty to provide an heir. I'll call on you soon. Perhaps we can visit some of our old haunts together."

When Reed could not spot any other acquaintance, he ordered a light repast to take the edge off his hunger and then left the club. On his way home, he made a courtesy call at the Hunthurst mansion, relieved to learn that both Helen and Violet were out for the day. The less he saw of Violet the better.

When Reed returned home, he was introduced to the new servants: Williams, his new butler; footmen Holmes and Gordon; maids Lil and Peg; and Mrs. Wickham, the new cook. Then he enjoyed a long bath in the brass tub and partook of an excellent dinner of roasted lamb, potatoes and assorted vegetables followed by a fruit cobbler with crust so flaky it melted in his mouth.

"Will you go out tonight, my lord?" Updike asked.

"I believe I will. I intend to visit a few of my old haunts. It's been a long time."

Dressed in ill-fitting evening wear, Reed left the townhouse and rode Ebony to one of the gambling establishments he had frequented in the past. He found a place at a gaming table and greeted the men, pleased to see that some were friends from his carousing days. But as the play progressed, he realized he was no longer the devil-may-care rogue who lived to gamble and womanize. The old thrill of the game was missing.

About the time Reed decided to go home, Gallard Duvall showed up. He spotted Reed at the gaming table and came forward to greet him.

"We meet again, my lord. How are Lady Helen and Lady Violet? Did they accompany you to London as they planned?"

"Hello, Duvall. The ladies did indeed accompany me to London."

"Then I will make an effort to visit them. Are you all staying at the Hunthurst mansion?"

"Only the ladies; I am quite happy at my bachelor quarters for the time being. Are you enjoying your stay in London?"

"*Oui*, very much. I met a group of émigrés like myself and attend salons and such with my fellow compatriots."

"I'm happy things are working out for you."

After a time, Duvall wandered off. His eyes narrowed, Reed watched him leave. No matter how hard he tried, he couldn't bring himself to trust the man. His appearance at Hunthurst Park was suspect. He would definitely bear watching in the future.

Shortly after midnight, Reed excused himself and left. He'd rather spend one night with Fleur than a thousand nights gambling and taking his pleasure with the nameless, faceless women he had enjoyed in the past.

Who was the man Fleur was attempting to rescue this time? Reed wondered. Porter had said it was personal. The man must mean a great deal to Fleur. Jealousy struck deep in his gut. He'd never felt jealousy before, but now it raged through him like an untamed storm.

After a good night's sleep, Reed spent the next day taking care of details associated with the succession. By the time he left the bank and finished with Jason's solicitors, he was legally and irrevocably the new Earl of Hunthurst. When he returned home, he found a note from Helen, asking him to escort her and Violet to the Washburn ball two days hence. While checking the rest of his mail, he found an invitation to the Washburn ball in addition to several other soirées to be held over the next few weeks.

As Earl of Hunthurst, it was his duty to attend at least some of the entertainments provided by the *ton*. He supposed the Washburn ball would be a good start.

The first of Reed's new clothing arrived the following

day. Thus, when he picked up Helen and Violet on the night of the ball in his recently purchased carriage with a newly hired driver holding the reins, he was decked out in the latest London style: tight-fitting black breeches, blue waistcoat, silver brocade vest with an abundance of lace spilling from his sleeves and neck. He disdained a wig and wore his dark hair tied back with a black ribbon.

Helen wore black, of course, embellished at the neck and sleeves with lace. Violet had chosen a pale yellow gown, close fitted, cinched under her ample breasts and dampened, making it nearly transparent. Although other ladies were similarly garbed, they seemed indecently exposed even to Reed's jaded tastes.

The moment their names were announced, Reed became the center of attention. His newly acquired title and social status made him fair game for every young girl looking for a titled husband. Reed led Violet onto the dance floor first. After two more dances with giggling young women who seemed unable to put two sentences together, he retired to the card room.

When it came time to leave, Helen rode home with friends, leaving Violet and Reed alone in the carriage.

"We don't have to return to the mansion, Reed," Violet purred. "I would love to see your townhouse. Helen won't mind. She approves of a match between us, you know. No one cares if we anticipate the wedding."

Before Reed guessed what she intended, she wrapped her arms around his neck, pulled down his head and kissed him. As quickly as possible, Reed removed her arms and set her away from him.

"Behave, Violet. I have no intention of wedding any time soon. You're wasting your time on me. Set your sights on someone who will appreciate your efforts."

Violet snuggled closer. "Make love to me, Reed. I know how to please a man. Let me prove how good we can be together."

Reed didn't want Violet, not even for a brief affair. Mentally, he shook his head. Brief affairs were all he had ever wanted in the past. Had imprisonment in Devil's Chateau addled his brain? He had joined Porter's organization as a lark, tired of the London whirl, gambling and ladies who weren't really ladies. Now he could barely stomach the thought of bedding the parade of women vying for his attention. What had happened to him?

The answer came to him in a blinding flash.

Fleur had happened to him.

What in bloody hell had she done to him?

✦ Chapter Eight ✦

Reed spent the next few weeks trying to find his new place in Society. He even agreed to squire Helen and Violet to a few events, which he found boring in the extreme. It was difficult to reconcile his new position in Society with the exciting life he had led as a spy.

Reed had even begged Porter for a new assignment but had been denied again. According to Porter, Reed was no longer of value to the agency. Reed believed the real problem was that Porter feared going head-to-head with Grandmamma if anything should happen to her grandson.

Violet's machinations to get Reed to propose were becoming more and more blatant. To avoid her, he began frequenting the gambling hells. When that palled, he tried some of the better houses of pleasure, where he invariably looked over every raven-haired beauty and in the end chose none of them. A few reminded him of Fleur, but none of them was her, and so he left, unsatisfied and wanting.

Reed's old carousing buddies now seemed like strangers to him. None had gone through what he had. None knew what living in hell felt like, nor had any of them wished for death as fervently as he had. More often than not he felt isolated and alone. No one could understand what he had gone through. No one knew about the demons plaguing him or the memories that left him deeply disturbed. Only Fleur had understood.

Reed had visited Porter on numerous occasions since his return, each time prodding the director to get Fleur out of France and find the man who had betrayed him. Each time he had been told that Fleur had been contacted but had asked for time to accomplish one more task. As for the traitor, Porter said he and his colleagues were working on it. Dissatisfied with the answer, Reed decided to find the traitor himself.

A few days after his last visit to Whitehall, Reed received a summons from Porter. Reed's hopes soared. His first thought was that Porter had changed his mind about using Reed's expertise as a spy. The second was that they had caught the traitor. There was a spring to his step as he was shown into Lord Porter's office a short time later.

"Thank you for coming so soon," Porter greeted him.

"Dare I hope you have an assignment for me? I'm bored to distraction."

Porter stood and paced to the window. He whirled around and said, "I have chosen you for this assignment because of your apparent interest in Fleur Fontaine."

Reed snapped to attention. "Has something happened to Fleur?"

"Not yet, but I received a frantic message from Peter Weldon. He says it's time to pull Fleur out, that if we wait any longer it will be too late."

"When do I leave?" Reed asked, gritting his teeth to stem his frustration. He'd wanted Fleur safely out of France for weeks.

"I'm of the opinion that we shouldn't delay. Can you be ready to sail on tonight's tide? Captain Skilling's ship is provisioned and waiting in London Pool."

"I'll be ready as soon as I return home and dress in something more appropriate than the fancy duds I'm wearing. Any other instructions?"

"Captain Skilling has all the details you need to know. Weldon's message was terse, but his urgency was unmistakable. If Fleur Fontaine's undercover work for us has been exposed, she needs to get out as fast as possible."

Reed gave a jerky nod. "I'll bring her back—you can depend on it."

The interview over, Reed made straight for his townhouse. Updike met him at the door. "I expect to be gone for a few days, Updike. I'll be leaving directly."

Updike nodded and followed Reed to his chamber. "I'll pack your bag immediately."

"A few necessities are all I need."

Updike's eyebrows shot up. "As you say. Am I to accompany you?"

"No, this is . . . I can't discuss this with you or anyone else."

Updike frowned. "Not another assignment, my lord. I thought you were finished with all that."

Reed began pulling clothes from his wardrobe. "It's not what you think."

"May I inquire what you're looking for in your wardrobe?"

"I'm searching for something nondescript to wear aboard ship. And boots, Updike. Those old ones in the back of my wardrobe will do."

While Updike rummaged around for the clothing Reed wanted, Reed opened the chest at the foot of his bed and retrieved a variety of weapons, including a pair of dueling pistols, a wicked-looking dagger and a sword.

"My word," Updike said with a gasp. "I hope you don't intend to use those weapons."

"Only if necessary, Updike, only if necessary. Have you found something for me to wear?"

Updike handed Reed a pair of black breeches, a white linen shirt and a black jacket. When he brought forth a snowy white cravat, Reed waved it aside. "I'm not going to a fancy ball."

Reed shoved his feet into his boots, strapped on his sword and began thrusting the remaining weapons beneath the belt. Before he left, he tossed a black cloak over his shoulders.

Updike shuddered. "You look like a proper pirate, my lord. Dare I hope you'll be careful?"

"I don't expect danger at this point, but I want to be ready should it arrive. Take care of things while I'm gone, Updike."

"You can depend upon me, sir. Be careful," he called as Reed strode out the door.

Captain Skilling was waiting when Reed arrived aboard his ship. He greeted Reed warmly and led him into his cabin to talk strategy while waiting for the tide to turn.

"Brandy?" Skilling asked as he shut the door behind them.

"I would appreciate it," Reed answered.

"Take a seat while I fetch our drinks. I could use something bracing myself."

Reed flopped into a chair, his mind occupied with thoughts of Fleur, wondering what kind of situation she had gotten herself into. Skilling handed Reed a goblet half filled with brandy and pulled a chair up to a desk covered with maps. Reed sipped thoughtfully as he waited for Skilling to speak.

"What did Porter tell you?" Skilling asked.

"Just the basics," Reed answered. "He said you'd provide the details."

Skilling nodded. "There's not much to tell. We're to set you ashore on the narrow strip of beach close to the cottage and put out to sea until the following night. Then we'll sail into the cove where we picked you up before and wait offshore for your signal. If you fail to appear, I'll take the ship to the alternate rendezvous site. If you don't signal us to send the rowboat for you at either rendezvous site after two consecutive nights, our orders are to return to England. The cliff near the cottage is steep; do you think you can manage? I doubt there is a path. If I set you ashore in the cove where the road is more accessible, you'd have a long walk to the cottage."

"Don't worry, I'll find a way up. And I'll bring Fleur to the rendezvous if I have to drag her all the way."

Skilling grinned. "I'm sure you will."

Reed took a hefty slug of brandy. "No matter what happens, I'm not leaving France without Fleur."

Before Skilling could reply, there came a knock on the door. "Come," Skilling called.

The first mate entered. "The tide is turning, Captain."

"Make preparations to get underway," Skilling ordered. "I'll take the wheel myself."

The first mate took his leave. "We'll talk later," Skilling said. "I'm needed on deck."

"I'll join you," Reed replied, rising. Though the captain's roomy cabin in no way resembled the tiny windowless cabins below deck, Reed would rather be out in the open.

Darkness hovered on the horizon as the ship left its berth and sailed down the Thames. Once into the channel, the schooner scudded before the wind at a fast clip. Reed found a place on an overturned barrel, dozing intermittently as Skilling guided the ship through the channel.

As daylight chased away the night, Reed rose and stretched. Skilling turned the wheel over to his first mate and invited Reed to breakfast with him. Reed followed Skilling into his cabin. Soon after, the cabin boy arrived with a breakfast of eggs, ham, bread and ale. It seemed the schooner was well provisioned for the short voyage.

Reed returned to the deck after breakfast and remained there despite a fine misting of rain and fog. Though he took his meals with the captain, Reed chose to wrap himself in his cloak and sleep on deck with the sailors. The wind was with them. They left the channel and turned south along the French coast, reaching their destination without encountering any French ships well after dark on the third day. The weather had cleared, though the moon was obscured by wispy clouds.

Captain Skilling ordered the sails furled and the anchor dropped. Reed prepared to leave the ship, waiting impatiently for the rowboat to be lowered.

"We'll be waiting for your signal tomorrow night," Skilling advised. "Just wave a lantern back and forth, and we'll launch the rowboat to pick you up. God go with you, Hunthurst."

Reed clapped Skilling's shoulder, then clambered down the ladder and into the rocking rowboat. The two sailors accompanying him shoved off and rowed toward the dark crescent of beach.

The moment the rowboat hit the beach, Reed jumped into the surf and waded ashore. The rowboat shoved off and soon disappeared into the darkness.

Reed searched the cliff rising above him, looking for the easiest way to scale it. After careful inspection he decided there was no easy way. He grabbed hold of the nearest tree root and started climbing, inch by careful inch. Loose sand caused him to lose his footing a time or two, but after stopping several times to catch his breath, he finally pulled himself over the crest.

Reed took a few minutes to rest and get his bearings before setting off. He knew exactly where he was. It was but a short walk to the lane that led to the cottage. He almost missed it in the inky darkness but recognized the hedge that lined both sides of the way and started down the rutted road. He had nearly reached the cottage when he heard a noise and drew his pistol. A man stepped out from a break in the hedge.

"Who goes there?"

Reed recognized the voice. "Antoine, is that you? I've come to take the countess to safety."

Antoine approached Reed and stared into his face. "Andre didn't tell us you would be the one to come for the countess. Thank God you arrived, *monsieur*."

"What are you doing out here?"

"I just relieved Gaston; he's sleeping in the stables. We take turns patrolling since the countess's last visit to Devil's Chateau. If soldiers approach, we can hear their horses before they arrive. A few minutes' warning is all the countess and Lisette need to hide in the hole beneath the ground."

Though Reed was boiling inside, he swallowed his rage and asked as calmly as possible, "Why in God's name would Fleur return to Devil's Chateau when she knew the consequences? I warned her before I left about her reckless behavior."

"She returned one last time because of you, *monsieur*."

"Me?" Reed gasped.

"*Oui, monsieur.* She knew how you hated to leave Doctor Leclair behind and wanted to free him for you."

"She took Leclair from the prison?"

"*Oui, monsieur.* He is still here and occupies your old chamber."

"Is he well?"

"He was in better condition than you were when we carried you out."

Reed glanced at the dark outline of the cottage. "I suppose everyone is sleeping, so I won't bother him. It's best that I make my presence known in the morning. Is the front door unlatched? I can sleep on the sofa in the parlor for what's left of the night. Meanwhile, prepare for a hasty departure. We are to meet the ship in the cove tomorrow night after dark."

"We will be ready, *monsieur.* The front door has been left unlatched in case Antoine or I need to enter quickly. I will continue to keep watch while you and the others sleep."

Reed headed toward the cottage. Nothing stirred, not even a breeze. An eerie silence hung in the air, raising the hackles on his neck. He glanced back at Antoine. Nothing seemed amiss, so he climbed the steps to the front door and turned the doorknob. It opened with only one tiny squeak.

Reed heard nothing, saw nothing as he felt his way to the parlor. He knew the layout of the cottage by heart and had no difficulty finding his destination. A chill slithered down his spine. The fire had died, taking its warmth with it. Removing a flint from a pouch in his pocket, he felt around for a candle, found one and struck a light to its wick.

Sighing wearily, Reed slumped down on the sofa and stared into the cold hearth. The thought that Fleur was asleep just down the hall warmed him. He hadn't stopped thinking about her since he had left the cottage all those weeks ago. She was everything to admire: passion and courage, temptation and desire, beauty and determination. Reed had to force himself not to tiptoe into her chamber, climb into her bed and make love to her.

Fear settled in Reed's chest. Despite Antoine's assurance, he couldn't help worrying about Fleur's safety. Anything could happen between now and tomorrow night. Reed removed his weapons, placed them near at hand and blew out the candle. He lay back and closed his eyes, hoping for a couple hours of much needed sleep. He had just started to doze when a light flared before his closed eyelids. His eyes snapped open and he found himself staring down the barrel of a pistol.

Fleur.

His gaze slowly rose to meet hers. As if spellbound, Fleur gazed back at him. Reed pushed the pistol aside. A smile in his voice, he said, "Be careful with that; it might go off."

Fleur gasped and released her grip on the pistol. "Reed! What are you doing here?"

Reed rose, took the pistol and candle from her hands, and set them on a side table. "Do you think I'd let anyone else come for you?"

A tremor ran through her. "How did you know?"

"Porter told me you were in danger and that it was time for you to leave."

Fleur stared at Reed as if he were an apparition. "I never expected to see you again."

"Are you sorry?"

"Sorry? No, how could I be?

"It was foolish and dangerous of you to return to Devil's Chateau," Reed scolded. "You tempted fate one time too many."

"I intended to leave after rescuing Doctor Leclair. I knew how much he helped you and wanted to get him out of there for you. And I succeeded."

"While I appreciate what you did for the good doctor, placing yourself in danger was foolish."

As if in defiance of his words, Reed's arms went around her, pulling her against his hard body. His lips came down on hers. Fleur felt as if she were sliding into an inferno, one she had never expected to feel again. His heat enveloped her thinly clad body; passion soared between them. It had always been like this with Reed, tense and volatile.

Reed's hands slid through her hair, loosening her braid and sending a shiny mass of black curls tumbling over her shoulders. He plunged his fingers through the silken strands, holding her head steady while he plundered her mouth. Fleur flung her arms around his neck, clinging to him fiercely, returning his kiss with every ounce of fervor she possessed.

Fleur broke off the kiss. "Not here." Grasping his hand, she led him down the dark hallway to her bedchamber. Once inside, they began tugging haphazardly at their clothes, turning and twisting in a dance of uninhibited desire.

He watched her with heavy-lidded eyes as she unbuttoned his jacket and pulled it down his arms. Reed drew off her dressing gown and tugged at the ribbon closing the neckline of her nightgown. It slid down her arms; she shrugged and it slid down her hips to puddle around her feet.

Fleur waited impatiently while Reed finished undressing. By the light from the dying fire, she studied his nude form.

"You've gained weight," she said, eyeing him with an assessing look.

"I'm nearly back to where I was before my imprisonment."

Reaching out, she ran her hand along the muscles of his upper body, enjoying the feel of his lightly furred chest. "I imagined how you would look once you regained your health and strength, and now I know. You're magnificent."

He looked into her eyes then, and Fleur saw desire flare in their silver depths, burning hotter than any fire. She shivered, unable to look away.

"I have lain awake thinking about making love to you every night since I left France. I've missed you, Fleur."

Fleur's breath hitched, then came out in a long sigh. "I've missed you too."

Slowly he slid his hands down her arms, his eyes lingering caressingly on her breasts. His fingers followed the direction of his eyes, lightly brushing over the lush curves. "You're more beautiful than I remembered."

Her nipples tightened in response, growing harder with each touch, each clever movement of his fingers. It seemed like forever since she had felt Reed's hands upon her. When he cupped her breasts in his hands, his thumbs stroking over her nipples, her body thrummed with pleasure.

Bending down, he kissed the tender curve of each breast, and then his mouth found her nipple, suckling her, arousing her until her knees trembled. As his mouth moved from nipple to nipple, she wanted it to go on forever, but she wanted him inside her more. She wanted everything, all of him at once, easing the ache inside her that his departure had left.

As if aware of her need, he eased a hand between her

legs, separating and caressing. She moaned, moving against him in response. "Take me to bed," she gasped against his ear.

His reply was to scoop her into his arms and carry her to the bed. He lowered her onto the mattress and followed her down, his body covering hers. At the touch of his flesh, she arched up, pressing her hips against his. She felt his rigid sex throbbing against her stomach. She opened her legs and invited him inside.

"Not yet," Reed said as he scooted down her body, his mouth poised over the wet heat between her thighs. Then he lowered his head and tasted her.

A moan ripped through her, turning her core to molten fire. Hunger for this man gathered hot and deep inside her, then shot like a lightning bolt through her body. She wound her fingers in his hair, holding him against her as she writhed beneath the wet lash of his tongue. She gave herself up to his passionate onslaught, surrendering willingly, eagerly to the power and strength of his body and her own desire.

"Reed!" His name was torn from her throat as he thrust his tongue inside her. When his thumb found the swollen bud above her cleft, she exploded. He crawled upward immediately, covering her mouth with his to catch and muffle her cries.

Fleur tasted herself on his tongue, mingled with his own special taste and scent. She climaxed again and again, until she had nothing more to give. Or so she thought until Reed lifted her knees, spread them and thrust his throbbing sex into her quivering center. Her muscles clenched around him.

Reed was so hard he ached. When he finally entered her, his relief was so immense he nearly ended it then and there. But he held on, determined to bring Fleur to the pinnacle again before he allowed himself the release he craved. He hadn't had a woman since Fleur; hadn't wanted one. But now she was beneath him and he wanted the pleasure to go on and on.

But as with all things, it had to end. He held on long enough to feel her fingers dig into his back, hear her call out his name as she reached that wondrous place where only lovers dwelt. And then he joined her, soaring to the skies as he emptied himself inside her.

Bloody hell, how could he have lived this long without truly understanding how deeply the bond of mutual desire could affect him? Or was it more than desire he felt for Fleur? He pushed aside the answer as he collapsed beside her, the air forced from his lungs in breathless gasps.

"God, I missed you," he said when his heart slowed to its normal beat.

Fleur turned toward him, resting her hand on his cheek. "I find that hard to believe. London must be filled with women eager to wed an earl."

"Indeed, but I find myself bored with the lot of them. I used every trick I knew to avoid marriage-minded mamas. Although I must admit, Grandmamma isn't happy with me. She is eager for me to provide an heir to the earldom."

Fleur turned away, well aware that she could never give Reed the heir he needed. Bearing Reed's children was not in her future. She was barren.

Reed cursed, realizing why Fleur had suddenly gone quiet. "I'm sorry, I didn't mean to offend you." He turned her around to face him.

"No need to apologize; I'm just overwhelmed to see you here."

Reed could tell she was lying but didn't press her. "It's almost dawn; Lisette will be up and about soon. She shouldn't find me in your bed."

"She knows about us. Nothing gets past Lisette. Don't leave yet." She reached for him. "There's still time."

Reed couldn't have left had he wanted to. The scent of their lovemaking filled his nostrils, provoking him in the most primitive way. He wanted her again. Now, before the household awakened and necessity parted them. He pulled her against him. She went willingly into his arms. But when he rose to mount her, she pushed him down and straddled him. Then she proceeded to arouse him with her hands and mouth to unparalleled heights of erotic pleasure.

Reed was nearly insensate with need when she finally lowered herself onto his engorged sex. She brought her mouth to his and swallowed his groan, much as he had done with her, and then she began to move. In a burst of renewed energy, Reed grasped her hips, pounding inside her, raising and lowering her to meet his thrusting loins. They came together in a thunderous blaze of glory, subsiding only when she collapsed against him, her cheek pressed to his heart.

They fell asleep, bodies melded, hearts entwined.

Reed awakened to daylight filtering through the narrow window. Damn, he'd overslept! As gently as possible, he lifted a sleeping Fleur off of him and placed her on the mattress, drawing the covers over her naked body. Then he arose and pulled on his clothes. Moments later, he stepped into the hallway, quietly closed the door and bumped into Lisette. Though her eyes were hooded, he knew what she must be thinking.

"I was wondering when you'd awaken. Come into the kitchen. Your breakfast is ready."

"You knew I was here?"

"*Oui*, Antoine told me, but the array of weapons on the parlor floor would have given you away in any case." She glanced at the door. "Is Fleur still sleeping?"

Reed nodded.

"*Bien*, let her sleep. She has not been resting well since you left."

With those words hanging in the air, Lisette turned and walked away. Reed knew she expected him to follow her to the kitchen, and he did. Antoine was sitting at the table when he arrived. He sat down, and Lisette placed a fluffy omelet and slice of fresh bread in front of him. Reed glanced at Antoine before digging in.

"Does Gaston know I'm here?" he asked around a mouthful of egg.

"*Oui*," Antoine answered. "He is keeping watch even as we speak."

"So you think the danger is great enough for a twenty-four-hour watch outside the cottage?"

Antoine popped the last of his bread into his mouth. "We have not been happy with the situation since the countess returned to Devil's Chateau for Doctor Leclair."

Reed agreed. "Perhaps you should get a few hours' rest. Tonight could be a long one."

Antoine nodded his compliance and left. Lisette poured herself a cup of tea and sat down opposite Reed.

"You are upset with me," Reed said.

"Not upset, *monsieur*, just worried about *ma chère petite*. What are your intentions toward Fleur?"

Their gazes met and held. "I mean your mistress no harm. Fleur is an adult. We enjoy each other; I will not abandon her."

"Will you marry her?" Lisette shot back.

Taken aback, Reed stuttered, "I-I . . . It's complicated. I need an heir."

"And Fleur has told you she cannot give you one."

"She believes it is so. Do you know something she does not?"

"*Non*, I am not a seer. I believe, however, that a woman is not always at fault for failure to conceive. Make of that what you wish."

"What are you two talking about?" Fleur asked from the doorway.

Reed looked at her and smiled. Despite the shadows beneath her eyes and the unrelieved black she wore, she was lovely. "Nothing of importance. Sit down and have something to eat. You'll need strength to get through the rest of the day and night. Have you packed?"

Fleur smiled her thanks as Lisette placed a plate of food in front of her. "Our last communiqué from Andre warned that we are under suspicion and should be prepared to leave at a moment's notice. There is little I wish to take with me. I'll have a small casket containing my jewelry but little else. Andre said someone would come for us, but we didn't know it would be you."

He touched her hand, feeling it jerk beneath his fingers. He smiled. He wasn't the only one who felt the jolt of awareness that passed between them.

"I am familiar with the cottage and surrounding area. The decision to come was an easy one. We'll leave after dark. Do all of you, including Doctor Leclair, intend to travel to England?"

"I can answer that for myself," Doctor Leclair said from the doorway.

Reed stood and greeted the doctor warmly. "I thought I'd never see you again, *mon ami.*"

"You are looking well," Leclair answered, giving Reed a measuring stare.

The last time Reed had seen Leclair, the doctor had been wan and emaciated, though he hadn't been beaten and tortured as Reed had been.

Leclair greeted the women and took a seat beside Reed. "As to your question, *mon ami,* I intend to remain in France. Since I am officially buried in the graveyard outside the prison walls, I will not be pursued. I hope to join my daughter and her family in Provence, in the south of France. Antoine and Gaston have agreed to take me as far as their village south of Paris, and I will make my way from there.

"Times are difficult. I can set up a small practice in my daughter's village and help with their living. My son-in-law has been reduced to working in the fields to support his family, and I wish to help out."

"Am I to understand that neither Antoine nor Gaston will travel to England with us?"

"They both wish to remain in France," Fleur answered. "They will take us in the wagon to the cove, then continue on to their village."

"What about you, Lisette?" Reed asked as Lisette placed Leclair's breakfast before him.

"I go where Fleur goes," the woman said stoutly.

"If those are the plans you have made, then I won't interfere."

Speaking in a low voice, Reed related the information concerning their departure. Once Reed was satisfied that everyone understood the plan, the small group broke up. Reed stood and followed Fleur to her chamber.

✤ Chapter Nine ✤

"What are your plans once you return to England?" Reed asked as he closed the door behind him. "Have you somewhere to go? A place to live?"

"My aunt still lives in the country, in Kent. I can stay with her until I decide what I want to do with my life. Lisette and I can live comfortably once I sell my jewels." She hesitated. "Perhaps Lord Porter can use me elsewhere in his organization."

Reed didn't like the sound of that. "If you'll let me, I'd like to provide for you—perhaps a small townhouse where I can visit you from time to time."

Fleur rounded on him. "You want to set me up as your mistress?"

Reaching for her, Reed pulled her into his arms, resting his chin on top of her head. He liked the smell of her but loved the taste of her even better. Reining in his wayward thoughts, he said, "I don't want to lose you, Fleur. I've missed you . . . desperately."

"I've missed you, too, but becoming your mistress is out of the question."

He moved her away so he could look at her face. "Why not if it's what we both want?"

"It's not what I want, Reed. I couldn't live with myself if I became a kept woman, even if it's *your* kept woman."

"I'd marry you if . . ."

Fleur placed a finger against his lips. "Don't say it. You know why it's impossible. I can't give you an heir." She lowered her gaze. "Besides, you don't love me. I saved your life. What you feel is gratitude, and I want more than that from a relationship."

"We're good in bed," Reed reminded her.

"How many other women have you said that to?"

Reed had the grace to flush. Whether he'd meant them or not, he *had* said those very same words to more than one woman. But somehow they had a deeper meaning when he said them to Fleur.

"That's not fair. With you it's different."

"I refuse to become mistress to any man. But if I did, it would be you. Accept that as a compliment."

"Very well, I won't press you. But the offer stands. I care about you and can't help worrying about your future."

"I'm not destitute, Reed. I have my jewels."

"I know you're not destitute. I expect Porter will present you with a substantial bonus for the work you've done on England's behalf. And if not, my own fortune is vast enough to reward you generously for saving my life."

"I don't want a reward from you, Reed. Seeing you alive and well is reward enough. What I did, I did out of loyalty to my country."

Reed kissed her hard, then released her. "You're a remarkable woman, Fleur Fontaine. My gut tells me we haven't seen the last of each other. Whatever the future holds for me, I sincerely believe you will be in it."

Fleur stared at the closed door long after Reed had left. More than anything she wanted to be with him. Not as his mistress but as his wife. Her hands fisted at her sides. Why did God have to make her barren? Had she been able to have a child, she might have had a good chance of becoming Reed's wife. She and Reed were indeed good in bed, but that wasn't all. Their attraction for each other was mutual; something stronger than simple lust drew them together.

Fleur's emotions had been engaged from the beginning. She had missed Reed after he'd returned to England, and she felt pangs of jealousy when she imagined him with other women, as she knew he must be. He was a virile man with healthy appetites. And he was handsome besides. She knew instinctively that women were throwing themselves at him, vying for his favors. Given those circumstances, how could he miss her as much as she missed him? How could he care for her as much as she cared for him?

Sighing, Fleur turned her thoughts in a more productive direction. She finished packing what remained of her jewelry in a small casket and went to find Lisette.

Reed spent most of the day with Doctor Leclair. They spoke of less pleasant times, of what they'd been forced to endure in Devil's Chateau, and of Leclair's plans for the future.

"I know my daughter and her husband will welcome me," Leclair said. "And I will enjoy being with my grandchildren. Perhaps my skills will be useful in their small village."

"I can't imagine anyone not appreciating your skills," Reed replied. "You saved my life, you know. I wish you would come to England with us. I hate to leave you here with your country still in turmoil."

"I will be safe enough in the south. My 'grave' lies outside Devil's Chateau alongside yours, if you recall. No one will be looking for me. But I thank you for your offer, *mon ami*. Without your friendship I would not have survived."

Reed clapped Leclair's shoulder. "Without your skill I would not be alive today."

Reed pulled a pouch filled with gold coins from his pocket and handed it to Leclair. "Take this." When

Leclair started to refuse, Reed said, "For your daughter and grandchildren."

Misty-eyed, Leclair accepted the pouch. "I thank you, and my daughter thanks you."

"It's nothing. If you ever need my help, send word and I will do my best to find a way to aid you."

Darkness fell along with a thick fog, and after partaking of Lisette's excellent meal, Antoine and Gaston returned to guard duty. With nothing left to do, Fleur wandered into the parlor. Lisette followed. The shutters had already been pulled closed; a candle provided the only light. Reed and Leclair joined them a few minutes later.

"We should wait awhile longer," Reed said. "We don't want to arrive at the rendezvous too early."

Lisette gave a wistful sigh. "I'll miss this cottage, but I won't miss the danger and turmoil we're leaving behind."

Fleur patted her hand. "We'll have a good life in England, I promise."

The words had no sooner left Fleur's mouth than Gaston burst into the parlor. "We have to leave. Now! Soldiers are headed our way. Doctor Defoe sent a lad from the village to warn us."

Reed reacted instantly. "Let's go! Everyone in the cart!"

Clutching her casket to her chest, Fleur grabbed her shawl, waited for Lisette to find hers and then both women raced out the door. Reed and Leclair followed. Gaston joined Antoine on the driver's bench while Reed and Leclair climbed into the bed of the cart with the women. The cart lurched down the lane.

As Antoine turned the cart onto the main road, Fleur peered into the encompassing darkness behind them. "Do you see anything?"

"No, not yet," Reed answered. "With any luck they'll stop at the cottage first. That should give us a little extra time. Let's hope Captain Skilling is waiting for us."

If the soldiers stopped at the cottage first, everything might *be fine,* Fleur thought. But what if the ship wasn't there to meet them? Their safety depended on too many uncertainties.

As if he were aware of her fears, Reed put his arm around her and squeezed her shoulder. His confidence buoyed her. Reassured, she leaned against him, grateful for his comforting warmth.

"We're here," Antoine called over his shoulder as he drew rein.

"I need to light the lantern. It's too dark to find the path to the beach without it," Reed observed.

While Reed struck a flint to the wick, Leclair assisted the ladies out of the cart. Once the lantern was lit, Reed jumped to the ground. *Adieus* were said all around. Reed shook hands with Leclair, then with Antoine and Gaston.

Suddenly the sound of hoofbeats cut through the stillness of the night.

"Go!" Reed cried softly. "Godspeed and good luck."

Leclair barely had time to climb back into the cart before it jerked forward and was lost in a swirl of darkness and mist.

"Follow me," he whispered to the women.

Holding the lantern high to light the way, Reed led the ladies down the winding path to the beach. Fleur clutched the casket containing her jewels close to her chest.

The well-worn path was fairly easy to navigate, even though it was steep and rock strewn. Reed reached the beach first and assisted the women. Aware that the soldiers were hard on their heels, Reed turned toward the sea, raised the lantern high and waved it back and forth.

"Let's pray the ship is waiting," Reed muttered. His greatest fear was that they had reached the rendezvous earlier than expected and the ship would not yet have arrived. Relief shuddered through him when an answering signal flared from the darkness beyond the cove.

"The ship is here!" Fleur cried, pointing toward the light. "How long will it take for the rowboat to reach us?"

"Not long, I hope."

"Look!" Lisette ventured, gesturing toward the top of the cliff, where a dozen lights winked in the breeze.

Reed immediately doused his lantern. "Soldiers," he whispered, pulling both women into the shadows beneath the cliff. "Let's hope it takes them a while to find the path."

They waited in breathless silence as the blinking lights at the top of the cliff spread out. An exultant cry warned them the soldiers had located the path.

"What will we do?" Fleur whispered frantically.

Reed dropped the unlit lantern and reached for his pistol, making sure it was loaded and cocked. "You and Lisette go down to the beach and wait for the boat. I'll hold them off as long as I can."

Fleur hesitated.

"Go, dammit!" Reed hissed, giving her a little push.

The soldiers had nearly reached the narrow strip of beach when Reed heard a scraping sound and someone called softly into the darkness, "Lord Hunthurst, where are you?"

Reed reacted instantly. He stuck his pistol in his belt, grasped each woman by the hand and pulled them toward the sound of the voice.

"I don't see the boat!" Fleur cried.

"This way," Reed replied, leading them unerringly toward the water's edge. A bullet pinged in the sand at their feet, then another and another. "Hurry!"

Reed all but dragged the women toward the boat bobbing in the surf. He could see it clearly now and altered his course a bit to the left as the soldiers grew closer, their bullets stirring up the sand and water around them.

As he waded into the waves, a sailor jumped into the water to help them. Reed pushed Lisette toward the sailor, then lifted Fleur into his arms, carried her to the boat and dumped her inside. The sailor did the same with Lisette.

"Stay down," Reed warned. Then Reed and the sailor jumped inside.

The soldiers splashed into the water behind them, but it was too late. The sailors had put their backs to the oars and the boat skipped over the waves, out of reach and out of pistol range.

They had made it!

"How did you get here so fast?" Reed asked one of the sailors.

"Captain Skilling had a hunch that you might arrive early and had the rowboat lowered as soon as darkness fell."

Thank God for Skilling's foresight, Reed thought.

"We're safe now," Reed said, helping the women onto the seat.

Fleur began to tremble. "That was close. If not for Doctor Defoe's warning, we wouldn't have had a chance. Though I always knew he wouldn't betray us, I wasn't sure he would be willing to protect us if the need arose."

Reed's arm came around her. "That part of your life is over, love. You are safe."

He shuddered to think what might have happened to Fleur had Porter not acted so fast to rescue her, and a cold dread settled in the pit of his stomach.

The rowboat bumped against the dark hull of the ship. A rope ladder was lowered from the railing. The sailors grasped it to hold the boat steady.

"You first, Lisette," Reed said. "Can you manage?"

"*Oui, monsieur*. I'm quite agile for my age." She placed one foot on the first rung and slowly ascended.

"Now you, Fleur," Reed urged. "I'll hold your casket while you climb."

When Lisette reached the top, hands grabbed her and hauled her up and over. Fleur started up the ladder with a great deal more speed and agility than Lisette. She, too, was lifted over the rail and set on the deck. Reed climbed up next, carrying Fleur's small casket under one arm, using the other to hoist himself up the ladder. He all but leapt over the rail, landing on the deck beside Fleur.

"Welcome aboard," Captain Skilling said.

"Thank God you came early," Reed replied.

"My gut told me you might meet with problems."

"Your gut was right. We received a warning that soldiers were on the way to the cottage and left posthaste." He turned to the women. "Captain Skilling, may I present Countess Fleur Fontaine and her companion, Lisette?"

Captain Skilling kissed Fleur's hand and made a bow toward Lisette. "Ladies, I salute you. You are courageous women. I have a cabin prepared for you below. Perhaps you would like to rest after your harrowing experience."

Fleur glanced at Reed. He nodded and handed the casket to her. "Thank you, Captain, we'd appreciate that."

Skilling motioned to a sailor standing nearby. "Wilford, show the ladies to their cabin. Someone will deliver tea to you later."

The ladies followed Wilford and soon disappeared down the hatch. Once they were out of sight, Reed said, "That was close. With luck, they won't have time to send a French warship after us."

"We're getting underway now," Skilling replied, pointing to men scurrying over the deck, working lines and unfurling sails. The first mate was at the wheel. Moments later, the sails filled with air and the ship bounded before the wind, heading north along the French coast.

For the first time since leaving London, Reed began to relax. Fleur was safe; he had accomplished what he'd set out to do and not a moment too soon. Now he could concentrate on finding the man who had betrayed him.

During the days at sea, Reed spent a great deal of time on deck with Fleur. Lisette had gotten seasick the moment she stepped aboard the sloop and hadn't left the cabin once. Though Reed wished for a private place to make love to

Fleur, nothing was available to them. So he contented himself with her company, and stealing an occasional kiss in a secluded spot.

The winds were favorable; the ship reached London Pool three days later in the dead of night. Lisette arrived on deck looking pale and shaky. Fleur clung to her arm to steady her.

"There's no berth presently available in London Pool," Skilling informed them. "Perhaps you should remain aboard until morning. Finding reliable transportation at this time of night is nearly impossible."

"I'd prefer to take my chances on land," Fleur said. "I want to get medical help for Lisette as soon as possible."

"Very well, Countess," Skilling agreed. "I'll anchor here and have you rowed ashore." He turned to Lisette. "Can you manage the ladder, *madame?*"

"If it means standing on firm ground again, I will manage well enough," Lisette replied shakily.

"I'll go first and help the ladies down," Reed said. He was over the rail in an instant, pausing halfway down the ladder, waiting for Lisette to descend.

Two sailors lifted Lisette over the rail, hanging on to her until she found her footing. Then she started down. Reed met her halfway, practically carrying her down the remaining rungs to the boat. When he turned back to help Fleur, she had already reached the last rung, her casket secured beneath one arm. Reed grasped her waist and swung her around, carefully placing her on the seat beside Lisette. He joined them as the sailors took up the oars.

When they bumped into the pilings of the quay, the sailors held the boat steady while Reed scampered up the stairs. As he helped the ladies onto the quay, Lisette all but collapsed against him.

"Convey my thanks to your captain," Reed called down to the sailors as they shoved off.

"We need to find an inn," Fleur said anxiously. "Lisette is ill."

"I'll hail a conveyance," Reed replied as he lifted Lisette into his arms and carried her along the quay to the deserted street. What he didn't say was that the chances of finding a hackney at this time of night were slim to none.

Lights winked from the windows of dockside saloons lining the street across from the quay. Reed considered securing a room in one of them but discarded the idea the moment it was born. The docks were no place for ladies, even with his protection.

Reed walked briskly along the dimly lit street. "We can't stay here; it isn't safe. Perhaps we'll find a hackney at the crossroad. Can you walk, Fleur?"

"I'm fine; it's Lisette I'm worried about."

"Do not worry about me, *ma petite*," Lisette said groggily. "I will be fine once I find my land legs."

Reed continued on, keeping a sharp eye out for footpads. He had his pistol, sword and a dagger hidden in his boot should he need them. Reed looked both ways at the first crossroad and saw nothing but empty streets. He continued walking. Fleur followed close on his heels.

Luck was with them. At the next crossroad he found a hackney parked along the curb, its driver sound asleep in the box. "You there!" Reed called. "Is this cab for hire?"

The driver woke with a start. "Eh, guv, you need a ride?"

"Indeed. Finding you is a welcome surprise. I thought I might have to walk all the way to Mayfair."

"Didn't think I'd find a fare this time of night," the driver said, scrambling down from the box. He pulled down the steps and held the door open. Reed handed Lisette in first, then Fleur.

"Where to, guv?" the driver asked.

Reed gave the address and climbed into the cab.

"Which hotel are you taking us to?" Fleur asked as the hackney rattled off.

"I'm taking you to my townhouse, love. You and Lisette will be safe there until you decide where you wish to live. I have a housekeeper and a full staff of servants to look after Lisette until she gets back on her feet. And I know Porter will want to see you once you are rested."

"A hotel will . . ."

"No, Fleur, a hotel won't do. I'm taking you to my townhouse."

Fleur wanted to refuse but couldn't bring herself to resist one more night with Reed. They'd had precious little privacy on the ship, and this might be the last time they would be together as lovers.

She sent him a telling look. "Very well, but this is only a temporary arrangement."

The streets were bereft of traffic, so they made it to Mayfair in good time. The driver let down the stairs. Reed exited first and handed the ladies down. Lisette staggered a bit but soon righted herself when Reed grasped her elbow to steady her. Reed remained behind a moment to pay the driver, then joined the ladies on the sidewalk.

He guided them to the door and rapped sharply. Several minutes passed before the portal was flung open by a man wearing a nightshirt and robe, holding a candle aloft. A grin spread from ear to ear the moment he recognized Reed.

He held the door wide. "Welcome home, my lord."

Reed ushered the women inside. "Thank you, Updike. As you can see, I've brought guests. The Countess Fontaine and Madame Lisette will be spending the night with us. Please wake the servants and have them prepare rooms for our guests. And would you fetch the housekeeper? Madame Lisette is ill. Perhaps Mrs. Peabody can prepare a tisane to help her sleep. We'll wait in the parlor until the guest chambers are made ready."

Updike scurried off to do Reed's bidding. Reed escorted the ladies to the parlor and seated Lisette in a comfortable chair and Fleur on a sofa. He built up the dying fire and settled down beside Fleur. Fleur felt the warmth of the fire and relaxed for the first time in days. It had been many years since she'd set foot in her native England, and her homecoming had proved emotionally draining.

"Are you feeling any better, Lisette?" Reed asked, concerned.

"*Oui, monsieur,*" Lisette answered weakly. "I'm glad we didn't spend the night aboard the ship as Captain Skilling suggested. I was desperate to feel solid ground beneath my feet. I swear I will never set foot on another ship as long as I live."

Reed chuckled. "You aren't the only person to suffer from *mal de mer.* It happens to the best of us. Your home is in England now, so you need never travel abroad again."

Shortly Mrs. Peabody appeared, wearing a flannel robe and wheeling in a tea tray. "I thought the ladies could use a nice cuppa before they retire, my lord."

"Thank you, Mrs. Peabody. I'm sure the countess and Madame Lisette appreciate your efforts on their behalf."

"Indeed," Fleur said, smiling at the housekeeper. "Tea is just what we need."

"I made up some sandwiches and included slices of lemon cake baked just this morning," Mrs. Peabody said. "Which one of the ladies needs a tisane?"

"Madame Lisette suffers from *mal de mer,*" Reed explained. "She could use something soothing to settle her stomach."

"I'll fix a tisane and bring it up to her room. Meanwhile, enjoy the tea."

"Will you pour?" Reed asked Fleur after Mrs. Peabody withdrew.

Fleur poured three cups of tea, added cream and sugar and handed one each to Reed and Lisette. Reed and Fleur sampled the sandwiches. Lisette averted her face from the food while they finished off the sandwiches and cake.

Updike entered the parlor and cleared his throat. "The guest rooms are ready, my lord. And may I applaud both ladies for their efforts in saving your life? I am eternally grateful his lordship didn't die in that horrible prison."

"Thank you," Fleur demurred. "I was happy to be of service to my country."

Reed offered an arm to each lady and escorted them to their chambers. He opened the door to the first room at the top of the stairs and ushered Lisette inside. A maid was waiting to help her. When Fleur started to follow Lisette, Reed held tight to her arm. "Lisette is in good hands. All she needs is rest."

Fleur took one look at Reed and lost the ability to think. The stark lines of his face were drawn taut with a hunger Fleur recognized immediately. She knew what he wanted, for she wanted the same thing. One last night in his arms; one final goodbye before circumstances parted them forever.

She nodded in understanding. That was all the encouragement Reed seemed to need. Sweeping her high in his arms, he carried her down the hall and opened the door to a chamber that Fleur recognized as being too masculine to be a guest room. A brace of candles sitting on a tall chest revealed a massive bed, heavy furniture, velvet drapes that appeared forest green in the dim light, and a thick carpet.

Reed set her on her feet. "If you're too tired . . ." His sentence fell off.

Fleur rose up on her tiptoes and kissed him on the lips. "I'm not too tired for you. Make love to me, Reed."

The invitation was eagerly accepted as Reed caught her head between his hands, brought her lips firmly against his and kissed her with fierce appetite and passion. With a sigh she slid her arms around his neck and melted into his kiss. This was what she wanted, what she had waited for.

"Let's get these cumbersome clothes off," Reed whispered against her lips.

With indecent speed he undressed her down to her shift and hose, and then even those came off. Meanwhile, Fleur worked diligently at the buttons on his coat, tearing the garment away. Reed helped her remove his shirt and boots, then struggled out of his trousers and smallclothes. Naked, they came together with unbridled passion, their hunger for each other too hot to be contained.

They made their way to the bed, falling upon the counterpane in a heap of tangled arms and legs. He shifted on top of her. She felt his erection pressing hot and heavy between her thighs. She opened her legs to welcome him into the moist heat of her core. Though she begged him with her velvet brown eyes to enter her, Reed chose instead to feast upon her sensitive nipples. Catching one nipple in his mouth, he circled it with his tongue, laving and suckling until Fleur thought she would expire from wanting. When he turned his attention to her other nipple, she groaned with impatience.

She heard Reed chuckle as he kissed his way down the taut line of her belly. Her fingers dug into his shoulders, and she arched against him as his mouth settled hotly over her womanhood. She stifled a scream when he circled the tiny pearl there with his tongue. He thrust the hot spear inside her, slowly at first, then with quick, hard strokes, his hands fondling her breasts at the same time.

Reed paced himself. His cock felt ready to burst, but he wanted to bring Fleur to the same high level of excitement he was experiencing before taking them both to paradise. He felt her tremble, felt her struggling toward orgasm, and his balls tightened in response.

He had to get inside her now before he embarrassed himself.

Surging up, he braced his hands on the mattress beside her head and entered her with one hard thrust. He shook with the effort to contain himself but found it wasn't necessary. Fleur was wet, hot and ready. With her head thrown back, her eyes closed, back arching, nails digging into his back, she was on her way to ecstasy.

"Now," Reed murmured against her lips. "Come now, love."

Wildness seized them both as he pounded inside her. Then her breath broke in a cry of completion. He watched her for one unbridled moment before the clamoring of his body forced his own release. With an exultant cry, he emptied himself inside her, the scent of their lovemaking swirling around him like a warm, wet caress.

Fearing his large frame was too heavy for her smaller one, Reed started to withdraw. With a small cry of protest, Fleur wrapped her legs and arms around him, refusing to let him go.

"No, not yet, Reed."

"I'm too heavy for you."

She shook her head. "No, you're just right. This may be the last time we'll be together like this."

Not if I have anything to do with it, Reed silently vowed.

❧ Chapter Ten ❧

Fleur awoke alone in a strange bed in a strange bedchamber. The room wasn't as large as Reed's, nor was the furniture as heavy and masculine.

A knock on the door interrupted her thoughts. "Come in," she called. A maid slipped through the door.

"Good morning, my lady. My name is Peg. If you're ready, I'll have a bath prepared for you."

"A bath sounds wonderful, Peg, thank you. Is Madame Lisette up yet?"

"She's still sleeping. Mrs. Peabody said not to wake her."

"Mrs. Peabody probably knows best. I'm sure her tisane was of tremendous help."

"Lord Hunthurst said to take your time. When you're ready, he'll be waiting for you in the breakfast room."

"Then I'll have my bath immediately," Fleur answered. She needed to make some decisions and the sooner the better.

Fleur's bath arrived shortly. The brass tub was rolled into the chamber and set up before the hearth. When it was filled with water that had been carried up by two burly footmen, Fleur sank into the tub and rested her head against the rim. But as much as she wanted to just lie in the warm water with her eyes closed, Fleur didn't linger. She needed to check on Lisette before joining Reed.

Fleur finished her bath and let Peg help her into the same black dress in which she had arrived. She couldn't wait to shed her widow's weeds. The color was associated with unhappy times, death and danger. All that was behind her now, and she didn't want to be reminded of past sorrows.

Reed was sitting at the head of the table when Fleur entered the breakfast room. She had already checked on Lisette and found her sleeping peacefully with a maid in attendance. Smiling in welcome, Reed rose and seated her on his right. A footman stepped forward to pour tea into her cup.

"Can I fetch you a plate?" Reed asked, gesturing toward the buffet set up on a sideboard. "Cook knows what I like and usually just sends a plate to me from the kitchen. But she wanted to do something special for my guests."

"Everything looks wonderful, and I am hungry. I'd like eggs, ham, a muffin and some kippers, thank you."

Reed filled her plate and set it before her. Then he filled one for himself and joined her. "I'd rather not have all these servants around," Reed said as he dismissed the footman. "I prefer to be alone with you."

They ate in silence for a time. Then Fleur said, "This is wonderful; thank your cook for me."

Reed grinned. "I'm delighted I can please you—" he paused—"in more ways than one."

His double entendre did not escape Fleur. It was all she could do to keep from blushing. "You're wicked, Lord Hunthurst."

"I try." Reed pushed his plate aside. "I sent word of your arrival to Lord Porter this morning, but there is no hurry to see him. You've had a harrowing experience, and Lisette needs time to recover."

Fleur put down her fork and picked up her cup, looking

at Reed over the rim. "Lisette and I need a place to live and new clothing to replace what we left behind. I need to sell my jewelry as soon as possible."

"There's no hurry. You and Lisette can stay here as long as you like."

"That won't do at all. These are your bachelor quarters; we don't belong here. What I need is for you to direct me to a competent modiste and a reputable jeweler who will give me a fair price for my jewelry."

"I will take you to the same modiste Helen and Violet use. She is known to keep ready-made outfits on hand for emergencies such as yours."

"Who are Helen and Violet?"

"My sister-in-law and her sister; they are currently residing at the Hunthurst mansion on Park Avenue. I thought it would be less stressful for me to stay at my bachelor quarters while they are in London. I shall accompany you to the modiste as soon as you're ready."

"What about my jewelry?"

"Don't worry. Trust me to take care of the matter for you."

Her chin tilted defiantly, Fleur pushed back her chair and rose. "I'm not your mistress, Reed. I can take care of Lisette and myself. I've been on my own a long time."

"I know it, love," Reed soothed. "There's no woman as independent as you. Until your life is more settled, let me take care of you the same way you took care of me. How soon can you be ready to leave?"

Fleur gave a resigned sigh. There was no arguing with Reed. "I'll fetch my shawl."

Moments later Fleur was seated beside Reed in his fancy phaeton, on her way to Bond Street. He pulled out of traffic and parked in front of a shop with a sign proclaiming it to be Madame Henrietta's Establishment for Discerning Women.

Reed set the brake, jumped down and walked around to hand Fleur down. Then he escorted her into the plush interior of the shop. Madame Henrietta herself met them at the door.

"Lord Hunthurst, welcome. Whom do you bring me today?" she asked in heavily accented English.

Fleur sent Reed a startled look. "You've been here before."

Reed shrugged. "I've been here a time or two with Helen and Violet. I sometimes act as their escort."

"Madame Henrietta, I present to you Countess Fleur Fontaine."

Henrietta's eyes sparkled. "Ah, a fellow émigré."

"No, not exactly," Fleur explained. "I am an Englishwoman once wed to a Frenchman. I am now a widow and have just recently returned to England."

"Ah, that explains the black gown. And now you are out of mourning and wish for something less depressing. Something in mauve or gray, perhaps?"

"No," Reed cut in. "The countess needs an entire wardrobe in a variety of colors, one fit for her station in life."

Madame Henrietta raised an elegant brow, as if to question Fleur's ability to pay for a costly new wardrobe.

"I will bring the countess's companion in for new clothing after she recovers from her *mal de mer*. You are to bill everything to me and send it to my man of business."

"Reed—Lord Hunthurst, I cannot accept your charity," Fleur demurred.

"We will settle this later, Fleur," Reed said for her ears alone.

Henrietta clapped her hands, and an assistant appeared from behind a curtain. "Take Countess Fontaine to a fitting room and measure her. I will be there directly."

Fleur sent Reed a speaking glance before following the assistant behind the curtain.

"Do not spare any cost," Reed informed the proprietor. "I want Fleur outfitted with walking costumes, ballgowns, day dresses, morning gowns, riding habits and appropriate undergarments. Do you have a gown or two already made up? The countess needs something decent to wear immediately."

Henrietta's eyes sparkled. "I do indeed. I have two ready-made gowns that would look stunning on the countess. One in blue-and-gold striped satin and the other in flocked muslin."

"Good. If they fit or can be altered quickly, we'll take them. As for patterns, I believe Fleur's taste to be impeccable. She will know which patterns and materials will look best on her. I'm sure she'll object to ordering more than two gowns, but do not listen to her. Watch her closely for her likes and dislikes and make up what she likes regardless of her wishes. You will be amply compensated for your attention to her needs."

"I understand perfectly, my lord."

Fleur returned a few minutes later. Henrietta seated her at a table with a pile of pattern books and fashion dolls while she collected material swatches. When Fleur paused overlong over a pattern or material swatch, Reed caught Henrietta's eye and nodded. In turn, Henrietta scribbled notes in her notebook. Thus the morning progressed. After Fleur had chosen two daytime frocks and a somewhat fancier one for nighttime outings, she pronounced herself finished.

Reed exchanged a look with Henrietta over Fleur's head that said otherwise. "Madame Henrietta has two gowns already made up that might fit you. Try them on, Fleur. Anything would be better than what you're wearing. Although black suits you rather well, I know you're eager for something colorful."

"The gowns I just ordered will be sufficient for my needs," Fleur demurred.

"Humor me," Reed said. "Surely you don't want to visit Lord Porter wearing widow's weeds, do you?"

Reluctantly Fleur agreed and accompanied Henrietta

behind the curtain. Both gowns fit her. She was particularly taken with the blue-and-gold striped walking dress.

"The gown suits you," Henrietta complimented.

Fleur thought so too. "It's lovely. I haven't worn a gown as pretty as this since . . ." Her words fell off. She didn't want to think of Pierre and the turmoil that followed his death.

"Will you wear it? I'm sure Lord Hunthurst will approve."

"It's far too costly," Fleur said, fingering the fine material of the skirt. "But," she added, "I do need something quickly."

"It's settled then. What should I do with the black gown you wore when you arrived?"

Fleur wrinkled her nose. "Donate it to charity."

Fleur never wanted to see it again. Somehow she would repay Reed for her new wardrobe. She hoped to gain at least five thousand pounds from the sale of her jewelry. The emeralds and sapphires were especially lovely. Then she and Lisette could retire to the country and live a simple life with her Aunt Charlotte.

Reed nearly lost the ability to speak when Fleur appeared from behind the curtain. Though she looked lovely in black, the fashionable blue-and-gold gown instantly transformed her. Her creamy complexion glowed. Her warm brown eyes sparkled mischievously as she spun around in a circle for his inspection and approval.

"That gown was made for you," Reed said. "No other woman would look as magnificent in it as you."

"Flatterer," Fleur teased. "It does feel rather wonderful to wear something attractive again," she admitted.

"Did the flocked muslin fit?" Reed asked. "Did you like it?"

"Oh, yes, but I like this one better."

"You shall have both," Reed decided. "Wrap the other gown, Madame Henrietta. We'll take it with us."

"No, Reed, there's still Lisette to clothe. I cannot afford both gowns with everything else I ordered."

"I said we'd discuss this later," Reed said rather sternly.

Before Fleur could reply, the door opened, admitting two women chatting animatedly with each other. Both were quite lovely. And when they saw Reed, they stopped talking and stared at him.

"Reed, where have you been?" the elder of the two asked. "You never showed up to escort us to that rout you agreed to attend."

Reed bowed before the women. "Forgive me, Helen. I was called out of town unexpectedly."

"You could have at least sent a message," the younger woman said, sending Reed a flirty smile.

Both women looked pointedly at Fleur, their curiosity blatant. "Forgive me again, ladies. I present to you Countess Fleur Fontaine. Fleur, this is my sister-in-law, Lady Helen Harwood, and her sister, Lady Violet Dewberry."

All three women made their curtsies. "Why have I never heard of the countess?" Violet asked. Her voice held an edge Fleur did not understand. Was the woman jealous of her? Was there an understanding between Violet and Reed?

Fleur's thoughts were shattered when Madame Henrietta handed the package containing the flocked muslin to Reed.

Violet glared at the package, then at Fleur. "You've never bought clothing for me, Reed. What is this woman to you?"

Reed gave an exasperated sigh. He didn't have time for Violet's foolishness. "I don't owe you an explanation, Violet. We must be going."

"Reed," Helen said, placing a hand on his arm. "Will you call on me? I need to speak to you about my allowance. It's insufficient for my needs. If you can purchase clothing for this . . . this woman, you can afford to be more generous with your brother's wife."

"That's enough, Helen. I'll call on you as soon as I'm able. Meanwhile, you might try curtailing your spending. Good day, ladies."

Grasping Fleur's arm, he escorted her from the shop. "Are you and Lady Violet an item?" Fleur asked.

"Lady Violet is nothing to me," Reed denied. "I'm unattached, even though Grandmamma is doing all she can to alter my unwed state." Reed handed her into his phaeton, climbed onto the driver's bench and took up the reins. "I'll introduce you to Grandmamma soon. You'll like her."

"Where are we going now?"

"A visit to the cobbler is in order, then on to the milliner. You need slippers, half-boots for walking and bonnets that aren't black."

"Reed, I can't afford all that!"

"Maybe not, but I can. You'll be decked out in the latest style when we call on Lord Porter tomorrow."

Her lips flattened. "I need to sell my jewelry before we do any more shopping."

Reed sent her a look that made her wonder what he was about. "Trust me to see to your jewelry, love. I'll take care of everything. If you go alone, you'll only be taken advantage of. Updike is knowledgeable about these things. I'll let him handle the sale. How much do you hope to gain from your jewels? Do you have a set amount in mind?"

"The emeralds and sapphires are Fontaine family heirlooms. I cannot put a price on them. Pierre presented them to me upon our marriage. Others I received as gifts. It's only due to Pierre's prior planning that I escaped with them intact. I don't expect to receive what they're worth, but I'm hoping for five thousand pounds for the lot."

"Hmmm, five thousand pounds seems reasonable enough. I'm sure Updike will do well for you. Shall we have something to eat before we finish our shopping?"

Reed took her to a popular inn, where they lunched on a delicious pigeon pie and berry cobbler floating in Devonshire cream. After lunch, Reed drove her to a cobbler on Bond Street where he ordered several pairs of slippers and stylish half-boots. Then it was on to the milliner, where Reed insisted she purchase several fashionable bonnets. By the time they returned to Reed's townhouse, Fleur's head was spinning. The whirl of shopping had exhausted her. After a visit to Lisette's chamber reassured Fleur that her companion was well on her way to recovery, she retired to her own chamber. She removed her gown so she wouldn't wrinkle it and collapsed on the bed. She had gotten precious little sleep the night before and fell asleep almost immediately. She didn't even have time to worry about how she was going to pay for all the finery she had purchased.

Reed retired to his study and summoned Updike. "Lady Fleur has some family heirlooms she wishes to sell. Emeralds and sapphires, I believe, along with some less valuable baubles. I've locked them away for safekeeping."

"You wish me to sell them for the lady?" Updike asked. "I know several establishments that buy valuables émigrés smuggle out of France."

"I'm sure you do, but I'm not going to sell Fleur's jewels. I just want her to *think* they've been sold. I'm warning you in advance in case she asks you about them. If she does, you're to tell her you're handling it."

Updike frowned. "What do you intend, my lord?"

"I'm going to give Fleur the money myself. I owe her more than I can ever repay. And since she won't accept my money, I'll keep her jewels in my safe until such time as she will agree to take them back."

"Very well, my lord, I will do as you say. Will the ladies be staying with us?"

"I doubt I can keep them here more than another day or two. Fleur is eager to move on."

Updike cleared his throat. "Ahem, you seem particularly fond of the countess. Why don't you marry her? Your grandmother would be ecstatic."

Reed stared down at his hands. He would marry Fleur in a minute if she could give him an heir. He thought about the obstacle that stood in his way and wondered if it really mattered. He could adopt any number of orphans and name one of them his heir. Or he could let his cousin Gallard inherit from him.

"My lord?" Updike said, reminding him of the question hanging in the air.

"It's complicated, Updike. Suffice it to say there are obstacles to a marriage between us." Reed stood. "That's all, Updike. I need to visit my bank before it closes."

Fleur opened her eyes, aware that someone had entered her bedchamber. "Are you awake, *ma petite?*"

"Lisette, what are you doing up?"

"Lying in bed does not make sense when one feels well. I feel perfectly fine now, Fleur. In fact, I intend to join you and his lordship for dinner tonight. I came to see if you are ready."

Fleur rubbed her eyes. "I will be as soon as I wash my face and put on my new gown."

Lisette fingered the fine material of the dress. "And a fine gown it is. Did you sell your jewels?"

"Not yet, but Reed has set Updike to the task. It seems he knows how such things are accomplished."

"Will we be moving to a hotel or inn soon?" Lisette asked.

"I shall post a letter to my aunt tomorrow. We will stay at a hotel until I hear from Aunt Charlotte. I'm sure she will invite us to join her in the country. She's a wonderful woman.

"I wrote her after Pierre died but didn't receive an answer. I sent several more letters through Andre but have no idea if they got through to her. I hope she is well."

"I hope so too. You know I will go wherever you go," Lisette assured her.

Fleur finished her ablutions quickly. Lisette was fastening her new striped silk gown when Peg came to fetch them for dinner. When they followed her to the dining room, they found Reed already there. He stood when the ladies entered.

"Lisette, how good to see you looking so well. Mrs. Peabody told me you were feeling better."

"I am quite cured, my lord. You have been very kind to us."

"I am the one who is in your debt." He seated them, then took his own place at the head of the table.

The first course was served, a delicious mushroom soup. The meal progressed to the dessert with little conversation. Reed dismissed the footman, then casually announced, "Updike got a good price for your jewels. He knew just where to take them."

Fleur's attention sharpened. "Already? Did he get as much for them as I hoped?"

"More. He sold everything for seven thousand pounds."

"Seven thousand!" Fleur gasped. "I shall thank him most profusely. That's more than I anticipated. Lisette and I will seek other accommodations tomorrow."

"There's no hurry," Reed said.

"I don't wish to intrude upon your life. Once I hear from my aunt, we will relocate to her home in the country. A little peace and quiet is what Lisette and I need right now. Unless," Fleur added hopefully, "Lord Porter has an assignment for me."

"You can forget about another assignment," Reed shot back. "I won't let you put yourself in danger again."

Lisette glanced from Fleur to Reed and back again to Fleur. "Excuse me," she said. "I believe it's time to retire to my bedchamber."

"I'll go with you," Fleur offered.

"*Non*, I know the way. Stay and converse with his lordship, *ma petite*."

Reed rose, pulled out Lisette's chair and handed her over to the footman waiting outside the door. "Please see Madame Lisette to her chamber." Once they were gone, he held out his arm to Fleur. "Shall we retire, my love?"

Fleur knew exactly what Reed had in mind. The hunger

in his expression spoke volumes. Her mouth went dry, and her skin felt so sensitive she feared she would shatter if Reed touched her. Unable to resist the sensual promise in his voice, she stood and placed her hand in the crook of his arm. When she dared to glance up at his face, her knees nearly buckled beneath her. His eyes were narrowed, his smile wolfish.

She felt a rush, a shiver, a soaring lightness in her chest. Her body seemed to come alive beneath his hot regard. Fortunately, she still retained a modicum of willpower.

"We can't . . . we shouldn't . . ."

Suddenly his mouth was so close to hers, she found it difficult to breathe.

She *wanted*.

Wanted him.

Wanted everything; anything she could get in the short time they had left together. His arms came around her, and she leaned in, sighing against his mouth as her body took on a life of its own. Then he kissed her, and any thought of right or wrong, should or shouldn't, fled out the window.

Reed ended the kiss. There was a smile in his voice as he said, "What were you saying about what we should or shouldn't do?"

"I . . . don't remember."

His silver eyes held a wicked gleam as he escorted her from the dining room and up the stairs to his bedchamber. He opened the door, scooped her into his arms and carried her inside.

"I can walk, Reed."

"I like the feel of you in my arms." He placed her on her feet beside the bed and began undressing her. "That gown becomes you, but I prefer you naked."

"Thanks to you and Updike, I shall be able to pay for my new wardrobe and Lisette's as well."

No answer was forthcoming as Reed concentrated on rendering both Fleur and himself naked. He rid them of their clothing with undue haste, then stood back to admire her. She was slim but not too slim, her breasts firm and round, her nipples a lush dusky rose. Her legs were long and shapely, and the nest between them dark and luxuriant.

Fleur returned his gaze, suddenly aware that this was no longer the same man she had spirited out of Devil's Chateau. Muscles corded Reed's belly; his shoulders seemed to have grown wider, his arms stronger, his legs sturdier. And rising from the thatch of dark hair at his groin was the most extraordinary display of masculine virility she had ever seen.

She stretched out her hand to caress him, leisurely exploring the hard surface of veins and silky smooth skin. Beneath her touch his sex swelled and flexed, rising hard and heavy against her palm.

"You're magnificent," she murmured.

He bent to nuzzle her nipple. "You're rather splendid yourself."

He fell back onto the bed and pulled her roughly on top of him. She gasped as her sensitive nipples brushed against the hair on his chest. Their hips met; the heat of his manhood probing between her thighs and the thumping of his heart against hers made her whimper with pleasure. How could she bear to part with this vital man she loved to distraction?

"Ride me, Fleur," Reed murmured into her ear.

Fleur rose slightly, grasped his cock in both hands, positioned it between her thighs and pushed down hard. He was seated so deep she could feel him touch her soul.

A groan gurgled in Reed's throat. "I could die a happy man right now."

Then he grasped her hips and guided her up and down over his erection to meet his frantic thrusts. They were both breathing hard. Fleur knew completion was coming fast for both of them. She tried to hold it off, wanting to keep him in her body for as long as humanly possible, to savor his possession, her power over him. She wanted the pleasure to go on forever.

But there was no holding back. When he lifted his head to suckle her nipples, spasms seized her, sending erotic sensations raging through her body. She was no longer Fleur Fontaine; she belonged body and soul to Reed Harwood, the Earl of Hunthurst, a man she could never have.

Reed felt her small explosions squeezing his cock and knew she had reached completion. A frantic wildness broke inside him as he raced toward oblivion. When she arched violently and cried out his name, he could hold back no longer. Grasping her hips, he surged into her warmth, again and again, until the storm within him broke and he spent himself inside her.

"Marry me, Fleur," Reed surprised himself by asking. Once he said the words he wanted to call them back. Marriage to anyone was a long way off. He wasn't ready to be leg-shackled yet, was he?

Tears sprang to Fleur's eyes. No man of rank or property or any hopes for the future wanted a woman who couldn't give him children. "Marry you? I cannot, and you know why. You owe it to your family and the earldom to provide an heir. And you don't love me. It's lust and gratitude that you feel."

"I don't know about love because I've never experienced it, but it's more than simple gratitude that I feel for you. As for heirs, I have a cousin, a Frenchman who recently showed up in England."

"You cannot mean that. No self-respecting Englishman would turn his earldom over to a Frenchman. Please, Reed, do not ask me again, for we both know what you suggest is impossible."

Fleur might be right, Reed realized. He certainly did not want Duvall to inherit. Too many things about his cousin didn't add up. And though he wanted Fleur in his life, he had spoken without thinking. Marriage was a big step, one he wasn't ready to take yet.

Reed allowed the subject to drop. "Go to sleep," he rasped. "We've both had a busy day."

Reed awoke with Fleur sprawled atop him. Rays of brilliant sunlight stretched their fingers through the windows. Damn, he'd overslept! Reed lifted a still-sleeping Fleur off him and laid her gently down on the bed. Then he rose, made his morning ablutions without waking her, dressed and went down to breakfast. Updike met him at the bottom of the stairs.

"I was on my way to awaken you, my lord. Your grandmother is here. It took a great deal of persuasion to convince her to wait for you in the parlor." His brows rose suggestively. "She wanted to pull you out of bed herself, and we both know why that wouldn't have been a good idea."

Updike was too knowledgeable for his own good. "What time is it?"

"Going on eleven."

"Good God, I didn't realize it was so late! Did Grandmamma say what she wanted?"

"She didn't say, and I didn't ask. One more thing you should know. Madame Lisette is with her. A tea tray was just rolled in, and they seem to be chatting quite amiably."

Reed spit out a curse. "I'd better get in there fast. No telling what Lisette is telling Grandmamma. I'll need coffee, Updike. Hot and black—to fit my mood."

Reed steeled himself before pasting a smile on his face and presenting himself to his grandmother.

"There you are," she said.

He marched over to the old lady and placed a kiss on her papery cheek. "I didn't know you were an early riser, Grandmamma. You didn't have to come here. I would have come to you had you summoned me."

She slanted a glance at Lisette. "I hadn't heard from you in several days and began to worry. I decided to come myself to see that you hadn't suffered a relapse after your nasty experience in France."

"As you can see, I am fine."

"Lisette tells me you brought her and Countess Fontaine out of France during a most difficult time for them. I thought you were finished with all that cloak-and-dagger business. Your time would be better spent looking for a wife. Not that I'm sorry you rescued two damsels in distress, you understand," she added, sending Lisette a condescending smile.

"This was one assignment I couldn't refuse, Grandmamma. Fleur and Lisette saved my life. It was my turn to save theirs."

The dowager glanced at Lisette. "Have you and the countess made plans for the future? There's quite a colony of émigrés in London. I have befriended many and often hold salons in my home for them. I'll send you and the countess an invitation the next time I hold one."

Lisette began chatting in fluent French with Grandmamma. Reed tuned them out, as he often did women's prattle.

Their conversation ended when Grandmamma turned her attention to Reed and said, "Well, now that your life has settled down, what are your plans for finding a wife?"

"I have none," Reed said flatly, recalling his ill-timed proposal and Fleur's refusal.

"That won't do at all," Grandmamma snorted. "I'll give a ball and invite all my friends with daughters or granddaughters of marriageable age. Yes," she said, "that's precisely what I shall do."

Before Reed could form an answer, a footman arrived with a pot of coffee. Reed poured a cup and drank it down, burning his tongue in the process. He poured himself another cup, blew on it and brought it to his lips. Before he could take a sip, Fleur breezed into the study.

"Updike said I would find you here." She twirled around, her skirts fluttering about her trim ankles. "How do you like my new flocked muslin? Oh," she gasped, stopping abruptly. "I didn't know you had company. Am I interrupting?"

"Not at all," Reed said, setting down his cup. "I'd like you to meet my grandmother, the dowager Countess of Hunthurst."

"Grandmamma, this is Fleur Fontaine, the woman who saved my life."

❧ Chapter Eleven ❧

Fleur made her curtsy to the dowager. "I'm pleased to meet you, my lady."

"No," the old lady insisted, "it is I who am glad to meet you. You are the reason my grandson is alive. I understand you are a widow. Please accept my condolences. Were you married long?"

"Five years, my lady."

"Five years! You must have been very young when you wed."

"I was seventeen. I lived in France for the entire five years I was wed to Pierre."

"Do you have children, Lady Fleur?"

"Pierre and I were not blessed with children."

The gleam that had entered the dowager's eyes when she'd first met Fleur died. Reed knew exactly what Grandmamma was thinking: Once Fleur admitted to not having conceived in all the years of her marriage, she was no longer a possible mate for her grandson.

"What are your plans? Obviously you cannot remain in Reed's quarters if you wish to preserve your reputation."

"Lisette and I intend to repair to the country as soon as I hear from my Aunt Charlotte. Until that time, an inn will suffice."

Reed heaved a sigh when Grandmamma didn't pursue the subject of Fleur's living arrangements. Turning to him, the old lady said, "I've decided to hold a ball in your honor a week from Saturday next. The invitations will go out to all my friends with marriageable daughters."

Before Reed could reply, the dowager took Fleur's hands in both of hers and said, "Because you and Lisette are dear to my heart, you are both welcome. I'll invite some eligible widowers with children for you to look over. You are still young; some man would be pleased to have you for a wife."

"Grandmamma, please," Reed chided, mortified by his grandmother's attempt at matchmaking. "For one thing, I'm not ready yet to settle down. I just escaped hell and need time to work it out of my system. Trust me, I'm not husband material right now. Hold off on the ball until a later date."

The dowager frowned, concern etching her wrinkled features. "Is there something you aren't telling me that I should know about your incarceration, Reed?"

"No, Grandmamma," Reed denied. "As you can see, I am fit as a fiddle. Let's just say I'm not in the proper frame of mind for marriage. Can we change the subject?"

"I understand, and will postpone the ball if you insist, but don't put me off too long." She rose with the help of her cane.

"By the way, a distant relative from the French branch of the family called on me recently. Gallard Duvall informed me that he is now living in London. I can't say I was impressed with the boy." Grandmamma sniffed.

"Actually," she confided, "I had him investigated and learned his claim is true. If you fail to produce an heir, Duvall is the next in line to inherit. Heaven preserve us if he ultimately ends up with the earldom. That branch of our family has never been favored by Society. Your father would turn in his grave if a distant cousin of his, and a Frenchman at that, ended up with the title and estate."

"I've met Duvall," Reed informed her. "He was staying with Helen during Jason's last illness. She said he was a great help to her."

"Be that as it may, you know what you must do."

Reed placed her hand in the crook of his elbow. "I'll escort you to your carriage, Grandmamma."

The dowager smiled at Fleur. "Thank you again for my grandson's life. If I can be of help to you, you have but to ask."

Fleur watched the dowager leave with a sinking heart. If she had had dreams of marrying Reed, his grandmother had just dashed them. Fleur had refused Reed's spur-of-the-moment proposal with good reason. She couldn't give him what he needed, no matter how right they felt together. If she wanted to wed, which she didn't, she would have to look to a widower who already had children, just as the dowager had suggested. Her hint couldn't have been broader.

"You look lovely in your new gown, *ma petite*," Lisette complimented. "I could tell by the look on his lordship's face that he thought so too."

For all the good it will do me, Fleur silently lamented. She had to forget Reed, just as he would forget her during his search for a young, fertile bride.

"I must write immediately to Aunt Charlotte," Fleur said. "We must not impose on Reed any longer than necessary."

"You aren't imposing," Reed said from the doorway. He strode into the room. "I hope nothing Grandmamma said upset you."

"Your grandmother said nothing that isn't true," Fleur replied. "We both know our living arrangement is temporary."

A frown puckered Reed's brow, then quickly disappeared. "I'm starving and I know you must be, too." He offered his arm. "Shall we have breakfast before calling on Lord Porter?"

Last night's strenuous activity had given Fleur a ravenous appetite. "Will you join us, Lisette?"

"I ate earlier with Updike and the others in the servants' dining room. I promised Cook I'd show her the art of French cuisine."

"I will see you later, then," Fleur returned. "We have plans to make concerning our future."

Reed escorted Fleur to the dining room. They filled their plates and sat down.

"Your grandmother loves you very much," Fleur said between bites.

"The feeling is mutual," Reed replied. "I'm glad she didn't offend you. She was rather insistent upon my marrying and setting up my nursery. But we both know I have demons to slay before I can wed anyone.

"I still have nightmares. Sometimes I dream I'm in a dark pit from which there is no escape."

Fleur searched his face. "Those dreams will pass in time."

"You have a calming influence on me, Fleur. I never have nightmares when you're in my arms. You're good for me."

Fleur gazed down at her plate. "I'm sure you'll find someone who will suit you better than I, someone who can give you children and please your grandmother." She rose. "I'll be ready to accompany you to Lord Porter's office as soon as I write a letter to my aunt."

Thirty minutes later, Reed's new coachman stood beside the carriage as they entered and closed the door behind them. The ride to Whitehall was short. Fleur and Reed were ushered into Porter's office immediately. Lord Porter stood to greet them, kissing Fleur's hand first, then shaking Reed's.

"You cannot believe how relieved I was to hear you had returned safely to England, Lady Fontaine," Porter said. "Did all go as planned?"

"Not quite," Reed explained. "Our escape was a close thing, but as you see, we stand before you unscathed."

"Thank you for seeing to my swift escape," Fleur said. "I am happy to be back in my homeland."

"I'm sorry about your husband, my lady. However, your service to the Crown is very much appreciated. Three of our men would have perished if not for you, Hunthurst among them. You have our heartfelt gratitude."

He pressed an envelope into her hand. "We realize that you no longer have your husband or his fortune to rely upon, so as a small gesture of our appreciation, please accept a draft in the amount of five thousand pounds, drawn on the Bank of England."

Fleur tried to hand the envelope back to Porter. "I never expected a reward for serving my country."

"Nevertheless, you shall have one. What are your plans, my dear?"

"I've written to my Aunt Charlotte and will post the letter after I leave here. Lisette and I hope to join her in the country soon."

Porter appeared startled. "Would that be Lady Charlotte Greenwood?"

Fleur broke into a smile. "Why, yes. Do you know her?"

The look of pity Porter gave Fleur set her heart to pounding. Had something happened to Aunt Charlotte?

"I've known your aunt for many years. I learned about you from her. Your letters to her were delivered to me, then sent on by special messenger. Please sit down, my dear. I hate to be the bearer of bad news."

A dark dread settled in Fleur's chest. She sank into a chair. "What is it? Has something happened to Aunt Charlotte?"

"The last letter I sent on to your aunt was returned. Your aunt died suddenly in her sleep several weeks ago. My man spoke with her doctor and confirmed that Charlotte died of heart failure.

"Her will was read after her death. She left her house

and estate to you. Unfortunately, there was little money left in her estate. I believe she lived on a small portion left to her by her father."

Reed reached for Fleur's hand, giving it a little squeeze. Fleur's voice broke on a sob. "Aunt Charlotte was my only living relative. She raised me. I cannot believe she is gone."

"I'm sorry to impart such sad news," Porter said. "Do you still plan to retire in the country?"

Fleur pulled herself together. She was truly on her own now. Thank God for Lisette. "I'm not sure what I'll do, unless . . . I'd like to keep busy. Do you by chance have another assignment for me?"

"As a matter of fact . . ."

"No!" Reed protested. "Fleur has done enough. Endangering her life again is out of the question."

Fleur ignored his outburst. "You were saying, Lord Porter? How can I be of use to you?"

"Fleur," Reed warned.

"Hear me out, Hunthurst," Porter said. "I've been trying to infiltrate the colony of émigrés with little success. My office has been actively seeking the man who betrayed you. The information we've gathered so far indicates that an émigré might be involved."

He directed his gaze at Fleur. "As the former wife of a French count, Lady Fontaine would be accepted by the émigrés.

"Where is this leading, Porter?" Reed growled.

"I need someone to attend salons and gatherings held for the émigrés, and it must be someone they will trust and open up to. All I ask is that Lady Fontaine ingratiate herself to those Frenchmen now living in London and listen to what they say. One of them may be a French spy."

"No," Reed said before Fleur could form an answer.

"It's not your decision, Reed," Fleur reminded him.

"So you'll do it?" Porter said excitedly. "We've been waiting for just this kind of opportunity."

"I'm sorry, Porter, but Fleur won't be available for any more cloak-and-dagger assignments. Since I was the one betrayed, I'll find the traitor for you."

Porter glared at Reed. "It won't be that easy."

"I feel strongly that the man who betrayed me is not an émigré," Reed asserted. "I'm convinced you'll find the man in our own ranks."

"I'll do it," Fleur said. "What do I have to lose?"

"Your life, for one thing," Reed bit out.

"I have no husband, no children, no one but Lisette will be affected by what I do."

Reed felt as if a hand had reached into his chest and squeezed his heart. Did Fleur care so little for her own life? Did she consider him no one? She was wrong. Dead wrong. He cared deeply about her. He couldn't bear it if something happened to her.

"Is there any way I can change your mind?" Reed asked. "You're young yet. You haven't even begun to live. Why place yourself in harm's way again?"

"This assignment is tame compared to what I did in France," Fleur replied. "I won't be in any danger." She turned to Porter. "I'll do it, my lord."

"You are a true patriot, my lady. I'll see that you receive invitations to functions that émigrés are likely to attend. Where can I contact you?"

"Lady Fontaine will be staying at Hunthurst mansion on Park Avenue," Reed said. "My sister-in-law and her sister are in residence now. I planned to move my entire household to the mansion soon anyway. There's no sense in keeping bachelor quarters when the mansion is roomier and more comfortable. There are sufficient chaperones in residence to protect Fleur's reputation."

"Reed, I cannot!" Fleur declared.

"You most certainly can. We'll spread the word that you

and Helen are old friends, and that she invited you to live with her until you decide where to relocate. I intend to protect you, Fleur, and having you nearby is the only way I can do it."

"What will your sister-in-law think? I hardly suppose she'll welcome strangers in her home."

"Helen and Violet live at the mansion because I allow it. I can assure you they won't object."

Porter nodded his approval. "It's settled then. I'll have your invitations sent to Park Avenue. Keep in touch, Lady Fontaine. I have high hopes that you can learn something to help our investigation."

They took their leave. Reed handed Fleur into the carriage, spoke a moment to the coachman and climbed in beside her.

"You know I can't live in your home, Reed. Whatever made you suggest such a thing?"

"It's the sensible thing to do. The story about you and Helen being childhood friends will fly. And my moving into the mansion is perfectly reasonable. Everyone will think well of me for sheltering two émigrés in my home."

Fleur heaved an exasperated sigh. "Do you always get your way?"

"Always, when it comes to something I want."

"Where are we going?"

"To my mansion on Park Avenue. The sooner we inform Helen and Violet of the imminent arrival of my special guests, the better."

The carriage pulled up in front of a spacious mansion barely visible behind high walls. Fleur began to fidget as Reed handed her down from the carriage. Before turmoil had erupted in France, she had lived in palatial comfort at the ancestral Fontaine chateau, but that seemed like a lifetime ago. This pretentious home was a far cry from Lisette's modest cottage. Reed must be enormously rich.

Reed opened the gate and ushered her inside. The three-story edifice loomed huge and imposing before her. They ascended the steps, passed between two enormous columns and arrived at the carved double doors flanked by glass panels. The door opened before Reed lifted the brass knocker.

A silver-haired butler wearing formal black livery bowed as Reed ushered Fleur inside. Fleur gazed with awe at the elegant entry hall that rose three stories high, its centerpiece a wide spiral staircase winding upward.

"Is my sister-in-law in, Hughes?" Reed asked.

"The ladies are in the drawing room, my lord. Shall I announce you?"

"Don't bother, Hughes. I'll announce myself." Grasping Fleur's elbow, he took three steps, then turned once again to the butler. "By the way, Hughes, I'll be moving into the mansion and bringing most of my staff with me. Please ask the housekeeper to have the master suite and two bedchambers prepared for two female house guests."

Though Hughes's expression remained unchanged, his blue eyes revealed a lively curiosity. "May I be the first to welcome you home?"

"Thank you, Hughes."

With his hand now resting in the middle of Fleur's back, Reed guided her into the drawing room, where two women were taking tea. She recognized them as Lady Helen and her sister, whom she'd met at Madame Henrietta's.

"Good day, ladies," Reed greeted them.

"Reed!" Violet cried, rising. "How splendid to see you again."

"I'm glad you're here, Reed," Helen said with several degrees less excitement than her sister. "I'm eager to discuss my financial situation."

"I believe you both know Lady Fontaine," Reed replied after acknowledging both ladies.

"We've met," Helen said coolly. "Why did you bring her here? Our discussion should be conducted in private."

"Really, Reed," Violet chided, "what *were* you thinking? This is a family affair; Lady Fleur has no business intruding."

"Perhaps I should leave," Fleur said, thoroughly embarrassed.

"You're staying," Reed replied, sending Violet a disparaging look. "Would you please pour tea for us, Helen?" He seated Fleur on a sofa and sank down beside her.

Helen hesitated, then did as Reed asked. Fleur accepted a cup along with a cold look, and sipped her tea gratefully. She had a feeling this meeting was not going to go well.

"I have something to impart to both of you," Reed began, setting his empty cup on the tea cart. "Fleur and her companion will be moving into the mansion tomorrow."

Helen's cup rattled in her saucer. "What? Are you mad?"

"Not at all," Reed said calmly. "Furthermore, I plan to move from my bachelor quarters to the mansion and to bring my staff with me."

"I won't allow her to move in here!" Helen protested.

"You won't allow it?" Reed said with deadly calm. "Might I remind you that this is my home, and that you and your sister are living here at my sufferance and expense?"

"I can understand why you would want to move into the mansion," Violet said, "but moving your mistress here is out of the question. Think of our reputation."

Wringing her hands, Fleur said, "Please, Reed, I told you this wouldn't work."

Reed's expression brooked no argument. "It will work if I say it will." He turned a scorching look on Helen and her sister. "Fleur is not—I repeat, not—my mistress. She has nowhere to go and might be in danger. I am keeping her close for a purpose."

"Indeed," Violet snorted. "I'm well aware of that purpose."

"That's enough, Violet! I won't countenance insults to Fleur's character."

"What are you involved in now, Reed?" Helen asked. "I thought you were finished with all that secretive business. I don't know what happened to you when you disappeared, but you've changed."

"What happened is none of your concern. I understand you need extra funds to supplement your portion. I will be happy to oblige if you accept Fleur and her companion without complaint. And that means being kind to them."

Helen's eyes narrowed thoughtfully. "How will you explain her presence in our home? I simply cannot tell my friends that she is here because you wish her to live with us. Our reputation is at stake." She sent Fleur a withering glance. "How do we know she is whom she claims to be? For all we know she could be a whore from the streets of Paris."

Fleur drew back as if struck. "How dare you! My late husband was Count Pierre Fontaine. His family is among the oldest and most prestigious in France. I come from good English stock. My father was a baron."

"So you say," Violet huffed.

"One more word out of either of you and I will insist that you remove yourselves from my home. The dowager house is being prepared for Helen's return as we speak, and Violet can return to her father's protection."

"You wouldn't," Helen gasped.

"Indeed I would. Now, if we're agreed, here is the story you will tell your friends. Fleur and Helen are childhood friends. They attended finishing school together before Fleur's marriage to a French count. She recently escaped the turmoil in France and is at loose ends. Since her husband and family are dead, you invited her to move into the mansion until she can make other arrangements. It's simple, really, and not at all far-fetched."

Violet greeted his words with a sneer. "Will you and Lady Fleur be sharing a bedchamber?"

"Absolutely not!" Fleur asserted indignantly. "This wasn't my idea. I was against moving here from the beginning. Reed thinks it's necessary, even though I don't agree."

"It is necessary," Reed growled. "Fleur saved my life. She's the reason I am standing before you. I owe her whatever protection I can offer. Do you understand? I'll hear no more mean-spirited remarks about Fleur and her companion. As for you, Helen, I'll provide you with an extra two hundred pounds a month while Fleur is living with us, even though my brother was quite generous with you in his will. I suggest that you spend less money on gowns and fripperies and limit your losses at the gambling tables.

"And you, Violet, I checked your circumstances and found you are in not in need of funds. Your allowance from your father is generous to a fault."

"Indeed," Violet purred, batting her eyes at Reed. "I'll bring a generous dowry with me when I wed, just as Helen did when she wed your brother."

Fleur was not fooled by Violet's subtle hint. Violet wanted Reed and would do anything to tempt him, even flaunting her fortune before him.

Reed rose. "Now that Fleur's living arrangements are settled, we'll be off. Fleur, Lisette and I will arrive tomorrow after breakfast. My household will follow in a few days."

"We already have a full staff," Helen protested.

"We'll make room," Reed assured her. "It's not as though I have a large staff. Besides, a house this big can use two cooks. As for the housekeeper, I believe Mrs. Court has been employed here beyond her usefulness. I will offer her a generous retirement and see her settled wherever she wishes."

Helen sputtered a protest until Reed held up his hand. "No more. Everything is settled to my satisfaction. Come, Fleur, it's time to leave."

The moment the front door closed behind them, Fleur

rounded on Reed. "How dare you force those women to accept me? Moving to an inn will suit me and Lisette just fine."

"I'll be the judge of that," Reed said as they approached the carriage.

Suddenly he froze. A familiar sound alerted him, a sound he had heard often enough in the past and hoped never to hear again. He pulled Fleur to the ground and fell on top of her as an explosion ripped through the air. A bullet whizzed past his head and lodged in the carriage door. He felt a momentary pain in his right arm, then numbness.

Frightened by the sound, the carriage horses reared and took off down the street with the coachman running after them.

Panting, Reed lay atop Fleur until he was certain the danger was past. "Are you all right?" he asked. He sat up and pulled Fleur across his lap.

Fleur lifted her eyes to Reed. Her bloody cheek and dazed expression told him that she was *not* all right. And the way she was holding her arms close to her side was not a good sign. Though he saw no blood to indicate the bullet had struck or even grazed her, it was obvious she had been hurt when he shoved her to the ground and landed on top of her.

"What happened?" Fleur asked.

"Someone took a shot at us."

"Who would do such a thing? Why would anyone want to hurt us?"

Reed's lips thinned. "That's what I'd like to know." He helped her to her feet. "Now do you understand why you need protection?"

Fleur brushed the dirt off her skirt. "How do you know the bullet was meant for me?"

That stopped Reed in his tracks. Did someone want him dead? Had his betrayer followed him to England? That didn't make sense. He could think of no reason anyone would want to kill him. He was no longer involved in covert activities. His spying days were over.

"I don't know."

"I say there, are you two all right?"

Reed glanced down the street and saw Gallard Duvall hurrying toward them.

"What happened here?" Duvall asked when he noted Fleur's dusty clothing and bloody cheek.

"Fleur tripped and fell," Reed lied, sending a warning glance at Fleur when she opened her mouth to explain. "Gallard, please meet Countess Fleur Fontaine. She's a childhood friend of Helen's and will be living at the mansion for the present. Fleur, Gallard Duvall is an émigré and distant relative."

Duvall made his bow. "Is there anything I can do to help, my lady?"

"I'm fine, thank you."

"What are you doing here, Duvall?" Reed asked.

"I'm on my way to visit Lady Helen and her sister. They have been kind enough to receive me. I usually take tea with them once or twice a week."

"Then we won't keep you," Reed said as he spied a hackney plodding down the street. He stepped to the curb and hailed it. "Please excuse us," he said as he gave his destination to the driver, handed Fleur into the cab and hopped in beside her.

Once inside, Reed produced a pristine white handkerchief and dabbed at the blood oozing from the scratches on Fleur's cheek. "Does it hurt?"

"I'm fine, Reed, don't fuss."

"What about your arm? I noticed you favoring it."

"I think I bruised it when I fell."

"Mrs. Peabody will take care of it when we reach home."

"Why did you lie to Mr. Duvall?"

"At this point, I don't trust anyone."

"But he's a relative of yours."

"A very distant one. I don't know enough about him or his background to confide in him."

"Have you ever met any of the Duvalls?"

He shrugged. "No, they never came to England before. I hope John Coachman managed to catch the horses before they got too far."

The hackney rolled to a stop. The driver opened the door and pulled the steps down. Reed paid him and escorted Fleur to the entrance. A footman opened the door before they reached it.

"Please summon Mrs. Peabody immediately, Gordon. Ask her to bring warm water and clean cloths," Reed ordered the startled footman. "And send Updike to me. We'll be in my study."

"Really, Reed, I told you I'm fine."

Once inside the study, Reed settled Fleur into a chair. "You don't need to make a fuss over a few scratches," Fleur persisted. "Lisette can . . ."

"*Ma petite*, what happened?" Lisette cried, bursting into the study. "I was with Mrs. Peabody when Gordon came to fetch her. She'll be here directly. How did you hurt yourself?"

"She tripped over the hem of her skirt and fell," Reed said. "She bruised her cheek and arm but is otherwise intact."

Lisette sent Reed a skeptical look. "I've never known Fleur to be clumsy. Oh, look at your new gown! The hem is ripped and so is the sleeve."

"Never mind the gown, Lisette. I'm sure it can be restored to its previous glory."

"Gordon told me Lady Fontaine was injured," Mrs. Peabody said from the doorway.

"Come in, Mrs. Peabody. Lady Fontaine suffered a scrape in a fall."

Mrs. Peabody clucked her tongue sympathetically as she cleaned the scratches on Fleur's cheek.

"That should do it," the housekeeper said as she stepped away. "Can I be of any further . . ." The words died in her throat when she noticed the jagged tear in Reed's coat sleeve and the blood seeping through it. "My lord, you're hurt! Take off your coat so I can see."

Reed stared down at his sleeve, surprised to see blood staining it. He'd been so worried about Fleur, he had forgotten his own pain. Now he remembered it. Though he knew the bullet hadn't lodged in his flesh, it must have cut a shallow groove in his arm. It stung like the very devil.

"It's nothing, Mrs. Peabody."

"It's something if it drew blood," Fleur contradicted. "Let Mrs. Peabody look at it."

"Fleur, I don't . . ." About that time Updike burst through the door.

"Gordon said you wished to see me, my lord."

Reed heaved a sigh of relief. "Updike, you're just in time. Mrs. Peabody, why don't you and Lisette take Lady Fleur to her room and treat any hidden bruises she might have. I noticed her holding her right arm."

"Reed, no!" Fleur protested. "I want to see if you're . . ."

"Do as I say, Fleur," Reed said in a voice that brooked no argument.

"What happened?" Updike asked once the door had closed behind the women.

"Help me off with my coat," Reed said. "Someone took a shot at me and Fleur. The bullet must have grazed me. Fleur injured her cheek when I shoved her to the ground. Thank God my reflexes are still good."

Updike eased Reed's coat off. "Did you see who did it?"

"No, though he must have been close. I was too concerned with keeping Fleur safe to worry about anything else. The explosion frightened the horses, which added to the confusion. The last I saw of the carriage, it was careening down the street with the coachman racing after it."

"Does someone wish you ill, my lord?"

"If I'm the target, I can handle it. But if it's Fleur, the would-be assassin had best beware."

❖ Chapter Twelve ❖

Fleur's arm was bruised but not badly injured. Lisette, Mrs. Peabody and Peg wanted to put her to bed, but she fought them and won. It was true her cheek stung fiercely but the pain was nothing she couldn't handle. Besides, she was desperate to check on Reed. Though he insisted the bullet had barely scratched him, she wanted to see for herself. To that end, she asked Peg to help her change her torn gown so she could find Reed.

"You had best do as she says," Lisette counseled Peg in halting English. "When Fleur makes up her mind, nothing will change it."

Fleur stood with waning patience while Peg fetched her blue-and-gold-striped walking dress and hooked her into it. Once the last hook was done up, Fleur hurried out the door and down the stairs with Lisette trailing after her. She entered the study without knocking and found it empty.

"May I help you, my lady?" Updike said from the doorway.

Fleur spun on her heel. "You can tell me where I can find his lordship."

"He's left the house, my lady."

"He left? What about his wound? Did he require the services of a surgeon?"

"No, indeed," Updike replied. "'Twas but a scratch. He changed his shirt and coat and left immediately."

"Where did he go?"

"I cannot say, my lady. His lordship didn't confide in me."

Fleur seriously doubted that. Updike seemed more than a simple valet. He was a butler, a confidant and apparently indispensable to Reed.

"Did he say when he would return?"

"No, my lady, though he did say not to expect him for dinner. He also said," Updike continued, "that you weren't to leave the house. Until the mystery of your recent . . . er . . . accident is solved, he wants you to go nowhere without proper protection."

Fleur gave an unladylike snort. How like Reed to think of her safety while disregarding his own. How dare he leave without telling her where he'd gone and why! This matter concerned her as well as him.

"Will you please tell him I wish to speak with him the moment he returns? I don't care how late it is."

Fleur failed to notice the speculative gleam in Updike's eyes. "I will give him your message, my lady. Might I suggest you and Madame Lisette take tea in the parlor? I'll have Cook include some tasty sandwiches and cakes to hold you over until dinner."

Grudgingly Fleur accepted the offer. She had missed lunch and was hungry.

"What do you think is going on?" Lisette asked once she and Fleur were ensconced in the parlor, an assortment of sandwiches and cakes placed before them. "I assumed the danger would be over once we arrived in England. Who would want to harm you?"

Fleur popped a tiny sandwich into her mouth and chewed thoughtfully. She swallowed, then said, "I cannot believe I am the one in danger."

"Then how do you explain being shot at?"

"The only explanation I can come up with is that Reed

was the target. In fact, I'm convinced of it. Now all I have to do is convince Reed."

Fleur spent the rest of the day curled up with a book. Later, she and Lisette ate off of dinner trays in her bedchamber rather than going down to the dining room. Lisette bid her goodnight and left after they had eaten. Fleur rang for Peg and asked that a bath be prepared. After she had washed her hair and bathed, she readied herself for bed.

Because Fleur had no chamber robe yet, she donned a shift and wrapped herself in a blanket. Then she sat in a chair before the newly stoked fire to await Reed's return. She didn't have long to wait. The clock on the mantle had just chimed ten when she heard the door open. Reed stepped into the bedchamber and closed the door behind him.

"Updike said you wished to see me."

Fleur rounded on him. "Where were you? Did you take a footman with you? What if someone used you for target practice again? Have you no sense at all?"

Reed pulled a chair up to the hearth and sat down. "One question at a time, please. I don't know why you're upset. I had my pistol in my coat pocket and a knife in my boot."

"You don't understand. You were the target of an assassination attempt today. Do you care so little about your own life?"

"What makes you think I was the target? It could have been you." He leaned over and touched her bruised cheek. "I hold myself to blame for your injury. I was too rough with you. Does it hurt?"

Fleur shrugged. "It stings but no serious damage was done. Do not blame yourself. You acted from pure instinct. You may have saved my life, though I doubt I was the target. There is no reason for anyone here to want me dead."

"What makes you believe I have enemies?"

"You were betrayed in France, for one thing."

Sighing heavily, Reed stared into the dancing flames.

"Lord Porter seems to feel as you do. He thinks I was the target. Neither of us knows why. I'm convinced there is a traitor within our ranks.

"Porter has assigned operatives to investigate," Reed continued. "We spent several hours this evening discussing the problem, including the possibility that French spies may be posing as émigrés. After I conferred with Porter, I visited Grandmamma. She counts many émigrés among her friends. I asked her to invite them to a salon Saturday next and to send you an invitation. Maybe you can learn something since you are considered one of them. You may even know a few of them. I will, of course, accompany you."

"While the salon sounds like a good idea, your attendance isn't required. In fact, it might hinder my efforts."

"How so?"

"Really, Reed, you're not an émigré and your presence could prevent people from speaking freely. No harm will come to me at your grandmother's house."

Reed sent her a look that told her he thought otherwise. "I cannot take that chance."

"Honestly, Reed, I've taken care of myself without your help since Pierre's death. I can do this on my own." She stood, indicating an end to their meeting. "It's late; I'm going to bed."

Forgetting she wore only a thin shift, she let the blanket fall away as she rose.

Reed's mouth went dry. His cock hardened instantly. With the hearth behind her, the dancing flames provided a showcase for her lush figure. Outlined beneath her transparent shift, her long shapely legs and the cleft between them drew his avid attention. Once he looked his fill, his gaze wandered upward to her breasts. Reed's breath seized when he noted how sweetly the flimsy material of her shift clung to her puckered nipples.

As if suddenly aware that Reed was staring at her, Fleur reached for the blanket.

"Don't," Reed said, reaching for her. "I like you just the way you are."

She gave a startled squeal when he pulled her into his lap. "How tired are you?" he whispered against her ear.

Fleur released a trembling sigh. "You need to leave."

"I know, but I can't help myself."

His mouth swooped down on hers without regard for tenderness or reserve. He wanted Fleur and wasn't ashamed to admit it. He thrust his tongue between her lips and heard her whimper when he stroked the tender inside of her mouth. He smiled inwardly when she arched her neck for his kisses. He didn't disappoint her as he trailed nipping kisses along the slender line of her throat. He pushed the sleeves of her shift down, giving his mouth free access to the tips of her nipples. He suckled her hard, flicking his tongue across the engorged buds.

Fleur's hands drifted to his head, her fingers sifting through the silken strands. Reed hardened even more. She had but to touch him and he went mad for her. His hand found the hem of her shift and eased it up along her thigh, baring her to his touch. He moved his hand between her thighs and caressed her cleft, finding her wet and ready for him.

He shifted her in his lap so that she straddled him, opening her to his exploration. She groped for the fastenings on his fly.

"Please," she gasped.

"I know what you want, love," Reed murmured. He helped her open the placket and release his erection. Her hand curled around him and stroked downward, from the head to his balls and back. Reed thought he would expire from pleasure. He would never get enough of this woman.

He could stand her tender torture no longer. Palming

her bottom, he lifted her slightly and eased his cock inside her. He groaned as she closed tightly around him. Head thrown back, she rode him hard, giving no quarter and asking for none. He gave her everything he had and then some. At the end, he took the reins from her, holding her hips in place as he pounded inside her, desperate now for release.

Fleur came first. He felt her body contract. Her arms. Her knees. Her thighs. Her inner muscles clenched around him and she cried out. Panting, Reed pumped harder, deeper, seeking his own pleasure. It came with a gush of hot liquid as he emptied himself inside her.

Fleur collapsed in a boneless heap against him. Reed fared no better. He felt as if every bone in his body had melted into a giant pool of liquid pleasure. When Fleur began to stir, he lifted her into his arms and carried her to her bed. Then he shed his clothes and joined her.

After a short rest, he began loving her again.

Fleur was alone when she woke the next morning. She stretched and smiled, remembering every blissful moment of the previous night. Though she recalled Pierre fondly, and they had been happy together, nothing about his lovemaking even remotely resembled what she and Reed had done in her bed last night.

After he carried her to her bed, she had taken the initiative. Blushing slightly, she recalled kissing every part of his body, caressing his erection with her tongue, taking him in her mouth and pleasuring him, and letting him return the favor. Everything they had done had been wonderfully arousing and not at all embarrassing. Reed released the wanton in her that neither she nor Pierre had known existed.

But being with Reed this way had to end when she moved into Reed's London mansion. Lady Helen did not like her, and Lady Violet was jealous of her. Besides, she had taken on another assignment and intended to devote all her time and energy to it.

Fleur was still lying in bed when Lisette poked her head into the room. "Are you ready to get up, *ma petite?* Lord Reed's luggage is being loaded into the carriage as we speak."

Fleur shot up. "How late is it? Why did you let me sleep so long?"

"'Tis only ten, but since we have very little to pack, his lordship said to let you sleep. Shall I send Peg to you?"

"Do I have time for a bath?"

"We'll make the time. I will see to it myself and ask Peg to bring up a breakfast tray so you can eat while the water is heating."

Lisette took her leave. Fleur lay back in bed, feeling somewhat guilty for causing the extra work. But she felt sticky from Reed's lovemaking and could smell his scent on her. It wouldn't take a genius to figure out what she had been up to if she skipped bathing this morning.

Fleur's breakfast arrived; she ate ravenously from a tray placed on her lap while a tub was being filled. Once Peg had carried off her tray and everyone except Lisette had left, Fleur got out of bed and eased into the tub.

Lisette regarded her with knowing eyes. "He was in your bed last night, wasn't he?"

Lying to Lisette had never worked. "Do you think worse of me for allowing it?"

"I could never think worse of you, no matter what you did. I cannot blame you for seeking pleasure where you may. Besides, his lordship is an honorable man. He will take care of you."

Fleur bristled. "I am perfectly capable of taking care of myself. I refuse to become a kept woman."

"As you say, *ma petite*," Lisette demurred. "But I fear you are falling in love with the rascal even though you know he will not wed you."

"Fear not for me, Lisette. I know precisely where I stand with Lord Hunthurst."

Reed was waiting for her when she arrived downstairs wearing the gold-and-blue walking dress. "I sent notes around to Madame Henrietta and the cobbler yesterday, instructing them to deliver your new wardrobe and slippers to Park Avenue. I wouldn't be surprised to learn the first of your gowns and most of the footwear we ordered have already arrived. Are you ready to leave?"

Fleur nodded.

Updike handed her the new bonnet that matched her gown. "We will see you in a few days, my lady. The entire household is moving to Park Avenue. 'Tis a move his lordship should have made when he returned from France."

Fleur tied her bonnet strings beneath her chin and smiled at Updike. "Thank you, Updike. I shall look forward to seeing a few friendly faces."

Reed grasped Fleur's elbow and ushered her out the door. "Where is Lisette?" Fleur asked.

"Waiting in the carriage with Peg. I'll follow on horseback."

"Ride inside with us, Reed. Why make a target of yourself?"

"Leave off, love," Reed said. "Just get into the carriage and let me worry about my well-being."

Fleur entered the carriage, muttering something about pig-headed men and their inability to take advice.

"Did you say something?" Lisette asked as Fleur settled her skirts around herself.

"Just talking to myself, Lisette."

The carriage rattled off. The ride was a short one, actually just around the corner. Fleur could have walked had Reed allowed it. He was waiting to open the door when the carriage arrived.

"*Mon Dieu*," Lisette said. "Why didn't you tell me we were going to live in a palace, *ma petite?*"

GET UP TO 4 FREE BOOKS!

You can have the best romance delivered to your door for less than what you'd pay in a bookstore or online. Sign up for one of our book clubs today, and we'll send you **FREE* BOOKS** just for trying it out...**with no obligation to buy, ever!**

HISTORICAL ROMANCE BOOK CLUB

Travel from the Scottish Highlands to the American West, the decadent ballrooms of Regency England to Viking ships. Your shipments will include authors such as CONNIE MASON, CASSIE EDWARDS, LYNSAY SANDS, LEIGH GREENWOOD, and many, many more.

LOVE SPELL BOOK CLUB

Bring a little magic into your life with the romances of Love Spell—fun contemporaries, paranormals, time-travels, futuristics, and more. Your shipments will include authors such as KATIE MACALISTER, SUSAN GRANT, NINA BANGS, SANDRA HILL, and more.

As a book club member you also receive the following special benefits:

- **30% OFF all orders through our website & telecenter!**
  (Plus, you still get 1 book FREE for every 5 books you buy!)
- **Exclusive access to special discounts!**
- **Convenient home delivery and 10 days to return any books you don't want to keep.**

There is no minimum number of books to buy, and you may cancel membership at any time. See back to sign up!

*Please include $2.00 for shipping and handling.

YES! ☐

Sign me up for the **Historical Romance Book Club** and send my TWO FREE BOOKS! If I choose to stay in the club, I will pay only $8.50* each month, a savings of $5.48!

YES! ☐

Sign me up for the **Love Spell Book Club** and send my TWO FREE BOOKS! If I choose to stay in the club, I will pay only $8.50* each month, a savings of $5.48!

NAME: _____

ADDRESS: _____

_____

TELEPHONE: _____

E-MAIL: _____

☐ **I WANT TO PAY BY CREDIT CARD.**

☐ VISA ☐ MasterCard. ☐ DISCOVER

ACCOUNT #: _____

EXPIRATION DATE: _____

SIGNATURE: _____

Send this card along with $2.00 shipping & handling for each club you wish to join, to:

**Romance Book Clubs
1 Mechanic Street
Norwalk, CT 06850-3431**

Or fax (must include credit card information!) to: 610.995.9274.
You can also sign up online at www.dorchesterpub.com.

*Plus $2.00 for shipping. Offer open to residents of the U.S. and Canada only.
Canadian residents please call 1.800.481.9191 for pricing information.
If under 18, a parent or guardian must sign. Terms, prices and conditions subject to change. Subscription subject
to acceptance. Dorchester Publishing reserves the right to reject any order or cancel any subscription.

JOIN NOW!

"It *is* imposing, I suppose, but if I have my way about it, we won't be living here long. The ladies of the house are suffering our presence only because Reed demands it. Raise your chin, Lisette, we cannot let them intimidate us."

The door opened. Several footmen came out to help unload Reed's luggage and carry it inside. Reed escorted the ladies through the gate and up the stairs. Hughes bowed and held the door wide for them to enter.

"Welcome home, my lord. We have been expecting you and your guests."

"Thank you, Hughes. Are the ladies in the drawing room?"

"They are. They have a caller. Shall I announce you?"

"A caller? Who is it?"

"A Mr. Duvall. I believe you know him."

"Indeed I do. No need to announce us, Hughes. We'll announce ourselves. Have the guest chambers been prepared as I requested?"

"Indeed they have, my lord."

"Which chambers will my guests occupy?"

"Lady Helen chose the green room in the east wing for Lady Fontaine. And for her companion, my lady suggested that we put her with Lady Fontaine's lady's maid in the servants' quarters on the third floor."

Reed scowled, not at all pleased with the arrangements. "She did, did she? We'll see about that. Madame Lisette is not a servant. She shall have the green room in the east wing. As for Lady Fontaine, I believe she will be more comfortable in the rose room in the west wing. Will you see that the chamber is made ready? And show Peg where she is to sleep."

"All the chambers have been cleaned and aired, my lord, in case you wished to change the arrangements made by Lady Helen. Delivery of Lady Fontaine's new wardrobe was made a short time ago. Everything was taken to the green room, but I will make sure everything is moved to the rose room and show the maid to her room in the servants' quarters."

"Thank you, Hughes." He offered an arm to each lady. "Shall we proceed to the drawing room?"

"You're here," Helen said when they entered the drawing room.

"Indeed. Hello, Duvall. I'm surprised to see you here this morning. Didn't you call yesterday?"

Duvall cleared his throat. "Lady Helen asked me to escort her and her sister on a shopping expedition this morning."

"Indeed I did," Helen said. "Once I saw all the boxes that arrived for Lady Fontaine early this morning, I decided Violet and I are in need of a new wardrobe. And since you have no time for us, I sent for Gallard to attend us. He arrived posthaste."

"I wouldn't think of disappointing the ladies," Duvall concurred.

"Good to see you again, Duvall," Reed drawled. "Duvall, ladies, allow me to present to you Madame Lisette, Fleur's companion."

Lisette curtsied and was acknowledged.

"Did Hughes inform you of the arrangements for your guests?" Helen asked. "I hope they are to your liking."

"They weren't to my liking, Helen. Since Lisette is not a servant, she shall occupy the green room."

"What about Lady Fontaine?" Violet asked. Her barbed gaze pierced Fleur. If looks could kill, Fleur would be dead. "She was to have the green room."

"Fleur shall have the rose room," Reed informed her. "The view from the windows is spectacular."

Violet objected vociferously. "But the rose room is . . ."

"Indeed it is," Reed agreed, cutting her off in midsentence.

Fleur wondered what had just taken place but held her tongue. She would find out soon enough.

"Since we are to be your guests, I'd prefer that we dispense with formalities," Fleur ventured. "I'd be pleased if you'd call me Fleur, and I know Lisette would prefer to be addressed by her given name."

"Of course," Helen acknowledged, "and you may call us Helen and Violet."

"Duvall, if you and the ladies will excuse us, I shall acquaint my guests with the house. I don't want to delay your shopping excursion."

Reed ushered Fleur and Lisette from the room.

"That went rather well," Reed said once they had quit the drawing room.

Fleur nodded. "But don't you think it strange that Duvall is making himself indispensable to Helen and Violet?"

"Better him than me," Reed retorted.

Fleur kept her thoughts to herself as Reed guided them through the mansion, explaining the function of each room as they passed through it. The first floor consisted of the drawing room, dining room, a huge ballroom, breakfast room, a well-stocked library and study. The modern, well-kept kitchen and servants' dining hall were at the back of the house, connected to the upper stories by servants' stairs. The second floor had an east wing and a west wing. Each wing held a total of five bedchambers. The third floor consisted entirely of several bedchambers occupied by servants.

"How will I ever find my way around?" Fleur wondered aloud.

"There are footmen stationed on each floor to direct you," Reed said. "My grandfather built this house, and my father and brother added improvements. We even have a water closet in each wing and modern plumbing."

"Amazing," Fleur replied, peeking into one of the water closets. "Our chateau had none of these amenities, though it was grand enough."

Reed stopped before a door in the east wing and flung it open. "This is your bedchamber, Lisette. You can stay here and rest or acquaint yourself with the servants below stairs. I know you feel comfortable around them."

Lisette grinned. "You know me well, my lord. I may be your guest but such lofty company unsettles me."

"I'll show you Fleur's chamber first and then you can do as you wish. Can you find your way to the kitchen and servants' dining hall?"

Lisette nodded, and they continued on to the west wing and Fleur's bedchamber. Reed opened the door and held it so they could precede him inside. Peg was already there, removing a bonnet from a large hatbox. "The chamber is beautiful," Fleur said, admiring the rose-colored drapery, flocked wallpaper and dainty furniture. Her gaze settled on the boxes Peg was busily unpacking. "Are those all for me?"

"It appears Madame Henrietta fulfilled her promise to have several outfits ready within the week. The rest will follow in a few days."

Fleur scowled. "I don't recall ordering so many gowns."

"You didn't, but I did."

Fleur frowned her displeasure. "I shall repay you every last farthing. I want to open a bank account today, if it can be arranged. It's time I purchased gowns and accessories for Lisette."

"I believe that can be arranged. Shall we plan on it after luncheon? I need to leave the house for a bit but shall return in time to take luncheon with you. If you need anything, just ring."

Lisette decided to stay and help Fleur and Peg unpack the boxes of new clothing. Lisette exclaimed over the fine silk stockings, filmy shifts, silk nightgowns, warm dressing robes and more gowns than Fleur remembered ordering. Included were a riding habit and boots, even though Fleur didn't own a horse, and bonnets and slippers to match nearly every outfit.

After, Lisette and Peg left to eat luncheon with the servants. Fleur freshened up and made her way to the dining room.

Reed was on his way home. It was nearly time for luncheon and he had promised Fleur he'd join her. He was riding Ebony down the street when he heard a coach behind him, approaching uncommonly fast for such a busy thoroughfare. At first Reed thought nothing of it. When he heard people cursing and shouting, he looked behind him and saw the coach bearing down on him, people, riders and conveyances scattering in its wake. A milkmaid leading a milch cow was forced off the road. The crowded street allowed scant room for maneuvering.

"Out of the way!" Reed shouted as he kneed Ebony into a gallop. Glancing over his shoulder, he saw the coach sideswipe a dray and send it crashing onto its side. And still the coach raced toward him. It was obvious now that he was the target of another unprovoked attack.

The coach was nearly upon him. He knew intuitively that people could be hurt and even killed if he plowed forward without a thought for life or limb. His mind searched frantically for an escape route. Looming ahead was a crossroad. Without a second thought, Reed veered to the right onto the less-crowded street. The coach followed. Then he saw it, a narrow alley wide enough for a horse but not a coach.

Reed did not hesitate as he reined Ebony into the maw of the alley. Aware that the coach could not follow, he slowed Ebony to a walk and picked his way around the garbage strewn in his path. He exited onto another street. Glancing over his shoulder, he noted with relief that he wasn't being followed. It took but a moment for him to get his bearings, and then Reed continued on to Park Avenue.

* * *

Fleur greeted Reed with a smile as he entered the dining room. "Have you been waiting long?" he asked, returning her smile.

"Not too long." She frowned. "You're out of breath. What happened?"

"Nothing at all." He sat down and shook out his napkin.

"I don't believe you. You may as well tell me. You know I'll hound you until you do."

"It's nothing really," Reed insisted, brushing her question aside. "Merely a little mishap on the road."

A footman placed a cold luncheon before them.

"Was another attempt made on your life?" Fleur demanded.

"I suppose you could call it that. It was nothing I couldn't handle. Forget it, Fleur. Where is Lisette?"

"She'll be ready to leave when we are." She bit into a piece of smoked salmon, chewed thoughtfully and swallowed. She decided to change the subject. "I will need the money you received for my jewels. I want to deposit it in the bank along with the bank draft Lord Porter gave me."

"That was one of my errands this morning. I had left your money in the safe at my townhouse and went to retrieve it."

They finished their lunch in silence despite the questions Fleur wanted to ask. Reed appeared distracted, so Fleur didn't prod him for answers. Lisette was waiting for them when they arrived in the foyer.

"I brought your bonnet, *ma petite*," she said. "I'm ready to leave when you are."

"The carriage is waiting," Hughes said.

Fleur was relieved when Reed entered the carriage behind her and Lisette. He didn't seem to realize his life was in danger. Or if he did, he wasn't doing anything to protect himself.

The shopping expedition was a success. Fleur opened a bank account, deposited her money and placed an order for a new wardrobe for Lisette with Madame Henrietta.

* * *

The following day found Fleur at loose ends. Because Helen and Violet made her feel unwelcome, she spent as little time as possible with them. Gallard Duvall had become a permanent fixture at the mansion. He had stayed for dinner last night and didn't leave until Reed made broad hints about the lateness of the hour. It seemed to Fleur that the Frenchman was far too interested in Reed's comings and goings. Fleur didn't like him.

It was only by accident that she learned her bedchamber connected to Reed's. No wonder Helen had wanted her to have the green room instead of the charming rose room she now occupied. Fleur hadn't noticed the adjoining door until she was preparing for bed that night. Curiosity got the best of her, and she opened the door to see where it led. It didn't take her long to realize she was in the master suite. It was twice the size of her chamber, decorated in dark colors with a huge bed against one wall and massive furniture situated around it.

"I wondered when you'd notice the door," Reed said from across the room. He had appeared suddenly from a small alcove Fleur assumed was a dressing room. He was wearing a robe, loosely belted at the waist. His feet were bare and his hair tousled from his bath.

"No wonder Violet objected to the sleeping arrangements. Why did you give me the chamber adjoining yours?"

Reed reached her in three long strides and pulled her into his arms. "You know why. Besides, Violet has no say in what I do or don't do."

"Any fool can see she's jealous of me."

"She has no reason to be. I'm not interested in Violet."

"She can give you the child you desperately need."

"I'm in no hurry to wed." His arms tightened around her.

Fleur pushed him away. "There's a matter I wish to discuss with you, and now is as good a time as any." She dragged in a steadying breath. "I believe that Gallard Duvall may be responsible for the attacks on you."

When Reed opened his mouth to speak, Fleur placed a finger against his lips. "Do not deny you had another close call yesterday."

"I wasn't in any danger. Forget Duvall. I am convinced my betrayer is one of Porter's agents." He reached for her again, but Fleur avoided him.

"I do not trust Duvall. He has ingratiated himself with Helen for a reason."

"Of course he has. He is a relative, after all. Helen says he was a big help to her during Jason's illness and after his death, when she was left adrift."

"Doesn't it seem odd to you that he showed up at your country estate just after your disappearance?"

"He's an émigré. They show up in England all the time. I helped a few escape myself."

"But . . . I still think . . ."

"You think too much," Reed said, dragging her against him. His kiss chased everything save his taste, his scent and his touch from her mind.

Fleur didn't leave Reed's bedchamber until he carried her to her bed shortly before dawn.

Fleur's dreamy expression, passion-glazed eyes and swollen lips gave ample proof of what had taken place in Reed's bed when she appeared at breakfast the next morning. Unfortunately, Violet noticed and took exception.

"Reed is mine, do you hear?" she hissed into Fleur's ear. "You cannot have him."

✦ Chapter Thirteen ✦

Fleur thought she had misheard, but when she glanced at Violet, she knew she hadn't been mistaken. The woman's feral look was too virulent to be mistaken.

Ignoring the remark, Fleur filled her plate, carried it to the table and sat beside Lisette. Snubbing them, Helen and Violet began chatting together about the latest gossip.

"Watch out for that one," Lisette whispered, nodding toward Violet. "I heard what she said."

When Reed entered the breakfast room a few minutes later, Violet gave him her full attention, coyly batting her eyes and touching his arm. Fleur turned away, more than a little disgusted by the blatant flirtation.

They were still in the breakfast room when Gallard Duvall was announced.

"Though it's a little early for visitors, you are welcome to join us, Duvall," Reed drawled.

"Forgive me, *mon ami*," Duvall said, "but I have some interesting news to impart."

"Please do join us, Gallard," Helen invited. "You are family, after all."

"Indeed," Reed concurred. "Fix yourself a plate. There's always room for one more."

Duvall didn't need a second invitation. He filled a plate from the sideboard and took an empty seat beside Fleur.

"What is your news, Monsieur Duvall?" Fleur asked. "Good tidings, I hope."

"I just learned that the dowager countess of Hunthurst is holding an afternoon soirée for my countrymen who fled the Reign of Terror and are now living in London. She has great sympathy for our plight."

Reed set his fork down and pushed his empty plate away. "Grandmamma is sympathetic to émigrés because of our French connections on Father's side of the family."

"Nevertheless, I wanted you to know I will be attending and hope to see you there."

"You know," Helen said, tilting her head thoughtfully toward the Frenchman, "I see no reason why you shouldn't live here with us as you used to in the country. You are Reed's cousin, no matter how distant, and you are renting a room in one of the less desirable sections of London."

"Oh, *non*, I could not . . ."

"Of course you can. Isn't that right, Reed?"

Lisette and Fleur exchanged glances, communicating without words their feelings about Duvall moving into the mansion. Fleur didn't trust Duvall, and apparently neither did Lisette. Fleur couldn't explain her distrust, except there was something about the Frenchman that didn't ring true.

Reed sent Helen a speaking glance that was more censure than approval.

Duvall, however, solved the problem. "*Non, non*, I have no wish to intrude. My quarters are sufficient for my needs, and I am among my own kind. But thank you for your kind invitation. I came to ask the ladies if they require my escort."

"Since I am attending Grandmamma's soirée, they will have my escort," Reed said.

"*C'est si bon*. Remember, I will be available if you need me." Duvall wiped his mouth with his napkin and rose. "And now I must bid you good day." Reed stood. "*Non, non*, do not rise, Cousin. I will show myself out."

Reed waited until Duvall left the room before addressing Helen. "You had no right to invite someone to live in my home without first consulting me."

Helen shrugged. "It was my home before it was yours. Besides, I happen to enjoy Gallard's company."

"Then enjoy it on your own time. If he needs monetary aid, I will help him because we are related, but that's as far as my hospitality extends." He pushed back his chair. "Excuse me, I have an appointment."

Good, Fleur mused, Reed was no more trusting of Duvall than she was. "Be careful," Fleur warned as Reed paused at the door and glanced back at her. Then he was gone.

"What was that all about?" Violet asked.

Fleur shrugged. "I merely wanted him to take care. Two attempts have been made on his life and the next one might succeed."

"Reed can take care of himself," Helen said, waving her hand dismissively.

"But I will take even better care of him when I become Reed's countess," Violet purred.

"I know your aspirations, my dear," Helen replied, "and I'm sure you will gain what you most desire."

"Excuse me, Violet," Fleur interrupted. "Does Reed know you plan to marry him? Shouldn't it be his decision?"

Though Violet sent Fleur a hostile glance, it was Helen who answered. "Men rarely know their own minds. Reed's grandmother is anxious for him to wed and produce an heir, and we all know she is partial to Violet. My sister has the proper bloodlines and a generous dowry; she is perfect for Reed."

Fleur didn't bother answering. She had no place in this

conversation. Excusing herself, Fleur rose and left the room. Lisette followed her out the door.

"Which gown do you intend to wear to the soirée?" Lisette asked as they climbed the stairs to Fleur's chamber.

"I thought the bronze silk might do since it's an afternoon affair. What will you wear?"

"The pale pink, I believe. It was delivered just yesterday."

The hours sped by with uncommon haste. While Lisette chattered away, Fleur's mind wandered to Reed. She hoped he was taking care of himself wherever he was. Fleur knew it was silly to worry about him, but she couldn't help it.

After Lisette left, Fleur wandered out to the garden. The weather was especially fine, and the sun felt good on her uplifted face. English weather was not always so pleasant.

Reed found Fleur sitting on a bench in the garden when he arrived home. "I've been looking for you," he said.

"Have you been home long?"

"No, I just arrived. Neither Helen nor Violet seemed to know where you were."

"Nor do they care," Fleur added. "They consider me an interloper."

He sent her a smile that warmed her heart. "I don't, and I'm the only one who counts. It's almost time for luncheon. We have a guest today."

"It's not unusual to have Duvall here for both luncheon and dinner. Helen quite dotes on him."

"It's not Duvall; it's my grandmother."

Fleur's heart sank. As Helen had pointed out, the dowager favored a match between Violet and Reed.

"Shall we go inside?" Reed asked, offering his arm.

Before she could place her hand in the crook of Reed's elbow, he pulled her into his arms and kissed her.

Fleur should have recognized the mischievous glint in

his silver eyes, but she didn't have time to absorb its meaning before his mouth claimed hers, delving deep with his tongue, setting her body on fire. She savored his kiss a brief few moments before pulling away.

"Stop it, Reed! Anyone looking out the window could see us."

A dimple appeared in his cheek. "You're right, of course. I can't seem to control myself around you." He extended his arm. "Shall we?"

They found the dowager in the drawing room, holding court. She greeted Fleur warmly. "I've come to extend a personal invitation to my soirée for French émigrés Saturday next. Reed can provide escort."

"I am not precisely family," Violet ventured. "Am I still invited?"

The dowager sent Violet a fond smile. "You, my dear, as you well know, head the list of women I'd be happy to welcome as Reed's countess. You are perfect for him in every way."

Fleur went still, her heart plummeting to her toes. Daring a glance at Reed, she wondered why he wasn't objecting to his grandmother's choice of bride for him. Did he intend to wed Violet? Did he have an understanding with her? Had Reed already proposed? What in God's name was she doing living in Reed's house, sleeping in his bed, when he already had a bride picked out?

Fleur leaped to her feet. "Excuse me, I don't feel well."

As she headed toward the door and the safety of her chamber, Violet called after her, "Perhaps something didn't agree with you."

Fleur didn't need to be reminded that she was an intruder, living with a family who cared nothing for her or her feelings. Never had it been driven home so clearly that she didn't belong here. She had become Reed's mistress, no matter how much she wanted to deny it. It was time to leave. She needed to concentrate on her assignment without the kind of distraction Reed provided.

Immersed in her thoughts, Fleur wasn't aware that Reed had entered her bedchamber until she heard him whisper her name. She whirled, surprised to find him standing behind her. "Go away."

"I never proposed to Violet," he said.

"Not yet, perhaps, but you will. If not Violet, then someone like her. It's time I left, Reed. Lisette and I will move to a hotel tomorrow."

He reached for her. She whirled away. "Be reasonable, love. I want you here. I'm not ready to wed anyone yet, no matter what Grandmamma says."

"Yet you want a mistress, and I'm convenient."

"It's not like that."

"What am I to you if not a mistress? I cannot bear any more of this, Reed. I'm leaving; don't try to talk me out of it. I wish you and Violet joy."

Reed reached for her again, and once again she eluded him. "No, don't touch me. You're not going to seduce me into changing my mind. I'm leaving, and that's final."

Reed realized Fleur meant it. Nothing he could say or do would change her mind. He could, however, offer her a safe place to live.

"If I cannot convince you to stay here, where you will be safe, then let me offer you an alternative."

"Alternative?" Fleur repeated suspiciously.

"Just so. My townhouse is unoccupied at the moment. It would be perfect for you and Lisette. And I'll even include the servants who were there when you arrived. Updike, Mrs. Peabody, Cook, the footmen and housemaids. They are superfluous here, anyway."

"If, and I stress if, I accept your offer, I fully intend to pay rent and not just a token fee."

"Agreed," Reed said. He mentioned a price that seemed

reasonable, that wouldn't stretch the limits of her income. He held his breath while she contemplated the offer. "The rent covers the salaries of the servants," he added. "That's how rentals are usually handled."

Fleur looked skeptical. "Are you sure? I'm not looking for charity. I have enough money to live comfortably. Once my assignment in London is completed, Lisette and I will repair to my aunt's manor in the country."

"I'm not offering charity. I need to find a renter or buyer for my townhouse; it's as simple as that."

"Very well, then. We'll move tomorrow."

"Stay until after Grandmamma's soirée," Reed said. "That will give the servants time to prepare for your arrival."

"Very well, I'll agree to those terms."

"Now that that's settled, shall we go in to luncheon?"

Fleur shook her head. "I can't face them right now."

Reed didn't press. "I'll have a tray sent up to you."

"Thank you."

Reed hesitated. "Fleur, I . . ."

"Go, Reed. There is nothing left to say. We both must forget the intimate part of our relationship and concentrate on finding our traitor."

Not bloody likely, Reed silently vowed. He wasn't ready to let go of Fleur.

The day of the soirée arrived. Peg helped Fleur into a fashionable bronze silk gown shot with silver; its high waist, scoop neck and tiny sleeves accented the slim shape of the skirt and her lithe figure beneath. Peg cleverly arranged her hair in a tumble of curls, held in place by a silver snood. At Fleur's request, Patsy didn't powder her hair, unlike Helen and Violet, who both sported elaborate powdered coiffures topped by huge ostrich feathers. It was all Fleur could do to keep from laughing.

On the other hand, Reed looked magnificent in a black

superfine coat and breeches that molded his muscular torso
and legs and other attributes. His pristine linen and metic-
ulously tied cravat were perfection itself. They all waited
in the hall for the town coach to be brought around.

The ladies piled inside the coach when it arrived. Reed
chose to ride Ebony rather than cram inside the already
crowded vehicle. When they arrived, they were announced
by the butler. The drawing room was bustling with activity.
Judging from the murmur of voices, Fleur deduced that
French was the language of choice for the majority of the
guests.

They headed toward the dowager, where she presided
over the salon from her thronelike chair. Duvall appeared
like magic and whisked Helen and Violet off to meet his
fellow émigrés. Fleur recognized an acquaintance of Pierre's
standing across the room, and she split from the group to
greet him while Lisette gravitated toward a cluster of her
countrywomen.

"Monsieur Barbeau, how nice to see you again," Fleur
greeted. "How long have you been in England?"

"Countess Fontaine," Barbeau said, kissing her hand. "It
is wonderful to see you alive and looking so well. I heard
your husband . . ." He gave a Gallic shrug. "So many bad
things happened. Please accept my condolences for your
loss. I just recently arrived in England." He shook his head.
"The turmoil in France is dreadful, just dreadful. Count
Dubois and I arrived together. We fled across the channel
in the dead of night. I do not believe you have met René.
Count Dubois, allow me to acquaint you with Countess
Fleur Fontaine."

Dubois, a haughty young man with aristocratic looks
greeted Fleur with a flourish. "Countess, how fortunate you
did not share your husband's fate."

"You knew Pierre, my lord?"

"*Non*, I did not have the pleasure. Are you French?
Somehow you do not have the look of a Frenchwoman."

"I am English, my lord. I moved to France with Pierre after we were wed."

Another couple joined their group. As they conversed together, Fleur attempted to judge their character. Were they grateful to England for offering refuge? As Fleur progressed from group to group, conversing, laughing, she began to realize how difficult her mission was going to be.

Many of the émigrés wore masks, not real masks but inner masks that shielded their private thoughts from the world. Could one of them be a spy? Her gaze sought Reed and found him. He was staring intently at her, eyes narrowed, his expression unreadable. She didn't see what had drawn his censorious attention until she realized Count Dubois had attached himself to her as she moved from group to group.

When Gallard Duvall approached and greeted her warmly, Dubois appeared discomfited, jealous even.

"I was not aware that you knew the countess, Duvall," Dubois said.

"She is a guest in my cousin's home," Duvall answered. "I see her on my frequent visits to Lady Helen Harwood and Lady Violet Dewberry."

"Ah, *oui*, I remember now. Your cousin is the Earl of Hunthurst. You are his . . . friend, Countess? Perhaps his *chère amie?*"

"You insult me, Count Dubois," Fleur huffed indignantly.

"Forgive me, it was wrong of me to assume."

"For your information, I am a house guest of the earl's sister-in-law."

Leaning close, Dubois said, "I understand Hunthurst recently returned to London from abroad, that he inherited the earldom from his deceased brother."

"It is not my place to gossip about the family," Fleur bit out. So saying, she stomped off. She didn't like Dubois, didn't even look back to see if he recognized the cut direct she had just given him.

"What happened?" Reed asked when he caught up with Fleur. "Did you learn something damaging about one of the émigrés?"

"Count Dubois was more than a little curious about you. I . . . didn't like his attitude."

"Did he insult you?"

Fleur noted Reed's clenched fists and the hard glint in his silver eyes and bit her tongue. Her assignment wasn't to make Reed jealous or force him to do something irrational.

"No, I just don't like him. I'm not particularly fond of Monsieur Duvall, either, but that doesn't mean either of them are suspect. I need more information before accusing anyone."

"I don't want you to put yourself at risk," Reed growled.

"Do you or do you not want your traitor?"

"You know I do."

"Then don't interfere," she said.

"Ah, there you are, Countess. I was looking for you."

Fleur smiled at Monsieur Barbeau. "Have you met his lordship?"

"*Non*, I have not had the pleasure."

Fleur made the introductions.

"I would be pleased if you would join me for a carriage ride through the park tomorrow, Countess," Monsieur Barbeau invited.

Fleur thought for a moment, then said, "I'd be delighted." She gave him the Park Avenue address. She could wait one more day to move. "What time will you call for me?"

"Does two o'clock meet with your approval?"

"It does," Fleur replied.

Barbeau beamed. "Until tomorrow, Countess. A pleasure to meet you, Hunthurst."

"Do you think that's wise?" Reed asked through clenched teeth.

"How else can I infiltrate their inner circle? I have accepted this assignment, and I intend to see it through."

"Porter doesn't expect you to place yourself in harm's way."

"Leave off, Reed. I can take care of myself. Look to your own safety. If you'll excuse me, I see Lisette standing quite alone and must attend her."

Reed was reduced to watching Fleur from afar while she flitted from group to group, conversing and flirting, or so it appeared to him.

When his grandmother beckoned to him, he went to her side immediately, reluctantly pulling his gaze from Fleur.

"You seem disgruntled, my boy. What is bothering you?"

"You know I don't enjoy these events, Grandmamma. I'm here because the ladies required my escort."

"You've paid more attention to Lady Fontaine than you have Lady Violet. Never say you are infatuated with the widow. She wouldn't be my choice for you, Reed, you know that. Anyone who remained childless after five years of marriage is not for you."

Annoyance darkened Reed's brow. "I'm not ready to wed yet, Grandmamma. Even if I were, Violet would not be my choice."

The dowager patted his arm. "Do not take offense, dear boy. I know you haven't fully recovered from your unpleasant ordeal in France yet."

"Just so," Reed muttered. Grandmamma didn't know the half of it.

Reed spent what remained of the afternoon observing Fleur from afar. Shortly before the guests started leaving, Violet sidled up to him, winding her arm in his.

"Don't you think it's time you turned your attention in another direction?" she purred.

Annoyed, Reed stared at her. Was he that obvious? Had everyone noticed his preoccupation with Fleur? "I wasn't aware I was paying attention to anyone in particular."

"I know Fleur is your mistress, and I don't hold it against you, but this has to stop if we are to be wed."

Reed removed her hand from the crook of his arm. "I don't recall proposing. Though I have nothing against you, Violet," he said, softening the blow, "I advise you to set your sights on another."

Violet sent him a coy look. "I shan't give up on you, Reed. I'm determined to have you for a husband. Fleur may have saved your life, but she isn't worthy of you. One wonders how many men she has consorted with in her line of work."

Reed went rigid. Rage consumed him. How dare Violet disparage a courageous woman like Fleur! No one knew how close she had come to losing her life for her country.

"Fleur's line of work was saving the lives of Englishmen. I wonder how far you would go to save a man's life."

"I'm not without honor, Reed," Violet huffed.

Reed was too angry to reply. "Would you please collect Helen and Lisette while I bid Grandmamma goodbye? It's time we took our leave."

"Wait, Reed. Forgive me for speaking my mind about Fleur. I admit I'm jealous of your attention to her, but I did not mean to judge her harshly or discredit her courage."

Reed nodded curtly and strode off. He made his farewells to his grandmother and searched the crowd for Fleur. He saw her in a corner conversing with Gallard Duvall and, to his astonishment, Henry Dempsey, another of Porter's operatives. What was *he* doing here?

He asked his grandmother how Dempsey had ended up on the guest list, only to be told she didn't know whom he was talking about. Reed didn't press the dowager even though Dempsey's appearance had taken him aback. Resolutely, he set off to break up the cozy threesome.

"I hate to intrude, Dempsey, Duvall, but the ladies are ready to leave," Reed said. "I've come to collect Fleur."

"A pity," Duvall said, squeezing Fleur's hand in farewell.

"A pity indeed," Dempsey concurred. "The countess and I were just becoming acquainted."

"Another time, perhaps," Fleur said, pulling her hand away from Duvall with some effort. She bid them farewell and took her leave.

"I'll join you in a moment, Fleur," Reed said. "I wish a private word with Dempsey."

"Allow me to escort you to the door," Duvall said, catching up with Fleur.

"What are you doing here?" Reed asked once he and Dempsey were alone.

"The same as you," Dempsey said, refusing to elaborate. "I understand Porter believes one of the émigrés is a spy and therefore a threat to our country."

"Porter has it wrong," Reed contended. "I believe . . ." His sentence slid to a halt. "It doesn't matter what I believe as long as we are both working toward the same end. How do you know Gallard Duvall?" he asked, abruptly changing the subject.

"I intruded upon the conversation between Countess Fontaine and Duvall and introduced myself to him. I tried to meet as many émigrés as possible today. The countess is a lovely woman, isn't she? I understand you and she are an item."

"You understand wrong, Dempsey. We'll talk later; the ladies are waiting for me."

Reed strode off, his mood considerably darker than it had been a few minutes earlier. He didn't appreciate Dempsey's attention to Fleur. Though Reed knew Porter was conducting a search for the traitor or double spy, he wasn't aware that Porter had involved Dempsey. He didn't know a great deal about Dempsey and was inclined to suspect anyone who knew about the operation.

Reed joined the ladies in the foyer and escorted them to

the coach waiting outside the door. Once he saw them safely into the coach, he mounted Ebony.

Violet poked her head out the window. "Aren't you coming home with us?"

"I have some business to attend to," Reed answered as he rode off.

"Well!" Violet exclaimed, settling back against the squabs. "That certainly was rude of him. Sometimes I don't understand Reed."

Fleur rolled her eyes and shared an amused glance with Lisette.

"Did you enjoy yourself, Fleur?" Helen asked. "You must have felt right at home among those poor displaced émigrés."

"Those poor displaced émigrés, both men and women, have survived the Reign of Terror, something you cannot begin to understand."

"I don't care to understand." Helen sniffed. "Of course I feel sympathy for those people, but their problems are not mine. I understand your involvement with them, Fleur, but they are not really your people either. Gallard Duvall, of course, is another matter. He's family."

"I was wondering," Violet said thoughtfully, "how long you intend to remain with us? I should think you'd be eager to visit your home in the country."

"Lisette and I plan to leave Hunthurst soon," Fleur informed them. "Peg is packing for us as we speak."

"Oh, you're leaving us?" Violet asked brightly. "I cannot say we'll miss you. Does Reed know?"

"He does. I have already told him of my plans. We'll be moving to a nearby townhouse in a day or two. I am not ready yet to leave London."

"May I ask where in London you will be living?"

When Fleur gave Reed's address, it took but a moment for the two women to understand the significance.

"You're moving to Reed's townhouse?" Violet shrieked. "Whore! Witch! You cannot have Reed. I've waited a long time for him."

Before Fleur could defend herself, Violet struck, digging a shallow groove in Fleur's cheek with her long fingernails. Fleur was not one to take abuse lightly. She struck out at Violet, slapping her across the face. Mouth agape, Violet reared back, cupping her reddened cheek. But before the fight got out of hand, the coach stopped and the coachman opened the door. Fleur spilled out the door first, with Lisette hard on her heels. Screeching like a wounded cat, Violet stumbled from the coach, supported by Helen.

"Reed will hear about this," Helen called as Fleur ran lightly up the steps and disappeared through the front door.

Meanwhile, across town, Reed was shown into Porter's office. He had ridden straight to Whitehall from the soirée.

"What is it, Hunthurst? You look upset," Porter said.

"Did you assign Henry Dempsey to Operation Traitor?" Reed asked without preamble.

Porter frowned. "To my knowledge, Dempsey hasn't received a new assignment. Why do you ask?"

"He was at Grandmamma's soirée. He hinted that you had asked him to take part in our investigation."

Porter drummed his fingers on the desk. "I may have mentioned the investigation to him. Perhaps he's as eager to find the traitor as you are."

"Perhaps," Reed agreed. "Have you considered that Dempsey, himself, might be the traitor?"

Porter laughed. "You're looking for the traitor in the wrong place, Hunthurst. I personally vouch for each and every one of my operatives. They have been thoroughly investigated before being brought on board, just as you were."

Still not convinced, Reed merely grunted. The meeting ended as abruptly as it had begun. Reed rode home in a contemplative mood. How in bloody hell was he going to find a traitor with so many suspects to choose from?

As he rode around to the stables behind the manor, he heard an explosion. Moments later he toppled from his horse and knew no more.

✦ Chapter Fourteen ✦

Reed awakened in a dark, cold place, a place where pain and the specter of death vied for his attention. He attempted to move and found his arms and legs shackled. He gnashed his teeth and waited for the bite of the lash.

"You can release him now." The voice bristled with authority.

Suddenly his arms and legs were free. Fearing he would find himself in hell, Reed forced his eyes open. He smelled her unique scent before the mist clouding his eyes cleared enough to see her.

Fleur.

"What happened?" Reed groaned.

The hand that touched his face was cool and reassuring. "John Coachman found you near the stables," Fleur explained. "He heard a shot and went to investigate. You were lying on the ground, blood seeping from your temple."

"Nothing serious, my lord," a male voice intoned. He turned toward the voice and recognized Doctor Freeman, the family physician. "Whoever shot at you missed the target," the doctor continued. "The bullet grazed your temple; lots of blood and some pain but not fatal. Once the headache passes, you'll be as good as new, except for the shallow wound along the right side of your head."

"Thank you, Doctor," Reed said, testing his arms and legs to make sure they still worked.

"You fought the doctor while he tried to patch you up," Fleur clarified. "Two servants had to hold you down."

She searched his face. "Where were you just now? You struggled so fiercely."

Reed glanced at the circle of people surrounding him. No one was close enough to see him shudder or hear him whisper, "I was in hell. Will I never escape that horror?"

"What did you say, Reed?" Violet asked, pushing Fleur away to reach his side.

Reed waved her question aside. "Nothing of importance, I assure you."

"I was so worried about you," she said, clasping her hands against her heart. "Why would anyone want to hurt you?"

Reed would like to know the same thing.

The doctor cleared his throat. "We should allow Lord Hunthurst to rest." He motioned to the footmen. "Help his lordship to his bed. I'll be up in a moment to give him something to ease the pain."

Reed started to protest, but the sharp pain in his head when he sat up made him more amenable to following the doctor's orders.

"Please listen to the doctor," Helen urged. "I'll send a message to Gallard. He will be such a comfort to us while you're recuperating."

"That won't be necessary," Reed bit out. He wasn't going to lie abed for long, not with a would-be assassin on the loose. He leaned heavily between two footmen while he was helped up to his bedchamber. Though it was Fleur he wanted with him, he resisted the urge to ask her to accompany him. It wouldn't be seemly. He made her aware of his feelings, however, by the look he sent her before he quit the room.

Fleur worried her bottom lip as she watched Reed being carried off. Once again, he could have been killed. Fleur silently vowed to renew her efforts to find those responsible. It was the least she could do for Reed before disappearing from his life.

Fleur debated all night about abandoning Reed and moving to the townhouse as planned. But when she found Reed sitting in the breakfast room in the morning, calmly eating, she realized he wasn't seriously hurt, making her decision to leave easier.

"Are you well enough to be out of bed?" Fleur asked as she filled her plate and settled in a chair next to Reed. Since they were the only two at breakfast, she felt she could speak freely.

"I feel fine," Reed said. "Doctor Freeman said to keep the bandage in place for a few days, and so I shall."

"Who do you think did this to you?"

"I wish I knew. I plan to call on Porter this morning to report the incident. I am beginning to believe that I am, indeed, the target of an assassin. The reason behind the attacks leaves me puzzled, however."

"Perhaps I will learn something when I go riding with Monsieur Barbeau this afternoon. He's to call for me at two. Tomorrow, Lisette and I shall move to the townhouse."

"I don't want you to leave," Reed said. "I like having you here."

Fleur stiffened. Of course he liked having her here. She was on hand to slake his lust. What could be more convenient? "I cannot stay here. Living in the same house with you raises suspicion and hinders my investigation."

Reed slammed his hand on the table. "Porter had no right to ask you to place your life in danger." The effort must have cost him, for he rubbed his right temple with the pads of his fingers.

"Does your head hurt? You should have rested another day or two as the doctor advised."

"My head feels fine," Reed snapped from between clenched teeth.

Fleur finished her breakfast and rose. "Do you mind if I borrow your carriage? Lisette and I wish to move some things to the townhouse."

"I was about to offer it to you. In fact, I'll go with you. I need to speak with Updike and the rest of the staff. When do you want to leave?"

"Ten o'clock, if that's agreeable with you."

"Ten o'clock is fine. I'll meet you in the foyer."

Fleur returned to her chamber to make sure everything was packed and ready to go. Peg had matters in hand so Fleur went in search of Lisette. She ran into Helen and Violet in the foyer.

"Reed said you're leaving tomorrow," Helen said. "It's for the best, you know."

"Indeed it is," Violet agreed. "People are beginning to talk about you. Most assume you are Reed's *chère amie*." She smirked. "They are not far off, are they? It's no secret you've been sleeping with him."

"I've no time for this conversation," Fleur replied, turning on her heel.

"Wait!" Violet called after her.

Fleur stopped but didn't turn around.

"Do you deny that Reed is moving you into his townhouse so he can visit your bedchamber without interference?"

Fleur didn't dignify Violet's question with an answer. A good part of her assumption was correct. Fleur *had* been sleeping with Reed, but she didn't intend for it to continue. One day soon she would move to the country and forget Reed.

No, not forget him. That wasn't possible. But she wouldn't see him again. Reed had to produce an heir, and she wasn't capable of giving him one.

Fleur found Lisette, and at precisely ten o'clock they met Reed in the foyer. Their trunks were being loaded onto the carriage as Reed handed both ladies inside and joined them.

"It really isn't necessary for you to come with us, Reed," Fleur pointed out. "The servants at the townhouse know we are coming and are capable of taking care of us. Don't you have business with Lord Porter?"

"I do. After I drop you off and speak with Updike, I shall continue on to Whitehall. I'm not really up to riding today." As if to prove his words, Reed winced and touched his temple when the carriage jerked forward and rattled off down the street.

Fleur made a clucking sound in her throat. "You shouldn't be out of bed. Your visit to Lord Porter can wait."

That blasted dimple appeared in Reed's cheek. "Don't fuss over me, love. I'm fine."

Fleur knew Reed wasn't as fine as he professed, but she ceased berating him. Reed being Reed, he would do what he pleased. He had suffered far worse and survived.

"We're here," Reed said as the carriage rolled to a stop. He stepped down and handed the ladies out. Two footmen rushed out of the house and began unloading luggage. Updike held the door open for them.

"Welcome, my lady, my lord," Updike greeted.

"Thank you, Updike," Fleur replied.

"Why don't you and Lisette direct the unpacking?" Reed suggested.

Fleur knew Reed wished to speak to Updike in private, so she nodded and went upstairs after Lisette and Peg, who had arrived earlier.

Reed waited until they were gone to speak. "I need a private word with you, Updike. Shall we retire to the study?"

Once inside the familiar room, Reed found the brandy in the usual place, filled two snifters and handed one to Updike. "Sit down, Updike."

The valet settled into a chair and sipped his brandy. "What's on your mind, my lord? Everything is in readiness for the countess and her companion, just as you asked."

Reed sat behind his desk, warming the brandy between his hands. "I'm appointing you, Peg, and the entire staff as Fleur's watchdogs. She's on a dangerous mission and could encounter people who do not have her best interests at heart. Therefore, there are some instructions I wish you to impart to the staff."

"I understand," Updike replied. "What do you wish us to do?"

"Make sure Fleur is accompanied wherever she goes. I want to know with whom she goes out and for how long she is gone. She is to accompany an émigré today on a carriage ride through the park. Send someone you trust to follow on horseback and provide help should she require it."

Updike frowned. "Do you believe Lady Fontaine to be at risk? Is there nothing you can do to prevent her from endangering herself?"

"The woman is too stubborn to listen to me."

"Might I inquire about the bandage you're wearing?"

"Another failed attempt on my life," Reed drawled. "It's not important."

"I should say it is important," Updike objected. "Perhaps my time would be better spent protecting you."

"No! I can take care of myself, Updike. Fleur cannot."

"As you say, my lord," Updike said with a hint of sarcasm.

"Is that mockery I hear in your voice?"

"Indeed no, my lord. If anyone can foil would-be assassins, it's you."

Reed's lips twitched with amusement. "Just so we understand one another." Updike rose to leave. "One more thing; I'm keeping a key to the front door."

"If you think it's necessary, my lord. However, a footman will be stationed at the door to admit you when you visit."

Reed's lips twitched again. "Let me phrase that another way. Everyone, including the servants, will be abed when I visit."

"But why would you . . ." Updike's brow rose as comprehension dawned. "Oh, I see. That's the way the wind blows."

"That's precisely how it is. I must be on my way, Updike. Follow my instructions and all will be well."

Fleur returned to the mansion in time for luncheon and to change her clothes for her carriage ride with Monsieur Barbeau. Peg helped her into a blue silk confection with short sleeves, a square neckline and high waist, embellished with embroidered rosebuds and trimmed with lace. Before she left the bedchamber, Peg handed her a matching bonnet and draped a silk shawl over her shoulders.

"Enjoy your ride, my lady," Peg called after Fleur as she left her chamber. "The weather is perfect for an outing."

Barbeau arrived at precisely two o'clock. His admiration was evident as he watched her descend the stairs. "You are a vision, Countess." He offered his arm. "Shall we?"

Fleur smiled and placed her hand in the crook of Barbeau's arm. They breezed past a footman, who held the door open for them. Barbeau handed Fleur into the carriage parked at the curb.

Fleur's smile slipped when she saw Count Dubois sitting on the seat opposite her. What was he doing here?

"Count Dubois expressed a wish to join us," Barbeau said. "I didn't think you would mind."

"Not at all," Fleur said, greeting Dubois with a forced smile.

They made small talk until the carriage entered the park and headed down the Serpentine. Then Fleur inquired, "Did both of you manage to escape the turmoil in France with your families?"

Barbeau and Dubois exchanged significant glances. "I am not wed and have no close relatives," Barbeau replied. "Count Dubois was the only one of his family to escape death."

"I'm sorry," Fleur said, patting Dubois's hand. "Shall we talk of more pleasant things?"

"Indeed," Dubois said, seizing the initiative. "I understand you will be moving to Hunthurst's townhouse soon. Did Lady Helen tire of your company? Or was the decision Hunthurst's?"

"Actually, it was my decision to leave," Fleur replied. "I had imposed long enough and felt it was time to find a place of my own. Lord Hunthurst was kind enough to lease me his townhouse."

"How convenient for you," Dubois said in a tone dripping with mockery.

"Is Lord Hunthurst in good health?" Barbeau asked.

The question startled Fleur. Did he know about the latest attack on Reed's life? "Fine, why do you ask?"

Barbeau shrugged. "No reason. I understand the Bonhams are holding a soirée tomorrow night. There's to be music. Will you attend? If you require an escort, I'd be happy to come for you in my carriage."

"I'll give you my answer if you will answer a question for me."

"Anything, Countess."

"Why are you so interested in Lord Hunthurst?"

"Gallard Duvall is a friend," Dubois answered in Barbeau's stead. "He speaks of Hunthurst often. He told us that attempts have been made on the earl's life. We are concerned about his well-being. Does he have enemies, Countess?"

"Not that I am aware of, but I know little of his lordship's affairs. I am merely an acquaintance of his sister-in-law."

"Rumor has it that Hunthurst recently returned from the Continent," Dubois probed.

"If he was in France, our paths never crossed there."

The questions about Reed ended abruptly as the conversation turned in another direction. The next hour passed pleasantly enough, even though Fleur's distrust of the pair grew with each passing minute. Yet why would either of these men want Reed dead? No matter how hard she tried, she could connect neither of them to Reed.

Apparently the drive through the park had come to an end as Dubois signaled the driver, and the carriage headed out of the park. It was a short ride to the mansion.

"You didn't answer my earlier question. May I escort you to the Bonham soirée tomorrow evening?" Barbeau asked as he handed her down.

"Very well, I accept your escort. You may come for me at the townhouse."

Barbeau beamed. "Excellent. I shall come by at nine tomorrow evening." He took her elbow. "I'll walk you to the door, Countess."

Fleur allowed him to escort her to the front door, which was promptly opened by a glowering Hughes. Fleur bid Barbeau goodbye and walked into the foyer. The butler promptly closed the door behind her.

"You're scowling, Hughes. Are you angry about something?"

"You've been gone nearly two hours. Madame Lisette was worried about you."

"I was in no danger," Fleur assured him, stripping off her gloves. "I'll find Lisette and let her know I am home. Please have the carriage brought around. I think Lisette and I will move to the townhouse immediately instead of waiting for tomorrow."

Fleur found Lisette in her bedchamber, packing the last of her belongings.

"Did you learn anything, *ma petite?* I don't like this game you're playing. Why did you have to accept another assignment when we could be living comfortably in your aunt's home in the country?"

"I was in no danger, Lisette. I learned a little more about Barbeau and Dubois today but nothing to connect them to Reed." She sighed. "I'm inclined to agree with Reed about the traitor coming from within the organization."

"Do you believe an English agent is involved?"

"At this point, I'm not sure of anything beyond the fact

that someone wants Reed dead. If you are ready, I'd like to move to the townhouse today instead of tomorrow."

"That suits me," Lisette agreed. "I do not like the atmosphere here."

After a somewhat heated discussion with Porter, Reed was no closer to naming his betrayer. Nevertheless, Porter was concerned about Reed's safety and suggested that he remain out of sight until the traitor was caught. Reed promptly refused.

He left Porter's office with little resolved. After, Reed visited his bank, his tailor and performed other errands, ending up at his club to partake of a lonely dinner. When anyone asked about the bandage, he said he had fallen down the stairs. No one dared question his excuse except his friend Viscount Tolland.

"Come now, Hunthurst, never say you expect me to believe you fell down the stairs," Tolland scoffed when Reed invited him for an after-dinner brandy. "What really happened? I heard that someone is taking pot shots at you. The betting books are filled with possible suspects. I even placed a bet myself."

Reed cocked an eyebrow. "Who, pray tell, did you bet on?"

Tolland laughed. "Why, Lady Violet, of course. You know how testy a woman can get when the marriage proposal she expects never materializes."

Reed threw back his head and laughed. "Are all the bets as ridiculous as yours? Really, Tolland, Violet isn't a violent woman, despite the alliteration."

Tolland shrugged. "Have you a better suspect?"

"I do not. I don't know how this kind of gossip gets started. It's all supposition. I'm not in danger." Though his reply wasn't exactly true, he hadn't connected anyone he knew to the unprovoked attacks upon his life.

Tolland stared pointedly at the bandage covering Reed's temple.

Reed gestured at it. "I told you, I fell down the stairs. Clumsy of me, I know, but it's the truth."

"So you say," Tolland drawled. "I'm your friend, Hunthurst. I'm at your service if you need my assistance."

"I appreciate that, Tolland."

"I thought I'd hit the tables at Crocket's tonight, and perhaps check out the women when the play becomes boring or the cards turn against me. Would you care to join me? You've been keeping to yourself too much of late. You need to get out and about more. You've changed since you returned from wherever it was you were."

Reed intended to refuse, until he recalled that Fleur would not welcome him to her bed when he returned home. She had made her feelings perfectly clear. She wanted to get on with her life, and she did not want him to be part of it.

"Why not?" Reed said. "Tell you what, Tolland. I'll return home to change my clothes and meet you at Crocket's around nine o'clock. Is that agreeable to you?"

"Perfect," Tolland replied. "I shall see you . . ."

Tolland's sentence fell off, his gaze settling on something beyond Reed. "I say, do you know that gentleman? He seems to be heading quite determinedly in your direction."

Reed glanced over his shoulder. "That gentleman is Count Dubois, an émigré."

"That's my signal to be off. Until tonight, Hunthurst."

Reed watched Tolland disappear out the door, already regretting the night of debauchery they had planned.

"Lord Hunthurst, how excellent to see you again. May I join you?"

Reed motioned negligently toward the chair Tolland had just vacated. "Be my guest."

Dubois sat down with a flourish, summoned a waiter and ordered brandy.

"What's on your mind, Dubois?"

"Nothing of importance, my lord. I saw a friendly face

and thought I'd ask if I might join you." He stared intently at Reed. "I saw Countess Fontaine earlier today. The woman is a delight. Have you known her long?"

Reed's hands gripped the edge of the table as jealousy rampaged through him. If the bastard touched Fleur, he'd kill him. "No, not long. She's a friend of my sister-in-law. I met her when I moved into the family mansion."

Dubois took a sip of brandy. "I understand she is leasing your townhouse."

"It was empty, so finding a trustworthy renter was most fortunate. Why is this of interest to you?" Reed drawled.

Dubois shrugged. "Just making small talk, *mon ami*. The countess has agreed to accompany my friend Barbeau to the Bonham soirée tomorrow night."

"Indeed," Reed said, barely able to speak through his clenched teeth. "Is that all you wished to tell me?"

"I hoped you could enlighten me concerning the countess. There is a mystery about her that intrigues me. Barbeau claims to have known her deceased husband but knows little about the lady herself. I wish to court her."

"I know even less about the countess than you do," Reed bit out. "It's none of my affair whether or not you court her." He pushed his chair back and rose. "If you'll excuse me, I have an appointment to keep."

Dubois rose too. "Certainly. I bid you *adieu*, my lord."

Reed strode away, barely able to contain his anger. If Fleur wished to accept another man's addresses, it shouldn't concern him. Except that it did. Fleur could be flirting with danger. Dubois could be a French agent with an agenda. Did she know she was putting herself at risk? He suspected she did, and that made him even angrier.

Dubois was not a stupid man. His questions about Fleur worried Reed. What was she up to? Was she delving too deeply into the Frenchmen's activities?

When Reed arrived home, Hughes handed him a note from Grandmamma. It was an invitation to attend a family dinner the following night. As he passed the parlor, Helen poked her head out.

"There you are, Reed. Did you receive Grandmamma's invitation?"

"Hughes handed it to me the moment I entered the house. How did you know it was from Grandmamma?"

"Violet and I were also invited. You'll escort us, of course."

Reed had reached the limit of his patience. "I'm afraid not, Helen. I have a previous engagement. I'll write my regrets to Grandmamma immediately and send it off with a footman. Do enjoy yourselves."

"You have to go!" Helen scolded. "Violet is counting on you."

"I'm sorry, Helen, but I don't exist solely to be at your beck and call."

"Did you know Fleur moved to the townhouse this afternoon?" Violet said.

Reed went still. He felt as if someone had punched him in the gut. "I thought she was moving tomorrow."

"She changed her mind."

He spun on his heel. "Have a nice evening, ladies."

"If you refuse to accompany us, I shall summon Gallard," Helen called after him. "He is family, after all."

"Give him my regards," Reed drawled.

Reed hated to disappoint Grandmamma, but he didn't enjoy being forced to squire Violet about. He was aware of her expectations where he was concerned and had no intention of being leg-shackled to her.

Reed left the house, arriving at Crocket's shortly after nine that evening. Tolland saw him enter and waved to him. Reed headed in his direction. The room was crowded and reeked of cigar smoke, unwashed flesh and strong perfume. The combination of smells made Reed gag. Why hadn't it ever bothered him before? Even worse, Reed felt as if the walls were closing in on him. Suddenly he couldn't breathe. Panic seized him, forcing him into that dark hell where pain and death reigned. Sweat popped out on his forehead, and he began gasping for air as his demons threatened to emerge.

"I say, are you all right, Hunthurst?" Tolland asked. "You don't look quite the thing."

Reed closed his eyes and forced himself to breathe. But when he opened them, nothing had changed. He was in hell.

"Forgive me, Tolland," Reed choked out, "but I must leave. I find I am unwell."

"Shall I accompany you home?"

"No, do not let me interfere with your evening. We will do this another time." So saying, he stumbled from the gambling hell.

Reed leaned against the building, dragging in deep, sustaining breaths. Why now? Why here? His sudden plunges into the dark abyss inside him had been sporadic since his return from France. What had triggered the panic attack this time? The answer came to him in a rush of enlightenment. Fleur had left him. She was no longer available to make his demons disappear.

Everyone was abed when Reed returned home. He retired immediately, pausing in the foyer to tell Hughes he didn't wish to be disturbed. The darkness was still upon him when he sought his bed.

Then the dreams came. He dreamed of beatings that continued long after he lost consciousness. Of being starved, of begging for water. Dreams of watching his fellow prisoners dying around him and being buried beyond the prison walls in unmarked graves.

Numbing coldness turned his limbs to lead. He fought against the returning horror. Bedclothes twisted around him like invisible manacles, hindering his movements. He refused to scream, bracing himself against the imaginary bite of the lash.

Reed jerked awake, fighting the sheets binding him to the bed. His nightmare had seemed so real, he could actually feel the pain left by another beating. Panting, he rolled out of bed. He hadn't had a nightmare like this in a long time.

He had to escape from the horror.

Reed leaped out of bed. With shaking hands, he dressed in the dark. He was out the door as the hall clock struck two. He hesitated. Where in bloody hell was he going to go at this time of night? Anywhere, he thought. Anywhere to escape the demons plaguing him.

Reed crept down the stairs and let himself out, closing the door behind him. The cool night air helped clear his head but did nothing to ease his tumultuous thoughts. Though he had no destination in mind, he walked with purpose in the light rain that had begun to fall.

Wet and shivering, Reed walked aimlessly. When he looked up to get his bearings, he was startled to find himself standing outside his townhouse, where Fleur slept snugly in her bed.

Without conscious thought, he reached in his pocket and found the key to the front door. Indecision rode him, but need won out. He climbed the stairs and fitted the key into the lock. The door opened noiselessly beneath his touch.

He closed the door behind him and leaned against it. He had to be insane to seek out a woman he couldn't have. Insane or not, he pushed himself away from the door and slowly climbed the stairs.

❧ *Chapter Fifteen* ❧

*F*leur awakened from a restless sleep, her heart pounding. She stared intently into the darkness, immediately sensing that she wasn't alone. A sensual stillness pervaded the chamber, charging the very air she breathed.

She recognized his scent, felt his soul reaching out to her. "Reed, is that you?"

A light flared. He had struck a flint to the candle sitting on the nightstand. The moment she looked into his face she sensed his terror. Something was terribly wrong. He was pale, his clothing wet and disheveled.

"Are you ill?" she asked, reaching out to him.

He gripped her extended hand and squeezed. "Fleur."

His voice held a note of uncertainty. Was he running from something? Had someone tried to harm him again? His silver eyes were dark as storm clouds, his pupils dilated. A thick, unsettling tension emanated from him.

"What happened?" Fleur asked. "Who let you into the house? Do you know what time it is?"

He let out a shaky breath. "I accompanied a friend to a gambling hell tonight. The moment I entered the crowded hall, the walls began closing in on me. Though I tried to gain control, the madness claimed me and refused to let go. My mind, my soul, my body descended into hell. It was pure torment. Memories of pain and darkness over-whelmed me. It was like the time we were forced to hide in the crawl space beneath the cottage in France."

His words came out in a choked whisper. "How long will I be forced to live with fear? I fled into the night, but the horror followed me. Eventually I returned home, but that didn't help. So I left the house and walked aimlessly in the rain. I didn't intend to come here, but this is where I found myself." He showed her the key he had used to let himself into the house. "I didn't surrender all the keys to you."

"I thought you were beginning to recover from your or-deal at Devil's Chateau."

"I thought so too. I even agreed to accompany my friend Viscount Tolland to Crocket's for some gambling and . . . whatever else struck our fancy."

Fleur's lips thinned. She knew exactly what "whatever else" meant. "Go on."

"I'd no sooner entered the stifling interior of Crocket's when I began to panic. I couldn't get out of there fast enough."

"So you came here."

"I need you, Fleur. Don't make me leave."

Fleur gazed into his eyes. The stormy gray mist had evap-orated; twin silver orbs returned her gaze with an intensity that crackled in the air between them.

"Do you want me to leave?"

Fleur could tell he was more himself now. The hollow-ness had left his eyes, and his jaw had relaxed. If she told him to leave, would he retreat to that dark place within him again? Who would help him if she asked him to leave? Besides, his clothing was damp from the rain, and his hair was wet and plastered to his head. Apparently he had left the house without a hat or coat.

Rain now lashed against the windowpanes, and Fleur knew she couldn't send Reed away in a drenching down-pour. Did she even want to? On one hand she was touched that Reed had come to her during his hour of need, and on the other she wondered how he would cope when he wed a woman who didn't know how to help him.

"You're wet," Fleur said. "You'll find a towel on the washstand. Dry your hair and take off those damp clothes."

Reed felt like an idiot. Showing his weakness to a woman was embarrassing. Only the knowledge that it was Fleur to whom he had bared his soul kept him from fleeing in shame. Would the woman he eventually wed run screaming from him the first time he retreated to his dark hell?

Reed found the towel and dried his hair. Then he began shedding his damp clothes, spreading them over a bench to dry. Even his smallclothes were damp, so he took them off too. He glanced over at the bed. Now that the madness had passed, he knew what he wanted but wasn't sure Fleur wanted the same thing. He needn't have worried. Fleur pulled the covers aside and beckoned to him.

"Come to bed before you freeze to death."

Suddenly Reed realized he was shivering. The fire had burned low, and the room held a definite chill. He had the presence of mind to throw some coal onto the dying flames before joining Fleur in bed.

She came into his arms, and he brought her against him. She was naked; her nightgown lay where she had tossed it beside the bed. He stopped shivering immediately. The heat of her body sank deep into his bones. He breathed deeply. Her scent was both familiar and arousing.

"This has to stop, Reed. I left Hunthurst so this wouldn't happen. It isn't right."

"You could have fooled me," Reed murmured. "This seems right to me."

"Your grandmamma . . ."

"I live my life according to my own needs," Reed replied. "Kiss me, my love. Chase away my fears. I need you."

"You don't need me. Time has a way of healing tortured souls like yours."

"You're not hearing me. I need *you*."

Lifting her chin, he kissed her, pressing his mouth to hers without regard for tenderness or reserve. He wanted to show her the passion that existed in his heart for her. The sudden surge of desire rose hot and needy and settled heavily in his groin. He went instantly hard, thrusting his hips flush against hers at the same time he plunged his tongue into her mouth.

She answered with equal fervor, sucking him deeper, drawing him into the wet heat of her mouth. He groaned, the ragged sound ripped from his throat. His hands spanned her waist. She was lithe and pliant beneath his touch, inviting further exploration. Though he felt he knew her body well, there was always something new and exciting to discover: the tiny freckle on her thigh he had failed to notice before, the perfect turn of her hips he had always taken for granted.

There was something special about Fleur that beckoned him, something indefinable but compelling. When he was with Fleur he became one with her in soul and body. Her touch healed his distraught mind and pierced through the darkness.

"You're mine, Fleur. Mine . . . mine . . . mine . . ."

Fleur wanted to deny his claim but knew in her heart that no man would ever move her as Reed did. Her whole body tightened as he lowered his head to suckle her right nipple. A deep primal moan escaped her lips as his fingers squeezed and pulled at her left nipple while suckling its mate. He laved and pulled until she cried out.

While he continued to suckle her, his fingers slid downward into her curls, parted the lush petals of her sex and stroked the hidden bud with a slow rhythm that sent molten heat surging through her veins. She felt a gush of moisture leave her body and bathe his hand. She was wet, ready and breathlessly waiting to be claimed by the man she loved. Her arms tightened around him, her legs parted of their own accord.

Her hand slid down his hip. She felt his staff harden against her thigh. Watching him closely, she moved her palm around to his inner thigh, then upward to his erection. A wildness broke in them both. Her hands were everywhere on him, touching, teasing, grasping. His mouth grazed over her body, tasting, suckling, taunting.

One by one Reed cast off the demons that had plunged him into unreachable depths of despair. Fleur's touch had freed him. Loving her was his salvation. Though her touch tortured him, it also brought him a measure of peace amidst the turmoil of clamoring hunger.

He positioned himself over her, his weight on his arms and knees as he released some of his burgeoning passion in a hard kiss. But it wasn't enough. He needed to taste more of her. His mouth left hers and took a downward path, pausing along the way to torment her with nipping little kisses that brought gasps and begging cries from her lips. When he reached the destination he sought, he lifted her legs to his shoulders and lost himself in the musky sweetness of her feminine heat. He swept his tongue over and around the tender, swollen bud nestling in her curls, then continued downward, parting the soft folds of her sex.

He laved her ruthlessly, lovingly until she climaxed, releasing the passion he had built inside her.

"Come inside me," she gasped.

Abandoning his succulent feast, he rose on his knees and stared down at her. She had never looked more beautiful. Her face was flushed, her lips swollen, her chocolate-brown eyes glazed with passion and her body rosy from his loving.

He reached down to cup her sex, letting his thumb play across the little nub of her pleasure. Fleur sprang to life with renewed arousal. The tip of his manhood nudged her, jolting her passion up another notch as he surged forward to fill her.

He continued to thrust; a fine sheen of sweat broke out

on his forehead. His kisses fell like sweet rain on her face and breasts as he drove her over the edge again. Her pleasure crested, and she reached for the stars a second time.

"Reed, come with me!"

He shouted his pleasure, his back arching as he flooded her with his seed. Their cries merged as she went limp against the pillow and he collapsed on top of her. Her arms came around him for a brief moment of bliss and then fell away.

His crushing weight lifted as he sagged to his side onto the mattress. Then he pulled her close, cradled her against him and promptly fell asleep.

Sighing, Fleur savored the moment of closeness, aware that it wasn't meant to last forever. She knew exactly what she needed to do and prayed for the strength to do what was right for both her and Reed.

Fleur let Reed sleep till nearly dawn. Then she gently shook him awake. He opened his eyes, smiled and reached for her.

She pushed him away. "No, Reed, it's time for you to leave. The servants will be up and about soon."

Reed glanced out the window. Dawn's gray fingers were peeling away the night. "There's still time." He reached for her again.

"Peg will be here any minute to open the blinds and build up the fire."

Ignoring her protests, Reed turned onto his back, grasped her about the waist and flipped her on top of him. Seconds later he was inside her, rekindling the fires of her passion. She began to tremble all over, and her protests turned into sighs of rapture.

Their coupling was fast and furious; she came in a blaze of soul-shattering ecstasy. Reed found his own pleasure a heartbeat later.

"*Now* it's time to go," Reed said, still breathing heavily as he lifted her off him and climbed out of bed.

Fleur watched as he poured water into a bowl and had a quick wash before gathering up his discarded clothing. She saw no sign of his former torment as he dressed and prepared to leave. Her heart skipped a beat when he glanced over at her and smiled. Then he returned to the bed, bent over and kissed her forehead. As he started to rise, Fleur clutched his sleeve with one hand and held out the other, palm up.

A frown gathered between Reed's brows. Stiffening her resolve, Fleur said, "The key, Reed, give me the key."

Reed's brows shot up. "Why?"

"Because this is my house, and I pay the rent. I should be the one to choose who may or may not visit."

"Are you implying what I think you are?"

"You can't keep sneaking into my home in the middle of the night. I thought I made it clear that the intimacy between us ended when I moved from Hunthurst."

"You decided that, not I."

"Give me the key, Reed. As long as I'm available to you, you'll never find a wife. Your grandmother deserves better than what we are doing to her. She wants to see grandchildren before she dies."

"Bloody hell!" Reed barked. "You enjoyed what we did as much as I. Why should we deny ourselves because of other people's wishes? Marry me, Fleur. You're the only one who makes me feel whole. Without you I am naught but a damaged soul."

Fleur felt herself shattering slowly from the inside. Why did life have to be so brutal? Why had fate turned against her? Being barren was her cross to bear; she would not share it with Reed, no matter how much she loved him.

She gazed into his eyes and willed him to understand. Her palm still in an upward position, she repeated, "Give me the key, Reed. You just think you love me because I saved your life and nursed you back to health. You'll know real love when you find it."

His sharp intake of breath nearly broke her heart. "Please don't make this any harder for me. You know this is right, Reed. I didn't turn you away last night because you needed me. You were lost and desperate, but you are a grown man, fully capable of destroying your own demons."

She knew her cruel words hurt him, but making Reed angry was the only way to end their intimate relationship.

Anger was exactly what Fleur got. Reed's lips flattened, storm clouds gathered in his eyes and the stark planes of his face grew sharp as rage and hurt consumed him. "How could you be so unfeeling? Have you no compassion? I bared my soul to you and you plunged a knife into it when I was most vulnerable." He laughed harshly. "The ultimate price of pleasure is dismissal."

He jerked the key from his pocket and slapped it into Fleur's palm with enough force to make her wince. "We're through, Countess. The greatest mistake of my life was proposing to you. I was foolish to think you cared." He sent her a withering look. "It shouldn't take you too long to find a new lover."

Reed turned on his heel and stormed out the door. Fleur burst into tears. The pain she suffered far exceeded Reed's. The lies she'd spouted ate at her like maggots. Reed would hate her for the rest of his life.

Reed strode down the stairs, his hurt nearly unbearable. He had mistakenly thought Fleur returned his feelings, though she had never said the words. What a fool he was. His grandmother wanted him to marry, and so he would. He really didn't care who he wed, even Violet would do. Yes, Violet was perfect. She wanted him, he wouldn't have to court her and Grandmamma would approve.

Reed reached the bottom of the stairs, saw Updike standing there and spit out a curse. "What are doing up so early?"

"It's not that early." He glanced toward the stairs. Disapproval resonated in his voice. "When did you arrive, my lord? Does the countess know you are here?"

Reed didn't feel compelled to offer an explanation. Let Updike form his own bloody conclusions. "It's none of your business, Updike. Furthermore, I no longer find it necessary to monitor Lady Fontaine's comings and goings. She may do what she pleases with whom she pleases." So saying, he slammed out the door.

Fleur was still hurting as she waited in her chamber for Monsieur Barbeau to arrive to escort her to the Bonham soirée. She had donned a violet, scoop-necked confection with puff sleeves and a fitted waist for the affair. When Peg knocked on the door to inform her that her escort had arrived, Fleur tied on her bonnet, picked up her shawl and left the room.

Her brows rose in surprise when Count Dubois met her at the bottom of the stairs. "What a fetching outfit," Dubois complimented.

"I thought Monsieur Barbeau was calling for me."

"Monsieur is suffering from a minor illness and asked me to step in for him. I hope you don't mind."

"Nothing serious, I hope," Fleur replied, hiding her dismay. She wasn't sure being alone in a coach with Dubois was wise.

"A nagging cough that troubles him from time to time. I'm sure he'll be right as rain in a day or two. Shall we go?"

"Yes, of course. It was kind of you to take Monsieur Barbeau's place."

"The pleasure is all mine." He assisted her into the coach and entered behind her.

"Does Hunthurst plan to attend the soirée?" Dubois asked once Fleur was settled.

"I'm sure I don't know," Fleur replied. "Why do you ask?"

Dubois sent her a sharp look. "I thought you and Hunthurst were . . . friends."

"Acquaintances," Fleur corrected.

"I asked Hunthurst if he had any objections to my court-ing you. He gave me his blessing."

"When was that?"

"Several days ago; I encountered him at his club."

"You wish to court me? Why?"

"Is that so strange? You're a beautiful woman. I am not without resources. I did not cross the channel penniless."

"I . . . have no intention of marrying again," Fleur stam-mered.

Dubois reached over and patted her arm. "You'll change your mind."

While Fleur chatted, danced and smiled at the soirée, her mind returned again and again to the fact that Reed had raised no objection to letting Dubois court her. And that was before she had put a period to their relationship. How could he ask her to marry him while blessing the count's plan to court her!

Fleur's spirits rose when she saw Henry Dempsey walk into the soirée. She wanted to question him, and now was her chance. She needed to find out what he knew about the attempts on Reed's life. She understood that Dempsey had been in France at the same time as Reed. She walked toward him but was forced to change directions when Gallard Du-vall approached Dempsey and struck up a conversation. Fleur wished she could hear what they were saying, but they had moved to an alcove at the far end of the ballroom.

A flurry of movement near the entrance caught her at-tention, and she turned her gaze in that direction. Reed had just entered with his grandmother on one arm and Vi-olet on the other. Helen followed behind. When Reed smiled down at Violet, Fleur's breath caught in her throat.

What had she expected? She had literally forced him out of her life and into Violet's arms. While Fleur watched him, Reed glanced up and saw her. Their gazes collided and clung. A smirk crossed his lips, and then he bent over and whispered into Violet's ear. She laughed up at him. Heartbroken, Fleur turned away and found Dubois standing behind her.

"Is something wrong, Countess?"

"I . . . yes, I have a terrible headache. I wish to go home."

His eyes narrowed on her, and then he smiled and nodded. "At once, my dear."

Dubois escorted her to the foyer. "Wait here while I fetch your shawl and summon my carriage."

Fleur couldn't believe she was fleeing because Reed was paying court to another woman. That was what she wanted, wasn't it? Indeed it was. Why then should she let Reed's courtship of Violet upset her? She had yet to converse with Dempsey and was eager to do so.

"Here is your wrap, Countess," Dubois said, draping her shawl over her shoulders.

Fleur turned to him with a smile. "My headache has suddenly disappeared. I'd like to stay, if you don't mind."

Dubois gave her curious a look but didn't question her miraculous recovery. He offered his arm, and she accepted his escort into the ballroom.

"Would you like something cool to drink?" Dubois asked.

"Thank you, I'm parched."

The moment he left her side, Fleur searched the ballroom for Dempsey. Instead of locating him, he found her.

"Countess Fontaine, we meet again."

"Hello, Mr. Dempsey. I'm glad I ran into you. I've been wanting to speak privately with you but never found the right moment."

"There is no time like the present. Would you care to step out on the balcony for a breath of fresh air? You are already wearing your shawl so the coolness of the night shouldn't prove a problem for you."

"Yes, fresh air is just what I need. We must hurry, though. My escort is fetching me something to drink."

He offered his arm, and they promenaded around the

perimeter of the ballroom and out the French doors onto the balcony. Only one other couple had ventured outside; Dempsey guided her to a far corner where they couldn't be overheard.

"What did you wish to say to me?" he asked.

"Has Lord Porter told you about the traitor within the organization?"

"Does Porter think there is a traitor in our ranks?" he shot back.

"No, but Reed believes there is. Porter thinks otherwise. He suspects one of the émigrés of being a spy."

"Interesting," Dempsey said without revealing anything. Count Dubois could be a suspect. So could his friend, Barbeau." He stared intently at her. "I am aware there are female agents in the organization; where do you fit in?"

"That's not important," Fleur demurred. "What do you know about Duvall?"

Dempsey looked distinctly uncomfortable. "Hunthurst's cousin? I hardly think . . ."

"I wouldn't count him out until he's proven innocent. Have you conferred with Hunthurst?"

"Why don't you ask *me* that question?"

Fleur closed her eyes and swallowed. Then she turned slowly to face Reed. "Have you conferred with Mr. Dempsey?"

"No, I haven't. I bear a message for you. Porter wants us to report to him tomorrow at four o'clock. Don't be late." His gaze shifted to Dempsey. "Porter did not request your presence, Dempsey."

He nodded curtly and strode off.

Fleur stared after him, a thoughtful expression on her face. "How long have you known Hunthurst?" Fleur asked Dempsey, dragging her gaze away from Reed's departing back.

"I was aware of his work for the organization but never knew him well," Dempsey replied. "We never crossed paths in France."

"Do you know Andre?"

"Sorry, I've never heard of him. Is he an agent?"

"Never mind, it's not important."

"Why all the questions? Do you suspect me of something, Countess? Please speak freely; I have nothing to hide."

Fleur glanced up and saw Count Dubois advancing toward her. "I have to go," Fleur said, hurrying off to meet her escort.

Fleur left the soirée in the count's company a short time later. Though she had learned nothing of importance, she had much to think about before her meeting with Reed and Lord Porter the next day.

To Fleur's dismay, Dubois insisted on walking her to her door. "May I call on you tomorrow, Countess?"

Though Fleur hated to encourage him, she felt she couldn't refuse. The meeting might lead to discovering something vital.

"I'll be at home between two and three tomorrow afternoon," Fleur said, affecting a smile.

"Until tomorrow then, Countess." He grasped her hand and lightly kissed her fingers.

Fleur pulled her fingers from his grasp as a scowling Updike opened the door. "Good evening, my lady."

Fleur waltzed inside. Updike, still scowling, closed the door in Dubois's face.

"Are you all right, my lady?" Updike asked.

"I'm fine, Updike. Thank you for waiting up. Has Lisette retired?"

A slow flush crept up Updike's face. "I believe so. I escorted her to her chamber an hour ago."

"Hmmm, I see." Actually, Fleur saw quite a bit. Updike was smitten with Lisette. She smiled all the way to her chamber.

Her smile died, however, when she recalled Reed's coolness toward her and his attention to Violet and realized she had no one to blame but herself. She prepared for bed with a heavy heart.

Fleur slept late the following morning. She didn't awaken until Peg arrived to open the drapes, letting in a flood of golden sunlight. She hadn't slept well. Erotic dreams of Reed had plagued her and she hadn't fallen asleep until nearly dawn.

"What time is it?" Fleur asked groggily.

"Almost noon, my lady. Lord Hunthurst is waiting for you downstairs in the study."

Fleur jerked upright. "Reed? Here? Help me with my toilette."

Twenty minutes later, Fleur had washed, dressed, had her hair twisted into a bun and was ready to confront Reed.

"You haven't eaten yet, my lady," Peg reminded her.

"So I haven't. Please ask Updike to serve tea for us in the study in twenty minutes."

Fleur's heart thumped erratically as she entered the study. Why was Reed here? After their passionate night together, their less than amiable parting and his coolness at the soirée, she hadn't expected to see him in her home anytime soon.

Reed arose from a chair before the hearth when she entered. "Countess," he greeted coolly.

"Lord Hunthurst. To what do I owe this visit?"

Bloody hell, they sounded like two strangers, Reed thought. Not the lovers they had been these past few weeks.

"We need to talk. Please sit down."

Fleur perched gingerly in a chair opposite him. "What is this about, Reed . . . my lord?"

Reed's lips twisted into a grim smile. If Fleur wanted formality, he would comply. "Porter is convinced that the man who betrayed me in France is an émigré. I believe our spy comes from within our own organization. In order to prove my theory, I need to demonstrate that Dubois and his associates are exactly who they seem to be and not spies."

"How do you intend to do that?"

"This is where you come in. Obviously Dubois is smitten with you. The Gibboneys, an émigré couple, are holding a fête next week. I'm hoping Dubois will ask you to accompany him. I want you to accept. While you keep him occupied, I shall break into his townhouse and search for evidence that could connect him to Napoleon."

"You think Dubois is a spy?"

"Not really. What I intend to do is eliminate the suspects one at a time until only the guilty party remains. I'll start with Dubois and work my way through the list of suspects."

"Who else is on the list?"

He counted off on his fingers. "Barbeau, Duvall and some of the émigrés with whom they are friendly. Perhaps even Peter Weldon, the man who calls himself Andre."

"You can forget about Andre. He played an integral role in your rescue from Devil's Chateau. He was the one who recruited me for Lord Porter's organization."

"I cannot discount anyone. Will you do as I ask?"

Fleur's answer was forestalled when Updike arrived with the tea tray.

"Will you join me? I slept late this morning and haven't had time to break my fast."

As Fleur poured tea into two cups, she eyed the accompanying sticky buns and buttered toast points hungrily.

"I've already eaten, but I'll have tea, thank you," Reed replied.

Reed watched Fleur take a dainty bite from her sticky bun, his gaze never leaving her mouth. He sipped his tea and waited until she finished the bun and licked the sugar off her lips with the tip of her tongue. His loins tightened, but he ruthlessly suppressed the desire welling inside him. "Will you do as I ask?" he pressed.

"What if the count doesn't invite me?"

"He will," Reed said grimly. "I watched him last night. He's fascinated with you."

Fleur couldn't disagree with Reed's assessment of Dubois's intentions toward her. "He wishes to court me. He's calling on me at two o'clock today."

Reed stared intently at her. "How do you feel about his paying court to you?"

She glared at him. "I told him I wasn't interested in marriage, even though you gave him permission to court me."

Reed hadn't realized he was holding his breath until he let it out in a whoosh. "What other answer could I give him? Finding the traitor is our primary concern. Duty must take precedence over personal feelings."

"If he asks me to the party, I will try to detain him at the affair as long as I can."

Reed rose. "Excellent. We won't mention this to Lord Porter until I find the proof I need."

"What about Mr. Dempsey? Is he one of your suspects?"

"I cannot discount anyone at this point." He affected a polite bow. "I will see you later at Whitehall."

"Congratulations on your imminent engagement to Lady Violet," Fleur said.

Reed didn't acknowledge her words as he strode out the door.

✦ *Chapter Sixteen* ✦

*D*ubois invited Fleur to attend the Gibboney party when he arrived that afternoon at precisely two o'clock. She accepted his invitation, and they made small talk for an hour before Dubois took his leave.

Mindful of the time, Fleur prepared herself for her meeting with Porter. She arrived at Whitehall a few minutes before four. Reed was already there when she was ushered into Porter's office.

Porter greeted her warmly. Reed merely nodded in her direction.

"What is this about, Porter?" Reed asked. "Have you found our traitor?"

"I wish I had good news, but I don't. Peter Weldon, the operative known as Andre, dropped out of sight shortly after Lady Fontaine fled France. I hoped all was well, but my hopes were dashed when Captain Skilling brought word this morning that Weldon has been seized and put to death."

"Oh, no!" Fleur cried. "The poor man. What happened?"

"I'm awaiting a report with more details, but I fear 'tis the work of our traitor. I don't know how or when his cover was blown. It could have been weeks or months ago. I'm so concerned I'm ordering my agents in France to come home until this is resolved. I cannot risk another good man until the traitor has been brought to justice."

Fleur glanced at Reed. His expression was grim; a white line had formed around his lips. She knew he was thinking about his own ordeal in Devil's Chateau.

"I haven't learned a blasted thing that could help us," Reed growled.

"Neither have I," Fleur admitted, "though I have a suspect or two in mind."

"Might I ask who they are?" Porter asked.

"Henry Dempsey and Count Dubois," Fleur answered, "though I have no proof either one of them is other than what he seems."

"I have no idea why you suspect Dempsey, Countess," Porter replied, "but I fear you are following a false lead. Dubois, on the other hand, is a distinct possibility. We've had our eye on him since his arrival in London."

"I want a list of all our operatives who had been or are still in France," Reed said. "Like Fleur, I believe Dempsey is a viable suspect."

"Though I respect your opinions, I shall await the final outcome before condemning anyone," Porter replied.

"Would Dempsey have knowledge of the Black Widow?" Fleur asked.

"Although he was in France during the time you worked undercover for us, I don't think he knew about your work there. Weldon was charged with protecting your identity."

"Why do you ask?" Reed inquired.

Fleur wasn't ready yet to relate her recent conversation with Dempsey. The man seemed to know far too much about her. That struck her as odd.

"Weldon was a good man," Porter continued. "I cannot afford to lose another agent. You and the countess must take care."

"I can't see how I'm in danger," Fleur retorted. "I am no longer a threat to anyone."

"Nor am I," Reed added. "None of this makes sense."

Fleur was about to mention Duvall but refrained. Duvall had a very good reason to want Reed dead. But since she hadn't spoken with Duvall at length, she couldn't voice an opinion.

The meeting was concluded soon after that. Reed offered her a ride home, and she accepted. Once he settled across from her, he said, "You suspect someone I hadn't considered, don't you?"

"Perhaps," Fleur hedged.

"Name him so we can coordinate our lists."

"Gallard Duvall," Fleur blurted out.

"I've already considered him, but he seems harmless enough."

"How, exactly, is he related to you?"

"The relationship is a tenuous one. My grandfather's younger brother, Raymond, married a Frenchwoman and moved to France before I was born. They started a whole new branch of the family. Duvall is Raymond's grandson. Grandmamma had him investigated, and apparently he is who he says he is. I've always known there was a French heir to the earldom, but it was of no concern until Jason died."

"Didn't you think it odd that Duvall turned up in England when he did?"

"Not particularly. England is a haven for émigrés. I'm not surprised Duvall found refuge here and looked us up. We *are* related, no matter how distant the connection."

The carriage rolled to a stop. "You needn't see me to the door," Fleur said. She accepted John Coachman's hand and stepped down.

"I'll contact you after the party to coordinate our findings."

"Be careful, Reed. Breaking and entering is against the law."

Reed smiled, revealing that enticing dimple in his cheek. "I'm not a novice at this, Fleur."

* * *

Reed worked his way around to the rear to the modest townhouse Count Dubois was renting on Court Street. All the windows were dark, enforcing Reed's belief that the Frenchman employed no live-in servants.

Reed had hidden himself in the shrubbery earlier in the evening and waited until Dubois left his house before finding a way inside. To Reed's frustration, none of the windows had been left ajar. It appeared that the émigré was an extremely careful man. Fortunately, Reed was an extremely talented one.

After finding the servants' entrance locked, Reed withdrew a slim piece of metal from his pocket and fitted it into the keyhole. It took him but a few minutes to spring the lock.

The door opened into the kitchen. The fire had been banked, but no one was watching it. Silent as a wraith, Reed pulled a stub of candle from his pocket and placed the wick against a hot coal. The wick caught and flared, revealing a door leading from the kitchen into the main part of the house.

Reed drew a sustaining breath and crept forward, his heart pumping furiously. Though he knew he wasn't back at Devil's Chateau, the pervasive darkness beyond the candlelight caused him a moment of panic. He clung to his sanity by imagining Fleur beside him, calming him.

Reed proceeded down the dark tunnel to the main hallway. The first door he tried opened into the study. Reed stepped inside and drew the drapes. Then he lit several candles and set to work. The desk proved no problem. The drawers were not locked, but they yielded little of interest. He did, however, find a note from Gallard Duvall. Reed read the meager contents and replaced it exactly where he had found it.

Duvall had requested a private meeting with Dubois. Since there was no date on the note, Reed had no way of knowing if the meeting had already occurred or was planned for a future date. Since there seemed to be nothing incriminating in the note, Reed dismissed it as being of little concern.

Working quickly, he finished with the desk and moved swiftly about the room, finding nothing to indicate Dubois was anything other than what he claimed. Blowing out all the candles but the one he was holding, Reed climbed noiselessly up the stairs, opening doors until he found the master bedroom. He went through the drawers there swiftly and expediently, carefully replacing each item he examined in the same place he had found it.

Nothing he had found so far was suspect. Then he began looking behind pictures for a safe. There was no safe in the bedchamber. He descended the stairs to the main hallway and entered the drawing room, where several pictures hung on the wall. He found the safe behind a painting of London Tower. Holding the candle close, Reed began fiddling with the combination. He'd no sooner begun when he heard a shuffling noise on the stairs.

"Is that you, my lord?" a sleepy voice called.

Reed blew out the candle and waited. Apparently Dubois did have at least one live-in servant. But fortunately the fellow decided not to investigate further, for his footsteps retreated, finally disappearing altogether.

Reed returned to the safe, this time working in the dark. It took longer than he expected, but eventually the tumblers slid into place. The safe held nothing but assorted pieces of jewelry and a cache of gold coins. Reed closed it and replaced the picture. Noiselessly he crept from the drawing room and made his way down the dark hallway to the kitchen, where he let himself out the same door he had entered. He even managed to spring the lock into place with the slim tool he had used to open the door.

Having found nothing to indicate Dubois was the traitor, Reed was convinced of the Frenchman's innocence and more certain than ever that the traitor came from within the organization.

While Reed searched Dubois's townhouse, Fleur made the rounds at the Gibboney party, asking subtle questions of the émigrés attending. Monsieur Barbeau was there, and so was Gallard Duvall. Duvall joined Fleur and Dubois near the refreshment table.

"Are you still a regular visitor at Hunthurst?" Fleur probed.

"*Oui*. I find the ladies delightful. I understand there might be a happy announcement soon."

"Announcement?" Fleur held her breath, waiting for Duvall's answer.

"Haven't you heard?" Duvall said, agog. "Lady Violet is anticipating a proposal from my cousin. The dowager is very pleased with the match."

Fleur felt as if someone had shot an arrow into her heart, even though she knew she had sent Reed straight into Violet's arms.

"How . . . wonderful," Fleur said, pasting a false smile on her face. Pushing aside her heartache, she decided it was an opportune time to probe Duvall for answers. "I understand you arrived in England in time to help Helen through her difficulties after her husband's death."

Duvall clucked his tongue. "Such a sad time. I was present when the former earl passed, you know."

Fleur's attention sharpened. "No, I didn't know. What brought you to England? Most of your countrymen had already fled France during the Reign of Terror."

Duvall shrugged. "I had no one in France. I lost most of my family and decided it was time to meet my English kin. I am the last of my line in France and was curious about my grandfather's people."

"Enough of this interrogation, I find it excessively boring. Duvall's story is no different from mine or any other Frenchman's," Dubois scoffed.

"I wasn't prying, my lord, merely curious," Fleur said.

"I find the countess delightful," Duvall insisted. "Perhaps she won't mind answering some of my questions."

Fleur became instantly wary. "What do you wish to know?"

"What kept you in France after your husband's death? Why didn't you flee to England after his passing?"

That question seemed to interest Dubois as well, for he cocked his head and said, "I wondered that myself, Countess."

Fleur searched for an answer that would satisfy them. "I fled our chateau after Pierre was imprisoned in the Bastille and went into hiding. I had no opportunity to leave the country until just recently. I was an Englishwoman in a country whose government was unfriendly with England. There was so much turmoil that I stayed in hiding until I thought it safe to flee."

"Before I left, I heard whispers about a woman who helped English spies escape prison," Duvall confided. "She was known as the Black Widow. Why didn't you seek her help?"

Totally flummoxed, Fleur could do little more than gape at Duvall. Was he trying to tell her something?

"Ah, *oui*," Dubois concurred. "I, too, heard of the woman. I often wondered about her identity."

Fleur pretended surprise. "Why, I never heard such a thing. How could a woman be so bold?" She waved her fan furiously in front of her face. "I wouldn't have the courage."

How could these two men know about the Black Widow? Fleur wondered. Unless . . . unless they were French spies in search of information. She was looking for a way to change the subject when Barbeau joined the group. Fleur excused herself and headed toward the ladies' retiring room. Her heart was beating furiously as she collapsed into a chair.

Once she had gained her composure, she rejoined the party. Soon after, the guests started leaving. Fleur and Dubois joined the exodus.

"I enjoyed the evening, Count Dubois," Fleur said as they settled into his carriage.

"I believe we have known each other long enough to dispense with titles," Dubois said. "Please call me René and I shall call you Fleur. How is it that you were given a French name?"

"It was my great grandmother's name. She came from France as a small child and settled in England with her parents."

"So you have French blood flowing through your veins."

"A very small amount."

"What prompted you to wed a Frenchman?"

"I met Pierre during my first season and fell in love with him. Business brought him to London."

"How romantic," Dubois remarked.

He reached over, grasped her hand and brought it to his lips. Fleur flinched and tried to extract her hand from his grasp, but he refused to release her.

"Have you changed your mind about taking another husband?"

"No, Count, I . . ."

"René, please."

"I have no intention of wedding again . . . René."

"You are young, too young to dismiss passion from your life. Since you don't wish to wed, will you take me as your lover, Fleur?"

Fleur's breath hitched. What had she done to give Dubois the impression that she was interested in taking a lover? If she couldn't have Reed, she would settle for no one.

"I'm not ready to talk of such things, René. I am still mourning Pierre."

Dubois laughed. "I doubt that, but I won't press you."

Fleur breathed a sigh of relief when the carriage drew to

a halt. The coachman opened the door and pulled down the steps.

"You don't have to see me to the door, René."

"It will be my pleasure," Dubois said smoothly. He stepped out and handed her down.

When they reached the front door, Fleur fumbled in her reticule for her key. She was so startled when Dubois reached for her and pulled her into his arms that she dropped her reticule, spilling the contents onto the doorstep.

"Wha . . . what are you doing?"

"I don't think a kiss is out of order, my dear. You already know my intention to wed you or become your lover, whichever you prefer."

Fleur started to protest but was forestalled when his mouth seized hers with brutal thoroughness, his unwelcome kiss and thrusting tongue nearly gagging her.

Abruptly he released her, his arrogant smile almost as sickening as his mouth had been. "That is just a taste of what we will enjoy if we become lovers. Good night, *ma petite*."

Too stunned to react, Fleur watched Dubois climb back into his carriage and disappear down the street. Taking a deep breath, she dropped to her knees to search in the dark for her key amidst the scattered contents of her reticule.

"Is this what you're looking for?" a deep voice asked from behind her.

Startled, Fleur fell back on her bottom with a thump. Reed stood over her, her door key dangling from his fingers. "Reed, you frightened me. Where did you come from? Were you spying on me?"

Reed gave a bark of laughter. "Why would I spy on you and your would-be lover when you clearly want nothing to do with me?"

He stretched out his hand. Fleur grasped it, and he pulled her to her feet.

He peered closely at her. "Are you hurt?"

She brushed the dust from her skirt. "I'm fine. What do you want?"

Reed fit the key into the lock and opened the door. "Shall we go inside? This is too public a spot for our discussion."

Fleur entered the house. Reed followed on her heels and closed the door behind them. "I thought you might want to know what I discovered in Dubois's townhouse tonight."

"You completed the search?"

"Indeed." He picked up the branch of candles Updike had left for Fleur and escorted her to the study.

"Did your search go well?" Fleur asked once the door closed behind them. "Did you find anything to suggest that Dubois is our spy?"

"I conducted a thorough search of his house and found a safe hidden behind a picture in the drawing room."

Excitement colored Fleur's words. "Did you find anything incriminating?"

Smiling at her enthusiasm, Reed studied her profile in the flickering candlelight, noting the slight tilt of her nose, the graceful arch of her neck and her ripe, slightly parted lips as she waited for him to speak. Her midnight hair was arranged artfully atop her head with a pair of loose curls curving over each shoulder. Her skin looked soft, luminous and luscious enough to taste. His fingers twitched with the powerful urge to touch her.

As their gazes met, he felt slightly off balance and struggled to keep his emotions in check. He was here to discuss his progress and nothing more.

"Reed, did you hear me? What did you find in the safe?"

Reed reined in his wayward thoughts. "Not a bloody thing that would help our investigation. The safe held jewelry and gold and little else. Your potential lover is a wealthy man. He should be able to keep you in comfort. I know from experience that he will be pleased with your talents in bed."

Reed knew he had crossed the line and wasn't surprised when Fleur hauled her hand back and slapped him. He wanted Fleur and couldn't bear the thought of another man possessing her.

"Forgive me, Fleur. I had no right."

His heart nearly broke when he saw moisture gathering in her eyes. He'd give anything to take his words back.

Apparently Fleur decided to ignore his apology and change the subject. "Am I to assume your lack of evidence proves that Dubois is not the man we are looking for?"

"It certainly makes his involvement less likely."

"I learned something tonight if you're interested."

Reed's attention sharpened. "Damn right I am. Something to help our investigation, I hope."

Fleur shrugged. "Make of it what you wish. Dubois, Barbeau and Duvall discussed the Black Widow with me tonight. They seemed to know everything but her identity and questioned me about my whereabouts during the years after Pierre's death."

A cold sweat broke out on Reed's forehead. "Remove yourself from the investigation at once! You are no longer safe. I shall inform Porter immediately that you are off the case."

"No! I'm going to see this through. Even if my identity is compromised, I see no reason why that should matter. My work in France has ended. I am a threat to no one."

Reed walked to the window and stared out into the darkness. "Now we're back to square one. If those men have knowledge of the Black Widow, any one of them could be a French spy."

He whipped around. "Why did you let Dubois kiss you? Have you feelings for him?"

Fleur gave a huff of exasperation. "He surprised me; I couldn't stop him."

"Did you enjoy his kiss?"

Fleur wrinkled her nose. Reed nearly burst out laughing. Fleur's face was so expressive it didn't take a genius to figure out that she'd hated Dubois's kiss.

"That's none of your business," Fleur snapped.

Reed flashed his dimple. "Your face says it all, love. You prefer my kisses to his."

"Conceited wretch," Fleur shot back.

He reached her in two long strides. Extending his hand, he stroked her cheek with the back of his finger. The satiny texture of her skin was nearly his undoing. "Do you miss me, Fleur?"

"I . . ."

"It's no use, my sweet; your eyes tell me you do. I miss you, too."

"You have Violet."

"Do I?"

"It doesn't matter, Reed. We can't be together."

Reed's dark brows shot up. "Do you really think so?" His expression turned serious. "I meant it when I said you're no longer a part of this investigation. I'm sure Porter will agree with me. Take Lisette and rusticate in the country until this is over."

Fleur's chin rose defiantly. "I'm involved too deeply to quit now. Please leave, Reed. I'm exhausted."

Reed didn't want to leave, but he knew that Fleur would never agree to what he *did* want. He knew he could slake his lust with Violet, but the thought of bedding her or any other woman made him physically ill. What in bloody hell had Fleur done to him?

Sending Reed away was the hardest thing Fleur had ever done. God help her, but she wanted him. He looked so handsome tonight, casually dressed in a black cloak, black breeches, black boots, and a white shirt open at the neck. No wonder she hadn't seen him hiding in the shrubbery.

Fleur didn't dare look into his eyes, for she knew what she would see and wasn't sure she could resist his seduction. Together they were magic.

"Very well, I'll leave if that's what you wish." His words came to her through the fog of desire building inside her.

She walked away from him but didn't get far. Reed pulled her around and into his arms. He stared into her eyes for the length of a heartbeat, then lowered his mouth to hers. Unlike Dubois's kiss, Reed's was intensely arousing as his tongue delved deeply into her mouth. Fleur groaned. She was shattering slowly from the inside.

Abruptly he broke off the kiss and stepped away. Staring at him, she touched her lips.

"Compare that to Dubois's kiss," he drawled. "Don't bother to see me out—I know the way."

Fleur didn't move until she heard the soft click of the door. As if in a dream, she moved slowly to the door and locked it. Reed's kiss made her realize it was far from over between them. Indeed, it had just begun.

The walk to Hunthurst was a short one. Reed let himself into the house and locked the door. The mansion was dark; everyone was abed. He walked into his study, threw off his cloak and poured himself two fingers of brandy. He swallowed it in one gulp, poured another and sank down in a chair in front of the fireplace. The soft glow of the dying flames played over his rugged features, revealing the anguish twisting his insides.

The picture of Dubois kissing Fleur replayed over and over in his mind. He'd wanted to grab the Frenchman by the neck and pull him off Fleur. He wanted to do other things, too, like kill the bastard. How could Fleur let Dubois touch her?

"Reed, do you mind if I join you?"

Fleur? For a moment he thought his fondest dream had come true. His heart sank when he realized it was Violet standing in the doorway, the scrap of material she called a nightgown revealing more than it concealed.

"What are you doing up?"

"I couldn't sleep. I heard you come in and thought I'd

join you." She walked over to the sideboard and gestured to the crystal carafe of brandy. "May I?"

"Help yourself."

She poured brandy into a snifter and sauntered toward Reed, stopping in front of him. The light from the dying fire behind her rendered her nightgown transparent. Every curve of her generous form was blatantly revealed to him. Though Reed stared, the sight did little to move him. How in bloody hell was he supposed to wed a woman who failed to arouse even the tiniest interest? How could he make an heir with a woman he didn't want?

"Do you see anything you like?" Violet purred.

"Go to bed, Violet."

Violet tossed back her brandy neatly and set the empty glass on the mantel. "I know you desire me, Reed. I don't mind if you want to anticipate our wedding." She sent him a coy smile. "I've been dreaming about making love with you."

"You forget one thing, Violet. I haven't proposed yet."

"Wedding me would please your grandmother. Would you deny the woman who saved your life that satisfaction?"

Before Reed realized what she intended, Violet plopped down on his lap and wound her arms around his neck.

"Do you realize you've never even kissed me?" She demanded.

"Frankly, it never occurred to me."

"Then it's about time you thought about it. Who knows, you might like it."

Why not? Reed thought. If Fleur didn't want him, why not kiss Violet? Perhaps Violet could help him forget Fleur's tempting mouth and lush body.

Seizing her face between his hands, he closed his mouth over hers. Though her taste was unfamiliar and not especially to his liking, he sincerely tried to lose himself in the heat of the moment. It didn't work. But when he tried to break off the kiss, Violet resisted. She grasped his hand and brought it to her ample breast. He felt her nipple swell against his palm and became faintly aroused.

"You *do* want me, Reed," Violet purred. "Take me to bed; I swear I will make you happy. You don't know how long I've waited for this moment."

"Are you a virgin, Violet?" Reed asked. He already knew the answer. She was too knowledgeable to be innocent.

Violet went still. "Does it matter?"

"It matters not at all to me. It *will*, however, make a difference to the man you eventually marry."

He stood abruptly, spilling Violet to the floor. "Good night, Violet. I'm sure you can find your way to your bed."

He stepped over her and walked away, leaving an enraged Violet sprawled inelegantly on the floor.

❖ *Chapter Seventeen* ❖

Reed paused before the window in his study, staring out at the rain. He had been working all afternoon on estate business and felt moody and out of sorts. Several days had passed since he'd dismissed Fleur from the investigation, and he hadn't seen her once. He wondered if she missed him as much as he missed her. Without Fleur to spar with, to tease, to love, to share information about the traitor, Reed felt at loose ends. He had ordered her off the investigation for a good reason, however.

There were too many suspects and not enough evidence to charge any one of them with treason against the Crown. Furthermore, several of the suspects had knowledge of the Black Widow's activities in France. That did not bode well for Fleur, even though she no longer posed a threat to the French Government. Reed sincerely hoped Fleur had backed off and ceased her investigations as he had advised.

Frustration gnawed at him. He was getting nowhere in his inquiries and neither was Porter. Nothing was falling into place for him, except for one thing. He had informed Helen and her sister that they were no longer welcome at Hunthurst. He was heartily sick of Helen's machinations and Violet's overt flirtation. They were both trying to arrange his life, and he didn't like it one bit.

Reed had given the women two weeks to pack up and leave. They could retire to the dower house in the country, move into their parents' London abode or rent their own lodgings. It made no difference to him. Helen was financially well off, thanks to Jason's will. She could set up her own household if she so wished. With the ladies gone, Gallard Duvall would have no reason to make himself at home at Hunthurst. Duvall fawned over Helen, and truthfully, Reed couldn't see the attraction.

Perhaps money was the key, Reed considered. Jason had left Helen a wealthy widow, and Duvall appeared to have no income. Oh, well, it didn't matter whom Helen favored as long as they left him out of the mix.

Reed turned away from the dismal scene outside the window and returned to his desk. Drumming his fingers against the fine-grained mahogany top, he wondered what Fleur was doing. Perhaps he should call on her, find out what she had been up to. He worried that she was probing where she shouldn't, or getting entangled in a situation from which she couldn't extract herself. Knowing Fleur, she had probably ignored his order to back off.

What was he going to do about her? Reed wondered, thrusting his fingers through his hair as he probed his mind for an answer. He knew what he *wanted* to do. He wanted to keep her with him forever and never let her go. He wanted to go to bed with her at night and wake up with her in the morning.

He wanted . . .

Fleur.

Rain battered against the windowpane. Thunder rolled in the distance. A strange restlessness seized Reed. That sense of being trapped and helpless began to stir. If he didn't do something, he would descend again into that dark and unbearable pit where madness dwelt. He didn't want to go there. A discreet knock on the door dragged him from the edge of a yawning abyss.

"My lord, a message has arrived for you."

"Come in," Reed called, glad for the distraction.

Hughes entered, bearing a silver salver containing a folded sheet of vellum. "Is the messenger waiting for an answer?" Reed asked.

"No, my lord. I sent him to the kitchen to dry off before returning. The message is from the dowager countess."

Reed stared at the vellum without opening it. "It must be important if Grandmamma sent a man out in this weather. I hope she isn't ill."

Since he hadn't been dismissed, Hughes waited while Reed read the dowager's note. Grandmamma wasn't ill, thank God. She did want to see him, however. Immediately. Reed glanced out the window and sighed. The rain was still drumming against the windowpane.

"Have the carriage brought around, Hughes." The butler bowed and retreated.

Fifteen minutes later, armed with an umbrella that did little to keep him from being drenched by the wind-driven rain, Reed dashed out to the carriage. Why had Grandmamma summoned him today of all days? He shook his head. No matter, he didn't dare disobey her summons. When she said immediately, she meant immediately.

It took longer than usual to reach Grandmamma's townhouse, due to the rain and heavy traffic. When the carriage rattled to a stop, Reed opened his umbrella and made a dash to the front door. It opened immediately; he stepped inside and handed his dripping umbrella to a footman.

"Her ladyship is waiting for you in her private sitting room," the butler informed him. "She said to send you right up."

Reed ascended the stairs, shaking water off his coat as he climbed. He knocked on Grandmamma's door and entered. The dear old lady was lying on a chaise longue before a roaring fire, sipping tea, her knees covered with a fur lap robe.

"There you are, dear boy. Do come in and sit down. I get a crick in my neck looking up at you."

Reed pulled a stool up to the chaise and sat down.

"You're wet," Grandmamma observed.

"In case you haven't noticed, it's raining. Quite heavily, in fact. Are you well? What can I do for you? You know I wouldn't venture out in vile weather like this for anyone but you."

Grandmamma gave a little shudder. "It is rather nasty out. I can't seem to keep warm on days like this. Take off your coat and hang it over a chair to dry. I don't want you to catch your death."

Grandmamma should have thought of that before summoning him on today of all days, Reed thought grumpily.

"Now, then," Grandmamma said as she poured tea into a cup and handed it to Reed, "tell me what you've been up to. You haven't called on me in ages."

Reed took a sip of tea, wishing he had a nip of something stronger in his cup. "I'm sure you didn't drag me out in inclement weather to ask me what I've been up to. What is this really about, Grandmamma?"

The dowager set down her cup and cleared her throat. "Very well, I'll tell you, but you won't like it. I'm disappointed in you, dear boy."

Reed cocked an elegant, dark brow. "How so?"

"You aren't doing your duty to the earldom."

It finally dawned on Reed what Grandmamma was talking about. "When did Helen and Violet call on you? They certainly didn't waste any time."

"Now, now, dear boy, don't get testy. It just so happens they did call on me. Helen was quite distraught. She said you turned her out of her own home."

"It's my home now, Grandmamma," Reed reminded her. "I allowed Helen and her sister to live at Hunthurst for Jason's sake, but they have outlived their welcome. Violet is becoming increasingly aggressive in her pursuit of me, and Helen is abetting her."

"You could do worse than Violet, Reed. She is perfect for you. Why can't you see it?"

"I don't love Violet, Grandmamma."

"Love? Are you saying you'll only marry for love?"

"Tell me, Grandmamma, did you love Grandfather? Was yours a love match?"

A dreamy expression crossed the dowager's face, and a tear slipped from the corner of her eye. "Believe it or not—for it wasn't the thing in those days—ours was indeed a love match. I fell in love with your grandfather the moment I laid eyes on him. He was so handsome, so dashing."

"Then you understand why I want no less for myself. I can never love Violet. She should find someone who will appreciate her. That man isn't me."

Grandmamma tapped her fingertips against her pursed lips. "Have you found a woman you could love?"

Reed stared off into space. He loved Fleur—he did, no matter how hard he tried to ignore his feelings. He didn't care about an heir. Besides, the fault might not be Fleur's. Perhaps her husband's seed was defective.

Reed was through lying to himself and especially to Grandmamma. Somehow he had to convince the two most important women in his life that Fleur was the only one he would wed, the only one he wanted.

"Reed, what are you thinking? You seem so far away. You weren't reliving that awful time in France, were you?"

"Not this time, Grandmamma. To answer your question, I have found a woman to love."

The dowager immediately perked up. "You have? Why

have you kept this joyous news to yourself? Tell me the fortunate girl's name so I can welcome her into the family."

"She hasn't agreed to become my wife yet," Reed said.

"I cannot imagine any woman refusing you," Grandmamma exclaimed, properly affronted. "Who has the nerve to refuse an earl of the realm? Do I know her?"

"You do know her, Grandmamma. She is Countess Fleur Fontaine."

"But . . . but," Grandmamma sputtered. "The woman is barren. She cannot give you an heir."

"You don't know that."

"By her own admission she was married five years without giving her husband a child."

Reed knelt before his grandmother and took her chilled hands in his. "Both you and Fleur have failed to consider that her husband might have been the one at fault. His seed could have been defective. Fleur feels as you do and refused to become my wife. Somehow I'm going to convince her to change her mind. I love her, Grandmamma. She's the only woman I want, the only woman I will wed."

"What if you marry her and she proves barren?"

A dimple appeared in Reed's cheek. "I'll adopt. London is full of orphans in need of a family."

Aghast, the dowager threw up her hands. "I cannot imagine an heir who does not have Hunthurst blood flowing through his veins."

"Fear not, Grandmamma, I haven't given up hope that Fleur will provide an heir for the earldom."

Grandmamma sighed. "Your mind is made up, then?"

"I'm afraid so. No one can take Fleur's place in my heart."

The dowager heaved a resigned sigh. "How can I deny you your heart's desire, dear boy?" She stroked his cheek. "You are all I have left in this world. I *do* want you to be happy, and if Fleur makes you happy, then you have my blessing. Your optimism is inspiring. I find myself believing in you, believing that your countess will provide the earldom with sufficient heirs to fulfill an old lady's dreams."

Reed kissed his grandmother's cheek and rose to his feet. "You're amazing, Grandmamma. I'm sure you will live to see several heirs enter this complicated world of ours."

"Must you leave so soon? It's growing late. Will you take an early supper with me?"

"Not today, Grandmamma, but I'll return soon and bring Fleur with me. I'm off to see her now. She has yet to agree to become my wife and I'm eager to change her mind now that I have your blessing."

"Go then. I remember what it's like to be young and in love. Tell Fleur I won't stand in her way. I'll even help her plan the wedding."

Reed took his leave, his mood considerably lighter after his conversation with his grandmother. It was still raining heavily as he ducked into his carriage. During the short ride to the townhouse, Reed rehearsed what he would say to Fleur to convince her to marry him. He hoped receiving Grandmamma's blessing would encourage her to accept him.

The carriage rolled to a stop. Reed didn't wait for the coachman to pull down the steps as he jumped to the ground. He didn't even bother with the umbrella.

"Go around to the back, dry off and have something warm to eat and drink," Reed told the coachman. "I don't know how long I will be. I will send for you when I'm ready to leave."

Updike opened the door before Reed reached it. "Come in out of the rain, my lord. 'Tis a day fit for neither man nor beast."

Reed stepped into the foyer, shaking the water from his shoulders like a shaggy dog. "Is Lady Fleur in?"

"The mistress and Madame Lisette are in the study. They prefer the cozy warmth of the study to the more formal rooms on dreary days like this. Shall I announce you?"

"No, I'll announce myself." He strode toward the study, stopped and turned to address Updike. "Please ask Mrs. Peabody to set another place for dinner and make sure John Coachman is taken care of in the kitchen."

A corner of Updike's mouth twitched. "Shouldn't you wait for Lady Fontaine to invite you?"

Reed flashed him a confident smile. "Don't be impertinent, Updike." So saying, he opened the door to the study and stepped inside.

Reed took in the homey scene with a single glance. Fleur was curled up on a sofa before the hearth, reading a book. Lisette sat beside her, bent over an embroidery hoop while she placed neat stitches on a piece of cloth. Fleur looked up, saw Reed standing inside the door and dropped her book.

"Reed! I didn't hear Updike announce you."

"He didn't," Reed said. "I'm announcing myself."

"Was there something important you wanted? I can't imagine anyone venturing out on a day like this unless there was some urgency for the visit."

Lisette must have taken that for a signal to leave for she rose, gathered up her embroidery and said, "Please excuse me. I need to confer with Mortimer about . . . something."

"Mortimer?" Reed asked once the door closed behind Lisette.

"Updike. Did you not know his given name is Mortimer?"

"Though he's been with me more years than I care to count, he never volunteered his given name."

"Sit by the fire and dry yourself," Fleur invited.

Reed lowered himself beside Fleur on the sofa and stretched his hands out to the fire.

Fleur knew Reed had come for a reason, but she was in

no hurry to question him. She wasn't sure she would like what he had to say. She was already angry with him for the underhanded way he had tried to boot her off the investigation.

She studied Reed from beneath lowered lids, admiring everything about him except his misplaced protectiveness. She hadn't taken his advice, of course. She had received both Dubois and Barbeau since Reed's edict and accepted an invitation to go riding in the park with Henry Dempsey when weather permitted.

Reed shifted his position and stretched out his legs. Fleur thought he had amazing legs. Long and lean with ropy muscles running down each thigh. A jolt of pleasure shot through her when Reed reached out, grasped her hand and brought it to his lips. Surely he wouldn't try to seduce her after she had turned down his marriage proposal, would he? She thought she had made herself clear; she wouldn't condemn him to a childless marriage when he needed an heir.

She tried to pull her hand free, but he wouldn't allow it. "What are you doing here, Reed?"

"I have something important to discuss with you."

"Does it concern the investigation?"

"This has nothing to do with the investigation. It's about us."

"There *is* no us, Reed. I thought I made that clear."

"You did, but things have changed."

"What things?"

"Grandmamma has given her blessing to our marriage." He waited for her reaction. It was not long in coming.

"Why would your grandmother give her blessing when she knows I can't give you an heir?"

"She knows no such thing and neither do you," Reed charged. "And since I cannot let you go, I see no reason for us not to marry."

Fleur took a shaky breath and tried to explain for the

hundredth time why she couldn't marry him. "I was married to Pierre for five years. Not once during that time did he get me with child. I'm barren, Reed. Why are you making this difficult for us? Why can't you just leave things the way they are and forget about me?"

"Tell me, love, can you forget about me?"

Fleur swallowed convulsively. Would Reed believe her if she lied? She doubted it. Therefore, she told the truth. "I'll never forget you, Reed."

"Good, there's no need to forget me. Have you considered the possibility that your husband's seed was damaged? Sometimes the man is at fault for failing to produce an heir. That's what I'm counting on, Fleur. If I'm wrong, we'll adopt. It's been done before, you know."

Fleur still wasn't convinced. "Your grandmother agreed to this?"

"My grandmother loves me. She wouldn't insist I wed a woman I didn't love."

Fleur went still, her eyes shiny with tears. Reed loved her. How could she refuse to wed the man she loved with every fiber of her being? The man who loved her in return? Still, she hesitated. Could it be true that Pierre was to blame for her failure to conceive a child? The idea was so new it left her breathless. If a marriage was childless, everyone assumed it was the woman's fault. No man alive would take the blame.

Reed's words gave her hope, but not much. She had lain with Reed countless times and still hadn't conceived. What made him think she wasn't barren?

"Reed, I don't think . . ."

He placed a finger against her lips. "Shhh. That's the problem, you think too much. Do you love me, Fleur?"

Fleur closed her eyes and thought about how lonely and bereft she'd felt these past few days without Reed. He'd become part of her life, part of *her*. Her love for Pierre paled in comparison to what she felt for Reed.

When she opened her eyes, she found Reed staring intently at her. "I do love you, Reed. To deny my feelings would be denying my heart."

Reed gave a whoop of joy. "We'll be married as soon as this business with the traitor is resolved. You soothe my soul and bring me peace."

After Reed's moving declaration, Fleur became too choked up to speak. She merely stared at him, her eyes misty with tears. Not even Pierre had loved her as deeply as Reed did. When she looked into his eyes she no longer saw shadows; she saw only happiness and . . . yes . . . love. She flung her arms around his neck and pressed her lips to his.

Reed reacted spontaneously, opening his mouth and drawing her into the kiss. She gripped his shoulders, drowning in sensation, flushed with the need to sink deeper into the abyss of pleasure.

"I don't know if I can control myself," Reed whispered against her mouth.

"Don't," Fleur gasped.

"I don't want to take you here. You deserve better. I want to undress you slowly, lay you down on a soft bed and arouse you until you're wild for me."

Her voice was a ragged whisper. "I want that, too."

"Then we're in agreement," Reed said as he scooped her into his arms and strode to the door.

"Reed! Wait! You can't carry me to my bedchamber at this time of day. What will the servants think?"

"Frankly, I don't care."

He opened the door and bumped into Updike, standing guard, no doubt. Updike stared gravely at Fleur and asked, "Do you require my help, my lady?"

Overcome with embarrassment, Fleur buried her face against Reed's chest and murmured, "No, thank you."

"What your mistress wishes to say is that we will require dinner for two served in Lady Fontaine's bedchamber at eight o'clock. Until then, we don't wish to be disturbed. Oh, yes, inform John Coachman that I'll find my own way home."

Updike stood firm, refusing to step aside. "Are congratulations in order, my lord?"

Reed laughed. "Indeed they are. Lady Fontaine and I just became engaged."

Beaming from ear to ear, Updike said, "Felicitations, my lady. May I tell Lisette?"

Once again Reed answered. "By all means; tell anyone you like. Now will you step aside?"

If Updike hadn't moved, Reed would have barreled past him.

"The whole household will know what we're up to," Fleur scolded. "Did you have to be so obvious?"

"Don't you think they already know about us? I've learned that servants know everything their employers do." He reached her bedchamber and opened the door. "Forget about them. Tonight is just for us."

He set her on her feet and closed the door behind them. Then he found a faggot and dipped it into the hearth. When it caught fire, he touched the flame to a candle. His eyes gleamed like silver when he finally turned to Fleur, lowered his head and lightly grazed her earlobe with his teeth. Then he nuzzled the soft skin behind her ear, inhaling the fragrant aroma of roses lingering on her skin. The scent weakened his knees and made him dizzy with need. Her arms circled his waist, melding their bodies together. If he didn't get her naked soon, Reed feared he would explode.

With gentle hands, he unfastened the tiny buttons holding together her bodice. When the last button was undone, the bodice fell away. He reached up and slid the sleeves down her arms. Desire darkened his eyes when he realized she was unfettered by a corset.

"No corset?" he whispered. "How fortunate for me."

"I knew no one would call on a raw day like this, so I dressed comfortably."

"Thank God for intelligent women." He stripped away her gown and then her chemise, baring her to his avid gaze. "Your beauty never ceases to amaze me," Reed said reverently.

"I'm no great beauty, Reed. The *ton* would consider me average looking. Lady Violet is lovely by Town standards."

He stared at her. High, full breasts beckoned his hands and lips. The indentation of her waist gave way to the sinuous curve of her hips. His gaze settled on the midnight tangle of curls at the apex of her thighs before continuing down her shapely legs to her graceful ankles.

"You're not just beautiful, you're exquisite. You underestimate your appeal."

"You talk too much," Fleur said as she set to work untying the complicated knot of his soggy cravat. His damp coat and shirt came off next, joining the pile of discarded clothing on the floor.

Reed caressed her back with long, slow strokes as she unbuttoned the placket on his breeches and peeled them down his hips. He gave her a dimpled smile as he kicked off his boots and stepped out of his breeches. Finally his erection sprang free. When she reached down and ran her fingers down his cock, he sucked in a sharp breath. Emboldened, she cupped his balls. His pleasure intensified until it bordered on pain. When he groaned, her hand stilled, and she looked up at him.

"Don't stop, please don't stop."

She stroked him again. Heat poured through him. Every muscle tensed and quivered as he flexed his loins and thrust himself into her hand. Wrapping her hand around him, she gently squeezed. His groin tightened painfully. Glancing down, he saw a pearly drop appear at the tip of his engorged sex.

"Enough," Reed said in a gravelly voice he barely recognized as his own.

Hooking his arm under her knees, he scooped her up, carried her to the bed and followed her down. His hand brushed over the curve of her bottom, then caressed the silken petals of her sex from behind, finding them already swollen and moist. With a deliberate lack of haste, he continued to arouse her. Turning her onto her back, he covered her nipples with his mouth and suckled, first one and then the other. Suddenly she pushed him away, startling him. If she asked him to stop, he thought he would surely die.

Reluctantly he reared up and stared down at her. Then he let out a bark of surprise when Fleur shoved him down and straddled him.

"Fleur, what . . ."

"You've had your turn; now it's mine."

Grasping his cock between her hands, she lowered her head and drew him into the hot cavern of her mouth. She tasted him with her tongue, lapping the pearly drop at the tip, arousing him unbearably with her lips and mouth.

"Minx!" Reed growled. "If you don't stop, this will end before it gets started."

Grasping her waist, he lifted her away and rolled her beneath him. He settled himself between her splayed thighs and braced himself on his elbows, staring into her eyes.

Fleur squirmed beneath him. "Please, Reed, don't make me wait."

The blunt tip of his erection brushed through the curls between her legs and over the dewy folds of her sex, teasing her unmercifully. Her fingernails scored his back in a silent plea. Gazing intently at her, he thrust hard and slid deep inside her.

And found heaven.

Her body gripped him like a velvet glove. As he began to

thrust and withdraw, she rose up to meet him, her breath coming in ragged puffs of air. His own breathing turned rough. Need scored him, and his thrusts became frantic. He glanced down at Fleur, relief pounding through him. She appeared to be on the cusp of climax. His control splintered.

"Come with me, Fleur. Come with me now."

He thrust hard, deep, imbedding himself to the hilt, then stilled, watching her. Her face was flushed, her lips parted. Her eyes were closed, her fingers bit into his back and her inner muscles clenched around him, squeezing his cock. The moment he felt her body go limp, he unleashed the passion clawing at him. Burying his face in the fragrant curve of her neck, he shouted her name and freed his seed.

When their shudders subsided, Reed found the energy to raise his head and look down at her. Fleur's eyes slid open, and she smiled at him.

"That was . . ."

"Incredible, magical," Reed suggested. "I promise it will always be like this for us."

A knock sounded on the door. "That will be our dinner," Reed said.

He rose and pulled on his breeches.

Fleur flushed a bright red when Reed opened the door, admitting Updike. Directing his gaze anywhere but at the bed, Updike walked into the room and placed the tray on the table.

"Will that be all, my lord?"

"That will be all, *Mortimer*."

Updike blushed as he drew himself up to his full height, bowed and made a hasty exit.

"You shouldn't have teased him," Fleur scolded.

"I couldn't help it." Reed glanced at the tray, then at Fleur. "How hungry are you?"

For a moment Fleur didn't know what he meant, until he started peeling off his breeches. "I'm ravenous, but not for food," she replied.

"I hoped you'd say that."

Reed had the presence of mind to lock the door before joining her in bed.

✤ Chapter Eighteen ✤

Fleur awoke to sunshine and a warm body snuggled against her back. The feeling was so blissful, she wanted to savor it as long as she could. A smile curved her lips as she burrowed deeper into Reed's warmth. He had made love to her last night in every way a man could love a woman.

Even more satisfying, Reed hadn't merely *made* love to her with his body, he *loved* her with his heart, and his grandmother had given her blessing to their marriage. Absolutely nothing could mar this day. It was the happiest of her life.

Reed was sleeping so soundly, Fleur didn't have the heart to awaken him. Carefully, she slid from the mattress without disturbing him.

Her stomach growled. She glanced at the untouched food that sat congealing on the tray and realized they had never gotten around to eating. She checked the clock on the mantel, surprised to see it was past ten. She couldn't remember the last time she had slept this late.

With as little noise as possible, she made a hasty toilette, dressed in a simple gown and left the bedchamber, closing the door quietly behind her.

She entered the breakfast room and pulled the bell pull;

Updike appeared moments later. He seemed surprised to see her alone.

He set a steaming teapot on the table. "Good morning, my lady. What would you like for breakfast?"

"I'm famished, Updike. I know it's late, but would you ask Cook if she has time to prepare coddled eggs, bacon, tomatoes and toasted bread? Oh, and maybe she would include one of those sticky buns I'm so fond of."

Updike bowed and left to convey Fleur's wishes to the kitchen. Fleur sipped her tea, a contented smile playing on her lips. She was going to be Reed's bride. It seemed like a dream come true.

Fleur dug into her breakfast when it arrived, savoring every bite. She was nibbling on her sweet bun when Updike announced visitors. Before she could ask who was calling, Lady Helen and Lady Violet barged into the room, followed by their toady, Gallard Duvall.

"Helen, Violet, what are you doing here? Isn't it a little early to be out calling?"

"This can't wait," Violet insisted.

"Have you eaten? Will you sit down and take tea with me?"

"No, we won't be long," Violet snapped. "We came to tell you what a bitch you are. You finally got Reed to toss us out on the street."

"I don't know what you're talking about."

Lashing out, Violet slapped Fleur across the face. Fleur reared back, more stunned than hurt. "Get out!" she ordered, struggling to control her anger. "How dare you come into my home and assault me? Updike, show the ladies the door."

"Stay where you are, Updike. The ladies will leave after I am done with them."

Reed stood in the doorway, casually dressed in an open shirt, breeches and, in an astonishing breach of etiquette, he was barefoot. Smiling at Fleur, he strolled into the room.

Violet gaped at Reed and blanched. Then without warning she rounded on Fleur. "Bitch! Whore! No wonder Reed didn't come home last night. He was with you, in your bed, doing God only knows what."

She raised her hand and would have struck Fleur a second time if Reed hadn't grasped her wrist in a bruising grip. "I won't allow you or anyone else to abuse my fiancée."

"Your fiancée?" Helen repeated, clearly stunned.

"You and the countess are to be married?" Duvall echoed, apparently as surprised as the ladies.

Releasing Violet's wrist, Reed returned to Fleur's side and kissed her cheek. "Yes, my fiancée. Aren't you going to congratulate us?"

"Wait until your grandmother hears this," Violet said indignantly. "She doesn't approve of Fleur, you know."

"You're mistaken, Violet. Grandmamma gave her blessing to our union."

Ignoring the stunned silence following his words, Reed pulled out a chair beside Fleur and sat down. "I'm hungry. Updike, will you ask Cook to fix me the same thing your mistress ordered this morning?"

"Right away, my lord. Shall I show your guests the door?"

"That's a splendid idea, Updike, though I'm sure they can manage on their own." He turned to Helen and Violet. "You have but a few days left to make other living arrangements. I suggest you make haste. I'm sure Duvall will give you whatever help you need."

"Indeed," Duvall said, patting Helen's arm.

"This way," Updike said in his haughtiest voice as he herded all three uninvited guests out the door.

Fleur turned to Reed and smiled. "That was rather unpleasant."

Reed returned Fleur's smile. Seconds later his smile turned into a frown as he gently stroked her reddened cheek. "She struck you! The bitch had the gall to raise her hand to you. I thought I arrived in time to stop her from abusing you."

"You did arrive in time. She would have struck me a second time if you hadn't intervened."

Reed's breakfast was served. "I'll make sure she never gets near you again."

"She didn't hurt me. Eat your breakfast before it gets cold." She poured tea into their cups. "Violet is the least of our worries. I'm much more concerned about the investigation."

"You're not involved in any of that anymore, remember? I dismissed you from the investigation."

"I chose to ignore you. What is our next move? Where do we go from here?"

"Your next move is to plan our wedding with Grandmamma. Mine is to find a traitor."

"Not without my help," Fleur argued. "You need me."

Reed laid his knife and fork down on his plate. "I don't want to lose you, Fleur. We're dealing with dangerous people. If they know about the Black Widow, they've already guessed the rest. The traitor may be out for your blood as well as mine."

Fleur shook her head. "It doesn't make sense. Why would we still be important to Napoleon's government?"

Reed shrugged. "I don't know, but I intend to find out."

"I wonder how long it will be before word of our engagement becomes common knowledge?"

Laughing, Reed wiped his lips with his napkin and tossed it down. "The news is probably making the rounds as we speak. Helen and Violet are notorious gossips. And you know how servants talk among themselves."

Reed rose, looked down at his bare toes and grinned. "My boots should be dry; I built up the fire and placed them and my coat in front of the hearth. It's time I left. I've begun an investigation into Henry Dempsey's background."

"Good, I've been suspicious of him from the beginning. I've been invited to Lady Ogleton's ball tonight. Shall we attend together? Perhaps we can learn something new. It's supposed be a well-attended affair."

"Good idea. We'll make our first appearance as a couple and keep our eyes and ears open. I'll call for you at nine."

He pulled her from the chair and into his arms. Then he kissed her soundly and took his leave.

"Good, you're alone," Lisette said from the doorway. "Mortimer said everyone had left."

"The tea is still hot. Will you join me?" Fleur asked, smiling at her friend.

"*Oui*, thank you," Lisette said as Fleur poured. "I passed his lordship in the hall. I understand congratulations are in order."

Fleur beamed. "I've accepted Reed's marriage proposal. He loves me, Lisette, really loves me. Even better, his grandmother gave her blessing to our marriage."

"Does Lord Hunthurst realize you cannot give him an heir?"

"Reed doesn't believe I am barren. He thinks Pierre was to blame."

Lisette glanced at Fleur's flat stomach. "One can only hope. When is the wedding to be?"

"Not until the traitor is brought to justice. We both need to concentrate on the investigation. Reed's grandmother wishes to help me plan the wedding."

Lisette gave Fleur a quick hug. "I'm so happy for you, *chèrie*. I know how much you love his lordship. I felt such sadness when you told him you wouldn't marry him. He must love you very much."

"What about you and Updike? You appear to be more than just friends."

Lisette giggled like a young girl. Fleur couldn't recall when her companion had appeared so happy.

"Mortimer and I have an understanding. I refused to make any commitment to him until your future is secure, and Mortimer understands."

Fleur squeezed Lisette's hands. "Everyone should have a friend such as you. Soon you and your Mortimer can plan your own future. Shall we stroll in the park today? After yesterday's rain, a walk in the sunshine will be just the thing."

Fleur and Lisette left the house a short time later. The distance to the park was a short one. As they strolled along the tree-lined walkway, they were hailed by Count Dubois and Monsieur Barbeau.

"Countess, Madame Lisette," Dubois greeted with a courtly bow. "Do you mind if we stroll along with you?"

"Not at all," Fleur replied. If luck was with her, she might learn something new to tell Reed tonight.

The sidewalk was wide, permitting them to walk four abreast for a time. But when the walkway narrowed, Lisette was forced to fall behind, allowing both men to flank Fleur.

"We heard the most startling news this morning," Dubois confided. "Say it's not true."

"Whatever are you talking about?" Fleur replied, pretending innocence.

"Monsieur Duvall told us you are engaged to Hunthurst," Dubois said, looking stricken. "That was rather sudden, wasn't it? I did not credit it since Hunthurst himself told me he wasn't interested in you."

"Monsieur Duvall is correct," Fleur said. "I am to wed the Earl of Hunthurst."

"I am devastated," Dubois cried, clutching his heart. "Why did you tell me you were not interested in marriage?" He paused for effect. "Duvall said he saw Hunthurst at your townhouse early this morning in a rather startling state of undress."

Fleur wasn't about to explain that. What she did or didn't do was no one's business but hers. "Are you questioning my reputation, Count?"

"Forgive me, Countess. I was deeply hurt and spoke out of turn."

"You are forgiven."

"Do you and Hunthurst plan to attend the Ogleton ball tonight?" Barbeau asked.

"That is our intention," Fleur replied.

Barbeau bowed. "Then we shall see you there. Congratulations on your engagement. I shall extend my good wishes to Hunthurst tonight. Come along, René. Let us leave the ladies to their exercise."

Dubois stared intently at Fleur before bowing. Fleur bobbed a curtsy to both men. A shiver ran down her spine as she watched them leave. Warning bells went off in her head, but which man should she be wary of? Common sense told her it was Dubois, but every instinct she possessed told her both men bore watching.

"What was that all about?" Lisette asked, catching up with her.

"Duvall told them about my engagement to Reed. Dubois didn't take it well. He was courting me, you see."

"Do you think he's a French spy?"

"Time will tell, although Reed believes it is one of Lord Porter's agents. If we don't solve this mystery soon, I fear for Reed's life. He's had several close calls already. He might not be so lucky next time."

"You think there will be a next time?"

"I sincerely hope not."

Reed appeared at the townhouse at promptly nine o'clock that night. He stood at the bottom of the stairs to await Fleur. She didn't keep him there long. His breath caught in his throat as she floated down the stairs toward him. She was a vision in violet silk trimmed with purple ribbon. The empire waistline, outlined with deep purple ribbon, fit snugly beneath her breasts and skimmed her shapely hips. Violet gloves covered her arms from fingertips to elbows.

"You're beautiful," Reed said, kissing her hands. "Every man at the ball will be envious of me."

"Not with all the young debs in attendance to distract them."

Updike appeared with a deep purple shawl and draped it around Fleur's shoulders.

"Don't wait up for us, Updike. We'll let ourselves in. And tell Fleur's maid she won't be needed tonight," Reed called over his shoulder as he ushered Fleur out the door and into his carriage.

"Did you make any progress today?" she asked once they were settled in the carriage.

"The men assigned to investigate Dempsey haven't reported their findings yet. I spoke with Porter again, but he refuses to believe one of his trusted men has turned traitor."

"I ran into Dubois and Barbeau in the park today," Fleur confided. "Duvall had already told them about our engagement and . . . well, you can imagine what else he said. Dubois seemed quite put out, but Barbeau didn't appear affected by the news. I must confess that I got the strangest feeling when we parted company."

"Stay away from them, Fleur. At this point we can't trust anyone."

When they arrived at the Ogleton's mansion, they had to wait in line before they could exit but finally the coachman let down the steps and opened the door. Reed stepped out first and handed Fleur down.

"It's going to be a crush," Fleur said.

"Unfortunately, yes. I wonder if Grandmamma will be here. She usually doesn't like venturing out at night."

"It's safe to say that Helen and Violet will be attending, accompanied by the ever-present Duvall."

Amusement colored Reed's words. "Who would think a second cousin twice removed, and a Frenchman at that, would be sniffing after Helen's skirts like a puppy dog?"

"Maybe he has true feelings for her," Fleur suggested.

The noisy crowd went silent when they reached the ballroom and were announced by a footman. All eyes turned in their direction. Fleur wanted to melt into the woodwork but somehow found the courage to raise her chin and smile. The buzz of conversation resumed as the crowd's attention turned elsewhere.

"Well, that's over," Reed whispered as they progressed into the room and Reed steered them toward a group of acquaintances. Introductions were made all around. Fleur followed the conversation but remained quiet and watchful.

"The next set is forming on the dance floor," Reed said. "Shall we join them?"

Since no public announcement of their engagement had been made, no one offered congratulations, though Fleur could tell by the covert glances and whispers that speculation was rife. It appeared the rumor mill had been busy grinding out gossip from one end of London to the other.

During the progression of the dance, Fleur spotted Dubois, Barbeau and Henry Dempsey. "What is Dempsey doing here?" she whispered when the dance steps brought them together again.

"Dempsey has connections, even though he lacks a title. I had the same connections before I came into my title."

"Did you notice the large number of émigrés in attendance?"

"It's all the rage now to invite émigrés to society events. Some came away from France with their fortunes intact and are being actively courted by the *ton*."

"Helen and Violet have just arrived," Fleur hissed. "Duvall is with them."

The sisters, trailed by Duvall, forged into the crowd. They tittered and gossiped behind their fans with each group they encountered during their progression.

"They're talking about us," Fleur whispered.

"Let them. Hold your head high; you've nothing to be ashamed of." The set ended, and they walked off the dance floor. "I'm parched, would you like something to drink?"

"Lemonade sounds wonderful. I'll visit the ladies' retiring room while you fetch our drinks."

"I'll be waiting for you beside the bust of Caesar. I don't want to lose you in the crowd."

Fleur located the meeting place and nodded. Reed soon disappeared into the crowd. Fleur realized she didn't know where the ladies retiring room was located and asked a footman. He directed her to the foyer and down a long hallway. When Fleur noticed Violet advancing toward her, she thanked the footman and hurried off. Glancing over her shoulder, she saw that Violet continued to close in on her. Not wanting to be cornered by her rival in the retiring room, Fleur ducked into the first door she came to. The room appeared to be a library. Light from a single candle barely illuminated the book-lined walls.

A breeze touched her cheek, and Fleur moved toward the open window to cool off. She intended to give Violet a decent amount of time before leaving the library and continuing on to the retiring room. She had no desire to run into Violet any time soon. The sound of male voices conversing in French wafted through the open window. Curious, Fleur flattened herself against the wall beside the drapery and eavesdropped on the conversation.

Apparently the men were standing right below the window for she heard their words clearly, even though they spoke in furtive whispers.

"We can wait no longer; he has to die." Fleur had to prevent herself from gasping. Were they talking about Reed?

"The man has more lives than a cat," the second man growled. "What is to be done about the countess?"

"If she gets in the way, she dies too."

"I agree. The woman deserves to die for her interference. He should have died in Devil's Chateau."

"We need to discuss plans for his demise, but not here. It's too public. Meet me tomorrow at our usual rendezvous. By this time next week, Hunthurst will be history."

Fleur began to shake. They *were* talking about Reed.

Who were they? Did she dare look out the window? When the voices began drifting away, Fleur waited a few breathless minutes before peeking out the window. She saw . . .

Nothing.

The men had slipped away into the darkness.

Mouth dry, heart pounding, Fleur remained frozen in place, unable to move, unable to think. She had just heard two Frenchmen plan Reed's death, but her mind and body refused to function. Finally her inertia gave way to terror. She had to find Reed.

She moved on wooden legs to the door. Her hands were sweating so profusely it took several tries before the knob turned. As luck would have it, she ran into Violet in the hallway.

"I wondered where you disappeared to," Violet snarled. "Is Reed in there with you?"

"No, I was by myself, not that it's any concern of yours. I needed a moment alone," Fleur had the presence of mind to say. "Is there something you want of me?"

"Indeed. I'm quite aware that you set your cap for Reed. You stole him from me. Everyone knows that you worked as a spy in France. I told all my friends about you. You'll never be accepted among the *ton*. Women of your ilk have no place in Society."

"I beg to differ," Reed said from behind Fleur.

Fleur's knees nearly buckled in relief. Reed was safe. They hadn't gotten to him yet.

"Fleur will soon become my wife," Reed said. "Grandmamma has influence, and she will see that Fleur is accepted by Society."

"I don't care about Society," Fleur huffed, anxious to whisk Reed off to safety. She began pulling him away. "My head hurts. I'd like to leave."

Reed stared at her. "We'll miss the midnight supper. Are you sure you want to leave?"

"Of course she wants to leave," Violet observed. "The gossips are having a field day at her expense. Only one kind of woman has the audacity to become a spy."

"A courageous one," Reed drawled.

Fleur tugged his sleeve. "Please, Reed, I want to leave."

Reed knew something was amiss from Fleur's expression. She looked upset, no, more than upset. She looked terrified. If Violet had done this to her, he would make sure the blasted woman suffered the consequences.

"Very well, we'll leave." He placed a hand in the middle of Fleur's back and guided her along the hallway to the foyer. He sent a footman for her wrap and another to fetch his carriage.

As luck would have it, Dempsey encountered them in the foyer. "Leaving already?"

"Fleur has a headache," Reed answered.

"I had hoped to find a moment alone with you," Dempsey said. "I've stumbled upon a man who claims to know the name of our traitor. Can we meet somewhere tomorrow?"

"Ten o'clock, Porter's office."

Dempsey shook his head. "No, that won't do. I'm not ready to reveal my source to our illustrious leader. He could ruin everything."

"Very well; tell me where and when."

"My source will only meet with us if it's a place of his own choosing. Are you familiar with the Crow's Nest near the docks?"

"I know it. Are you sure he wants to meet there? The place has an unsavory reputation."

"Do you want this information or not?"

"Don't go!" Fleur pleaded. "I have a bad feeling about this."

"Women!" Dempsey laughed. "They're afraid of their own shadow."

Reed studied Fleur's face, recognized her anxiety and forced himself to ignore it. "What time?"

"Ten o'clock tomorrow night. I'll set everything up. My

contact expects to be paid for his information, so don't come empty handed."

Reed nodded grimly. "I'll be there."

Nodding curtly, Dempsey retraced his steps to the ballroom. Reed took Fleur's wrap from the footman and placed it around her shoulders. Then he guided her through the door and into the carriage.

"All right, Fleur, what is this about?" Reed asked once they were seated. "You don't have a headache, do you?"

"I do now," Fleur replied. "You can't meet Dempsey tomorrow, Reed. It could be a trap."

"Do you know something I don't?"

"Before I tell you, answer me this. Does Dempsey speak fluent French?"

"Of course he does. Only men fluent in French are sent to the Continent. Why do you ask?"

Fleur clutched Reed's sleeve. He stared into her eyes and frowned. "You're frightened! Tell me what's upset you. Did someone try to intimidate you? Was it Violet?"

"Violet followed me to the ladies' retiring room."

"Bloody hell," Reed bit out.

"No, this isn't about Violet. I wanted to avoid a confrontation with her, so I slipped into the library. The window was open, and I moved toward it to cool off. A conversation taking place outside the window drew my attention, and I stepped closer to eavesdrop. They were speaking in French."

Her hand tightened on his sleeve. Reed peeled her clenched fist away and held it between his hands. "What did they say that frightened you so?"

"They were planning your death."

Reed went still. "Are you sure? Absolutely sure?"

"I know what I heard, Reed. I understand and speak French fluently."

"Did you get a look at them?"

"No, I was afraid to show myself in the window. I didn't

look until the men stopped talking. By then they had disappeared into the darkness."

"Did you recognize the voices?"

"No, and that's what frightens me so." A sob caught in her throat. "Don't you understand? Those men want you dead!"

Reed remained calm despite Fleur's panic. "Did they say why they wanted me dead?"

"Does it matter? Just knowing they're planning your death should be enough to warn you away from your meeting with Dempsey."

"Word for word, tell me what was said."

Fleur took a shaky breath and repeated the conversation to the best of her recollection. "I distinctly heard them say you were the man they wanted dead. That's why you can't meet with Dempsey."

"I have to, love. It may be my only chance to learn who put me in Devil's Chateau. I have to find out what Dempsey's source knows about the traitor. Judging from the conversation you overheard, there could be more than one."

The carriage rolled to a stop. John Coachman opened the door and pulled down the steps. Reed handed Fleur down and accompanied her to the door. She fumbled in her reticule for the key. Reed took it from her shaking fingers, fit it in the keyhole and opened the door.

"I'm not leaving you tonight," Reed said.

Relief shuddered through Fleur. If Reed was with her, danger wouldn't be stalking him. At least he'd be safe one more night.

Reed closed and locked the door behind them. Then he handed her the candle Updike had left for her, scooped her into his arms and carried her up the stairs. "Don't worry, love," he whispered into her ear. "I don't plan on dying any time soon."

Tears clogged her throat. "Promise?"

"Promise," he repeated. They reached her room. "Open the door; my hands are full at the moment."

Shifting the candle to her left hand, Fleur reached down with her right and opened the door. Reed carried her inside, set her on her feet, plucked the candle from her hand and placed it on the nightstand.

"You're not taking this threat to your life seriously," Fleur charged.

"My love, how much more serious can I get? I'm serious about undressing you. I'm serious about taking you to bed and serious about making love to you."

He turned her around to reach the tiny buttons on the back of her gown.

"I'm going with you tomorrow night," Fleur said stubbornly.

Reed's fingers stilled. "Like hell you are! You're going to stay home where it's safe."

"Don't shut me out of this, Reed. Let me help you. What if Dempsey has set a trap for you?"

"If it's a trap, I want you out of it. I can take care of myself."

"You've suspected Dempsey all along, haven't you?"

"Hmmm," he mumbled, neither agreeing nor disagreeing.

Her gown fell away, then her shift. Reed lifted her and sat her on the edge of the bed while he peeled off her garters, hose and shoes. His gaze remained intent upon her as he shed his own clothing. When he stood before her naked, Fleur reached for him. He shifted away and pushed her down on the bed so that her legs hung over the side. Then he knelt between them.

"We're not through talking yet," Fleur resisted.

"We are as far as I'm concerned. Open your legs, my love, I want to taste you."

When Fleur didn't obey fast enough, he grasped her legs and draped them over his shoulders. The sight of her lush feminine folds sent a shaft of raw lust spearing through him. He bent his head to her. Fleur's last thought as Reed's tongue, mouth and hands worked their magic on her, was that somehow, some way, she would save Reed's life, even if she had to risk hers to do it.

✤ Chapter Nineteen ✤

Fleur awoke with a smile on her face, recalling every sensual moment of the night before. Her smile lasted until she realized she was in bed alone. Reed had left without awakening her. It didn't take a genius to realize he had sneaked off before she could pester him about his meeting with Dempsey. He knew she wanted to accompany him and that she trusted Dempsey no more than he did, but he was being stubborn about involving her.

When and if Fleur saw him later in the day, she promised herself she would convince him that he needed her. He wasn't invincible; everyone needed someone. Why did Reed insist on meeting Dempsey in an unsavory place when he knew he could be walking into a trap?

Fleur scooted to the edge of the bed and started to rise. The moment her feet hit the floor, a wave of nausea struck. It happened so suddenly she barely managed to pull out the chamber pot in time. Peg entered the bedchamber while Fleur was still retching.

"Oh, my lady, you're ill!" She rushed to fill a glass with water from the pitcher and handed it to Fleur. Fleur took it gratefully and rinsed out her mouth.

"Shall I send Gordon for a physician?" Peg asked anxiously. Fleur sat back, relieved that the nausea had already passed. "No, that won't be necessary. I feel much better now. It must have been the salmon I had for supper last night. Is anyone else ill?"

"No, my lady. Cook made the salmon especially for you because she knows how fond you are of it. Madame Lisette doesn't like fish; she ate boiled beef along with the help."

"Oh, well, whatever it was seems to have passed."

Peg's gaze swept over Fleur; a troubled look wrinkled her brow. "As you say, my lady, but I would eat lightly this morning if I were you. Dry toast and tea sounds just the thing. My sister often found it helpful."

The hint passed right over Fleur. "I shall do as you say, Peg, thank you."

While Fleur prepared for the day, she began to make plans. Whether or not Reed wanted her help, he was going to get it.

Even as Fleur was making plans concerning Reed's meeting with Dempsey and the informant, Reed was finalizing his. On the walk home after he left Fleur, he decided against involving Porter at this point since he was convinced he could handle the situation on his own.

It was just past dawn when Reed let himself into his mansion. The servants were just beginning to move about. Reed climbed the stairs to his chamber and reached for the bell pull. Hughes appeared a short time later, exhibiting surprise at the early morning summons. Reed ordered a bath.

Reed lolled in the hot water, recalling the love he and Fleur had shared the night before, every erotic moment. He smiled inwardly, pleased that Fleur had finally agreed to marry him.

When the water grew cool, Reed stepped out of the tub and dried himself. Then he dressed in the clothes Hughes had laid out for him. Reed laughed when his stomach growled. He had worked up an appetite last night and hoped breakfast was ready and set out on the sideboard for him.

Reed needn't have worried. His staff was efficient if nothing else. Apparently his valet had alerted the cook when he had called for a bath. A footman stood nearby to pour his tea, and he helped himself to a heaping plate of eggs, ham, kippers, tomatoes and toasted bread.

"Are the ladies still in residence?" Reed asked the footman. He'd been so busy of late he hadn't paid much attention to their comings and goings.

"Lady Helen and Lady Violet requested that their luggage be carried downstairs this morning. I believe Mr. Duvall is to call for them later and take them to their new abode."

"Thank you," Reed said as he turned to the morning paper lying beside his plate. He really didn't have time to dawdle this morning; he wanted to be tucked up in his study before the ladies came down. He wasn't in the mood for a confrontation right now.

Luck was with Reed. He finished his breakfast and went directly to his study, leaving orders with Hughes that he not be disturbed. Reed delved immediately into his plans for tonight's rendezvous with Dempsey and the informant. He had no intention of seeing Fleur before the meeting. He knew she would try to talk him into taking her with him, and he was adamant that it wasn't going to happen. It was best that he stay away from Fleur today.

It was nearly eleven o'clock when Reed asked Hughes to summon the head groom and John Coachman to his study. Some ten minutes later, both men appeared before him.

The two were burly, strong and capable of taking care of themselves. They were also good, faithful men whom he trusted.

"Do either of you know how to handle a pistol?" Reed asked without preliminary.

John Coachman stepped forward. "I do, my lord. I'm quite handy with a gun."

Bates, the head groom, shook his head. "I've not had enough practice to hit anything I aim at. But I'm right handy with a cudgel, if I say so meself." He held up his beefy fists. "And me own two fists are as good as any weapon."

"Are you both willing to help me with a situation that could become dangerous? Before you answer, know that I'll be armed and that I've had plenty of practice with pistol, knife and sword."

"You can count on me," John Coachman replied.

"Me too," Bates echoed. "Tell us what you want us to do, my lord."

"I'm to rendezvous with two men tonight at ten o'clock. We're to meet at the Crow's Nest, a rather unsavory saloon near the docks. The meeting is vital to me. It concerns information I've been seeking for some time."

"We're yer men, my lord. How can we help?" Bates inquired.

"I want you both to accompany me and lend a hand should I need it. Once we arrive, you are both to hide in the shadows near the front door of the saloon and remain out of sight. If I come out and look like I'm in trouble, your help will be greatly appreciated."

"You can count on us," John said.

"We will all wear dark clothing. When I come out of the saloon, wait for my signal before acting. John, bring the carriage around at nine-thirty."

Reed opened a drawer and handed John a pistol and several bullets. "Load and prime the weapon beforehand so it will be ready should you need it. Can you find a cudgel, Bates?"

Bates grinned. "Aye, my lord, I've a thick one tucked away in my quarters."

"Any questions?" None were forthcoming. "Very well, I'll see you both tonight."

Shortly after the men left, Hughes announced Monsieur Duvall. Sighing, Reed told Hughes to show him in.

"I've come for the ladies, Hunthurst," Duvall said importantly. "I hope you have no objections to my helping them move to their new townhouse."

"No objection at all."

Duvall seemed disinclined to leave. "I've become fond of Lady Helen and her sister."

"How fortunate for them," Reed mocked.

His sarcasm rolled over Duvall. "I will take good care of them. Someone in the family should take responsibility for your brother's widow. I am more than happy to assume the duty that should rightfully be yours."

Reed stiffened. Had Duvall just insulted him? "Be careful, Duvall; my good nature can be stretched only so far."

"I meant no insult, Hunthurst. We are cousins. Until you produce an heir, I am the next in line for the earldom."

Reed's eyes narrowed. "I wondered when you were going to bring that up. Just so you know, Duvall, I have no intention of putting a period to my life just yet."

Duvall backed off immediately. "*Non, non,* you mistake my meaning. I want us to remain on good terms."

"Keep the ladies out of my life and I shall be forever grateful. Marry Helen if you wish; you have my blessing. Or if Violet is your preference, she is yours for the taking."

Duvall beamed. "Thank you, *mon ami.* I will collect the ladies and be off. *Adieu.*"

Reed remained thoughtful after Duvall's departure. What made Duvall think he cared what Helen and Violet did or did not do? True, Helen was Jason's wife, but both she and her sister had interfered in his life. If Helen were dependent on his largesse, it would be different, but neither woman lacked funds.

Reed worked at his desk another hour, then asked Hughes to serve luncheon in his study on a tray. He didn't want anyone bothering him while he went over his plans for this evening's rendezvous. He wanted to be prepared for a trap should that be Dempsey's intention.

Tonight would either prove or disprove whether Dempsey was a traitor to the Crown. If he were the guilty party, the reason for the attempts upon Reed's life became clear. Dempsey knew Reed was tracking a traitor and that the trail might eventually lead to him. But who was his partner? That part presented a mystery. While either Dubois or Barbeau could be French spies, that didn't necessarily mean they had a reason to want him dead. He was no longer a threat to France. The puzzle wouldn't fall into place until he had all the pieces.

Fleur paced the drawing room, angry that Reed had forbidden her to go with him. She squared her shoulders. He left her no alternative. Just because he didn't want her involved didn't mean she had to obey him. She summoned Updike and Gordon, filling them in on Reed's plans, aware that of all his employees they were the two he trusted most.

"Gordon and I will attend to his lordship's safety," Updike said firmly. "You can trust us, my lady. Give us his lordship's direction."

"I will give it to you before we leave. Reed insisted upon doing this alone; that's why I'm enlisting your help without his knowledge. I don't trust the men he's dealing with."

"The traitor, you mean," Updike sniffed. "I am quite aware that his lordship was betrayed in France. Gordon, here, knows what's what. Don't worry, we'll arm ourselves and be on hand should his lordship need us."

"Thank you, I knew you'd want to help. I think we should arrive at the rendezvous before his lordship. We can park the carriage nearby and see what develops."

"If you'll pardon my saying, my lady, you won't be accompanying us," Updike maintained. "I don't believe his lordship will walk into a trap unprepared. He'll have a plan in mind; you can depend on it."

"A plan that doesn't include me," Fleur argued. "Either I go with you or no one goes. Only I know where Reed is to meet Mr. Dempsey."

Updike eyed her narrowly. "His lordship doesn't want you involved with good reason."

Frustration gripped Fleur. "Do you want to help or not? I'm fully prepared to go it alone. I can handle a pistol as well as any man."

Gordon and Updike exchanged speaking glances. "Very well," Updike agreed. "What time do you wish to leave?"

"Nine o'clock. That will give us a head start on Reed. Bring a weapon if you have one."

The men nodded and departed. Lisette joined her a short time later, her face set in determined lines.

"Mortimer told me about your plans. You're not going. Let the men handle this."

"I have to do this, Lisette. Don't try to stop me. Reed's life may be in danger."

"Very well, if you insist on this folly, I'm going with you."

"No, Lisette, you're staying here. Involving too many people is not a good idea."

"Do not do this, *ma petite*," Lisette begged. "I'm sure Lord Reed can handle things on his own. He will be angry if you interfere."

"I'll have to take that chance, Lisette. I love Reed too much to let him walk into danger alone." She held up her hand when Lisette opened her mouth to argue the point. "That's enough, Lisette. My mind is quite made up."

The day passed too slowly for Fleur's peace of mind. Eight o'clock came and went, then eight-thirty. Updike and Gordon left to collect their arms and prepare the carriage. Fleur slipped her own pistol into her pocket, donned her cloak and bonnet, and waited in the foyer.

Moments later, Fleur heard a pounding on the door. Since the butler and footman were in the carriage house, she answered the summons herself. Surprise scarcely described what she felt when she saw Duvall standing on the doorstep. He was highly distraught and appeared nervous.

"Monsieur Duvall, what brings you here at this time of night?"

"Lady Fontaine, forgive me for intruding, but a terrible thing has happened."

The blood froze in Fleur's veins. What terrible thing brought Duvall here in such a state? "What is it, Monsieur Duvall? How can I help you?"

"It's my cousin, Hunthurst."

Fleur's hand flew to her mouth. "Dear God, has something happened to Reed?"

"I went to Hunthurst Manor tonight to fetch some things Lady Helen left behind during her move. Hughes let me in. Hunthurst appeared on the gallery and leaned over the railing to see who had called. *Mon Dieu*, I do not know how something so tragic could have happened."

If Duvall didn't get to the point soon, Fleur feared she would throttle him. "Tell me, *monsieur*, and leave nothing out."

Duvall wrung his hands. "As Hunthurst leaned over the railing, I heard a crack, and suddenly the railing gave way. Hunthurst plunged to the floor below."

"No!" Fleur cried.

"The entire household is in a dither," Duvall continued. "A physician was summoned and Hunthurst was carried up to his chamber. I followed, of course, willing to do anything I could to help. He was bleeding profusely from his head and seemed quite out of it. When I heard him mutter your name, I knew you'd want to be with him."

"Oh, yes," Fleur exclaimed. "I'll go to him as soon as the carriage is brought around."

"There's no time to waste," Duvall said. "My carriage and driver await us at the curb."

"Thank you, thank you," Fleur cried as she fled out the door past Duvall. Duvall hurried after her. He helped her into the carriage, climbed in after her and shut the door.

Fleur was so worried about Reed that she failed to notice the direction in which the coach was traveling. Five minutes later, at precisely nine o'clock, Updike and Gordon parked the carriage in front of the townhouse and waited for Fleur to appear. When she did not, Updike went to fetch her. After a thorough search of the house, it was determined that Fleur was nowhere to be found.

Updike made the decision to find Reed and tell him about Fleur's sudden disappearance. When he arrived at the mansion, he learned that Reed had already left on some mysterious mission and that none of the house servants knew where he had gone. Since Updike had no idea where or how to contact Reed, he returned to the townhouse in a state of abject terror. Lisette would have his head for this; he dared not think what his lordship would do.

At precisely ten o'clock, Reed stepped out of his carriage and glanced about, looking for signs of a trap. He saw nothing to rouse his suspicion, except for an unmarked vehicle parked across the street in front of another saloon much like the Crow's Nest. The Crow's Nest itself was as disreputable as any saloon Reed had ever seen.

"You know what you have to do," Reed said in an aside to John and Bates. The men immediately melted into the dark shadows.

Reed checked his pistol, made sure his sword was in position for quick withdrawal and walked into the saloon. Reed spotted Dempsey sitting at a table in the common room teeming with boisterous, tipsy customers. Reed stood just inside the door, getting the lay of the land, so to speak.

He found it strange that Dempsey was alone when he'd promised to bring the informant with him.

Aware of potential danger, Reed remained alert, his gaze darting about for signs of covert movement. No one appeared to be paying attention to him. When Dempsey motioned him over, Reed approached his table.

"Sit down, Hunthurst," Dempsey invited.

"You're alone," Reed growled as he pulled out a chair and lowered himself into it.

"Our informer is not a trusting soul. He's waiting in the alley behind the saloon for us. He fears the traitor might learn of our meeting and seek his death."

"You're mad if you think I'm going out in the alley with you. That's a perfect setup for a trap. If you don't produce the man, I'm leaving."

Dempsey stared at him, clearly agitated. "Very well, Hunthurst, you've forced my hand."

"Which hand is that, Dempsey? Is it the one where you reveal your identity as a traitor to the Crown? You're the one who betrayed me, admit it. Did you think you were above suspicion?"

Clearly Reed's words shocked Dempsey. "You suspected me? What did I do to rouse your suspicion?"

"It was a combination of many things. Lord Porter refused to believe one of his own men could turn traitor, but I am not so naïve. You're despicable, Dempsey. Why did you do it?"

"Money, of course, is there any other reason? The French paid well for information, and I had access to secrets others did not. I knew the names of every spy working in Paris and throughout France."

"Bastard," Reed hissed. "Justice will be served. There is no informer, is there? You've set a trap and expected me to walk into it. It won't work, Dempsey. I'm one step ahead of you."

Dempsey smirked. "Are you? We'll see about that." He rose. Reed pushed back his chair and gained his feet.

"There's something outside I wish to show you."

"Is this another trick, Dempsey? You may as well give yourself up, for I won't fall for your lies."

A grin lifted the corners of Dempsey's mouth. "Will you not? How fond are you of your fiancée?"

Reed's right hand shifted to his pocket, where he'd placed his pistol. "I wouldn't if I were you," Dempsey warned. "My partner has orders to kill Lady Fontaine if anything happens to me."

"I don't believe you. Fleur is tucked away in her bed, where she belongs."

"I beg to differ. My partner has her in his carriage, all nicely trussed and gagged. You did notice another carriage parked across the street when you arrived, did you not?"

"Even you wouldn't stoop so low as to drag a woman into this."

"Would I not? The Black Widow has a price on her head in France. I stand to collect a hefty reward for her capture or death."

Reed went cold. Was Dempsey telling the truth? Did he have Fleur? "Hurt Fleur and you're a dead man." His voice was low and deadly.

"Why did you betray me? Why do you want my death when I am no longer a threat to Napoleon?"

"Your death is not as important to me as it is to my partner."

Reed went still, his hand hovering near his sword. "Your partner? Name the bastard."

"Come with me and find out."

Reed was torn. If his enemies had Fleur, he couldn't afford to take chances. He would have to go along with Dempsey. Thank God he'd had the foresight to bring men along with enough sense to follow his orders.

"Very well, I'll play your game."

"This is no game, Hunthurst, this is very real."

Bound and gagged like a Christmas turkey, Fleur cursed herself for an idiot. How had she allowed herself to be tricked by Duvall? Like an irrational fool, she had believed him when he'd said Reed had been hurt, and to make matters worse, she hadn't paid attention to where he was taking her. It wasn't until she became aware that the ride to Hunthurst Manor was taking too long that she realized she had fallen for the oldest trick in the world.

When she had confronted Duvall, he reacted quickly. Before she could gather her strength to struggle, he'd pulled a rope from beneath the seat and bound her arms and legs. When she opened her mouth to scream, he had stuffed a rag into it.

Fleur knew where Duvall had taken her. When she smelled the stench of the Thames, she realized they were somewhere in the vicinity of the docks, probably near the Crow's Nest. It didn't take a genius to figure out why she had been abducted. Dempsey had set a trap for Reed, and she was the bait. Furthermore, Dempsey and Duvall were in cahoots. Dempsey was a traitor and Duvall a French spy. Why hadn't she seen it before? Because her inclination had been to place Dubois in the role of spy and to ignore Duvall as an annoying but harmless hanger-on.

"It shouldn't be long now," Duvall said. "We'll soon have Hunthurst right where we want him."

Fleur tried to speak, but the gag cut off her words.

"I planned all this, you know," Duvall bragged. "Finally I'll get what's coming to me. And you, Madame Black Widow, will get what you deserve. Your rescue of Hunthurst undid all my careful planning to end his miserable life.

"I even helped his brother to his final reward, did you know that?"

Horror-stricken, Fleur stared at Duvall in disbelief. Duvall was a monster—no, worse than a monster. Did Reed know what he was walking into? She prayed he wouldn't fall into the trap Duvall and Dempsey had set for him.

Reed kept his wits about him as he followed Dempsey out the door and into the dank, dark night. From the corner of his eye he saw John and Bates edging out from the shadows. With a shake of his head, he indicated that they should remain hidden. He had to think of Fleur above all else. He had to know if she was in danger before summoning help.

Dempsey prodded Reed toward the carriage that had been parked across the street but was now parked in front of Reed's own conveyance.

"Turn over your sword and whatever else you're carrying," Dempsey ordered. He held out his hand. "Knowing you, you have a concealed weapon somewhere on your person."

"Why should I? Show me proof that Fleur is inside the carriage as you claim and I might consider it."

Suddenly the shade was rolled up and a lamp flared inside the carriage. Reed blinked and stepped close enough to peer through the open window. What he saw nearly brought him to his knees. Bound and gagged, her eyes wild with fright, Fleur half sat, half reclined against the squabs.

Reed lurched forward, reaching out to open the door of the carriage and rescue his love. Dempsey grasped his arm, pulling him back. "I wouldn't if I were you. Make another move like that and there will be consequences."

"Damn you!" Reed snarled. "Release her at once."

Dempsey chuckled. "I don't think so, Hunthurst. You see, we have you and your lover where we want you. Both you and the Black Widow have been thorns in Napoleon's side, each in your own way. I am neither rich nor titled. The reward for the Black Widow should set me up for the rest of my life. And my partner has even more to gain from your death than I do."

"Who is this mysterious partner of yours, Dempsey? When will I meet him?"

A face appeared in the window. Stunned, Reed staggered back. "You! We are cousins, Duvall. Why do you want me dead?"

"Are you so naïve that you don't realize I want the earldom for myself? You were supposed to die in prison when I left France. Did you know I helped your brother to his final reward? Until you survived Devil's Chateau against all odds, no one stood in my way of inheriting the earldom."

Duvall had killed his brother! Enraged, Reed reached for Duvall, eager to wrap his hands around the traitor's neck and squeeze the life from him. The pistol pressing into Reed's side effectively cooled his anger.

"I wouldn't do that if I were you," Dempsey hissed. "Hand over your weapons and get into the carriage. If you cooperate, we might consider letting your lover go."

Reed recognized a lie when he heard one; they both would die. But remaining alive was his only chance of helping Fleur. He removed his sword from its scabbard and handed it to Dempsey.

"The pistol, if you please," Dempsey snapped. "I know you too well, Hunthurst. You wouldn't venture out with only one weapon at your disposal."

Reed reached in his pocket, removed his pistol and handed it to Dempsey.

"Anything else?" Dempsey asked.

"You've got everything," Reed growled.

Apparently Dempsey wasn't satisfied, for he proceeded to search Reed's person. Reed held his breath, hoping Dempsey wouldn't discover the wickedly sharp blade hidden in his boot. He didn't.

"Now get in the carriage," Dempsey said, opening the door and pushing Reed inside. Reed didn't struggle. As long as he and Fleur were together and alive, there was a good chance they could remain that way.

"What makes you think we won't be followed?" Reed drawled as he settled down beside Fleur.

"The streets are deserted; I saw no coachman or servants lurking about your carriage. Obviously you came alone," Duvall said.

Reed said nothing. He knew John Coachman was intelligent enough to follow him.

Dempsey scrambled into the driver's seat and took up the reins. The carriage rattled off down the street.

Reed glanced at Fleur, trying to convey a confidence he didn't feel. "Untie Lady Fontaine. Keeping her bound and gagged is cruel and unnecessary."

"She'll stay as she is for now."

Reed swallowed a curse. "Where are you taking us?"

"To a place you won't be found. Once we're sure we're not under suspicion for your disappearance, we'll dispose of you and your lover."

"At least tell me how you two came to be partners," Reed said. "You and Duvall are unlikely allies. How did a spy for the Crown and a nobody like Duvall meet?"

Duvall stiffened angrily. "I beg your pardon! I've always known I was third in line to the earldom after you and your brother. I was working in Paris as a minor official when I stumbled across Dempsey. I learned he was selling information to us and sought him out. When he mentioned that Reed Harwood was working undercover in Paris, I immediately jumped on the news. Together we arranged for you to be apprehended and imprisoned in Devil's Chateau. Soon after, I left for England to put a period to your brother's life.

"You can imagine my shock when you showed up in England alive," he continued. "I thought you had died an ignominious death in Devil's Chateau. After you assumed the earldom, your death became my mission in life. When

Dempsey returned to London, we teamed up for a mutual cause."

"In London," Dempsey revealed, "I learned that the new Earl of Hunthurst was alive and well and that the Black Widow had fled to England. Eventually we put two and two together and came up with Countess Fontaine. It wasn't difficult."

"You are both beyond despicable," Reed snarled. "You, Dempsey, betrayed your own country for blunt, and you, Duvall, wanted a title badly enough to kill for it. What will you do next?"

"I plan to retire once I collect the reward for disposing of two of France's enemies," Dempsey revealed.

"And I will become Earl of Hunthurst. Quite a feat for a French nobody," Duvall mocked. "Once you announced your engagement to Lady Fontaine, it became imperative to kill you before you produced an heir."

Fleur whimpered beneath her gag. Reed reached over and patted her bound hands, trying to convey confidence. He still found it difficult to imagine Duvall and Dempsey as cohorts. The only thing clear about this entire fiasco was that greed drove both men.

"We're here," Dempsey said as the carriage rolled to a stop. Dempsey opened the door and stepped down. Duvall followed. "Get out," he ordered, motioning to Reed.

Reed hesitated. "What about Fleur?"

"She's coming too. Don't try anything funny—Dempsey has a gun trained on you."

Reed stepped down and reached for Fleur. "Trust me," Reed whispered as he lifted her out of the carriage. "I'll get us out of this."

Reed took a few moments to get his bearings. Though he didn't know exactly where he was, the rundown buildings and narrow, garbage-littered streets spoke volumes about their location: the slums of London. Holding Fleur in his arms, Reed was prodded down a narrow alleyway between buildings. He tried to avoid unidentifiable piles of refuse as he walked. Midway down the alley, he was told to halt before a narrow door in one of the deserted buildings.

Dempsey opened the door. "Inside," he growled.

Still cradling Fleur in his arms, Reed stepped into a dark, dank hole that stank of abandonment. His emotions shut down; his old terrors roared to life.

A gurgling sound erupted from his throat as he plummeted down . . . down . . . down, into hell.

✦ Chapter Twenty ✦

The door slammed shut behind them and a bar slid into place outside. Immediately, Fleur reached up and tore the gag from her mouth. She felt Reed's body tense, heard an animal sound erupt from his throat and cried, "Reed, put me down."

Silence.

"Reed, put me down and untie me."

Nothing.

"Reed, you're frightening me."

His body was stiff, his breath coming in short gasps. She felt him retreat to a place within himself she couldn't reach. What would it take to keep his demons at bay?

"Damn it, Reed, don't do this to yourself. You're not in Devil's Chateau. That part of your life is over. Don't go back there."

Though she couldn't see him, Fleur sensed him looking at her. Little by little she felt his muscles ease, as if he were fighting to regain control.

"Fleur? Thank God you're here!"

Fleur released a heartfelt sigh. "You left me for a minute there. What were you thinking?"

He shuddered. "You don't want to know. Forgive me, love." Carefully he set her on her feet.

Fleur swayed on her bound legs and would have fallen if

Reed hadn't reached out to steady her. "Please untie me, Reed. We need to find a way out of here before our captors return."

Reed's trembling hands slid down her arms to her hands. They were bound tightly, the knots secure.

"Hurry, we don't know when they will return."

"I don't need to untie the ropes; I can cut them with my blade."

Fleur feared Reed had really gone off the deep end. "Dempsey took your weapons before you entered the carriage."

"Not the knife in my boot. Dempsey must be losing his touch. I never would have missed such an obvious hiding place. Give me a second to remove the blade and I'll have you free in no time."

Reed bent, found his weapon and reached for Fleur's hands. He positioned them carefully before slicing through the ropes.

"Thank you," Fleur said, rubbing the circulation back into her wrists.

"Now for your legs." Reed felt down her skirts until he reached the place where a rope had been wound tightly around her calves. With great care he placed the blade beneath the layer of ropes and sliced outward. The ropes fell away.

Fleur felt as if a great weight had been lifted from her, leaving pain in its wake. She stifled a sob as she attempted to massage her calves.

Reed knelt in front of her. "Hang on to my shoulders and let me do that for you." He placed his hands beneath her skirt and rubbed vigorously. "Better?"

"Much better. What about you? I feared . . ."

"Once I realized I wasn't alone, that you were with me, I was able to bury my fears." His arms went around her. "You have a calming influence on me, my love. You give me the courage I need to put my demons behind me."

"You're strong, Reed. You could conquer your fear of dark places on your own."

She felt Reed's shoulders stiffen. "I *could* manage on my own, but I rather like having you with me when terror strikes."

Abruptly he released her and stepped away. "Shall we explore our prison? You need to walk a bit anyway to get the blood circulating in your legs. Give me your hand."

Their hands met and meshed. "You lead, I'll follow," Fleur said.

"First, I need to know how large a room this is. I can tell by the sound of our voices that the room isn't large. The darkness is so complete, I'd guess there are no windows. Let's start at the door and circle the room."

With one hand outstretched and the other clasping Fleur's, Reed shuffled forward until his hand came in contact with the door.

"We'll start from here. I'll count our paces to get an idea of what we're dealing with. Be careful, I don't know what obstacles we'll encounter."

Fleur stretched out her free hand to avoid bumping into things as she walked at Reed's side.

"I've reached a corner," Reed said. "Now let's walk down the side wall." Hand in hand, they shuffled along together.

Suddenly a clatter broke the silence. She heard Reed curse and felt him bend down. "What is it?"

"I bumped into a bench. I'm going to have a bruise on my shin, but that's the least of my worries." He pulled her toward the bench and eased her down. "Wait here, I'll return as soon as I've finished exploring."

Fleur felt him drift away. She listened for his footsteps, sucking in a relieved breath when they came to her loud and clear. She was beginning to share his fear of this place.

Fleur began talking, rambling, really. She had no idea afterward what she'd said. Then he was with her again, settling down beside her. Her fear receded, though her heart was still pounding.

"The room is roughly six feet by ten feet," Reed informed her. "There are no windows. Except for this bench, it is empty."

"Do you have a plan?"

"I'm still thinking."

"I don't understand why they didn't kill us instead of bringing us here. Not that I'm complaining," she added.

"It wasn't convenient for them. They want to make sure they are seen in public so no one will connect them with our deaths. I believe they've hired thugs to do their dirty work. It was probably hired thugs who made those attempts on my life. Fortunately the killers weren't skilled. The stews are full of men eager to do anything for enough blunt. My guess is that Dempsey and Duvall made sure they were seen elsewhere when their men were trying to kill me."

"How long do you think we have?"

"They won't risk killing us in daylight, so I expect something to happen before dawn. We have a few hours yet. Can you stretch out on the bench and sleep?"

At the moment, sleep was the last thing on Fleur's mind. "I don't think so."

"Lean against me and relax. I need time to think. I have my blade; that will be of some help."

"Your blade will be of little use against more than one man."

"We'll face that hurdle when we come to it." His arm came around her shoulders and hugged her close. "Rest while I consider our options."

Reed sounded so confident, Fleur allowed herself to relax against him. As she leaned toward him, she felt something poke into her side. Excitement raced through her when she realized what it was. "Reed, I have a pistol in my pocket. It's loaded and primed. Thank God Duvall didn't think to search me."

"That's my girl," Reed murmured. "I should have known the Black Widow wouldn't leave home unarmed. The pistol and knife give us much better odds. They won't expect us to be armed."

Feeling more confident than he had since their imprisonment, Reed said, "Perhaps we should both get some sleep. We need to be alert when our captors arrive."

Though Fleur was certain she couldn't sleep, she leaned into the comfort of Reed's body, closed her eyes and knew no more.

Lisette was beside herself with worry when Updike informed her that Hunthurst had already left for his meeting. She knew deep in her heart that something terrible had happened to her beloved Fleur.

"You must go to his lordship's rendezvous site, Mortimer," Lisette urged.

Updike shrugged helplessly. "The countess failed to give me the direction. She wanted to make sure I didn't go without her as I threatened."

Lisette wrung her hands. "You must find *ma petite*."

Updike headed for the front door. "Stay here with Madame Lisette," he ordered Gordon. "I'm going for help."

Updike ran to the carriage. Before he could climb onto the driver's bench, Reed's carriage came careening around the corner. Updike waited impatiently for it to roll to a stop.

"Is his lordship with you?" Updike called up to John Coachman.

John leapt down from the carriage. Bates joined him. "They got him!" John exclaimed. "Those bastards got his lordship."

"Was the countess with him?"

"Aye," John replied. "I saw her face in the window before the bastards took them away. His lordship handed his weapons over without a peep of protest and got into the carriage."

"I recognized one of the men but not the other."

"Tell me what happened. Don't leave anything out."

John launched into an explanation. "The man in the carriage with the countess was that Duvall bloke. When I saw his lordship give up his weapons, I pulled out my pistol and edged from the shadows where his lordship told me to wait. When he shook his head, I knew he wanted me to remain where I was. I think he was protecting the countess."

"Did you follow the carriage?"

John looked properly affronted. "Of course I did. Do you take me for a fool?"

Updike grew excited. "Good man! Can you direct me to him?"

John nodded eagerly. "Aye, I can take you there. We had to hang back a ways to keep from being noticed, but we were able to get close enough to see them disappear down an alley."

"Then what did you do?"

John and Bates looked at one another. "We waited until Duvall and the other bloke left in the carriage without his lordship and the countess. Then we came straightaway here to ask you what to do. Since his lordship didn't confide the particulars to us, we didn't know what else to do."

"There's no time to waste. Stay here, I'll take care of this. I know his lordship better than either of you."

Updike climbed into the carriage, took up the reins and sped off down the street. He knew where Lord Porter lived. He had heard the name brought up in conversation with Hunthurst often enough. Lord Porter was the only person capable of helping Hunthurst and his fiancée.

Fifteen minutes later, Updike stood before Lord Porter's townhouse, pounding on the door. It took considerable effort to rouse someone, but eventually an irate butler opened the door.

"What do you want at this ungodly time of night? Come back at a decent hour."

"Tell your master I need to see him on urgent business. It's a matter of life and death," Updike said before the door closed in his face. Updike wasn't to be deterred. Lives were at stake. He jammed his foot in the door.

"What's the meaning of this?" Porter shouted from the top of the stairs. "Can't a man get a decent night's sleep?"

Updike pushed past the startled butler. "Lord Porter, I'm Updike, Lord Hunthurst's man. His lordship is in serious trouble. I've come to beg your help."

Porter descended the stairs, his nightshirt flapping about his ankles. "Hunthurst, you say? What has he gotten himself into now?"

Updike told Porter everything he knew, which wasn't all that much. "So you see, my lord," Updike finished, "the pair of them are in grave danger."

Porter cursed fluently. "I cautioned Hunthurst about getting in over his head. He wasn't supposed to move against the traitor without my knowledge. Did the men who accompanied Hunthurst to his rendezvous recognize anyone?"

"They recognized Mr. Duvall, his lordship's cousin, but didn't know the second man. That's all I can tell you, my lord, except that Lord Hunthurst and Lady Fontaine desperately need your assistance."

Porter nodded curtly. "They shall have it. I'll need time to summon help. Return in an hour with the men who can lead us to Hunthurst and we'll take it from there."

Reed held Fleur close as she dozed against his shoulder. He had no idea how long they had been in this dark hole, but each minute seemed like an eternity. Fleur had no idea how difficult it was for him to control the panic racing through him. When he heard a scraping noise outside the door, his panic was replaced by cold reality.

Their captors had returned.

"Wake up, sweetheart," Reed whispered against Fleur's ear. "We're about to have company."

Fleur awakened instantly. It took a moment for her to remember where she was, but when she did she clutched Reed's sleeve and hissed, "What are we going to do?"

"Listen carefully," Reed instructed. "I don't know how many men Duvall and Dempsey have brought to do their dirty work, but they'll need light to see us. They'll probably bring a lantern or torch. That means we'll be able to see them too."

The bar scraped across the door.

"Remove your gun from your pocket and hide it in the folds of your gown. I've hidden my knife in my sleeve; a flick of my wrist will place it in my hand. If more than one man enters the room, I'll need a moment to assess the situation. Wait for my signal before you shoot."

The door burst open. All Reed could see was a nimbus of light spreading out from a lantern.

"There's a hook on the left beside the door," someone ordered in heavily accented English. "Hang the lantern there so you can see what you're doing. Hurry, it will soon be light."

Duvall.

Reed blinked as his eyes adjusted to the light. Immediately he saw two thugs standing in the doorway, brandishing wicked-looking knives. Duvall stood behind them.

"Steady, love," Reed whispered.

"There they are," Duvall rasped, pointing at them. "Kill them."

"Where is your partner, Duvall?" Reed taunted. "Is he too cowardly to show his face while your hired killers make short work of us?"

"Dempsey is keeping watch on the street."

"You're both cowards," Reed ridiculed.

Duvall nudged the thugs. "You have your orders. They

may fight; especially Hunthurst, but you are more than his
match. I'll wait outside the door. Come out as soon as you
finish them off."

The men, both lumbering brutes, stalked menacingly
toward their prey. Reed waited until the last possible moment
before hissing, "Now, Fleur! Aim for the man on the left."

From that moment on, everything seemed to happen at
once. Both men went down. Fleur's bullet found its mark
in one man's chest while Reed's blade protruded from the
second man's throat. Duvall appeared in the doorway, a
stunned expression on his face. Reed started toward him,
then stopped abruptly when Duvall produced a pistol and
pointed it at Fleur.

Reed shoved Fleur behind him. "You only have one bullet, Duvall. You'd better aim for my heart because if you
don't kill me, I'm going to kill you."

"At this distance, I can't miss."

Reed shoved Fleur to the ground and crouched low,
preparing to launch himself at Duvall. Then all hell broke
loose. Two men jumped Duvall from behind. His pistol exploded. The bullet whizzed past Reed's ear and thudded
into the wall behind him. Reed flung himself on top of
Fleur to protect her.

Duvall went down. Reed glanced up and saw Lord Porter
standing in the doorway. "Take Duvall and the traitor
Dempsey away," Porter bit out. The disgust in his voice was
palpable.

"Are you and your lady all right, Hunthurst? We got
here as fast as we could."

Reed climbed to his feet and helped Fleur to hers. "Are
you hurt, love?"

"I'm fine," Fleur said weakly. "Just a little out of breath."

Reed didn't care who was looking as he brought Fleur
into his arms and kissed her soundly. "You're also a great
shot and more courageous than most men." He kissed her
again before answering Porter's question. "We're both well,

Porter. But if you had arrived a few moments later, it would have been too late."

Reed stepped over the two thugs sprawled on the floor. "These two are dead. They're hired killers. What about Dempsey?"

"We got him. He'll pay with his life for betraying the Crown."

Reed ushered Fleur out the door and into the dim light of a misty dawn.

"You can explain how you managed to keep your weapons later. I assume you're anxious to take your lady home. Your man Updike and the two servants who followed you here are waiting with your carriage at the end of the alley. Without them, we wouldn't have known where to find you."

They exited the alley in time to see Porter's men shove Dempsey and Duvall into a waiting wagon.

"Thank God you're safe," Updike said with a shaky sigh. "Where shall we take you, my lord?"

"To the townhouse, Updike," Reed replied as they piled into the carriage. "You're all going to get a fat bonus for tonight's work."

Updike closed the door and climbed onto the driver's bench beside John Coachman. Bates jumped onto the tiger's perch and hung on as the carriage rattled off down the street.

Everything had happened so fast that Fleur's world was still spinning. It seemed incredible that she and Reed were alive and Duvall and Dempsey had been taken into custody.

Suddenly the murky confines of the carriage started to fade as dizziness and nausea struck at the same time. Fleur's stomach lurched up into her throat. "Stop the carriage!"

Reed must have noticed Fleur's paleness for he rapped on the roof, and the carriage rolled to a stop.

"I need to get out!"

Reed flung open the door and stepped out. He held his arms up and Fleur jumped into them.

"I'm going to be sick," Fleur gasped. Leaning over, she emptied the meager contents of her stomach into the gutter. She heaved until she had no more left. Then she collapsed into Reed's arms.

Reed handed her his handkerchief and supported her while she wiped her mouth. "Don't faint on me now, sweetheart. This nightmare is over. The traitor is as good as dead, and my cousin will hang for his crimes. He deserves death for what he did to my brother."

Fleur leaned against him while Updike stood nearby, wringing his hands.

"Do you feel better, love? Shall we go home?" Reed asked.

Fleur nodded weakly. Reed scooped her into his arms, placed her inside the carriage and climbed in beside her. "We're ready, Updike." Updike closed the door and returned to the driver's bench.

"I'm sorry you had to go through this ordeal," Reed said, smoothing her hair away from her damp forehead. "Do you still feel ill?"

"This isn't the first time I've been sick," Fleur admitted. "My stomach has been upset a lot lately, usually in the morning. I don't know what's wrong with me. I feel fine most of the time."

A worried look creased Reed's brow. "I'll send Updike for a physician as soon as we arrive home."

"I'm sure it's nothing," Fleur protested.

"I'm not taking any chances with my future wife."

True to his word, Reed sent Updike for the physician and had a worried Lisette put Fleur to bed the moment they arrived at the townhouse.

Lisette and Peg helped Fleur wash and ready herself for bed.

"Why didn't you tell me you were ill, *ma petite?*" Lisette asked as she fluttered about Fleur.

"It's not the first time my lady has been ill," Peg ventured.

Lisette sent Fleur a concerned look. "You've been sick before? Why didn't you tell me?"

"I was sick yesterday morning, but then I felt fine."

Lisette and Peg exchanged knowing looks.

"*Ma petite*," Lisette began. "Is it possible . . . Could you be . . ."

A knock on the door interrupted Lisette's question.

"The physician is here," Reed called through the door. "May I come in?"

"Come in, Reed, but truly, I feel fine now."

Reed opened the door and ushered a dignified man carrying a black bag into the bedchamber. "This is Doctor Fielding. He'll take a look at Fleur to make sure nothing serious is wrong with her."

Lisette swallowed a smile. "I'm sure it is nothing serious, my lord."

"Please leave me alone with my patient," Fielding said, shooing everyone from the chamber and closing the door behind them.

Reed paced the corridor outside Fleur's chamber, his concern palpable.

"Do not worry, my lord, I am convinced Fleur is not ill," Lisette said. "In fact, Peg and I believe that Fleur is . . ."

The door opened. Doctor Fielding stepped out into the corridor and closed the door behind him. Reed's heart jumped into his throat. What if Fleur was seriously ill? How could he bear it?

"How is she, Doctor?"

"No need to worry, my lord. Your lady is in good health and will get through this with flying colors. I understand she's been under a great deal of stress lately." He wagged his head. "Not good. Not good at all for a woman in her delicate condition."

Panic seized Reed and refused to let go. "How serious is it?"

The doctor smiled. "Most people count it a blessing. See that she stays calm, eats well, gets plenty of rest and exercises in moderation." He sent Reed a stern look. "You do intend to wed the lady, do you not?"

"Of course, as soon as it can be arranged."

The doctor leaned close. "I suggest sooner rather than later. By my estimation, your fiancée is two months into her pregnancy."

Reed staggered backward. "Fleur is pregnant? She's carrying my child?"

He heard Lisette and Peg tittering behind him and realized they had already arrived at that conclusion.

Reed grasped the doctor's hand and pumped it vigorously. "Thank you, Doctor. Updike will see you out and pay your fee with a little extra for arriving so quickly."

Reed rushed headlong into Fleur's bedchamber and closed the door behind him. He found her sitting up in bed, a dreamy smile lighting up her face.

"Did the doctor tell you?" Fleur asked, bursting with excitement.

Reed searched Fleur's face. She looked more radiant than she had a right to after her terrifying ordeal. There was no sign of the sickness she had suffered earlier. He reached the bed in three long strides and gathered her into his arms.

"He did. Didn't I tell you your worries about being barren were premature, that the fault could be Pierre's?"

"I'm so happy that I can give you an heir," Fleur said.

"Marrying you makes me happy. I love you, Fleur. It didn't matter to me if you were barren. That's how important you are to me."

As if to prove his words, he lowered his mouth to hers and kissed her. His emotions were so raw, so close to the surface that Reed struggled to contain the tears that threatened to fall. Fleur didn't even try. Her tears flowed freely down her cheeks.

Tenderly, Reed brushed the moisture away with the pads of his thumbs. "Don't cry, sweetheart."

"These are tears of happiness. I love you so much. It frightens me to think that I almost drove you away."

Reed chuckled. "I wasn't going anywhere. You couldn't have chased me away, no matter what you did or said." He laid her back against the pillow. "And now, my love, you need to rest. Peg will bring a tray up to you, and then I want you to get some sleep. While you're napping, I'm going to make my report to Porter. Then I intend to obtain a special license and call on Grandmamma to invite her to a wedding. How does the day after tomorrow sound?"

Fleur sighed happily. "It sounds wonderful. But how can you possibly arrange it in so short a time?"

Reed laughed. "With determination and a great deal of luck."

Peg knocked on the door and poked her head into the room. "Cook fixed my lady something to tempt her appetite."

"Come in, Peg. I was just leaving. Make sure Lady Fleur cleans her plate; we don't want her fainting from hunger. And then she's to rest."

Reed placed a tender kiss on Fleur's forehead and strode out the door.

Lord Porter listened intently to Reed's explanation of the past events and expressed his gratitude for Reed's help in capturing the traitor and unmasking a spy. He assured Reed that Dempsey and Duvall would likely hang for their crimes. Reed invited Porter to his wedding two days hence and took his leave.

The special license was easy to procure when one had the blunt to pay for it. In a surprisingly short time, Reed had the license tucked in his pocket, had arranged for a clergyman to perform the ceremony and was on his way to pay his grandmother a visit.

Reed was ushered promptly into Grandmamma's sitting

room. She greeted him warmly, stretching her hand out to him. "Dear boy, you have sorely neglected me. Have you brought your fiancée? She and I were to plan your wedding."

Reed kissed his grandmother's wrinkled cheek. Then he pulled up a chair and sat down beside her. "I have startling news to tell you, Grandmamma, some of it bad but most of it good."

The old lady eyed him warily. "Don't keep me in suspense. What is it?"

"Gallard Duvall hired thugs to kill me. He wanted the earldom. He failed and is now in custody. The man who betrayed me in France is also in custody. It's over, Grandmamma. I can wed the woman I love and live happily ever after. My service to the Crown is finished. Henceforth, I will devote my life to my estate and my family."

Grandmamma shook her head. "I never did trust that Frenchman. Please do not tell me the details of Duvall's machinations, for I fear my poor heart cannot stand it."

"Are you ready for the good news?" Reed asked, grinning. Grandmamma nodded. "Fleur and I are to be married at Hunthurst the day after tomorrow. The gathering will be small—just you, Lisette, Lord Porter and the servants. You will attend, won't you?"

Grandmamma searched his face. "Why the hurry? I was so looking forward to planning a grand affair."

Reed cleared his throat, hoping his grandmother would understand. "There is a need for haste, Grandmamma."

The dowager's eyes lit up. "Ah, now I understand. You and your bride anticipated the wedding night and are now expecting the consequences." She batted his arm playfully. "You sly dog. And here I was concerned that your lady was barren. It turns out she simply didn't have the right partner. Nothing short of death will keep me from your wedding, dear boy."

Reed took his leave, eager to return to Fleur. He found her sitting in front of the fireplace in her bedchamber when he arrived. She looked rested and radiant, much to Reed's relief.

"I asked Updike to serve our supper in your bedchamber tonight. Is that all right with you?" Reed asked.

"Perfect." Fleur sighed. "Did you call on your grandmother?"

"I did, after I procured a special license and arranged for a clergyman to perform the ceremony. Grandmamma was a little put out that she couldn't plan a grand affair, but she soon came around. She's thrilled for us. I also invited Lord Porter. Is there anyone else you'd like to ask?"

A mischievous glint appeared in Fleur's green eyes. "I'd like to invite Lady Helen and Lady Violet."

"Why? They tried their best to destroy our relationship."

"But they didn't. You cannot fault me for wanting to gloat."

"I'll see that they receive invitations. Is there anything else I can do for you?"

"Oh, yes," she said a little breathlessly. "Make love to me, Reed. I want that more than anything right now."

Reed didn't have to be asked twice. He loved her with all the passion in his body, with his whole heart and soul, with every fiber of his being.

Fleur responded in kind, her heart soaring with happiness. Her future with Reed and the children they would share stretched before her in endless harmony and timeless love.

✤ Epilogue ✤

Fleur's wedding day couldn't have been more perfect. By some miracle, she didn't experience morning sickness and the sun shone brightly, with no sign of rain on the horizon. The ceremony was blessedly brief and the wedding breakfast following the ceremony delightful.

Grandmamma smiled ecstatically throughout the ceremony and breakfast. Before the ceremony, she had whispered to Fleur that she hoped to live long enough to see the birth of Reed's heir. That had produced a round of tears over Jason's death, but her happiness soon overcame her sorrow.

Reed had no intention of telling Grandmamma that Duvall had hastened Jason's death, for he doubted the old woman could take the shock. But Porter knew, and it would be brought up at Duvall's trial. As for Lady Helen, she gave no indication at the wedding that she and Fleur had been anything but good friends. Helen had found herself in an awkward position. Her friendship with Gallard Duvall had been duly noted and remarked upon, causing grist for the gossip mill. She needed to be on her best behavior. Lady Violet chose not to attend.

Fleur and Reed planned to leave for their country estate the following day to await the birth of their child. When they walked hand in hand to their honeymoon suite that night, Reed presented Fleur with a wedding gift. He surprised her with the jewels he was supposed to have pawned. His thoughtfulness brought tears to her eyes, which Reed promptly kissed away.

Seven months later, Reed and Fleur's son arrived with little fanfare and a minimum of pain. The new viscount was christened Jason Edward three weeks later. A grand celebration was held at Hunthurst Park in his honor, with neighbors, friends and tenants feasting and reveling until the wee hours of the morning.

No one was more pleased than Grandmamma. She had achieved her goal. She had lived to see her great grandson and the heir to the earldom. Little did she know on that happiest of days that she would live to see two more sons born to Reed and his wife.

Hand in hand, the happy parents bid their guests goodbye and climbed the stairs to their bedchamber, where they celebrated their miracle child by making love.

JOYCE HENDERSON

Kalen Barrett could birth foals, heal wounded horses, and do the work of two ranch hands, so she was hired on the spot to work at the Savage ranch. But the instant attraction she felt to sinfully handsome Taylor Savage terrified her. Each time she glimpsed the promise of passionate fulfillment in Taylor's heated eyes, she came a little closer to losing control—but he always held back the words she longed to hear. If he would only give her his heart, she would follow him body and soul...

TO THE EDGE OF THE STARS

ISBN 10: 0-8439-5996-7
ISBN 13: 978-0-8439-5996-3

To order a book or to request a catalog call:
1-800-481-9191
This book is also available at your local bookstore, or you can check out our Web site www.dorchesterpub.com where you can look up your favorite authors, read excerpts, or glance at our discussion forum to see what people have to say about your favorite books.

DAWN MacTAVISH

Lark at first hoped it was a simple nightmare: If she closed her eyes, she would be back in the mahogany bed of her spacious boudoir at Eddington Hall, and all would be well. Her father, the earl of Roxburgh, would not be dead by his own hand, and she would not be in Marshalsea Debtor's Prison.

Such was not to be. Ere the Marshalsea could do its worst, the earl of Grayshire intervened. But while his touch was electric and his gaze piercing, for what purpose had he bought her freedom? No, this was not a dream. As Lark would soon learn, her dreams had never ended so well.

The Privateer

AVAILABLE JANUARY 2008!

ISBN 13: 978-0-8439-5981-9

JOY NASH

THE DRUIDS OF AVALON

Hidden away on a misty isle, steeped in the teachings of The Lady, they used enchantment to stem the tide of the invaders while battling a still darker enemy.

CHALYBS

It was the Roman word for bright iron, and Marcus had long been struggling to forge of it a mighty weapon. Though his workmanship surpassed all others, the right combination of heat and force eluded him...until a familiar silver-haired beauty appeared beside his anvil. Gwendolyn's lithe body aroused in him a white-hot fire, a need fanned ever higher by her nearness. Though he could not help remembering the golden glow of a wolf's eyes when he looked into her hypnotic gaze, he knew he must surrender body and soul to her mysterious powers, for only with Gwen guiding his hammer could they create...

DEEP MAGIC

AVAILABLE JANUARY 2008

ISBN 13: 978-0-505-52716-5

SHIRL HENKE

What happens when a beautiful lady gambler faces off against a professional card shark with more aces up his sleeve than the Missouri River has snags? A steamboat trades hands, the loser forfeits his clothes, and all hell breaks loose on the levee. But events only get wilder as the two rivals, now reluctant partners, travel upriver. Delilah Raymond soon learns that Clint Daniels is more than he appears. As the polished con man reverts to an earlier identity—Lightning Hand, the lethal Sioux warrior—the ghosts of his past threaten to tear apart their tempestuous union. Will the River Nymph take him too far for redemption, or could Delilah be his ace in the hole?

The RIVER NYMPH

AVAILABLE FEBRUARY 2008!

ISBN 13: 978-0-8439-6011-2

EMILY BRYAN

BARING IT ALL

From the moment she saw the man on her doorstep, Lady Artemisia, Duchess of Southwycke, wanted him naked. For once, she'd have the perfect model for her latest painting. But as he bared each bit of delicious golden skin from his broad chest down to his—oh, my!—art became the last thing on her mind.

Trevelyn Deveridge was looking for information, not a job. Though if a brash, beautiful widow demanded he strip, he wasn't one to say no. Especially if it meant he could get closer to finding the true identity of an enigmatic international operative with ties to her family. But as the intrigue deepened and the seduction sweetened, Trev found he'd gone well beyond his original mission of...

DISTRACTING the DUCHESS

AVAILABLE MARCH 2008!   ISBN 13: 978-0-8439-5870-6

C. L. WILSON

LORD OF THE FADING LANDS

Once he had loved with such passion, his name was legend....Tarien Soul. Now a thousand years later, a new threat calls him from the Fading Lands, back into the world that had cost him so dearly. Now an ancient, familiar evil is regaining its strength, and a new voice beckons him—more compelling, more seductive, more maddening than any before. As the power of his most bitter enemy grows and ancient alliances crumble, the wildness in his blood will not be denied. The tairen must claim his truemate and embrace the destiny woven for him in the mists of time.

ISBN 10: 0-8439-5977-0
ISBN 13: 978-0-8439-5977-2